BACILLUS

BACILLUS

CLASSIC STORIES OF THE MICROBIAL AND CONTAGIOUS

Edited by

CHAD ARMENT

COACHWHIP PUBLICATIONS

Landisville, Pennsylvania

Bacillus, edited by Chad Arment

ISBN 1-61646-104-7
ISBN-13 978-1-61646-104-1

CoachwhipBooks.com

CONTENTS

STORIES

NOVEL

THE MASQUE OF THE RED DEATH
EDGAR ALLAN POE

The "Red Death" had long devastated the country. No pestilence had ever been so fatal or so hideous. Blood was its Avatar and its seal—the redness and the horror of blood. There were sharp pains, and sudden dizziness, and then profuse bleeding at the pores, with dissolution. The scarlet stains upon the body and especially upon the face of the victim, were the pest ban which shut him out from the aid and from the sympathy of his fellow-men. And the whole seizure, progress and termination of the disease, were the incidents of half an hour.

But the Prince Prospero was happy and dauntless and sagacious. When his dominions were half depopulated, he summoned to his presence a thousand hale and light-hearted friends from among the knights and dames of his court, and with these retired to the deep seclusion of one of his castellated abbeys. This was an extensive and magnificent structure, the creation of the prince's own eccentric yet august taste. A strong and lofty wall girdled it in. This wall had gates of iron. The courtiers, having entered, brought furnaces and massy hammers and welded the bolts. They resolved to leave means neither of ingress or egress to the sudden impulses of despair or of frenzy from within. The abbey was amply provisioned. With such precautions the courtiers might bid defiance to contagion. The external world could take care of itself. In the meantime it was folly to grieve or to think. The prince had provided all the appliances of pleasure. There were buffoons, there were improvisatori, there were ballet-dancers, there were musicians, there was beauty, there was wine. All these and security were within. Without was the "Red Death."

It was toward the close of the fifth or sixth month of his seclusion, and while the pestilence raged most furiously abroad, that the Prince Prospero entertained his thousand friends at a masked ball of the most unusual magnificence.

It was a voluptuous scene, that masquerade. But first let me tell of the rooms in which it was held. There were seven—an imperial suite. In many palaces, however, such suites form a long and straight vista, while the folding doors slide back nearly to the walls on either hand, so that the view of the whole extent is scarcely impeded. Here the case was very different; as might have been expected from the prince's love of the bizarre. The apartments were so irregularly disposed that the vision embraced but little more than one at a time. There was a sharp turn at every twenty or thirty yards, and at each turn a novel effect. To the right and left, in the middle of each wall, a tall and narrow Gothic window looked out upon a closed corridor which pursued the windings of the suite. These windows were of stained glass whose color varied in accordance with the prevailing hue of the decorations of the chamber into which it opened. That at the eastern extremity was hung, for example, in blue, and vividly blue were its windows. The second chamber was purple in its ornaments and tapestries, and here the panes were purple. The third was green throughout, and so were the casements. The fourth was furnished and lighted with orange, the fifth with white, the sixth with violet. The seventh apartment was closely shrouded in black velvet tapestries that hung all over the ceiling and down the walls, falling in heavy folds upon a carpet of the same material and hue. But in this chamber only, the color of the windows failed to correspond with the decorations. The panes here were scarlet—a deep blood-color. Now in no one of the seven apartments was there any lamp or candelabrum, amid the profusion of golden ornaments that lay scattered to and fro or depended from the roof. There was no light of any kind emanating from lamp or candle within the suite of chambers. But in the corridors that followed the suite, there stood, opposite to each window, a heavy tripod, bearing a brazier of fire that projected its rays through the tinted glass and so glaringly illumined the room. And thus were produced a multitude of gaudy and fantastic appearances. But in the western or black chamber the effect of the fire-light that streamed upon the dark hangings through the blood-tinted panes, was ghastly in the extreme, and produced so wild a look upon the countenances of those who entered, that there were few of the company bold enough to set foot within its precincts at all.

It was in this apartment, also, that there stood against the western wall, a gigantic clock of ebony. Its pendulum swung to and fro with a dull, heavy, monotonous clang; and when the minute-hand made the circuit of the face, and the hour was to be stricken, there came from the brazen lungs of the clock a sound which was clear and loud and deep and exceedingly musical, but of so peculiar a note and emphasis that, at each lapse of an hour, the musicians of the orchestra were constrained to pause, momentarily, in their performance, to hearken to the sound; and thus the waltzers perforce ceased their evolutions; and there was a brief disconcert of the whole gay company; and, while the chimes of the clock yet rang, it was observed that the giddiest grew pale, and the more aged and sedate passed their hands over their brows as if in confused reverie or meditation. But when the echoes had fully ceased, a light laughter at once pervaded the assembly; the musicians looked at each other and smiled as if at their own nervousness and folly, and made whispering vows, each to the other, that the next chiming of the clock should produce in them no similar emotion; and then, after the lapse of sixty minutes, (which embrace three thousand and six hundred seconds of the Time that flies,) there came yet another chiming of the clock, and then were the same disconcert and tremulousness and meditation as before.

But, in spite of these things, it was a gay and magnificent revel. The tastes of the prince were peculiar. He had a fine eye for colors and effects. He disregarded the *decora* of mere fashion. His plans were bold and fiery, and his conceptions glowed with barbaric lustre. There are some who would have thought him mad. His followers felt that he was not. It was necessary to hear and see and touch him to be *sure* that he was not.

He had directed, in great part, the moveable embellishments of the seven chambers, upon occasion of this great *fête*; and it was his own guiding taste which had given character to the masqueraders. Be sure they were grotesque. There were much glare and glitter and piquancy and phantasm—much of what has been since seen in *Hernani*. There were arabesque figures with unsuited limbs and appointments. There were delirious fancies such as the madman fashions. There was much of the beautiful, much of the wanton, much of the bizarre, something of the terrible, and not a little of that which might have excited disgust. To and fro in the seven chambers there stalked, in fact, a multitude of dreams. And these—the dreams—writhed in and about, taking hue from the rooms, and causing the wild music of the orchestra to seem as the echo of their steps. And, anon, there strikes the ebony clock which stands in the hall of the velvet. And then, for a moment, all is still, and all is silent save the voice of the clock. The dreams are stiff-frozen as they stand. But the echoes of the chime die away—they have endured but an instant—and a light, half-subdued laughter floats after them as they depart. And now again the music swells, and the dreams live, and writhe to and fro more merrily than ever, taking hue from the many-tinted windows through which stream the rays from the tripods. But to the chamber which lies most westwardly of the seven, there are now none of the maskers who venture; for the night is waning away; and there flows a ruddier light through the blood-colored panes; and the blackness of the sable drapery appalls; and to him whose foot falls upon the sable carpet, there comes from the near clock of ebony a muffled peal more solemnly emphatic than any which reaches *their* ears who indulge in the more remote gaieties of the other apartments.

But these other apartments were densely crowded, and in them beat feverishly the heart of life. And the revel went whirlingly on, until at length there commenced the sounding of midnight upon the clock. And then the music ceased, as I have told; and the evolutions of the waltzers were quieted; and there was an uneasy cessation of all things as before. But now there were twelve strokes to be sounded by the bell of the clock; and thus it happened, perhaps, that more of thought crept, with more of time, into the meditations of the thoughtful among those who reveled. And thus, too, it happened, perhaps, that before the last echoes of the last chime had utterly sunk into silence, there were many individuals in the crowd who had found leisure to become aware of the presence of a masked figure which had arrested the attention of no single individual before. And the rumor of this new presence having spread itself whisperingly around, there arose at length from the whole company a buzz, or murmur, expressive of disapprobation and surprise—then, finally, of terror, of horror, and of disgust.

In an assembly of phantasms such as I have painted, it may well be supposed that no ordinary appearance could have excited such sensation. In truth the masquerade license of the night was nearly unlimited; but the figure in question had out-Heroded Herod, and gone beyond the bounds of even the prince's indefinite decorum. There are chords in the hearts of the most reckless which cannot be touched without emotion. Even with the utterly lost, to whom life and death are equally jests, there are matters of which no jest can be made. The whole company, indeed, seemed now deeply to feel that in the costume and bearing of the stranger neither wit nor propriety existed. The figure was tall and gaunt, and shrouded from head to foot in the habiliments of the grave. The mask which concealed the visage was made so nearly to resemble the countenance of a stiffened corpse that the closest scrutiny must have had difficulty in detecting the cheat. And yet all this might have been endured, if not approved, by the mad revelers around. But the mummer had gone so far as to assume the type of the Red Death. His vesture was dabbled in *blood*—and his broad brow, with all the features of the face, was besprinkled with the scarlet horror.

When the eyes of Prince Prospero fell upon this spectral image (which with a slow and solemn movement, as if more fully to sustain its *rôle*, stalked to and fro among the waltzers) he was seen to be convulsed, in the first moment with a strong shudder either of terror or distaste; but, in the next, his brow reddened with rage.

"Who dares?" he demanded hoarsely of the courtiers who stood near him— "who dares insult us with this blasphemous mockery? Seize him and unmask him—that we may know whom we have to hang at sunrise, from the battlements!"

It was in the eastern or blue chamber in which stood the Prince Prospero as he uttered these words. They rang throughout the seven rooms loudly and clearly; for the prince was a bold and robust man, and the music had become hushed at the waving of his hand.

It was in the blue room where stood the prince, with a group of pale courtiers by his side. At first, as he spoke, there was a slight rushing movement of this group in the direction of the intruder, who at the moment was also near at hand, and now, with deliberate and stately step, made closer approach to the speaker. But from a certain nameless awe with which the mad assumptions of the mummer had inspired the whole party, there were found none who put forth hand to seize him; so that, unimpeded, he passed within a yard of the prince's person; and, while the vast assembly, as if with one impulse, shrank from the centres of the rooms to the walls, he made his way uninterruptedly, but with the same solemn and measured step which had distinguished him from the first, through the blue chamber to the purple—through the purple to the green—through the green to the orange—through this again to the white—and even thence to the violet, ere a decided movement had been made to arrest him. It was then, however, that the Prince Prospero, maddening with rage and the shame of his own momentary cowardice, rushed hurriedly through the six chambers, while none followed him on account of a deadly terror that had seized upon all. He bore aloft a drawn dagger, and had approached, in rapid impetuosity, to within three or four feet of the retreating figure, when the latter, having attained the extremity of the velvet apartment, turned suddenly and confronted his pursuer. There was a sharp cry—and the dagger dropped gleaming upon the sable carpet, upon which, instantly afterwards, fell prostrate in death the

Prince Prospero. Then, summoning the wild courage of despair, a throng of the revelers at once threw themselves into the black apartment, and, seizing the mummer, whose tall figure stood erect and motionless within the shadow of the ebony clock, gasped in unutterable horror at finding the grave-cerements and corpse-like mask which they handled with so violent a rudeness, untenanted by any tangible form.

And now was acknowledged the presence of the Red Death. He had come like a thief in the night. And one by one dropped the revelers in the blood-bedewed halls of their revel, and died each in the despairing posture of his fall. And the life of the ebony clock went out with that of the last of the gay. And the flames of the tripods expired. And Darkness and Decay and the Red Death held illimitable dominion over all.

THE MICROBE OF DEATH

RUDOLPH DE CORDOVA

I am a murderer.

A murderer—the slayer of life. I, Sutherland Huntingdon, a doctor of medicine, a master in surgery, a recognized power in the scientific world, a man whoso business, whose duty, according to the popular idea, is to save life, not take it.

I, an educated man, a murderer, guilty of a crime which a foolish public is taught, is almost cajoled into believing, will disappear with education.

Fudge! Murders like that I have committed will last as long as the world, as long as life or love, which means life and passion.

I am a murderer. I write the words again to see how they look; to glory in my deed.

I have revenged myself upon my enemy. Revenge is sweet. No one knows how sweet until he has tasted it.

I have slain my enemy; the one man on earth I hated; the man who robbed me of all that made life sweet.

In the olden days was it not accounted great to kill a foe? Did not our ancestors rejoice in the net, and even drink their wine out of the skulls of those they had slain?

Wherein are we different today? We kill the enemies of our country in war; in a cause with which we may have no sympathy we destroy men who have never done us a wrong—whom we have never seen. We are heroes then; the country votes us ribbons, medals, money: gives us honor. A man comes into our lives and makes earth hell. We kill him for the wrong, and we are villains;

the country calls us villains, fiends, and demands our lives; gives us death.

But I at least am free from that. It cannot know my crime. Crime! How curious is the habit into which we mechanically drop, when we are not on the alert, of using words we hear the rest of the world employ! Crime, forsooth!

To-day I am a murderer. Through all eternity I shall be what I am. What a thought! Through all eternity! Through years the contemplation of whose very number numbs my brain and leaves me dazed, confused.

Yet I have not felt remorse.

What is remorse? Fear of detection. I can never be found out. Why, then, should I feel remorse?

Even if I were to confess I should not be believed. People would only declare I had gone out of my mind. I should be locked up as a lunatic.

What a sensation for an hour—what a headline for a newspaper, "A Famous Doctor Mad"! But I shall not confess.

And yet I killed Harrison Everard.

I, Sutherland Huntingdon, his friend—to use the glib word which so often masks an enemy—I killed Harrison Everard, whose short obituary is before me as I write:

> "Harrison Everard, M.D., M.S., Dead.
>
> "Dr. Harrison Everard, whose death we regret to record, was one of the most original and brilliant of the younger physicians in the city.
>
> "Yesterday he was in the enjoyment of his usual excellent health and engaged in the active pursuit of his profession, in which he would undoubtedly have been a shining light had he been spared.
>
> "His death was due to cerebro-spinal meningitis, but no one knows the origin of the disease. He had been performing a post-mortem examination early in the afternoon with his friend Dr. Sutherland Huntingdon, and at its conclusion the two gentlemen started for a walk, but being overtaken by

the thunderstorm, they parted to ride home in different cars, after agreeing to meet to-day to discuss the notes on the case, as Dr. Everard himself had an engagement for the evening.

"So much for the mutability of human plans. Long before the hour appointed for the interview Dr. Everard was lying cold and stiff in death.

"Early in the evening he complained of headache and his temperature began to rise. He told his wife he thought he must have contracted a cold in the storm, and got her to give him some quinine. This produced no effect, for in a little while his head was worse and his temperature higher, so he went to bed. An hour later he became delirious, and Mrs. Everard, being alarmed, sent for a physician, who applied the usual remedies.

'Then Dr. Sutherland Huntingdon was summoned in consultation. He diagnosed acute spinal meningitis, and though he tried to encourage Mrs. Everard, it was plain from the first he did not anticipate a favorable termination of the disease.

"All that human skill could do and science could suggest was tried without avail, and after suffering terrible agony the unfortunate young man died at about nine o'clock this morning.

"Dr. Everard, who had been married only a couple of years, leaves no children. His widow is prostrate with grief."

Who, reading that notice, could suspect even for a moment his death was planned by me—executed, too, by me?

Who could suggest its reason was revenge? Yet so it was.

My friendship was a mask of hatred stronger than death, for it still survives. I hate him now as I hated him when first I saw him.

Presentiments are out of fashion nowadays. "They exist only in women's novels," people think. Even I laughed at the idea before I felt it. "Presentiments—bosh! Why should impending evil reveal itself to us in emotion?"

I ask the question as credulously now as incredulously then. I can offer no answer which will satisfy the inquiring mind. I merely state a fact when I say I felt the presentiment that this man meant the ruin of my happiness when I first saw Harrison Everard over three years ago.

Let me go back to the events which preceded that day.

I had been spending a few weeks in England, the happiest weeks that ever linked themselves in my life, for just before my departure from New York Agatha Brodair had promised to be my wife. She had planned the trip some months before, and when she accepted me I naturally made my arrangements to accompany her and her mother.

A physician with a good bank account may indulge in the luxury of a holiday.

Her father had died many years before, and although her mother became thereby her natural guardian she did not submit to much interference from headquarters, and generally managed her own affairs herself.

I cannot describe the time we spent abroad. No words of mine could ever paint the joy of those days, when she seemed wrapt in me and I was wrapt in her.

Those who have really loved will know the ecstasy of that communion when her wish was my command, her smile a guerdon far beyond the greatest honor a king can give.

You whose souls have not been touched with that holy fire would only smile—nay, even laugh outright—were I to attempt to describe the emotions, the myriad thoughts of love, the joyous plannings for the future, which each moment would suggest as we wandered down some shady lane, here lighted with bright sunshine, there mottled by shadows cast by the branches of overhanging trees which, as it were, greedily gathered in the light and danced in the breeze, murmuring the while as if they, too, were whispering of love.

The memory of those days will last with me until death in mingled bittersweet, but never a word will I speak of them, for only at rare intervals do I lift the curtain of recollection and gaze upon the ashes of what was my greatest treasure.

Our holiday was drawing to an end when I was asked to take charge of a gentleman who had been ill and was returning on the *Umbria,* on which our passage was booked. The fee offered was large; I accepted, for he would not require much attention.

We went down to Liverpool on Thursday, preparatory to sailing on Saturday, and late on Friday night my patient had a relapse. It was impossible for him to start the next day or for me to leave him.

I talked the situation over with my intended and her mother. I tried to get them to delay their departure, but certain affairs demanded their presence in New York, and to my inexpressible regret they were reluctantly compelled to decide to go that afternoon.

I got a friend to watch my patient while I went to see them settled on the steamer.

After depositing their handbags, etc., in their stateroom, we went to the saloon to talk for a few minutes before the bell rang for visitors to go on shore. As we reached the foot of the staircase leading from the deck a gentleman stepped down; there was a pause as he and we stopped each to allow the other to pass. Our eyes met, and in that instant, without any reason at all, I felt a sharp sting, it could hardly be called a pain, dart through my heart, which seemed to stop, and a dread, a nameless horror came over me. I almost shuddered, and my flesh crept all over. I could not understand it.

We passed on, and in talking I remarked how signally his presence had affected me, and how strangely I disliked this unknown man.

Presently the bell rang. The time had come for us to part, but it would only be for a few days, we felt, and we consoled ourselves with the thought of the joy our meeting would bring.

The next morning a telegram came from Queenstown, and on Monday such a letter as I naturally expected from the woman I should soon call my wife.

On Wednesday my patient died, and after duly notifying his relations I made my arrangements, and left on Saturday for New York.

We had a fine passage, and early on the following Sunday we were landed. There was a great crowd on board, and, eager to see the girl I had parted from two weeks before, I decided not to wait until the luggage was sorted, but to go to her at once and return to pass my trunks through the Customhouse in the afternoon. I therefore went, as fast as the Elevated could carry me, up Sixth Avenue to my hotel, where I expected a letter telling me where I should find her and her mother, for they had given up their flat before leaving, and were not sure where they would stop.

I found the eagerly looked-for letter, and went to my room to gloat over its contents alone.

I opened it, and I remember how I turned hot and cold as I read.

My God! how can a woman be as false as that?

She swore she loved me when we had parted at Liverpool; she had told me of her "deep, undying" affection; she repeated it in her letter from Queenstown.

And in the one I held that day—the day I expected to bring me nothing but joy—she merely said she had something serious to tell me, and asked me to call that evening.

What could that something be? Again I had that dreadful sinking at my heart, that sinister foreboding of disaster.

It was hours until the time she had appointed, but they were going out of town for the day, she said, without mentioning where, and I could do nothing but wonder and possess my soul in such patience as I might summon to my aid.

I went back to the dock, gathered my trunks together, had them examined and sent home. That took a couple of hours, but I still had to wait until afternoon waned into evening before she would be back.

The time wore on slowly enough, but at last the hour came, and I went to her.

What a story for an ardent lover to hear!

Briefly this: She loved me no more; or rather she had found, after months of constant intercourse, she had never loved me. She loved another with all her soul; that other, Dr. Harrison Everard. He was the man whose presence had filled me with a nameless horror, with a presentiment of evil, when I saw him at the foot of the stairs of the *Umbria*.

She had discovered all this love during the week they were at sea. He was "her affinity"—also discovered during that week; "the being ordained to make her life complete"—discovered during that week.

She wished, though, that, for the sake of what had been, I "would still remain her friend"— "become their friend."

"Their friend"—think of it! Friend of him, the man who had robbed me of the woman I loved better than life!

Friend to her, the woman who had blasted all my hopes, and wanted to crown the ashes with a lie!

Friend to a faithless woman, and the man for whom she was unfaithful!

Friend! How many know the meaning of the word?

The most misused, the greatest in the language.

All that night I paced up and down my room. I looked out of my window at the night. Black! All nature seemed attuned in sympathy with me.

Not a star, not a glimmer of the moon was in the sky; not the reflection of a light from the street reached my straining eyes. Everything was black. The universe seemed filled with the gloom that pressed upon my heart, that overwhelmed my soul. It seemed as if the world had gone hack to primeval chaos, and I alone, a lost spirit, was standing looking at eternal night and nothingness.

I threw myself upon the bed, and for the first, the only, time in my life I sobbed aloud.

When next I looked out a glow was in the east.

It was the strangest lighting of the day I ever saw—against the gloom a blood-red streak.

In a moment flashed into my brain the wild thought which has at length been realized:

"Blood—his blood—his life for my soul!"

In that moment, too, with that thought of murder came a fearful revulsion of feeling, a change as unaccountable as strong.

I hated her as I hated him.

I set down this fact. In that moment the woman for whom, immediately before, I would willingly—nay, with joy—have gone to death and damnation, assumed another shape; from angel she was transformed to fiend, a fiend gnawing at my heart, seeking to tear out my soul, and succeeding, too, in her devilish desire.

Which was most to blame?

Harrison Everard, who had stolen her love from me, or she who, though she had sworn to be loyal to me, had broken her oath and been faithless to the bond which united us, to the love of one which she had declared had beautified her life?

Not on him alone should my vengeance be wreaked, but on her—even more on her. On him a short, a sudden punishment—death, which must come to all sooner or later.

On her its consequences, the bitterness of disappointment, the blasting of her life, the numbing of sensibilities awakened by a love such as she had declared she bore to him—as she had before sworn she bore to me.

The pain of living on in loneliness to which she had condemned me should be hers, too.

That was my thought then.

And through the bitterness of hatred and the thought of vengeance, somehow, welled up love. It permeated all the hate as water added to a bucket filled with pebbles permeates them with another element without displacing or changing what was there before.

Love and hate—intense, the one as the other—struggled in my soul, and through them grew the thought: "But not death now; wait—wait until they have been married for awhile, and she has learned to lean on him. So will the sting be sharper, deeper, longer-lived."

But how to accomplish my purpose without discovery?

And with the question came the answer, "Her request. 'Be our friend,'" she had said.

So be it. She had furnished me the opportunity; the means could wait, for no vulgar murder should stain my hands; no electrocution chair should be my lot.

Respected by the world, I should live my natural length of days; regretted, a benefactor of my kind, I should die, and my memory be heaped with honors.

Poor credulous, foolish world!

I looked out again at the sky; the blood-red streak had spread, and through it shot a shaft of bright white light—a sign, it seemed to me, of the double punishment, the double vengeance, I should wreak, and a promise of the achievement of my purpose.

I went that day and was introduced to Harrison Everard, whom I congratulated on his happiness.

We met frequently—always a bitter pain to me.

I took them out to suppers and the theatres.

We were "friends"! We made merry over the idea of my dislike of him when I first saw him, for she told him of it, and we laughed at the notion of belief or notice of first impressions.

For months I suffered beyond description. I scarcely ate; I scarcely slept, or else sank into a dull, heavy stupor from which I awoke unrefreshed in body and brain, for I dreamed always—dreamed awake as well as asleep. If I attempted to read I did so mechanically; my eyes passed over the pages line by line, but not an idea was registered on my mind; if I talked my thoughts wandered away, and I would give the most haphazard answers if I replied at all. Nothing interested me.

A black pall, as it were, hung over my life, and its gloom oppressed me; always the thoughts, "She does not love me; she has never loved me; she loves him." I could not escape them, or the dull, heavy load which weighed down my whole existence.

I thought of seeking relief in suicide. In the grave, I knew—at least I thought I knew—peace is to be found.

But why suicide?

Why should I cut short my career, dash from my lips the brimming cup when I had only just begun to quaff the elixir of success with which it was filled, for which I thirsted? No, I must drink deep of that before I shall be satisfied.

Besides, when he is dead (I said to myself), may she not, after a time, come back to me, and may I not know something of the happiness he will taste?

Oh, fatally weak love—hatred! How like a weathercock it makes a man!

Could I really dream of such a possible unraveling of this tangled web?

Would I even take her then if she would consent? Who knows? Even I would not hazard an opinion, although I hated her then as deeply as I loved her before.

Time alone can tell. Time that bound them closer still.

* * *

When they were to be married I arranged to be called out of town to see a patient.

Men will get ill at inopportune moments. Physicians must be summoned. What physician but will give up an entertainment, a pleasure, at the call of duty!

I could not go to their wedding. That would have been more than I could bear.

Of course I sent a present—and a very elaborate one.

When they had been married some time I grew calmer. Even the sting of great grief does not last forever, and in time we can look without much pain on the wound which once ached so sorely.

As I became more composed I began to rouse myself to the thought of vengeance. As a cobra coils itself asleep, but when aroused the head rises from the mass, poises itself for a moment—there is a sudden, lightninglike movement—a puncture somewhere, and in a few minutes, coma—death: so I—I was a cobra. A subtle poison, ill understood, but powerful beyond anything found in nature—a poison allied perhaps to some arrowhead venom used by barbaric Africans—was to be my weapon.

For years I had been engaged in the study of bacteriology, in which science all the world knows I have won a reputation, a place among the famous men.

I have a laboratory stocked with all the apparatus required for research in this field, where I cultivate germs of all sorts and examine them under the microscope.

One day, while examining a solution containing microbes derived from a sheep that had died of anthrax—splenic fever, as it is more commonly called—the idea came, toward the carrying out of which I bent all my energy, directed my every thought.

Energy and thought are better employed than in that way—the destruction of human life? To what do we devote our energy, to what do we give our thought, for what do we work day and night, straining every fibre, muscular and mental, racking every faculty, if not for the gratification of our senses, the accomplishment of our desires, the achievement of our will?

What though I kill a body? How many in the pursuit of their desires kill a soul, a dozen, a score, a hundred souls?

It is in their way, an obstacle in their path; it must go down, not by fair means, but foul, and down it goes, and other souls with it, and that is called success, the thing the world ranks highest upon earth, the thing for which to barter all that is best and noblest in life.

Crime like mine—I write the word again to meet the popular prejudice, to take the view of the world—society, the world, recognizes and decries; it raises up its grimy hands in horror at such deeds and calmly winks at him who murders—again the popular word—a soul; it may, nay, probably does, even pat him on the back or beat its hands together in applause, or bend its neck for him who has achieved his will to walk upon.

But then society, with smug complacency, recognizes only bodies; without a soul itself, what should it know of souls? What is my soul—your soul—a thousand souls?

The universe of souls is nothing in the balance against one body.

And yet men—men who say they have brains and heart and soul—men can rush, struggle, fight and fall fighting for society's rewards. They sacrifice father, mother, wife, children; worse than all these, perhaps, they sacrifice self, under this modern car of Juggernaut.

Damn society. It makes fools of men and marks the great so far below the little.

But my own soul?—Well, let that be murdered. I torture hers, and I must pay the penalty. Here and hereafter, everywhere, we reap as we sow, we suffer as we give suffering, we receive as we pay.

I ask no one to receive my propositions.

Never have I sought to impress my views on others.

I see the consequences of my act; I believe what I have stated. I have weighed all in the balance of my mind. Is the deed worth the payment? I calmly answer, Yes.

I pause and ask myself this question: How far must we regard murder contemplated as a "crime" against the moral law, the law of the invisible but potent power?

How far?

When shall I find the answer?

* * *

I set to work with revived interest in my bacteria, especially in the bacteria of anthrax.

The anthrax bacillus is undoubtedly one of the most potent in its effect; perhaps that is the reason why it is so common in every laboratory. It is a standard article, and can be kept dried for months and years, as potent when revived as if used fresh. Yes. Scratch a needle upon the medium upon which it has been kept—a piece of gelatine—stick that needle into a guinea pig—the animal specially designed by nature for the scientist's slaughter—or inject a drop or two of a solution containing anthrax germs, and the disease breaks forth with undiminished virulence, and in a few hours the animal is dead.

I made the experiment dozens of times, always with success from any point of view.

Science is selfish in its contemplation. It looks only on one side of the picture, it hears only one side of the argument; we shut our ears and eyes to the guinea pig's objections.

In time I came across a sheep suffering with the disease in the most virulent form I had ever seen it.

It seemed as if fate were working for me—with me.

I took a few drops of the blood, mixed them with solutions of gelatine in test tubes and allowed them to develop under the most favorable conditions.

I watched them with loving interest as the feathery thread spread onward in the mass and formed a filmy scum upon its surface.

A little solid jelly in a tube—a whitish substance on the top. No more. It looked so insignificant.

Yet death lurked within a scrap of that insignificant-looking scum; not death whose gentle fingers soothe and caress the weary, spirit-broken frame until the worn-out child of earth sinks on her ample breast and finds sleep and rest—peaceful, long hoped for, too long delayed; not death whose clarion call rings loud above the battle's thunder, stirring the blood, stimulating the heart, until man rushes on, proud, defiant, with head erect, impetuous, eager to meet the grisly foe, and from the bony hands receive a crown of glory as he falls; but death with swift-hurrying footsteps; death remorseless, agonizing, grim, who terrifies the watchers with a numbing sense of impotence, of impossibility of escape from his all-conquering presence, even though he delays upon the road to shoot an arrow now on this side, now on that.

And yet men boast of all their power. What is their vaunting worth when something infinitesimally small, indiscernible as a distinct object, except with powerful glasses, can lay that power in the dust?

I dried some of the blood itself on microscope slides, and put them away carefully as a sort of reserve fund in case of need.

The time was approaching.

From one of the tubes I removed a minute quantity of the developed virus and injected it into a rabbit.

Of course the animal died; more rapidly, too, than any of the others on which I had before experimented.

I took a needle and rubbed the point upon the gelatine; then I stuck it into another rabbit's ear.

It died even more quickly than in the former case.

One day I started for a walk and took with me a piece of the gelatine which grew a whole colony of anthrax germs from the direct cultivation of that blood drop. The gelatine I put into a carefully closed little box, to preserve its precious inhabitants from harm.

I was walking with an army in my waistcoast pocket, an army powerful for action as any furnished with the deadly weapons of to-day; as numerous, perhaps, as the combined soldiers of any country.

I was going to make an experiment on a larger scale than ever before, and at another man's expense—whose, I neither knew nor cared.

Passing a store, I noticed a fine, large, strong horse standing in a cart in front of the door.

Crowds were hurrying on; men and women jostling, elbowing their way along, intent on their business; some resenting the passage of the few moving more rapidly in their endeavor to force a pathway through the close ranks; most following in the slow, steady stream of humanity, gazing at the wares exhibited in the windows.

Where could a better opportunity occur? Where is one less observed than in a crowd?

In an instant came the thought, "Try your needle prick on one of these, make your experiment on a human subject and be sure of the effect."

This thought, which sprung full-armed from my brain like Minerva—I had already drawn the needle over the scrap of gelatine—I killed in its birth.

What had any of the crowd done to me that I should bring sorrow to their families?

In that moment I held in my hand a godlike power, the power to destroy—a power as potent as the thunderbolt of the heathen Jove himself forged by misshapen Vulcan, and yet so slight. A needle, a tiny bar of polished steel devised for the most inoffensive domestic use, yet in my hands remorseless as fate itself in dealing out swift death.

No, no; the crowd was safe from me. My vengeance was directed against one house—not against mankind at large.

I am a man—no fiend.

Sweep on, then, men and women. Laugh and talk, jostle and be jostled, elbow your way along; break your necks in the pursuit of the chimera happiness, or stumble over each other as you rush with outstretched arms after the will-o'-the-wisp called gold. Sell honor, yours and that of those yon love best, for place, and barter repose and content for ashes in bright-colored packets tied with gaudy ribbons and labeled with a lie.

Your fathers did it before you; so did theirs. Your children will follow in your footsteps; so will theirs.

How long will it continue?

Through eons of centuries, no doubt. But what care I? I have but to do with my time. Let the time to come do with itself.

So I thought.

Then I looked again at that strong horse.

I got in the way of a man; he pushed me on one side. I pretended to slip, and as I did so I stuck the needle into the horse's lip. He dashed his head up at the sudden prick, but did not attempt to move, so slight was the pain. I had passed a strong piece of silk through the needle's eye to remove it quickly, but I need not have feared it would be imbedded in the poor brute's lip, for I scarcely touched the mucous membrane.

I knew where the horses belonging to that store were stabled, and next afternoon I passed the place. I went in, and, as if I were a newspaper reporter, made some inquiries as to the number kept, the amount of work they did, etc., and remarked casually that I had noticed two or three very fine animals in the firm's vans the day before. The man to whom I was talking told me one of the best had just died with most curious symptoms, which they could not understand, and after only a few hours' illness.

Presently they dragged the carcass out.

It was the creature I had inoculated.

The trap was made; the bait prepared. All that remained was to set it.

When?

I must await my opportunity.

* * *

Ever since I had determined on my vengeance I had omitted no opportunity of associating Harrison Everard with my work.

Did I need a consultation, I sent for him.

Was it necessary to perform a post-mortem, I got him to help me, either letting him use the knife while I made notes, or I used the knife while he wrote.

"The medical twins" we might have been called.

Professionally we "went coupled." It was even rumored we should soon enter into partnership.

Whatever, then, might happen, no one would dream of looking at me as the author of his death.

But who would imagine that his death was other than an accident?

The time was ripe.

The opportunity was at hand.

She and he had been married over two years by this time, and though he and I met often professionally I had not been to their house more than a few times. I was invited, but I could not accept hospitality from her, so I pleaded work and the experiments I was making for the book I had already begun. All doctors write books nowadays.

Ten days ago I was sent for to attend a patient. He was dangerously ill. I summoned Harrison—we called each other by our Christian names—to a consultation.

We agreed to watch the case together and meet daily, for the disease was obscure and complicated. Constant vigilance was necessary if the patient were, by any possibility, to be saved, which even then seemed doubtful.

We went each day to his bedside, and one or the other would remain and watch him for awhile after our chat.

He was a curious man, alone in the world, the last of his family, and he requested that if he died during this illness we would perform an autopsy to learn exactly what had been the trouble, and then have his body cremated. All this, he informed us, he had ordered in his will, so there should be no possibility of neglect; but still he begged us to be sure to follow out his wishes.

Of course we promised.

After a week his symptoms took another turn, and he began to suffer awful pain. We gave him hypodermics of morphine.

Three nights ago I was aroused by an urgent message that he had suddenly developed alarming symptoms, and the nurse feared the end was near.

I went with all haste to him, but before I left I put into my pocket a tiny tube containing a solution, in pure sterilized water, of the same generation of the anthrax blood drops I had used in my previous experiments—experiments which had resulted so famously.

When I arrived I saw death was certain.

It was three o'clock.

A black night. It was quiet, too, there, high above the street. In an apartment on the eleventh floor even of a New York house the city's roar becomes a hum, if it be heard at all. But in the dead hours of the night when everything is hushed, except the bell of an occasional car which rumbles up and down the avenue with a belated roysterer or hard-working journalist returning home, all is peaceful.

There was not a sound in the apartment save the ticking of the clock on the mantel, that seemed to call off the seconds left for the poor fellow on the bed, whose heavy breathing was the only other sound which broke the silence.

I watched the dying man, who was now unconscious.

Five o'clock boomed from a neighboring church, and I roused myself with a start from the half-doze into which I had fallen.

The breathing was quieter, the pulse scarcely discernible, the face ashy pale; he could not live an hour more; the end might come at any time.

I took the tube from my pocket and a hypodermic syringe.

The clock upon the mantel kept up its dull, monotonous record of the seconds as they flew.

I drew into the syringe some of the fluid with its potent germs, turned up the sleeve of the dying man's shirt, pressed on the vein just at the bend of the elbow of his left arm, and as it swelled I stuck the needle into the blood vessel in the direction of the circulation and injected the contents.

He did not know what I was doing; his brain had stopped performing its functions; he was a mere machine.

Nothing that I could do would hasten his death. I used him for my purpose. He was the means to my end.

In half an hour he was dead.

I returned home, and as I walked along the quiet street, here and there awakening into life and activity, I looked up at the sky, and there in the east the sun was rising, undimmed by a single cloud, and in its brightness I read the promise of a day of triumph—a day in which all I wished for most on earth would occur, in which I should achieve the reward of patience and observation.

My vengeance was at hand.

As soon as I got home I wrote to Harrison and told him of our patient's death, suggesting twelve o'clock for the autopsy.

He agreed.

I went to breakfast and ate heartily. Death has no influence on a physician's appetite, or some of us would eat but little. After breakfast I bandaged up a finger and put on a glove stall, as if I had cut myself, for I knew he would not then let me use the knife for fear of poisoning the wound.

We met and went to work. I gave him the tools at his request, as he insisted I should take the notes and run no risk of infecting my (supposed) cut.

I knew that body was swarming with anthrax bacilli as virulent as they could be.

It held death for thousands of men, could a needle stuck in a vein prick them deep enough to draw but a single drop of blood.

And Harrison Everard had his hands in that body. A touch with one of the knives, he was using, and my vengeance would be accomplished.

But how to do it. Knock against his arm. Yes; but that would most probably make a cut, and he could blame himself or me for carelessness.

No; I would rather not do it that: way if I could help it.

In looking over his shoulder I noticed that, in cutting through the ribs, he had left a jagged edge on one. If I could get him to strike his hand on that!

As he was taking out the heart I saw him leave his knife in the cavity, and as he put his hand to regain it I turned suddenly and spoke to him; he started and struck the back of his hand against the edge of the chest cavity, and a tiny spicule of bone broke off in his little finger.

I removed it for him. It did not even bleed. He took no notice of it and went on with the operations; each moment making it more certain he would introduce hordes of bacilli into his system through that slight puncture, such is their minute size, while their virulence, in inverse ratio, would make an illness, if not death, certain, though only a few entered his body.

We finished our work and prepared to leave. As we did so we noticed that the sky had suddenly grown overcast. Black clouds lowered and scudded quickly before the hot, oppressive breeze.

Almost as we stepped out into the street the storm broke—there was a vivid flash of lightning, a deafening peal of thunder, which had scarcely died away when another flash and another peal startled us by their intensity, and huge drops of rain began to fall. Before we reached the corner the drops had quickened into a heavy downpour, and the thunder rolled incessantly.

It seemed as if the elements were at war and keeping up a perpetual cannonading in the sky.

We stepped into a doorway and waited until the storm was over, but even in the few steps we had walked our clothes were wet and our shoes soaked.

In a little while the rain ceased, and we were able to start on our homeward way; we parted at the corner, after agreeing to meet to-morrow morning at eleven to talk over the case.

"To-morrow morning at eleven." This morning.

"Will he keep the appointment?" I thought, as I watched him jump lightly enough on to a car, and I smiled grimly at the question as I stood waiting for my car to come up.

Then my scientific training getting the ascendancy, I dropped the humor, and looking beyond at the reality in a serious way, I asked myself: "Which will it be, delirium, unconsciousness or death itself when eleven o'clock to-morrow comes?"

"It should be death," I heard myself mutter, "if the big experiment can be relied on approximately as to time, 'death or very near it,'" and I hummed the last three words to the tune of a popular song I used to hear in the streets with that catch phrase. I laughed half aloud at the odd conceit as I swung on to the step of the car going my way, which had just reached the corner.

His death—my victory—and a comic song.

Then my thoughts reverted to the storm, which had passed as rapidly as it had arisen. It seemed as if the elements had, at the same moment, been saluting me with the loud salvos of artillery which greet a conqueror on his return after a brilliant victory, and firing a volley for the loss of a hero, while the mutterings of the thunder might have been muffled drums beating over his grave.

Even the elements inspired me with the idea of the success of the vengeance I had taken. I reached home and lunched heartily. Then I set to work.

I suppose people would be surprised, incredulous, horrified, perhaps, if they knew I did not trouble myself any further about Harrison Everard.

Why should I?

There was no reason for me to speculate as to his fate.

By all my calculations he was doomed; his death was certain.

But even if he should, by some chance, escape, what matter? He knew nothing of the trap I had laid for him; he suspected nothing.

If I failed I could try again and again.

Patients die; even my patients.

Post-mortems must be made.

It was not the last opportunity I should have. No, not by scores.

Time was not an element to be considered. Now or a little later could make no difference, so long as we both lived.

He was mine—his life mine.

The pain, the consequences of his death, hers—mine.

Why, then, should I be anxious or troubled about him?

No; I worked and was absorbed in my labors until the time came to visit my patients. Then I went and examined them with cool head, steady hand and quiet nerves. I never thought of him.

It is remorse—fear of detection—which makes a man's hand tremble, his knees shake, his voice quaver.

I returned home, read, went to bed, and slept till they woke me at the summons from Mrs. Everard.

Then I knew that I was the victor, and I hurried to the house to see him and study his symptoms. My scientific training would not permit me to neglect so excellent an opportunity to watch the case.

About eight o'clock last night, as I learned when I was summoned, he complained of a headache, and his temperature began to rise. In an hour he was in a high fever and the pain had increased. He told his wife he must have taken cold through getting wet on his way home, and went to bed.

In another hour he was delirious, and Mrs. Everard sent for a physician. He blistered Harrison, and later put on an ice cap.

Of course the treatment was futile.

The anthrax bacilli were at work.

He succumbed, as I foretold when I arrived, for they sent for me early in the morning.

At nine o'clock he was dead.

There had been no local symptoms to show that septic matter had entered the circulation. Not a lymphatic was inflamed; there was not a single red line on his white arm, as generally happens when poison gets into the system in this way.

I did not mention the incident of the spicule of bone. Why should I complicate the deed with the story of its cause when there was no need?

Harrison Everard dead!

"So perish all my enemies!" I could have cried; and as I looked down upon the whitened face again, I felt the gleam of triumph come once more into my eyes.

She was prostrated by the shock, and remained in her room. I have not seen her, but I sent a message by her mother—the smooth, smug message of emptiness and loss with which people are expected to intrude upon one's grief and blamed if they omit.

I left and returned home while they were making the arrangements for the funeral.

I promised to be present.

I shall see him borne in the black casket to the city where rich and poor, happy and wretched, good and bad, the world-esteemed fiend and the world-despised demigod, sleep the long sleep.

I shall exult as I see the casket go down, down, scraping the sides of the earthy pit, tilting a little here, then righting itself again as another rope is loosened, until at last it lies upon its bed.

I shall hear the earth cast on the lid, rattling as it falls, or echoing with a dull thud should the day be wet.

And I will cast earth on it; the last office the living can give to the dead will be from me a parting infamy—the last shot to an expiring foe.

Then I shall go back to work, to augmenting the reputation I have won by my bacteriological researches.

If the world but knew to what a use I put my knowledge!

And she! Shall I see her soon, and after a few months of mourning strive to win her love again? or shall I look on from afar and watch her suffer still, and hate her more for all I have done to her, for all she has done to me?

Who knows?

THE STOLEN BACILLUS

H. G. WELLS

"This again," said the Bacteriologist, slipping a glass slide under the microscope, "is a preparation of the celebrated Bacillus of cholera—the cholera germ."

The pale-faced man peered down the microscope. He was evidently not accustomed to that kind of thing, and held a limp white hand over his disengaged eye. "I see very little," he said.

"Touch this screw," said the Bacteriologist; "perhaps the microscope is out of focus for you. Eyes vary so much. Just the fraction of a turn this way or that."

"Ah! now I see," said the visitor. "Not so very much to see after all. Little streaks and shreds of pink. And yet those little particles, those mere atomies, might multiply and devastate a city! Wonderful!"

He stood up, and releasing the glass slip from the microscope, held it in his hand towards the window. "Scarcely visible," he said, scrutinising the preparation. He hesitated. "Are these—alive? Are they dangerous now?"

"Those have been stained and killed," said the Bacteriologist. "I wish, for my own part, we could kill and stain every one of them in the universe."

"I suppose," the pale man said with a slight smile, "that you scarcely care to have such things about you in the living—in the active state?"

"On the contrary, we are obliged to," said the Bacteriologist. "Here, for instance—" He walked across the room and took up one of several sealed tubes. "Here is the living thing. This is a cultivation of the actual living disease bacteria." He hesitated, "Bottled cholera, so to speak."

A slight gleam of satisfaction appeared momentarily in the face of the pale man. "It's a deadly thing to have in your possession," he said, devouring the little tube with his eyes. The Bacteriologist watched the morbid pleasure in his visitor's expression. This man, who had visited him that afternoon with a note of introduction from an old friend, interested him from the very contrast of their dispositions. The lank black hair and deep grey eyes, the haggard expression and nervous manner, the fitful yet keen interest of his visitor were a novel change from the phlegmatic deliberations of the ordinary scientific worker with whom the Bacteriologist chiefly associated. It was perhaps natural, with a hearer evidently so impressionable to the lethal nature of his topic, to take the most effective aspect of the matter.

He held the tube in his hand thoughtfully. "Yes, here is the pestilence imprisoned. Only break such a little tube as this into a supply of drinking-water, say to these minute particles of life that one must needs stain and examine with the highest powers of the microscope even to see, and that one can neither smell nor taste—say to them, 'Go forth, increase and multiply, and replenish the cisterns,' and death—mysterious, untraceable death, death swift and terrible, death full of pain and indignity—would be released upon this city, and go hither and thither seeking his victims. Here he would take the husband from the wife, here the child from its mother, here the statesman from his duty, and here the toiler from his trouble. He would follow the water-mains, creeping along streets, picking out and punishing a house here and a house there where they did not boil their drinking-water, creeping into the wells of the mineral-water makers, getting washed into salad, and lying dormant in ices. He would wait ready to be drunk in the horse-troughs, and by unwary children in the public fountains. He would soak into the soil, to reappear in springs and wells at a thousand unexpected places. Once start him at the water supply, and before we could ring him in, and catch him again, he would have decimated the metropolis."

He stopped abruptly. He had been told rhetoric was his weakness.

"But he is quite safe here, you know—quite safe."

The pale-faced man nodded. His eyes shone. He cleared his throat. "These Anarchist—rascals," said he, "are fools, blind fools—to use bombs when this kind of thing is attainable. I think—"

A gentle rap, a mere light touch of the finger-nails was heard at the door. The Bacteriologist opened it. "Just a minute, dear," whispered his wife.

When he re-entered the laboratory his visitor was looking at his watch. "I had no idea I had wasted an hour of your time," he said. "Twelve minutes to four. I ought to have left here by half-past three. But your things were really too interesting. No, positively I cannot stop a moment longer. I have an engagement at four."

He passed out of the room reiterating his thanks, and the Bacteriologist accompanied him to the door, and then returned thoughtfully along the passage to his laboratory. He was musing on the ethnology of his visitor. Certainly the man was not a Teutonic type nor a common Latin one. "A morbid product, anyhow, I am afraid," said the Bacteriologist to himself. "How he gloated on those cultivations of disease-germs!" A disturbing thought struck him. He turned to the bench by the vapour-bath, and then very quickly to his writing-table. Then he felt hastily in his pockets, and then rushed to the door. "I may have put it down on the hall table," he said.

"Minnie!" he shouted hoarsely in the hall.

"Yes, dear," came a remote voice.

"Had I anything in my hand when I spoke to you, dear, just now?"

Pause.

"Nothing, dear, because I remember—"

"Blue ruin!" cried the Bacteriologist, and incontinently ran to the front door and down the steps of his house to the street.

Minnie, hearing the door slam violently, ran in alarm to the window. Down the street a slender man was getting into a cab. The

Bacteriologist, hatless, and in his carpet slippers, was running and gesticulating wildly towards this group. One slipper came off, but he did not wait for it. "He has gone *mad!*" said Minnie; "it's that horrid science of his"; and, opening the window, would have called after him. The slender man, suddenly glancing round, seemed struck with the same idea of mental disorder. He pointed hastily to the Bacteriologist, said something to the cabman, the apron of the cab slammed, the whip swished, the horse's feet clattered, and in a moment cab, and Bacteriologist hotly in pursuit, had receded up the vista of the roadway and disappeared round the corner.

Minnie remained straining out of the window for a minute. Then she drew her head back into the room again. She was dumbfounded. "Of course he is eccentric," she meditated. "But running about London—in the height of the season, too—in his socks!" A happy thought struck her. She hastily put her bonnet on, seized his shoes, went into the hall, took down his hat and light overcoat from the pegs, emerged upon the doorstep, and hailed a cab that opportunely crawled by. "Drive me up the road and round Havelock Crescent, and see if we can find a gentleman running about in a velveteen coat and no hat."

"Velveteen coat, ma'am, and no 'at. Very good, ma'am." And the cabman whipped up at once in the most matter-of-fact way, as if he drove to this address every day in his life.

Some few minutes later the little group of cabmen and loafers that collects round the cabmen's shelter at Haverstock Hill were startled by the passing of a cab with a ginger-coloured screw of a horse, driven furiously.

They were silent as it went by, and then as it receded— "That's 'Arry 'Icks. Wot's *he* got?" said the stout gentleman known as Old Tootles.

"He's a-using his whip, he is, *to* rights," said the ostler boy.

"Hullo!" said poor old Tommy Byles; "here's another bloomin' loonatic. Blowed if there aint."

"It's old George," said old Tootles, "and he's drivin' a loonatic, *as* you say. Aint he a-clawin' out of the keb? Wonder if he's after 'Arry 'Icks?"

The group round the cabmen's shelter became animated. Chorus: "Go it, George!" "It's a race." "You'll ketch 'em!" "Whip up!"

"She's a goer, she is!" said the ostler boy.

"Strike me giddy!" cried old Tootles. "Here! *I'm* a-goin' to begin in a minute. Here's another comin'. If all the kebs in Hampstead aint gone mad this morning!"

"It's a fieldmale this time," said the ostler boy.

"She's a followin' *him*," said old Tootles. "Usually the other way about."

"What's she got in her 'and?"

"Looks like a 'igh 'at."

"What a bloomin' lark it is! Three to one on old George," said the ostler boy. "Nexst!"

Minnie went by in a perfect roar of applause. She did not like it but she felt that she was doing her duty, and whirled on down Haverstock Hill and Camden Town High Street with her eyes ever intent on the animated back view of old George, who was driving her vagrant husband so incomprehensibly away from her.

The man in the foremost cab sat crouched in the corner, his arms tightly folded, and the little tube that contained such vast possibilities of destruction gripped in his hand. His mood was a singular mixture of fear and exultation. Chiefly he was afraid of being caught before he could accomplish his purpose, but behind this was a vaguer but larger fear of the awfulness of his crime. But his exultation far exceeded his fear. No Anarchist before him had ever approached this conception of his. Ravachol, Vaillant, all those distinguished persons whose fame he had envied dwindled into insignificance beside him. He had only to make sure of the water supply, and break the little tube into a reservoir. How brilliantly he had planned it, forged the letter of introduction and got into the laboratory, and how brilliantly he had seized his opportunity! The world should hear of him at last. All those people who had sneered at him, neglected him, preferred other people to him, found his company undesirable, should consider him at last. Death, death, death! They had always treated him as a man of no importance. All the world had been in a conspiracy to keep him under. He would teach them yet what it is to isolate a man. What was this familiar street? Great Saint Andrew's Street, of course! How fared the chase? He craned out of the cab. The Bacteriologist was scarcely fifty yards behind. That was bad. He would be caught and stopped yet. He felt in his pocket for money, and found half-a-sovereign. This he thrust up through the trap in the top of the cab into the man's face. "More," he shouted, "if only we get away."

The money was snatched out of his hand. "Right you are," said the cabman, and the trap slammed, and the lash lay along the glistening side of the horse. The cab swayed, and the Anarchist, half-standing under the trap, put the hand containing the little glass tube upon the apron to preserve his balance. He felt the brittle thing crack, and the broken half of it rang upon the floor of the cab. He fell back into the seat with a curse, and stared dismally at the two or three drops of moisture on the apron.

He shuddered.

"Well! I suppose I shall be the first. *Phew!* Anyhow, I shall be a Martyr. That's something. But it is a filthy death, nevertheless. I wonder if it hurts as much as they say."

Presently a thought occurred to him—he groped between his feet. A little drop was still in the broken end of the tube, and he drank that to make sure. It was better to make sure. At any rate, he would not fail.

Then it dawned upon him that there was no further need to escape the Bacteriologist. In Wellington Street he told the cabman to stop, and got out. He slipped on the step, and his head felt queer. It was rapid stuff this cholera poison. He waved his cabman out of existence, so to speak, and stood on the pavement with his arms folded upon his breast awaiting the arrival of the Bacteriologist. There was something tragic in his pose. The sense of imminent death gave him a certain dignity. He greeted his pursuer with a defiant laugh.

"Vive l'Anarchie! You are too late, my friend. I have drunk it. The cholera is abroad!"

The Bacteriologist from his cab beamed curiously at him through his spectacles. "You have drunk it! An Anarchist! I see now." He was about to say something more, and then checked himself. A smile hung in the corner of his mouth. He opened the apron of his cab as if to descend, at which the Anarchist waved him a dramatic farewell and strode off towards Waterloo Bridge, carefully jostling his infected body against as many people as possible. The Bacteriologist was so preoccupied with the vision of him that he scarcely manifested the slightest surprise at the appearance of Minnie upon the pavement with his hat and shoes and overcoat. "Very good of you to bring my things," he said, and remained lost in contemplation of the receding figure of the Anarchist.

"You had better get in," he said, still staring. Minnie felt absolutely convinced now that he was mad, and directed the cabman home on her own responsibility. "Put on my shoes? Certainly dear," said he, as the cab began to turn, and hid the strutting black figure, now small in the distance, from his eyes. Then suddenly something grotesque struck him, and he laughed. Then he remarked, "It is really very serious, though."

"You see, that man came to my house to see me, and he is an Anarchist. No—don't faint, or I cannot possibly tell you the rest. And I wanted to astonish him, not knowing he was an Anarchist, and took up a cultivation of that new species of Bacterium I was telling you of, that infest, and I think cause, the blue patches upon various monkeys; and like a fool, I said it was Asiatic cholera. And he ran away with it to poison the water of London, and he certainly might have made things look blue for this civilised city. And now he has swallowed it. Of course, I cannot say what will happen, but you know it turned that kitten blue, and the three puppies—in patches, and the sparrow—bright blue. But the bother is, I shall have all the trouble and expense of preparing some more.

"Put on my coat on this hot day! Why? Because we might meet Mrs. Jabber. My dear, Mrs. Jabber is not a draught. But why should I wear a coat on a hot day because of Mrs.—. Oh! *very* well."

THE PURPLE DEATH

WILLIAM LIVINGSTON ALDEN

Last winter I occupied a small villa in one of the towns of the Italian Riviera. To me it is a very delightful little town—partly, because it is extremely picturesque and, partly, because it is as yet almost unknown as a health-resort. You can live there without constantly hearing the cough of the consumptive, and when you do meet an occasional foreigner, he does not instantly begin to discuss the condition of his bronchial tubes, or to inquire as to the state of your own lungs.

Thank. Heaven! my lungs and bronchial tubes are perfectly sound. My only trouble is insomnia, and it was for this that I sought the perfect repose and stillness of my sleepy little Italian town. There was but one other foreigner in the place, so I was told; and as I was assured that this foreigner was phenomenally strong and well, and was, moreover, a German, and hence presumably unable to converse with a man wholly innocent of any knowledge of the German language, I did not find fault with the fact that he was to be my next-door neighbour. I saw him in his garden a day or two after my arrival, and was struck by his singular resemblance to the portraits of Von Moltke. Although he looked to be at least seventy years old, he was tall, and straight as an arrow, and his face, which had something of the firmness and rigidity of sculpture, was that of a man in perfect health and of an indomitable constitution. Even if I had not already heard him called "the Professor," I should have known him at first sight as a man of culture. Intense thought and unremitting labour had chiselled those clear-cut features. I made up my mind that, instead of avoiding him, I should like to make his acquaintance, and I found myself hoping that he could speak English, or that, at all events, I could understand his French.

Twice during the first week of my residence next door to the German I saw after midnight a light in his garden, and heard the sound of a spade. It is one of the advantages of insomnia, that the patient learns to know the things of the night as well as those of the day. Had I been able to sleep as soundly as other people, I should never have noticed this mysterious midnight lanthorn or had my hearing sharpened sufficiently to note and identify the sound of a spade. What was the professor doing at so late an hour in his garden? Clearly, he could not have been engaged in gardening or ditching. Even a German philosopher would not be capable of getting up at one o'clock in the morning to plant cabbages, or to improve the drainage of his garden. The only plausible explanation of his conduct was that he was engaged in burying something which he had reason for burying secretly. I knew that he lived absolutely alone, without a single servant. Hence, he could not be a murderer, who made a practice of burying his victims at night. Then, again, he was a scientific person, and, of course, had no money for safe-keeping in the earth. The third time that I saw my neighbour's lanthorn in the garden, I discovered that I had an object in life, which was to find why he dug in the earth at an hour when, as he supposed, all his neighbours were asleep.

The mystery solved itself a few days later, and proved to be disappointingly simple. The arrival at my neighbour's door of a hamper of rabbits, and another of guinea-pigs, showed me at once that he was engaged in studies which involved the death of numbers of those unhappy little animals. Of course, when his guinea-pigs and rabbits had fulfilled their mission in life, it became necessary to bury their remains; and the professor wisely performed this task at midnight in order not to offend the prejudices of those curious people who believe that vivisection is merely a form of vice in which inhuman men indulge purely for recreation. I had seen the professor, and I could have sworn that he was a kindly and gentle man. If his guinea pigs and rabbits were cut down in the prime of life, I felt sure that they died in the interests of humanity, and their fate gave me no pain.

My acquaintance with the professor—whom I will call Professor Schwartz, for the reason that it was not his name—grew up gradually. We began by exchanging polite commonplaces over the garden wall, and I found that he spoke English perfectly. We were both methodical in our habits, and were accustomed to smoke in our gardens every afternoon at about the same hour. Gradually we passed from the discussion of the weather to more interesting themes, and, finally, the professor accepted my pressing invitation to come and inspect a plant growing in my garden, of the name of which I was ignorant. When I returned his visit, I accidentally discovered that, like myself, he was a devotee of chess. That put the finishing touch to our acquaintance, and we fell into the invariable habit of playing chess, every evening, from seven to nine.

I found him extremely interesting. He was a physician, though he had long since ceased to practice medicine, and had devoted himself, so he old me, to the study of bacteriology. He was, moreover, a man of wide culture; and there seemed to be hardly any subject of which he had not a more or less thorough knowledge. But what charmed me in the man was his kindness of heart. His philanthropy was not bounded by any of the limitations of race or creed. The sufferings of the poor touched him profoundly, whether they were Germans, Italians, or Frenchmen. His love for animals was unmistakable, in spite of the fact that he daily inflicted tortures on the unfortunate subjects of his experiments. I had a collie, between whom and Professor Schwartz a deep affection sprang up, and the man was never so happy as when the dog sat by him with its head resting on his knee. There is no reason why I should hesitate to say that Professor Schwartz came, in time, to be sincerely attached to me, for there can be no doubt of the fact. I wondered that such a man should live so completely alone; but once, when I spoke of the matter to him, he gravely replied that a man should live for the benefit of others, and that his studies were of much more importance than his pleasures could possibly be.

One day, my collie came into my room, evidently suffering the greatest agony. He was swelled out to twice his ordinary size, and he had hardly sufficient strength to drag himself to my feet, where he lay moaning. My first thought was of my neighbour's medical skill, and I rushed over to his house, and implored him to come to the aid of the poor dog. The man came instantly, bringing with him a huge bottle of some disinfecting fluid, and showing an agitation which surprised me in one who had spent so much of his life as a practicing physician. The dog was dead when he reached the room where I had left him, and the professor instantly poured the entire contents of the bottle over the carcass, and then sent me for his spade. When I returned, he carefully removed the dog's body to the garden, and buried it, exercising the greatest care not to touch it, except with the spade. Then he went to his house, bidding me remain in the room where the animal had died, and when he returned he disinfected the room and everything in it with chemicals that caused a thick but entirely respirable smoke. To my inquiry as to what was the matter with the dog, he merely replied that the animal had been poisoned, and asked me if I had seen the dog digging in his garden. I had seen nothing of the kind, but I saw that the professor suspected that the animal had dug up the remains of some guinea-pig or rabbit that had died of an extremely infectious disease. This explained the elaborate care with which disinfectants had been used, though I could not but think that my friend had been unnecessarily alarmed.

I had been acquainted nearly two months with this mild and lovable vivisectionist, when one evening our conversation fell upon Anarchism. The usual bomb had just been exploded in Paris, and I was expressing a good deal of indignation at the miscreants who did such things.

"The Anarchist means well," replied Professor Schwartz; "but he is hopelessly stupid. He attacks the wrong people, and he uses absurdly inefficient weapons."

"What do you mean by saying that he attacks the wrong people?" I asked.

"Just what I say," he replied. "The Anarchist wants to kill men who have money—capitalists, and small or great shopkeepers, and employers of labour. These are the very people who are most necessary to the existence of humanity. If the Anarchist tried to kill labouring men, he would be working for the emancipation of the race from poverty and misery; but he cannot see this."

"I hardly see it myself" said I. "Do you mean that the true way to lessen suffering is to kill the sufferers?"

"Yes and no," said Professor Schwartz. "My dear friend, listen to me. All the poverty on this earth is the result of over-population. Why does the Italian labourer work for two francs a day, and spend his whole life in a state of semi-starvation? The Anarchist says that the labourer is oppressed by the capitalist. That is rubbish. A man works for two francs a day because there are so many workmen that the price of labour is wretchedly low. Halve the number of workmen, and you would more than double the wages of the remaining ones. The same thing is true of the men in this town who make a miserable living by raising vegetables. Each man has a little morsel of ground, and he can hardly raise enough to keep himself from starvation. Reduce the numbers of these small proprietors one-half, and you would double the amount of land which each one would cultivate, and thus double their aggregate incomes."

"That sounds very mathematical," I answered; "but I haven't that sublime confidence in figures that I had when I was younger."

"Any man who sees things as they are must admit," continued the professor, disregarding my interruption, "that the world is horribly over-populated. If a pestilence should sweep off two-thirds of the workmen in Europe, the survivors would be able to live in comfort. Now, the Anarchist doesn't see this. He would kill off the capitalists—the very men who employ labour, and make it possible for labourers to live. I, on the contrary, would not harm a single man who has money to pay to others, but I would remedy this fatal overpopulation—an evil which grows worse and worse every year. Your English Malthus had a glimpse of what was coming, but he did not foresee what the remedy would be."

"Then, there is a remedy?" I asked.

"Yes. Did I not tell you that the remedy is to reduce the working population? The man who discovers how to do this most swiftly and effectually will be the greatest benefactor this world has ever known."

It rather amused me to hear this man, whom I knew to be gentle and tenderhearted, actually insisting that about one-half of the population of the globe ought to be murdered; but I thought little of it at the time. I knew how fond some men are of propounding bold and startling theories, which they themselves would be the very last to dream of carrying into action. Here was a man, whose business in life had been to heal the sick, and so to prolong the existence of the weakest specimens of the human race. And now he was saying that the extermination of millions of healthy, vigorous men was the one thing that the world needed! It was another illustration of the inevitable bee which, sooner or later, gets into the bonnet of every scientific man.

I have said that Schwartz lived completely alone. A man in good health can do this, but if he is taken ill he soon finds that he must depend on the help of others. One afternoon Professor Schwartz did not appear in his garden, and when I went to his house, in the evening, he did not come as usual to open the door. Suspecting that he was ill, I went to the side of the house, where I knew his room was situated, and called to him. He answered, but without showing himself at the window. He was not quite well, he said, but assured me that he would be able to see me the next day, and that in the mean time he should want no assistance. He would not consent to see me; and I went back to my villa somewhat uneasy, and half determined to break into Schwartz's house the next morning in case he still refused to open the door.

That extreme measure, however, did not prove to be necessary. When I called at his house in the morning, he opened the door, and invited me to come in. He was looking wretchedly ill, but he assured me that his attack was over, and that there was not the slightest cause for uneasiness. He took me into his library, and tried to converse with his usual ease. The attempt was a failure, and I saw that, besides being weak from the effect of his illness, he was both preoccupied and troubled. Finally, I asked him to tell me frankly what was the matter, and to permit me to be of any service that might be possible.

He remained silent for a little while, and then he said—

"My dear friend, I have made up my mind to trust you. My illness has shown me that it is no longer safe for me to keep my secret absolutely to myself. I shall die suddenly, and possibly very soon. In that case there must be some one who will know how to prevent the catastrophe which would otherwise happen to this pretty little: town, where I have spent so many happy hours. Give me your word that what I shall tell you shall remain a secret so long as I live."

I gave him the desired promise—rashly, as I now know, but without dreaming of its nature.

He rose from his chair and told me to follow him into his laboratory. There was nothing remarkable in the appearance of the place. I had once before seen the laboratory of a bacteriologist, and it closely resembled Professor Schwartz's except that the fittings of the latter were rather more elaborate and complete. On one side of the room was a series of shelves filled with carefully-sealed glass tubes, containing what I assumed to be gelatine. Schwartz called my attention to these, and said—

"If you should find me dead, or dying, some day, I want you to take every one of these tubes, break them one by one in a bucket full of the liquid which you will find in yonder glass jar, and then bury the contents of the bucket, glass and all in the earth not less than four feet deep. Do this with the utmost care, making sure not to break a single tube except under the surface of the liquid, otherwise I cannot answer for your life. You perfectly understand me?"

"Perfectly," I said; "and I will promise to carry out your wishes. The tubes, I presume, contain the microbes of various diseases."

His face lightened up with a glow of enthusiasm.

They contain the microbes of diseases," he replied; "but the diseases are nearly all new. They are inventions of my own, and some of them are infinitely more deadly than any disease known to the medical profession. You remember the death of your dog? The poor fellow died of a disease which is absolutely new, and which kills in less than six hours. If that disease were once introduced into any city in the world, it would spread so rapidly that in a week the place would be depopulated."

"I do not understand what you mean by newly invented diseases," said I. "How is it possible for a man to invent a disease?"

"Allow me to sit down," said the professor, "for I am too weak to remain standing. The answer to your question is very easy. Certain diseases are produced by certain microbes, and hitherto bacteriologists have confined themselves to trying to discover the specific microbe of each disease, and to find a remedy that will kill the microbe without killing the patient. No one but myself has ever tried to develop the deadly powers of known microbes. Look at that tube numbered 17. It contains the microbe of typhoid fever, but I have cultivated it until it will produce the disease in twenty-four hours after the microbe is taken into the system, and will kill the patient infallibly in twelve hours more. That is only one of a dozen similar successes that I have obtained. Then I have crossed different microbes, or rather cultivated them together, so that they have become capable of producing a new disease, partaking somewhat of the character of each of the diseases which the same microbes, if cultivated separately, would produce. It was I who invented, in this way, the present variety of influenza, by crossing the microbes of malarial fever with those of pneumonia. I was living in St. Petersburg at the time, and I accidentally dropped the tube containing the germs of influenza. Some one must have found it and opened it, for when the influenza broke out I instantly recognized it as my own invention."

"I have always heard," I ventured to remark, "that the influenza is a disease which has appeared in Europe several times during the present century."

"There have been epidemics of a disease called influenza," he replied, "but they differed from the present one. They lacked the symptoms of malarial poisoning, which are characteristic of my own influenza. I have always been very sorry that I lost that tube, for an epidemic of influenza can do no possible good, and does great harm. But to come back to what I was saying before we spoke of influenza. Look at tube number 31. It contains microbes that will produce a disease having some of the characteristics of hydrophobia, and some of those of dropsy, while it also has symptoms which are entirely new. It was one of the earliest of my new diseases, and would certainly be very efficacious, should it ever become epidemic. I have, however, invented other diseases which are far superior to it. Here is a tube," he continued, taking it almost lovingly in his hand, "which contains my *chef d'œuvre*. The microbes are a cross between those found in the venom of the *tuboba*, the most deadly of all known serpents, and those of the Asiatic plague. By the way, I am the first man to discover the existence of microbes in snake-venom. I call the new disease which these crossed microbes produce the 'Purple Death,' for the reason that the body of the person who is attacked by it becomes purple before death. It kills in less than thirty minutes, and there is no remedy which has the slightest effect upon it. As to its infectious qualities, it is the king of all diseases. If I were to break this tube while we are in this room together, you and I would be dead within an hour, and from this house the infection would spread so rapidly that in two days, at furthest, not a human being would be left alive in this poor little town. Think what would happen were we Germans to use these microbes in our next war with France. A single bomb filled with the Purple Death, and thrown within the lines of a French army, would render a battle an impossibility. Before six hours were over there would not be left in an army of four hundred thousand men survivors enough to bury the dead!"

The man's eyes sparkled with pride. His weakness had almost vanished while he was talking, but suddenly he sank back on his chair, and feebly begged me to assist him into the other room.

When he was lying on the sofa, and had somewhat regained his strength, I asked him what possible good he expected to accomplish by adding to the number of diseases which already afflicted humanity.

"I have told you," he said, "that I am a philanthropist, only, unlike other philanthropists, I have intelligence and, I hope, the courage of my convictions. You have heard me say that all the poverty and misery of the world are due to over-population. Well, I have there in my laboratory the remedy for this evil. I can, with merciful swiftness and with absolute certainty, reduce the population of Europe to a half, or a third, of what it now is. I have only to take my Purple Death, and scatter the teeming gelatine on the sidewalk of the most crowded street of your London. It will dry quickly, and under the trampling of hundreds of feet it will become pulverized, and the particles will float in the air. That very day the physicians will find themselves in the presence of a disease wholly unknown to them, and against which medical science can achieve nothing. In a few days London will be silent. The working-classes and the poor will be dead, and every one who can possibly fly from the stricken town will have fled. When the pestilence has spent its force we shall hear no more of the unemployed workmen in London. There will be more work than workmen can be found to do, and the very street-sweepers will receive wages that will permit them to live almost in luxury.

"Or, say that I wanted to decrease the population of Berlin. I simply place some of that gelatine in an envelope, and send it through the post to the head workman in some factory. He opens it, and the Purple Death breaks out among the workmen. Nothing can stop it until it has run its course. Of course, a percentage of capitalists and employers of labour will fall victims to the disease, but its ravages will be chiefly confined to those who have not the means to escape from the city. Did I not tell you that the Anarchists select the wrong victims, and that their favourite dynamite is absurdly ineffective in comparison with the weapons that I can use. Now you see that I told the truth. Man, the lives of half Europe are in my hands!"

I made no reply. The vastness of the man's horrible scheme stunned me. I had not the least doubt that he spoke the truth, and I had promised to remain silent while his devilish project was carried out.

Presently he resumed—

"I do not want my weapons to fall into hands that would use them ignorantly. That is why I have asked you to destroy every one of those deadly tubes in case I should die without having been able to destroy them myself. I made the discovery yesterday that I may die at any minute, and I am physician enough to be sure of what I say. If I should find myself dying, and should have the time and strength to act, I should set this house on fire, and blow out my brains. So, if you should happen to find my house burning, you will take no measures to check the flames. But I fear that I shall not have the time to do this myself, and so I rely on your help."

"How long since you invented the Purple Death?" I asked.

A troubled look passed over Schwartz's face. "Nearly two years ago," he replied.

"Why have you delayed to use it?" I asked, a sudden hope that the man was not quite so mad a he seemed to be, springing up within me.

"As yet it has killed no one, beside the guinea-pigs, except your dog," he replied. "The dog must have been digging where the guinea-pigs are buried, and so contracted the disease."

"But why have you not carried out your scheme of depopulating the world during these two years?"

"My friend," replied the professor, "I am not so strong as I believed myself. The truth is, I have lacked the courage to begin the work. I have been like a surgeon whose nerves will not permit him to perform a painful operation, although he knows that it is the only means of saving the patient's life. But I shall delay no longer. I may have very little time to live, and, besides, now that I have told you all, my secret is no longer safe. Oh, I do not for an instant doubt your word, and I have perfect confidence in your friendship, but when a secret is known to more than one person it is no longer a secret. But I will have more courage. In another week I shall be as well as ever, and then I will begin the work of redeeming the world from poverty. Now I must ask you to leave me, for I must try to sleep. By-the-by, you will find a duplicate key of my door hanging on a nail in the hall. Take it with you, and don't hesitate to use it in case of necessity."

I left the professor, and returned to my house, in a most unenviable state of mind. I had not the slightest doubt that what he had told me was strictly true. Granting that the man was mad—and surely no sane man could have calmly proposed the murder of hundreds of thousands of unoffending men—still the death of my dog was sufficient evidence that Schwartz's claim that he had invented microbic poisons was true. I had given him my word to remain silent. If I kept my promise I should be accessory to the crimes which he unquestionably meant to commit. If I betrayed him, I not only broke my word, but I made it certain that either he would be condemned to a madhouse, or would be sent to the gallows. I could not determine what it was my duty to do, and I spent a night of more terrible anxiety than any criminal ever spent who knew that the gallows awaited him in the early morning.

All night long, and far into the next day, I ceaselessly debated the question what ought I to do. Towards noon, not having yet heard any sound of life in my neighbour's house, I took the key, and, entering, went up to his bedroom. He was lying in bed, with the bedclothes drawn up close to his chin, and I spoke to him, but he did not answer. When I touched his forehead I found that he was dead and cold. He had evidently died soon after going to bed, for the body was already perfectly rigid.

I did not lose a moment in destroying the tubes in his laboratory. I placed them carefully, one by one, in a bucket filled with the disinfecting fluid which he had shown me, and broke them with a blow of a marble pestle. When this was done, I carried the bucket into the garden and buried it deep with its contents. I should then have been ready to send my servant to notify the authorities of Professor Schwartz's death had it not been for one thing. The tube containing the Purple Death was missing from its place on the laboratory shelf, and I had been totally unable to find it. So long as this remained above ground, all that I had done was comparatively useless. Doubtless the tube would be found by the officers whom the Syndic of the town would send to search the apartment, and take charge of the dead man's effects. Then it would be broken, purposely or accidentally, and the frightful consequences that Schwartz had predicted would be inevitable.

I searched every corner and cranny of the house without finding the tube. Finally I began to hope that the professor had himself destroyed it, fearing that he was near his end, but that he had been unable to destroy the rest of his poisons. Comforting myself with this solution of the mystery, I went to his bedside to smooth the bedclothes before sending for the police, and in so doing I found the Purple Death clasped firmly in his hand!

It was impossible to loosen the dead man's grasp, and, after vainly making the attempt, I gave it up, fearing to break the tube in the effort. I called my servant, and told him to go first for the village doctor, and afterwards to notify the police, and then I sat down to await events.

The doctor arrived promptly, and proved to be a very intelligent man. I told him the whole story that the professor had confided to me, with the exception that I did not hint at the use to which the dead man had proposed to put his terrible inventions. The doctor found no difficulty in believing what I told him, and it evidently gave him a profound respect for his deceased *confrère*. He agreed with me that it would be dangerous to meddle with the tube which the corpse clasped in its rigid hand, and promised me that even if an autopsy should be necessary, he would see that the tube remained undisturbed. I think he was a little shy of coming too closely in contact with the body, lest the professor should have died of one of his new diseases. At any rate, he decided to accept my theory that Schwartz had died of heart-disease, and persuaded the Syndic that an autopsy would be quite superfluous.

Professor Schwartz was buried within twenty-four hours, with the Purple Death still in his right hand, The police were easily persuaded that it contained some holy relic, and that it would be impious to meddle with it. When the funeral was over, I left the place as soon as I could pack my boxes, and surrendered the lease of my villa. I have never seen it since, and never want to see it.

On my way back to England I passed through Berlin, where I went to see an eminent bacteriologist, and asked him how long microbes inclosed in a tube containing gelatine would retain their vitality. His answer was, "For ever, so far as is at present known." That answer has poisoned my whole life. Six feet underground, in the grave of Professor Schwartz, lies the Purple Death, waiting until the day when the cemetery will share the fate of all cemeteries, and be cut up into building lots. Then the tube will be exhumed and broken, and the pestilence that is to sweep away the teeming millions of Europe will begin its work. Sooner or later, this is morally certain to happen. I have sometimes thought of exhuming the coffin of Professor Schwartz, and searching for the fatal tube, but to do this would be to invite the catastrophe which I dread, for in all probability the tube has become unsealed by this time. My only hope is that an earthquake will some day bury the cemetery too deep for any spade to reach the grave of my poor mad friend.

THE PLAGUE SHIP
JACK LONDON

"What's this! What's this! Do you wish to kill the man? Such treatment is too heroic. Bah! An emetic of ipecacuanha, fifteen grains of powdered calomel and as many of quinine, and then castor oil! Why my dear madam, you know absolutely nothing about medicine!" and the speaker glared indignantly at her.

She flushed, half hurt, half angry, but smothering her feeling, replied, "What do you take the case to be? Typhus?"

"No. It's merely a bilious fever, made the more severe by this d—, I beg your pardon, this infernal weather."

"Bilious fever! Ha! Ha! Ha!" They had withdrawn from the side of the sufferer, and she burst forth into merry peals of laughter.

"Yes, madam, I repeat it. Bilious fever. Bilious fever! Do you hear? Bilious! Bilious! Bilious fever!"

"My dear sir, though I do not know you, from the wondrous knowledge you display I'll call you doctor. Then doctor, let me ask you if you have ever heard of black vomit, or, if that does not come within your technical nomenclature, yellow fever?"

"What symptoms does the man evince. Madam Know-It-All?"

"Miss Know-It-All, if you please. Languor, chilliness, muscular pains, headache, fa—"

"Precursors of any febrile attack. You evidently do—"

"Face flushed, eyes suffused then congested, nostrils and lips red, tongue scarlet, temperature 105, loss—"

"Loss of appetite, hot skin, thirst, nausea, restlessness, and delirium—all the usual accompaniments of any high fever—go on Miss—Miss—"

"Miss Know-It-All. But all these militant symptoms have ceased and he is now in a state of prostration and collapse. This, the *stadium*, is as you know the great characteristic of yellow fever."

"Collapse! Bah! Convalescence. The man is recovering but weak, and here I find you have given him ipecacuanha, calomel, quinine and castor oil. Where's the ship's doctor? I'll have you out of here!"

"As for the ship's doctor, he's sick too, with bilious fever I suppose. And for you, who are you, pray? Don't rest under the hallucination that you are still walking your hospital, wherever it may be. I am as competent as you; nay, have a diploma as well as you: and as to this case, have had too much experience to be mistaken."

"Madam—A—A—Miss—I—I—I—I'll see the captain at once. You're a–a–a—don't know your business!" And in choleric wrath he left her in pursuit of the chief officer.

The steamer *Caspar* had left the West Coast, with a clean bill of health and in first class order, for San Francisco. But fortune had illy favored her and from the first day her voyage had been one of trials and tribulations. She had been fearfully overloaded with both cargo and passengers. So low did she float in the water that she seemed and behaved like a log. All buoyancy was lost: she was dead, plunging through instead of rising to the great seas she had met with. In this condition she had encountered a storm, broken her propeller shaft, and been blown hundreds of miles out of her course into the Pacific. The engineers had worked night and day but could effect no permanent repair. They would manage to run the engines a few hours, then their patches would give away and they would be forced to stop twice as long to again make ineffectual repairs. They were still far out of their course and even the captain did not know when they would get back. To make it worse, they had been blown into an unfrequented portion of the ocean, far from the beaten paths, and could look to no outside source for assistance.

There were 158 first class passengers and only berths for 95. Many of the ladies were forced to sleep on lounges and settees, while the gentlemen literally floored and walled the smoking saloon when bedtime came. While it was thus rather hard on the first class passengers, it was worse on the second, and in the steerage it was frightful. Some of second-class berths were directly over the screw and so close to the Chinese quarters as to be rendered almost uninhabitable by the fumes of opium and otherwise abominable stenches. In the after-lower-deck, it was more like a cattle ship. Four Chinese, half a score of Negroes, and quadruple as many white people, the majority of which were seasick, were crowded into this hole. So far down was it, that there was no ventilation save through the ports, which more often were bolted down than otherwise.

And now, in the fierce tropic heat of midsummer, to cap their misery, fever had broken forth. While many were hasty in proclaiming it the terrible yellow jack, the more clear-headed, cognizant of their horrible condition, naturally attributed it to that. The ship's doctor, a too efficient and too poorly paid man, had been the first to come down, leaving the passengers and men to take care of themselves. Their endeavors had been spasmodic and erratic. A fifth of the crew were down and the rest were on the verge of mutiny, threatening to take to the boats. The firemen and stokers were as bad, no longer yielding subordination to their officers. The Chinese, while none were taken ill, continued to stolidly smoke their opium, turning a deaf ear to the protests of the passengers and the commands of the captain, which they knew could not be enforced. The first officer, in despair, had taken to whiskey and was now locked up in a fit of horrors, while the rest of the officers were nearly crazy in their impotency. The passengers were just beginning to awake to their danger; but as yet, save for the isolated efforts of the couple that quarreled over the diagnosis, had done nothing.

Doctor Chandler, who maintained it was bilious fever, had yet to meet his thirtieth birthday. He was returning from an expedition to Peru, on which he had been absent a year. Long retired, in fact, except for his hospital experience, he had never taken up a practice; for the same hand that educated him, had, on its demise, endowed him with an ample fortune. Possessed of a scientific worship for good sanitation—it was his hobby—to the absence of it he attributed, under various names, the sickness which had fallen on them.

Miss Appleton, while possessed of a diploma, had perhaps not as much experience in hospitals, but of Southern origin, she had gone through an epidemic of yellow fever in New Orleans and was familiar with all its symptoms. She was a woman not more than twenty-five, beautiful as the word goes, but owing more to a pleasant, forceful personality than to her physical charms. Traveling with her aunt, as soon as the disease had manifested itself, she deserted her to the attention of a maid and threw herself into the breach. And thus, just as she had attempted her first case, had she encountered Doctor Chandler, who had similarly awakened and who was in search of his first patient.

Several days had elapsed and things were going from bad to worse. At last, everybody had been forced to acknowledge that the disease was yellow fever, even Doctor Chandler, who had become very contrite and usually begged Miss Appleton's pardon every other time they met. Though rather rash and headstrong, he was really a good fellow at heart, and soon the twain were on the best of footings. He was generous and self-sacrificing to a fault and devoted himself night and day to the struggle. Maud Appleton easily penetrated his brusque exterior and grew to understand and like him. Still, they occasionally quarreled over methods of treatment, nor, it must be confessed, was she always in the right.

In the meanwhile, the ship's doctor, several of the stewards and cooks, and quite a number of the passengers and crew had succumbed and been given hasty sea burial. The captain had caught the contagion and lay helpless in his stateroom, leaving only the second and third officers to manage the men whom every day saw the more unruly and boisterous. Save the two doctors and the dozen or so that had volunteered as assistants, the passengers were sunk in a state of lethargic horror. At first they had been panic stricken, but that had now subsided and they had become stolidly indifferent to the course of events. They recognized no ties except those of blood, and selfishly struggled for their individual creature-comforts—few, it must be acknowledged, they obtained, for each hour the discipline grew more lax and nothing could be obtained from the stewards and waiters without liberal tipping. In short, the plague ship had become a floating hell in which brute struggled with brute for survival.

Sick and giddy, Miss Appleton had staggered from out the fetid atmosphere below-decks, and now was leaning over the rail in a vain effort to catch some refreshing breeze. The *Caspar* lay in the trough of the sea idly rolling to the smooth swell. She had no steerage-way; the quartermaster had deserted the wheel; the engineers had given up the struggle; and despair had settled upon the ship. The heat was suffocating, and as Maud panted for breath she was approached by the indefatigable Doctor Chandler, who had new cause of quarrel concerning the treatment of one of her patients. But they quarreled good-naturedly now, more in pleasant badinage and sharp repartee. Amid all their misery, it had become their one source of pleasure—a contest of wit and skill, in which personality was lost in the keenness of professional zeal. Though their methods were quite diverse, he had lost as many patients as she, while in the number of recoveries she was one the better of him—the patient over which they had had their first dispute being now in the last stage of convalescence. This rankled the doctor, in a professional way, and did not in the least abate his faith in his treatment, while he ascribed her success to a phenomenal streak of luck, which gave her the patients that would have recovered any way.

But while they enjoyed themselves in their merry dispute, affairs of moment were approaching a crisis. The crew had long before deserted their stuffy fore-castle and camped on deck beneath sails spread as awnings. Later they were joined by the stokers, oilers and firemen, who brought along their sea-bags and blankets. Here, in full view of the terrorized passengers, they played cards, fought, cursed God and man, and refused all duty. Too powerful to break, the officers were forced to send their meals to them and to pray that they would not take to the boats. For all their lawlessness, however, they maintained a crude organization and enforced their rules with terrible penalties. Whenever one fell sick, he was carried away to the fore-castle and attended upon by shifts appointed for that purpose. Only this morning, the remainder of the cooks, waiters and mess-boys had deserted and come forward to join them. As the crowd of them, carrying all the paraphernalia for an improvised camp, came marching along the deck, they had received an otherwise than cool reception.

"I say, lads, what the — are we to do for cooks and mess-byes and grub?" queried one of the tars.

An instant sufficed for the mutineers to grasp the situation. With belaying pins and sheath-knives they drove the would be deserters, bag and baggage, back to their duty, incidentally breaking a few heads and creating a momentary pandemonium. This incident had given the shifty second and third officers their cue, which they were soon to utilize with such disastrous consequence.

The mutineers quickly gave full intimation of their next procedure. They took possession of the boats; saw to it that they were seaworthy; and looting the hold, provisioned them. The passengers crowded the after-decks in a terror-stricken mass, while a few of the more clear-headed grouped round the officers and placed themselves at their service. As the day proceeded, the panic grew: several mutineers they saw fall to the deck, overcome by the heat and the dread yellow jack. These were quickly carried away to the improvised hospital while their comrades worked the faster in completing their preparations.

Nor was this the only trouble which threatened. The three score Chinese between decks, who till now had manifested no discontent, were ripe for revolt. The contemplated desertion of the cooks and waiters had left them without food for twenty-four hours, and the officers had been forced to lock them in. Left to their fate, their yells and curses penetrated throughout the ship and at any moment they were expected to break forth. To add to the terror, the sick and dying, actuated by some subtle impulse, had broken out in loud cries and wailing.

It was at this moment that the officers put into execution the plan they had conceived. Why not turn these two destructive forces, which threatened them, against each other? The sailors were in just the mood for a fight, and as they never lost any love for their

Asiatic brethren, it would not take much to precipitate one. The second officer argued that if they left the ship, those that remained would be at the mercy of the Chinese, and, since they were bound to take to the boats, it were best to be left behind in safety by cleaning the Chinese out. And again, he thought if the conflict were severe enough, the ranks of the mutineers would be so decimated, that he could conquer them with the help of the passengers, engineers, cooks and stewards.

Maud and Doctor Chandler had concluded their quarrel with the customary assurance of good comradeship and an agreement. Each was to choose a patient that had just come down and take exclusive control, brooking no interference and applying their own method in its extremity. As chance had it, they chose a pair which had just taken to their berths: a young Californian and his sister, returning from a visit to their father, an extensive mine-owner in Peru. She selected the young man, and he, the sister. Leaving the deck, they were elbowing their way among the passengers who had been sent below by the second officer. Amid the confusion on every side, as they entered the saloon, anarchy and hell broke forth.

The hubbub which the Chinese incessantly maintained had ceased for a space; but now, redoubled in fury, it arose, amid the crashing of heavy bodies and the splintering of wood. They heard the rapid revolver snots of the two engineers set to guard them, followed by terrible oaths and shrieks of agony. Then the passageways were thronged and the yellow devils, inflamed with blood, were upon them. At this juncture, the door of the first officer's stateroom flew open, and he sprang out, an awful sight to behold. He was evidently suffering the tortures of *delirium tremens*: his eyes were set and dilated; his gigantic body convulsed with nervous spasms; his mouth a mass of froth and blood. Throwing himself into the doorway, armed with nothing but a huge battle-axe (some curio of his), he held the fiends at bay. The fleeing passengers blocked the other exit while those that remained beheld a wondrous struggle. Among the Chinese were some of the most redoubtable highbinders and hatchet-men of the coast—mercenary and trained fighters for the societies to which they owed their allegiance. Unlike the average Chinese, they were not cowardly: murder and bloodshed was their profession.

His battle-axe described flaming circles of steel as it flew back and forth, hither and thither, on its mission of death. At first, the marauders had rushed to their certain fate; but now they drew back, leaving several of their number beneath his feet. Into the narrow passage they knew he dare not pursue for lack of space in which to wield his great weapon. Stepping to the fore, their leader prepared to finish the struggle. It seemed as though David had come forward to face Goliath. His appearance belied his reputation as the wonderful Ah Sen, the fiercest of all hatchet-men: slender and effeminate of form, his delicate face seemed more that of a smooth-faced boy or woman, than that of a notorious desperado. Seizing the proffered knives of his men, thrice he cast one, full at his opponent. They leaped from his hand like rays of glancing light, turning half way round in mid air and burying themselves in the first officer's breast. Yet he seemed not to feel them. Again he tried; but this time, aiming at the throat, it hurtled past still intent on its mission and sank between the shoulders of one of the ladies, struggling in the press at the other door. The highbinder, evincing not the slightest irritation at his failures, changed the method of attack. Seizing a hatchet, with the speed of the lightning, it pursued the path of its predecessors. Full on the forehead, it struck the giant, who swayed, tottered, sank to his knees: like a cat. Ah Sen followed his weapon to his fate. For one second the giant was endowed with the full vigor of his strength, and in that second, Ah Sen encountered him. There was no struggle. Rising to his feet and totally disregarding the knife which entered his side, he seized the slender-necked celestial by the head with both his hands—once—twice—his body whirled in giddying orbit round his head. There was a snap of bones and rending of flesh and Ah Sen sank to the floor, his neck wrung like a chicken's. The next instant he was joined by his antagonist, who fell beside him, literally hacked to pieces by a score of knives and hatchets.

In the meantime, the officers had been busy persuading the mutineers to do the one act of mercy before they left the ship. The celerity with which the contagion spread and its malignancy, had put them in a fright, terrible to behold in strong, fearless men. They had been loth to listen, doggedly proceeding with the work of launching the boats, all bent upon their departure, but when the noise of the combat reached them and they knew that the Chinese were up, they forsook their tasks, hastily armed themselves with cutlasses distributed by the first officer, and sprang to the rescue.

Dividing into two parties, after killing a few stragglers which they caught murdering and robbing the passengers, they hemmed the remainder in the great saloon. Here, aided by the firearms of the officers, a short but sanguinary conflict ensued, ending in the complete annihilation of the Asiatics.

Exhilarated by their success; their fiercest passions aroused by the battle and blood; all the brutishness of primeval man burst forth and the sailors were in the mood for any mischief. Blood-stained and panting, they grouped about the ringleader, who, qualified with all the attributes that go to make the sea-lawyer and popular demagogue, addressed them in a short but very trite speech:

"Ho! My lads! We've blasted the heathen and saved the ship—never say die says I—we've saved the passengers too—ain't it so? (Interruptions of "Aye, aye, that we have.") and in saving their bloody necks, we save their treasures too—what say ye? (An' where do we come off? Aye, that's the ticket!) Hold your jaw, Jack Gunderson: I'm coming to that. Yes, where do we get off? The company? (Ha! Ha! Ha! The skinflints! They'll pay us—see us with Davy Jones first!) Aye, my lads, that's not true enough: they'd see you in hell first, a-simmering like pork-chops in the galley. But here's the proposition: let the blasted passengers keep their bloomin' lives and us their treasure. What say ye, mates?" A burst of applause and cries of "A loot! A loot!" signified that it had been answered in the affirmative.

Charybdis had saved the passengers from Scylla to engulf them himself. It was not destruction, however, for quickly overcoming the officers and the remnant of their supporters, they assured the passengers of their good will and desire for suitable reward. The latter they at once proceeded to appropriate.

The sailors fell to their work with a vengeance, and in the scenes which followed, there was much mingling of the ludicrous and the tragic. Staterooms were ransacked, baggage of all descriptions turned upside down and inside out, and articles of wearing apparel appropriated; nor did they hesitate to personally despoil the passengers. Maud's aunt, an old lady, yet vigorous in body, mind and invective, led two of the tars, intent on her magnificent earrings, a merry chase. She finally sought refuge in the stateroom of the Senor Morella, an Honduras patriot, martial of aspect and afflicted with a wooden leg—a memento of his latest insurrection. He lay in his berth, dying, with his artificial limb unstrapped but near him. Seizing this redoubtable weapon, she laid about her with such will and good purpose, as to down the robbers as fast as they stuck their heads inside. Quite a crowd ceased their looting to enjoy the fun. But the "old she-devil," as they delightfully termed her, held her own against all comers.

As usual, the men broke into the spirit room, and while some became good-natured and jolly, others became the more violent. Fearing injury to her aunt, Maud hurried forward to persuade her into giving up her jewels, accompanied, of course, by Chandler, as protector. He was quickly dispossessed of his gold repeater and diamond links—little incidents which he scarcely heeded, so intent was he on guarding Maud. She, however, failed in her mission, barely missing being brained by her somewhat confused and belligerent relative. Though frustrated as a peacemaker, she well succeeded in involving herself and protector in new troubles. One of the sailors, a big, hulking brute, rendered amorous by the too-frequent caress of certain plainly labeled bottles, threw his arm about her waist and drew her to him. Quick, full on the lips, he kissed her.

In that moment did the doctor become cognizant of a new sensation—a sensation he knew to be different from any he would have felt, had it been a woman other than her. A swift shoulder-blow, and the man lay in a heap on the floor. The next instant he was on his feet, cursing and glowering malignantly at the doctor, who, in the heat of his anger, made as though to repeat the performance.

To Maud, events followed like a flash: the fellow's cutlass hissed through the air; a comrade interposed another; the blow was broken but still fell upon Chandler's head; and when she beheld the rush of blood, she experienced a strangely-intense and solicitous anxiety for him.

"A breeze! A breeze! My hearties! Fair wind for Mexico!" came a cry from above. A second saw the mutineers on deck, springing into the boats which lay along side. The *Caspar* was deserted.

In the bloodstained cabin, amid the weeping and shrieking of women, the wailing of the fever-stricken, and the curses and groans of the dying combatants, Chandler, bathed in a baptism of blood, and Maud, flushed and fainting with what had transpired, sprang or rather tottered and fell into each other's arms. There, in that moment of horror, with all the hideousness of the present and terror of the future upon them, they confessed their newly-discovered and mutual love.

Many days had elapsed. Helpless, the *Caspar* drifted about with her cargo of misery and death. No help had come: none was expected, save through the safe arrival of the deserters in Mexico, which was merely problematic. In the absence of this disorderly element, the survivors had settled down to an orderly existence, systematized everything, isolated forward the fever patients, and were getting along far better than might have been expected from people in their condition. As a traveler in Yosemite loses all conception and appreciation of height and distance, so had they lost all horror of their situation. Continually facing death, they had come to fear it not; and great indeed must have been the occurrence which could have surprised them from out their placidity. They had not broken under the strain but merely accustomed themselves to it. In fact, they were progressing finely, and too much could not be attributed to the two doctors, who, while loving, still quarreled over methods.

Meanwhile, Maud and the doctor, while in no wise neglecting their other cases, devoted themselves night and day to the particular ones of the brother and sister. They had been very sick, but never, even in the worst of crises when the toss of a penny would have almost decided life or death, had the two physicians even dreamed of consulting each other. They had put into the fullest operation their favorite methods, and so strong was their professional rivalry, that they abided the result with far more anxiety than is usually the lot of the patient to receive from its physician. In fact, so extreme had the contest become, that they devoted all their spare time to the nursing, scarcely seeing each other, save to quarrel about the merits of their respective schools or to twit each other, as the case might be, on any bad signs which might have been manifested. Still it seemed as though the superiority of either was not to be thus exemplified, for neither patient had died, and both were now fairly convalescent. Nevertheless, each had been surprised at the zeal displayed by the other, and now, when all danger was past, all doubts vanished, their surprise grew as their zeal flagged not.

The days took their allotted course, slipping silently, imperceptibly, each into the other, while no new incidents or happenings arose to vary the monotony of their existence. In truth, the gods had smiled upon them in their distress. The *Caspar* encountered no storms while the fierceness of the epidemic began to abate. Perhaps, because everybody, with the miraculous exception of the two physicians, had been either killed or cured. Everything was on the mend: nothing was apprehended except bad weather, and even in that the *Caspar* stood a fair show of remaining afloat. In case of storms, small sails had been prepared by which to heave to and ride them out. With the dwindled company and the great boilers, the engineers had no difficulty in maintaining the fresh water supply, while, as part of the cargo was composed of food, little was to be feared from starvation. Slowly the summer dragged on, but quickly the sick list grew smaller, till finally, amid great rejoicing and festivity, it had become totally negated and the ship thoroughly fumigated.

But while everything was so bright, Maud found herself tormented by strange thoughts and discovered an inconsistent vein in her nature which she had never dreamed of. Again and again she summoned herself to judgment, but always to judge in vain, for in despair, she invariably threw the case out of court. Sometimes she came to herself and was appalled at the thoughts which had risen uncalled in her mind, at the visions she unconsciously contemplated. Her life became one tangled mesh of self-analytical whys and wherefores, its and musts, pros and cons. The more she endeavored to reason with herself the more entangled and confused she became. Cold memories of some possible past mistake caused her to often shudder, to avoid the present, and to fear the future which must be shaped by the impress of that possible wrongdoing. Still she could not find the heart to blame herself: she could only not understand.

As it fared with her, so fared it with Chandler. He also found himself involved in a sea of seeming self-inconsistency. But he behaved differently from Maud—she was a woman. His masculinity and choleric disposition asserted itself, and not only did he clearly see his past mistake, but he grew enraged and waxed indignant at himself, often cursing the son of his father with such sublime abstraction from self as to be truly startling. Still, in the obscurity of his mental vision, he could see so far and no farther. If he could have seen beyond, doubtless he would not have figuratively kicked himself so often, nor would his life had been tinged with savage melancholy which now gnawed at his heart-strings so unceasingly.

With these inward ills tormenting them, their intercourse with each other was not exactly that of fond lovers; and their very cognizance of this but increased the pitch of their misery. They constantly upbraided themselves after the many such unsatisfactory meetings, as being the causes of the same—nor was this the less severe, for each unselfishly and ignorantly pocketed all the blame, deeming the other to have been the person injured. Under such circumstances, he became gloomy and irritable, while she well hid hers beneath a mask of gaicty and enthusiasm in all the little social events on shipboard. Very naturally, this diversity of mood drew them the farther apart.

And so, while the collective prospects of the little community went from good to better, their individual affairs traveled with unseemly haste from bad to worse. Logically, this stretching out to the extremes must reach an end sometime, and both, intuitively recognizing this, pondered expectantly over the outcome. To make matters worse, they no longer quarreled: this new state of affairs was maintained with the stiff awkwardness of self-consciousness, from which each suffered the more acutely, never suspecting the other to be in the same dilemma. So affairs rapidly approached a crisis, and one night, when the situation had become almost absolutely unbearable to both parties, the electric searchlight of a man of war, sent out in quest of them, vaguely foreshadowed to each a cessation of their troubles.

The passengers were crowding the weather rail of the *Caspar*, devouring the lights of the vessel in the offing and feasting their eyes upon its dim, bulky loom. Amid this scene of boisterous rejoicing, Maud felt strangely out of place. It jarred upon her—this gregarious mass which clustered like bees on every hand. She became aware of a longing for solitude. Yielding to the mood, she slipped away and climbed to the deserted bridge.

Similar had been the feeling of Chandler, and similar the action. He burned from one side as she did from the other. Face to face, with the glare of the searchlight shining full upon them, they met, midway on the bridge. The next instant and they were in darkness. He had taken her hand, yet they spoke not as they gazed on the dancing lights, heard the merry scream of the boatswain's whistles upon the battleship, and dimly discerned a boat as it sprang to the man of wars-man stroke. Nearer and nearer it came; but it was with a strange apathy that they watched it. The next moment and it would be alongside. Seemingly, they both resolved and spoke at the same time. What each said seemed to startle the other. Surprise, doubt, assurance, gratification, happiness, in turn were mutually delineated upon their countenances. What was said they only knew, but it was with light steps and joyous faces, all wreathed in smiles, that they joined their companions of the now-to-be-abandoned plague ship.

Extract from the *San Francisco Daily Herald* of six weeks later:—

> At the Palace Hotel, the consummation of a happy romance, strangely connected with the ill-fated *Caspar*, is about to be attained. Miss Maud Appleton—an M.D. by the way—of New Orleans, and Doctor Chandler of Boston—the two that rendered such effective service in overcoming the plague on the Caspar—are to marry respectively, Mr. Charles Waldworth, Stanford '93, and his sister, the charming Miss Waldworth, of local social note. It is whispered that Mr. and Miss Waldworth, while ill with the fever, were made test cases for a professional contest between the two M.D.s, and so strenuous and successful were their efforts, that the fruition is the happy dual marriage to be celebrated shortly. But more of this anon.

THE PLAGUE-SHIP *TUPISÁ*

GEORGE GRIFFITH

The ride from Magdalena to San Pablo is one of the most wearisome on the journey from Pacasmayo, the coast town, into the Interior, as it is always called in Peru, that is to say, the eastern slopes of the Andes, where the fertile Montaña region stretches away in range after range of magnificently wooded mountains, until the mountains become hills, and the hills melt softly away in the boundless plains of the Amazon.

First, a slow, toilsome ascent of three or four thousand feet; then an even more toilsome descent into the next valley, out of which the next ridge towered up, cutting a clear edge against the sky. At last, however, San Pablo hove in sight—a cluster of white houses in the middle of a green patch far away across an enormous valley three parts up the side of a great ridge about eleven thousand feet high, the last that had to be crossed before the giants of the Andes proper came in sight.

It looked a lovely spot from the distance, but when four hours' more riding brought me to it, I found it just as forlorn and shabby and smelly as all the interior towns of Peru are. It was just about the last place on earth in which I should have expected to stumble across as tragic a sea-yarn as I have heard in the course of somewhat extensive wanderings; and if my man Patricio had not had what he called *una familia*, by which he meant relations, there, I should have gone by another and less difficult route, and the story which is set out hereafter might never have been retold in English. I carried a *recommendacion*, or letter of introduction, to the cura, or parish priest, of San Pablo, which Patricio had secured for me from the governor of the town we had slept at the night but one before, Magdalena. This cost me an advance of two dollars, which went to entertain the *familia*, and Patricio did it in such style that the next day he was quite unfit to travel. So, too, as it happened, was my mule, which was suffering from a gall consequent on the constant shifting of the saddle in the ascents and descents. And that is how I came to spend the day with the cura.

Now, the cura of a pueblo, or township, in the interior of Peru is not, as a rule, the sort of person I should choose for a host. He is usually dirty, dissipated, and degraded—little better, indeed, than his Indian flock, a goodly proportion of whose blood often flows in his veins. But this man was a gentleman, evidently a descendant of one of the old Spanish families which lorded it in Peru in the days of the Viceroys. He was of fair height and good carriage, with a grave, strong face, and, although he did not strike me as being much past middle age, his tonsure was perfectly white. His house was only a four-roomed cottage, built of mud and thatched with maize straw, but it was newly white-washed, and it was very clean; in fact, it was the only really clean house that I entered during my fourteen days' journey. It stood a little way from the village in a pretty, neatly kept garden, and on one side of it there was a piazza commanding a view of simply indescribable grandeur.

By the second evening we had become quite good friends, and he allowed me, after many gentle protestations, to add a bottle of Moquegua, the Burgundy of Peru, to our modest supper. As we sat out on the piazza afterwards, finishing this and smoking our ever-succeeding little brown cigarettes in the delicious coolness of the early evening, we somehow got back into a previous conversation on the Chilian war, which, by the way, seemed to be the last of the world's events that my host had any clear knowledge of.

"The Chilenos were guilty of some terrible cruelties during that war, I have been told," I said, after a little pause.

The remark was really a sort of feeler, for I knew that there were many dark stories told about that bitter struggle, and perhaps this sad-faced, white-haired exile might know some. It was just the time and place, too, for a story, for the moon was getting up and making the mountains look dim and ghostly, and the fireflies were flashing in the shadows under the edges.

"Yes, señor. That is true; but war is war, you know, and Spanish blood is hot. It is fire when it is pure, but it is molten lava when it is mixed with the Indian. Yes, truly there were many horrible things done. I was down yonder then," he went on, motioning with his hand toward the far-away coast across the dim ridges below.

"And therefore, perhaps, you saw some of them?" I said insinuatingly, as I refilled his glass. "You know, Señor Padre, I am a storyteller by trade, and—"

"And therefore," he said, with one of his grave, gentle smiles, "when you meet any one on your travels who knows any stories, you like to hear them, eh? Well, yes, that is good. You know, we Spaniards are great story-tellers, and we would rather hear stories than read them. Yes, as I told you, I was down yonder in the war time, and I saw some things and heard of others—things that you could write much about if you knew them. Let me think, now."

He looked out over the mountains, and up at the big bright stars which seemed to hang in clusters down from the firmament, as they always do at considerable altitudes in very clear air. I thought I saw his face harden in the dim light, and his placid brow wrinkle into something like a frown. Then he turned to me, and said rather abruptly—

"Señor, have you ever heard the story of the plague-ship that came from Panama?"

I had heard some vague rumours of the sinking of a plague-stricken steamer off the coast when I was down in Lima, but either no one that I met knew much about it, or no one cared to talk of it, so I said, without any attempt to conceal the curiosity he had aroused—

"I have heard such a thing mentioned once or twice at some of the ports, but I have never heard the story, if, as you say, there is one."

"Yes," he said, "there is; and, as you have nothing else to do just now but listen, I will tell it to you, if you please; and when you go back to England you can write it, and it will show the English people that even in poor, ruined, despised Peru there are born men who know their duty, and can do it, no matter what the cost. Now, this is the story of the plague-ship—

"It was nearly the end of the war, and the Chilian fleet had captured or destroyed nearly all the poor little navy that Peru had, but there was one vessel which had so far escaped scot free. She was the *Huarura*, a fast merchant steamer which had been armed as a cruiser with good guns, both heavy and light, and, thanks to her speed and good handling, she had done not a little damage to the Chilian shipping and coast towns. She was commanded by a captain of the Peruvian navy, Riccardo Caldera, a man who was then about thirty.

"I must tell you, for the sake of the story, that his father's brother was a merchant in Valparaiso. His own home was in Lima, and before the war Riccardo had often visited his uncle. Now, at his house, about three years before what I am going to tell you about happened, he had become acquainted with the daughter of another Chilian merchant, Señorita Carmen de Salta. To be short, she was very beautiful, and the two fell in love. Her parents were well pleased, for his blood was good and his family rich. Many Peruvians, you know, were still rich before the war.

"But Doña Carmen was still very young, and they insisted that there should be no talk of marriage until she had been to Paris to finish her education, as you know many sons and daughters of our good families here do. To this, of course, Caldera consented gladly, though the parting was sorrowful. She went, and then came the war, and Caldera saw the clouds of battle rise up between him and his hopes of happiness; for war *is* war between the South American peoples, you know, and the hatred that it leaves is bitter.

"Well, the war went on, as every one knows, all to poor Peru's disadvantage, both on land and sea, until Caldera's ship remained the only one that still flew the Peruvian flag. One day, when she was cruising off the southern coast, well away from the land, towards which she only approached at night-fall, she sighted a steamer chasing a sailing-vessel. Caldera put on steam, and ranged up close to the steamer. The sailing-ship hoisted Peruvian colours as he passed, and the steamer hoisted Chilian. That was enough for him. He opened fire as soon as he came within range, and so they fell to.

"The Chilian was a vessel something like his own, a passenger-ship made into a cruiser, and in the end he sank her; but just as she was going down she fired a parting shot after the sailing-vessel, which, by an unhappy mischance, tore a great hole in her stern, and caused her, too, to begin to sink. Almost the last shot before this had damaged the propeller of the *Huarura*, but she could still steam, though slowly, and Caldera at once went to the help of the sailing-ship.

"He found that she was from Islay, and that she had over a hundred fugitives, mostly women and children, on board, who had fled from Islay when the Chilians destroyed Mollendo, and were hoping to make their way to Panama. He took these, with the crew, out of the sinking ship on board the *Huarura*, and promised to carry them to Panama himself, since the Chilians held all the coast now, and, having no orders from the Government, he felt free to do what he thought best for his countrymen in distress.

"So, as there was no possibility for him to get the damage to his propeller made good nearer than Panama, he set out northwards at such speed as he could make with his rescued countrymen on board. This had happened early in the morning, and towards the middle of that afternoon he sighted the smoke of a steamer coming southward, keeping far out as he was for fear of the war-vessels on the coast. He kept on in his course towards her, trusting to his guns in case she should be an enemy, since he had now no more speed left. When the strange vessel came within clear view, he saw that she was a small old passenger-steamer of the Chilian line, which he recognized as one called the *Tupisá*. But there was no flag flying on her, nor, as they came closer, was any attempt made to hoist one.

"He thought this strange, but he saw something stranger still as he came closer, for then, from the bridge through his glasses, he could see that there were people fighting on her decks, some forward and some aft, and he saw that some one in the forward part on the upper deck was trying to hoist a flag, and others were trying to prevent him; but he could see no signs of guns, and so he steered close in, and then he saw a man and a young girl with revolvers in their hands, keeping back a small throng of men, while another man fastened on the flag and dragged it up.

"As soon as the wind took it, it opened out, for it was not tied up as flags usually are—but that, of course, I need not tell you—and when it opened out, he saw that it was yellow. It was the flag of plague, and as it went up the men made a rush forward at it, crying horribly, as if to pull it down again, and the girl and the man fired two or three times each, and drove them back. And then the other man, when he had pulled up the, flag, ran into the wheel-house, and presently dragged out a big blackboard, and held it up on the rail. Caldera turned his glasses on it, and saw the dreadful word "Verole" [*Smallpox*] in big white letters on it. Then the two ships came very near together. The girl, after she had fired away all the shots from her revolver, turned round towards the *Huarura*, and spread her arms out and screamed—

"'Verole! Verole! We are plague-stricken, nearly all of us! Keep away! Some hope to escape, and would board you! Keep away!'

"Then, agonized as the voice was, Caldera, stricken with wonder and horror, recognized it. He turned his glasses on the girl, and recognized her too. It was Carmen, his own Carmen, his promised wife, there on the plague-ship. How she came there, of course he knew not; but she was there, and that was true enough and horrible enough for him.

"Then she saw him standing on the bridge of the *Huarura*, and screamed out again

"'Riccardo! Riccardo caro! Keep away from us! Do not try to rescue any! The verole came on board at Guayaquil. The ship is a pest-house. Keep away! If you cannot, then sink us, for we must die!'

"Now, señor, you will easily see that no man could well have been placed in a more dreadful position than poor Caldera was by these words. He was a gentleman with pure Castilian blood in his veins, and he was also a patriotic son of Peru. He loved this heroic girl as only a Spaniard can love, and he saw her now, in this awful situation, for the first time for three years. He would have given his life—nay, his soul, to save her, but he had a hundred women and children dear to others and his own gallant crew to guard. If the ships touched, the stricken ones would leap on board, bringing horrible disease and death with them. Nay, if even a boat passed from one to the other, the infection would come with it.

"He had seen, too, that the *Tupisá*, slow as she was, was faster a little, a very little, than his own half-crippled ship, and that if he sought to escape her, she must sooner or later overtake him. What hope was there, then, for those under his care save in the last awful resort to the guns?

"Still, even now, he could not bring himself to give the word to fire. Instead, he altered the course of the *Huarura*, and steamed away, shouting back to Carmen—

"Throw yourself overboard, Carmen mia, you and those who are still clean, and we will save you. You others, keep off, or, by the holy saints, I will fire! I would save you if I could, but I have women and children here, and I dare not.'

"Seeing that the *Huarura* was trying to get away, those who had taken the *Tupisá* changed her course and steamed after her. Then Caldera gave the order, and the guns, large and small, swung round, and the muzzles went down. Again he and his officers shouted their warning, and, to show that they were in earnest, a shot was fired across the *Tupisá*, but too high to do any harm. Still she came on, slowly gaining on the *Huarura*. Carmen had fled up on to the bridge, where two or three men, and among them the one who had put out the blackboard, were keeping back the crowd with revolvers, but they could not steer the ship from the wheelhouse, because the mutineers had broken the connection, and were steering with the after-wheel.

"At last, when the *Tupisá* was getting very close, those on the bridge had fired all their cartridges away, and so they, too, began to shout to Caldera to fire because of what he had said about the women and children. They were brave men, you see, señor—men who would rather die themselves than bring death on the innocent. And Carmen cried out, too, praying her lover, by the love he bore her, and by all things holy, to forget his love and do his duty. And while she was crying out thus, there was a rush from the deck to the bridge—a rush of men with faces horrible to behold. There was a fierce fight—a fight with living death for awhile—and then Caldera, his heart torn with agony and his brain reeling with despair, saw one of those deaths in human shape seize Carmen and clap his hand over her mouth.

"The same moment the word 'Fire!' left his lips. The great guns roared out, and a shell burst right under the bridge of the *Tupisá*, blowing it and all on it to fragments. Another pierced her side, and tore a great hole down to the water-line, and at the same time the shot and bullets from the smaller guns fell like a hailstorm on her decks, striking down the already stricken, men and women alike, for there were women also on the *Tupisá*, since she was a passenger-ship—horrible work, señor—work, you would think, for devils, not for men; yet what would you what else could be done?"

"Nothing, I suppose," I said, speaking for the first time since the cura had begun. "It was a hideous situation; but, after all, Captain Caldera did his duty. Of course, the *Tupisá* went down?"

"I am glad you think that, señor," he said very softly; "I am glad you think that. Yes, the *Tupisá* sank, and every soul with her. Some of the stricken wretches swam for the lives they had already lost. They were shot in the water that their agony might not be too long; and then the *Huarura* went on to Panama. That is all."

"You have told me a strange and terrible story, Señor Padre," I said, "and I will tell it again on the other side of the world for the sake of the heroes who did their duty, and of that brave girl who did hers so well."

I should have stopped there, but I didn't, and I said—

"But, if you will pardon my curiosity, Señor Padre, you have told the story as only an eye-witness could have told it. May I ask if that is true?"

"Yes, señor, that is true," he said, rising from his seat and holding out his hand. "I was one of those on board the *Huarura*. Now, *buenos noches!* We have sat late, and you have far to ride to-morrow."

Then I saw the mistake that I had made, and said "Good-night," and went to bed.

At sunrise the next morning the cura brewed me a cup of tea with his own hands, and when I had drank this and the usual *copa* as stirrup-cup, he gave me his blessing, and I started out, with Patricio looking red-eyed and repentant, on my way to scale the pass over which Pizarro and the Conquerors had marched three hundred and sixty years before to seize the last of the Incas in the midst of his victorious host.

Three months afterwards I was sitting with my friend Major Harris on the verandah of the English Club at Callao, telling him of the cura and his story.

"Yes," he said, when I had done, "that is quite true. Señorita de Salta went on board the *Tupisá* at Panama. She was on her way home from Paris. That was found out after the war from the agent's passenger-list. When the war was over, Caldera resigned his commission and entered the Church. I heard afterwards that he devoted himself to teaching the Indians in the Interior, and from what you tell me, I have no doubt that you heard the story from his own lips."

DR. COX'S DISCOVERY
HERBERT D. WARD

Last July I boarded the stanch steamer *Boston* for Yarmouth. There was the usual medley of cooks and waitresses returning from a two weeks' vacation, and of tourists eager for a taste of foreign soil at the cheapest rates. For the most part the faces were common and uninteresting; so, when we passed Boston Light, I fled a group of howling children, whom the swell, I hoped, would soon silence, and, choosing a seat above the screw, fell to reading a most fascinating account of Doctor Broca's discovery of the serum of intoxication.

Like so many other physicians of the modern school, I am an enthusiast over the many microbe theories that tumble over each other in the order of their discovery. What will not the bacillus be responsible for next? Absorbed in the resistless fascination of this speculation, I raised my eyes from my pamphlet, and looked straight into those of a man not ten feet away.

His was a most remarkable face; it conveyed the immediate impression of intolerable anguish. His eyes were sunken, burning with unquenchable intelligence; they looked as if they were vainly seeking compassion, and had lost all hope; the high forehead seemed glazed, as if covered with stretched parchment; his cheeks were hectic and hollowed; the beard, wandering of its own free will, showed the mouth, whose passionate form and sensitive outline, embittered at the corners, indicated a noble character that had been blasted by some extraneous fatality, or by perjured love. The man might have been thirty, but looked fully fifty. His seemed an age of ambition undone, of plans miscarried, and of future disrupted.

For fully two hours we sat there side by side without speaking. I had now ceased speculating upon Doctor Broca's serum, and was filled with curiosity regarding my vis-à-vis. At last, unable to stand the tension any longer, I handed him the pamphlet, and said: "If you are interested in medical discoveries, you will find this of momentous importance to society, if what he claims can be proven."

The stranger's eyes lighted with recognition as he glanced at the title. "Ah, Doctor Broca!" he exclaimed. "I knew him well. I worked with him and Pasteur and Koch before I went to Vienna. I am Doctor Cox."

Through the lobes of my brain there flitted a reverberation of that name. It was associated with the reports of foreign medical journals, and with some remarkable experiments. Indeed, there flashed upon me the association of the name with a discovery that was to revolutionize humanity, and which would be given out at some future time. So I greeted the stranger with that effusion which mediocrity pours upon genius, and gave him my unknown name.

I had never studied abroad, and knew nothing of the incandescent lights—those saviors of humanity—except by reports. Doctor Cox greeted his brother physician with as much cordiality as his reserve could command. Evidently he was pleased not to be alone upon the ship.

"You look as if you had overworked," I said, introductorily.

"No," he answered, with pathetic weariness, "I have not overworked, I have overdone." This distinctive phrase did not detract from the mystery that surrounded the man. We talked for an hour or two before the gong sounded. His deep eyes glowed as he retailed with intimate knowledge the history of Pasteur's and Koch's wonderful experiments. And, as he forgot his own misery, his youth came back before my eyes just as some desiccated plants are suddenly resurrected by a few drops of water.

"Doctor!" I ejaculated, as the last vibration of the gong passed by. "You are suffering from some terrible calamity; you have given up your future, and it is killing you. Anyone with the blindest eyes to symptoms can see that. I wish you cared to confide in me." I felt more like a girl than a man in my impulse, and breathed rapidly. I could distinctly feel my blood accelerating, and expected nothing less than a curt reply, if not an immediate withdrawal.

But Doctor Cox looked at me long and searchingly, until my eyes became blurred, and I could no longer distinguish his features. Then he said, kindly: "Thank you for your interest. After supper, when the rest have retired, and the moon is well up, I will tell you my story, and you can judge whether you can be of assistance to me or not." With that he bowed and left. I cannot now account for my friendly aggression, or for his flood of confidence to a stranger, except for the mysterious fact that natures change upon the high seas.

With what impatience did I await the night! Food was impossible; but time, that flies too fast for the condemned, at last accommodated the waiting. With an ill-assumed air of indifference, I strolled to the stern. Doctor Cox was sitting smoking impetuously. Without a word of greeting, and with startling abruptness, he began his story.

The churn of the tireless screw, the velvet line of smoke, the sheen of the moon upon our quarter, the quiet sea whose horizon was veiled by a tenuous mist: these are my only memories in connection with the marvelous tale which I was permitted to hear.

"I will not burden you," he said, "with the story of my whole life. I will simply say that I am a graduate of Harvard College and Medical School. Ten days after I got my diploma, authorizing me to kill or cure under the law, my father died, leaving me an income that made me independent. In a month I was in Paris, and devoted my nights as well as days to investigation and experiment. I became familiar with the Pasteur School and all that it aimed to accomplish. In the same way I spent two years as Doctor Koch's assistant in his laboratory in Berlin.

"Feeling the need of hospital practise to supplement my laboratory experiments, I went to Vienna, that Mecca of all physicians. In less than a month I met Elsa. Elsa was the most superb woman

I had ever seen. She was a perfect type of blonde. She had all the stateliness of a Margaret, all the piquancy of a Lili, and all the seductiveness of an Undine. She was tall and svelte. Her eyes were star sapphires, and her lips bows of roses. At one moment she could be stately as a princess, at another clinging as a bride. Capricious as the Mediterranean, yet steadfast as the Gulf Stream, she was a woman to be won by hurricane and calm, by volcano and by ice. I became immediately infatuated with her, and was soon on intimate terms with her mother.

"Madame Von Krakenburg was the widow of an Austrian captain of noble blood, and lived a proud life of genteel poverty, which she fancied she hid from all her friends. The only one she deceived was herself.

"In a natural way it came about that I soon hired the whole of her top floor, and so became an inmate of that delightful household. This household consisted only of Elsa, her mother, and an aged Newfoundland dog, called Max. This dog had a strange habit that had grown upon him like the mange, a hatred of Elsa's mother; at the time of my entrance into the family this had become a mania. This extraordinary aversion was undoubtedly due to senility. Devoted to Elsa, Max would growl asthmatically, and show his toothless gums whenever the mistress of the house came into the room. The dog never allowed Elsa to be touched by anyone but me without fierce demonstrations of resentment. I had been provident enough to bribe him the first day I called with sugar pellets.

"One morning I received a summons to go to the hospital to see a patient who had just been brought in. I arrived in time to find a man dying of old age. A careful diagnosis showed that he had absolutely no disorder or ailment. For years I had been looking for just such a case, for I had developed a theory that age was nothing but a disease caused by the ravages of a bacillus which had never yet been seen. Up to this time I had never found a case whose fatality did not result from either disease or accident; but before me lay a man perfect in all his functions, yet so old that his years had long since passed the century-mark. Feebleness without senility, death without impairment of functions—the suspension of the breath of life without a visible cause—here was the opportunity for my years of training. It was the unique case that might solve the insoluble problem. That night the life of the man flickered out while I held him in my arms; and in a moment I was absorbed over specimens of his blood that I had wrung from his reluctant veins. Fancy the feeling of the man who after superhuman efforts discovers the North Pole, or who has lived to see an almost impious theory accepted as a law of the universe! With eyes glued to the microscope, that night I understood for the first time the saying that a day is as a thousand years unto the Lord. In the viscid fluid before me floated the microbe of old age, and in my hands lay the secret of eternal life!

"I must have lost my head; for, when I came to, I found myself in the wintry night, running like a madman home in order to perpetuate in my own laboratory that precious colony of immortal germs. It was icy, and in crossing a street I slipped and fell. At that fatal moment a dozen sleighs darted by on the return from some cursed revel. Ah, if they had only known how they trampled on eternal life! We commit the unpardonable sin in blindness, and giggle and chatter, while Azrael points his shining sword at us, prophetic of our doom.

"When I arose, dazed with the momentous misfortune, the hurricane of hoofs had passed, sweeping with it my slides and specimens—hostages to humanity of undying youth—that had been flung from my hands when I fell. In vain I groped and searched; the discovery had passed me by, illuminating my soul for a brief moment like a blinding flash of lightning, leaving me in greater darkness than before.

"For two months I lay delirious. Elsa and her mother watched over me. During my convalescence, the manner of the mother puzzled and troubled me. She was a splendid woman of about forty-five, in the prime of her vigor, and at times of excitement not looking much older than her daughter. She must have been beautiful in her youth, and indeed I had heard from General Van Fersen that the court of the Emperor held no fairer maid of honor when she was eighteen.

"It was at the time of my greatest depression and perplexity that Elsa told me that the old elephant in the Zoo had died that morning. In an instant I was well. The microbe that I had once held and lost might be found again. Elephants are well known to live to a marvelous age. Fortune, whose daughter I had, alas! kissed, was restoring to me her fitful favors.

"'I must hurry,' I said. 'Have the stove in my laboratory heated. I must see that elephant.'

"'You will take care of yourself?' Madame Von Krakenburg put her hand imploringly upon my arm. But Elsa only pouted. With a hurried assent I jumped into the drosky, and was gone.

"My disappointment only whetted my ambition. Somewhere in the world my great discovery was beckoning me. Somewhere the limit of existence was reached, and at that limit would be found the microbe of old age. I got in the habit of calling it 'my macrobiote.'

"'Madame,' I said one day after supper, 'I am going to leave you for a few months, or even for a year or more. I have a mission to perform for humanity. I have made a great discovery. It must be verified. It may take much or little time; in the meanwhile I wish to keep my rooms intact. If I return successful I shall be hailed as the greatest benefactor the world has ever seen—next, of course,' I said, reverently, 'to the historic Savior. In that case I shall ask you for the hand of your daughter Elsa.'

"Madame Von Krakenburg became very pale, but Elsa looked me straight in the eyes.

"'Mama,' Elsa said, after a long pause, 'I shall marry Carl, and no one else.' She arose, with royal dignity, and held out to me her hand, and I kissed it.

"They accepted my high claims and the necessity for my departure with a beautiful faith, and made suitable preparation.

"The next morning I read an account of a large whale which had been captured alive on the shores of the Baltic. My opportunity called me. I hastily packed in a special case all the apparatus for making and preserving cultures. It seemed as if Elsa's arms could not be untwined from my neck, and that my eyes were fascinated by her beautiful face; but later, when I bade Madame Von Krakenburg adieu, it seemed as if her lips had lost the power of detachment. What did that passionate kiss mean to her? What would it mean to me? Thrilled, but troubled, without another look at my weeping fiancée, I tore myself away, and rushed into the street.

"I need not detail my search for the oldest life the world had in existence. Birds, beasts and reptiles passed under my microscopic gaze. Impatience and disappointment were the travail of my mind, and what hope was left was rapidly dispelled through travail of the body. The carp, the turtle, the snake, the whale, the elephant, the cockatoo—in short, any animal supposed to live longer than the time allotted to average life, underwent a vigorous scrutiny. You know as well as I do that old age comes to animals as well as to man without a feeling of desire to be old. It is therefore abnormal, and it must be a disease. We all fight it. At last, overcome, we accept it with resignation. It occurred to me that this unconscious or even sentient antagonism to old age might be a means itself for hastening its advent, for it is a universal law that what we dread we invite. Every now and then there occurs a rare case where old age comes with a desire for it. Such a clod of a man ought to live forever, for to him there is no waste of the brain and body tissue. The one I found in the hospital may only exist once in a century. I therefore decided to give up animals, and continue my search in plants. They have a circulation of the vital fluid, and may attain an extraordinary age. It has been stated by the greatest botanist that they have morality as well as sagacity. What is an elephant of a hundred years to a tree of a thousand?

"The decision made, I hurried to the Island of Kos, and to its little capital, for there is supposed to exist the oldest tree in the world. It was especially fitting that I should give this historic and guarded monument of ancient civilization a careful inspection, for it is undisputed that under its shade over two thousand years ago Hippocrates wrought his healing arts, and that four hundred years before, Æsculapius, his ancestor, the father of human medicine, beneath its limbs cured the superstitious of their diseases.

Supported by columns of masonry, surrounded by a fountain, and railed from the populace, this most ancient living relic challenged the modern discoverer. Did the bacillus of old age course sluggishly in its atrophied veins? Had this wonderful tree stored in its heart the lore of the ancients? And would it yield up the secrets of eternal life to a disciple of Pasteur?

"This memorial relic of Grecian paganism is probably the most pathetic example of old age in the world. Its enormous trunk is only a hollow shell, and from its scaly bark only a few green shoots struggle for a starved existence. To gather one or two of these became literally the object of my future life. In vain I tried to bribe the zealous guards. No money could accomplish my purpose, for the tree had been worshiped by the simple inhabitants for many centuries; besides, it was the source of the island's greatest income.

"I soon found myself an object of suspicion, and dogged with a persistence that characterizes the bigotry of the Levant. Fortunately, at the critical moment of failure and despair, an Englishman, whom I had met pleasantly in Paris, sailed in on his yacht. I explained that I needed a few twigs of that almost dead descendant of an unknown age for museum purposes, and told him how matters stood.

"Nothing pleases an Englishman more than a spice of adventure in which the superstitions of an inferior race are trampled upon. A few nights later, in a hurricane of wind and rain, a small party of us landed, and made for the sacred tree. The frightened guard was gagged and bound, ladders were hastily unlimbered, and in a few minutes the priceless twigs, oldest known specimens of living growth, were concealed in my breast-pocket. The next morning before sunrise we were in the open ocean, with only purple spots on the distant horizon.

"But all night long my eyes were glued to the microscope, searching in vain for that microbe of old age which I had once held in my possession, and which now seemed to have eluded me forever.

"In three months, after I had eliminated all the possibilities of Europe, I was encamped amid the giant redwood-trees of California; for, after all, it was forced upon my reluctant imagination that the United States not only held the tombs of the most ancient civilizations the world knows of to-day but it also possesses within its fastnesses inorganic life that antedates the Montezumas, the Incas, the Greeks, the Egyptians, the Cliff-dwellers, and even the Mayas—that mysterious race, contemporary with the inhabitants of submerged Atlantis, and cousins to the shepherd kings, who antedated the ancient monarchs of Egypt by many thousands of years.

"I stood, surrounded by the gigantic sequoias, and seemed to be transported into that antediluvian age when ferns scraped the sky, and when dragons were not myths but were fearful realities. It did not take me long to run to earth, or rather to air, the oldest group of this strange species that have been appropriately called 'sempervirens.' At Felton, near Santa Cruz, I soon found myself in a mystical circle of sequoias, more ancient than the Stonehenge, and whose birth perhaps antedated the sacred tree of Kos. The redwood is the natural receptacle of germs and microbes, for, like the fauna of arid zones, its veins contain much water and no resin. Pierce its cells, and it bleeds like an ox at the sacrifice. With infinite pains I selected the oldest of this prehistoric group. There it stood, pointing straight to heaven. Its base was over a hundred and twenty feet in circumference, while its huge fronds swept the pure air hundreds of feet above me.

"I had hardly pitched my tent at the base of this eternal monument, wondering what strange history it had witnessed and had disdained to record during its thousands of years of life, when a party of scientists rode up for purposes of investigation. These confounded college expeditions headed by the inevitable professor! How did I know that under the disguise of a blessing they were about to bring upon me a life's curse? How ignorantly and how buoyantly we walk into the traps that Fate is ready to spring upon us!

"That evening I drew the ichor from the sequoia's veins. It flowed elastically, nay, too eagerly. It lacked the inertia natural to senility. It dawned upon me, even before I prepared the fateful slide, that perhaps the gigantic specimen, born before Abraham was conceived, had not yet arrived at even a respectable old age. Cyclone, fire, flood, the ruthless axe of civilization—these may murder the redwood-tree, but age has not yet wreaked her vengeance on that sublime order.

"My microscope, the most powerful made in Paris, showed, alas! undoubtedly this astonishing fact, that the oldest sequoia known had not yet reached middle life. If it were permitted to live on, it would in all probability witness the rise and bemoan the fall of our boasted American civilization. For such curves of progress and degeneracy are but ephemeral instances during its transcendent vitality.

"'What's the oldest thing alive?' I asked the professor next morning, as I smoked my pipe, trying to calm my vibrant nerves. As his students were off bug-hunting, we had a quiet moment to ourselves. The professor was one of those lean, spry men, whose eyes burn within their cavernous sockets, whose cheeks are high and hollow and hectic, and whose gaunt jaws are covered by fine, gray, unkempt hair. Driving, yet kindly, a bundle of watch-springs, yet philosophic, he combined the solidity of continental learning with the irrepressible originality of American expression.

"'Lichens,' he said, sententiously, as if he were about to deliver a lecture. 'There are some lichens that never die.'

"'Explain.' I looked at him, trying to control my breath. Little did he know how I suffered during those few seconds of anticipation.

"'Take the verrucariaceous apothecium,' he began, lightly, as if he were discussing corn.

"'Yes?'

"'Have you ever been to the Grand Cañon? No? It's a pity. When you go, if you are fortunate, you will see on one of the walls a huge grayish green stain, extending two to three thousand feet in circumference. It is the apothecium. There may not be more than ten specimens in the hundreds of miles of gorge. When the river first flowed, and cut its first depression, this lichen had its birth. As the Canon deepened, the lichen followed its fall. As the erosion averages one foot every thousand years, and the Canon is about three thousand feet deep, you can easily calculate the age of your friend.'

"'Three million years!' I exclaimed, ecstatically.

"'Precisely.' He took a leisurely contemplative puff.

"'But how can it exist on and on indefinitely?'

"'It is because the spores are developed in the thecæ, which constitute, with the paraphyses, the hymenium.'

"'Ah, I see.'

"'If the interior of the conceptacle were not thickly dotted with converging filaments—'

"'Of course!'

"'It continually throws off spore-like bodies, found within the spermogonium—'

"'Spermatia?' I hazarded.

"'Exactly so. It thus became perpetual in its cellular reproduction.'

"Why had I not thought of lichens before? Taking their nourishment from the air, they contain the elemental principle of life as much as a violet, a tree, an elephant, a man. I saw the end of my search and sorrows. I saw in the desert of cathedral rocks, amid the fastnesses of the Grand Cañon, the everlasting fount of eternal youth, the secret of which I alone held in my possession.

"Engendered in the hour the glacier receded from the North American Continent, and alive in the day of King Edward, and in the aggression of Emperor William, and in the might of Roosevelt, it beckoned me to its arid heart.

"'I should think it would be about dead by this time,' I said.

"'Not at all.' The professor waved his hand, lightly, as if a hundred thousand years more or less were a mere turn of the palm.

"'I suppose they will be living when the ice age comes again and engulfs them with the rest of us.'

"'When will that be?'

"'In about ten million years or so.'

"'Then the apothecium is hardly past its teething, so to speak.'

"'Hardly.'

"When I looked up again into the sympathetic and puzzled eyes of the professor, I burst into violent laughter, the hysterics of despair.

"'Now,' said the college professor, strolling up to my tent the next morning, with a shrewd glance worthy of a professional palmist, 'I have been watching you, and I wouldn't take your disappointment so bitterly. Perhaps I can help you.' He held a square pasteboard box in his hand. The box was perforated with holes. 'You are searching for the last throes of life. Is that not so?'

"I nodded, moodily.

"'I suppose its some new germ theory that you bacillus bigots are running to earth.'

"'I suppose so,' I said, warily.

"'And the subject must have lived longer than the number of years supposed to be allotted to the species.'

"'Much longer,' I said, decisively.

"'Well, here's a toad.'

"'A toad!' I said, contemptuously. I fell back against the trunk of the redwood-tree.

"'I suppose you've heard of toads being found imprisoned in coal-seams.' His tone implied indulgent sarcasm.

"'Of course, I have heard of such things, but there are no authenticated cases. It's all tommy-rot. Greville experimented encasting toads and frogs in clay and plaster of Paris, but none ever lived over a month.'

""But still such toads have been found, and here is one whose authenticity is beyond question. I saw it dug out of a coal-seam, fifteen hundred feet under the surface.'

"The professor spoke with such sane assurance that I was aroused as if by a shock of electricity.

"'That was six months ago. I have carried him with me ever since. He has taken only two meals since his rescue. I want to show you his case. There, hold the box carefully. You can take the cover off; he can't move.'

"With the reluctant eagerness natural to a cautious scientist, I gazed upon this world-old specimen. It seemed indeed the gift of an unknown age. The only signs of life were the infrequent heavings of the puffy chest, showing that the lungs could still work. The skin was warty, rough, and wrinkled beyond imagination, and the eyes were glued shut. I touched the animal reverently. It was as cold as the age of ice.

"'Here,' said the professor, interrupting my stare, 'this may convert you. This nodule fell beneath my feet at the end of one of the drifts which I was investigating. Thinking that it might be a fossil, I carefully broke it with my hammer, and the toad fell out on my palm.' The dark bluish slate showed the perfect outlines of a fossil toad. The stone had become the living amphibian's shroud.

"'There is no doubt in my mind,' continued the professor, gravely, 'that this batrachian was born in the Carboniferous age, when coal was forming. Burrowing in clay to hibernate during a winter, it was overwhelmed in one of Nature's stupendous catastrophes, following on the heels of the Devonian period, and thus was included in the coal-formation. It may, and it may not live more than a few hours or a day. Now, young man, tell me what you want?'

"'Only a drop of its precious blood! My God! Professor, only one drop, and I'll be satisfied!' Shaken with an anxiety and wild excitement which I could no longer repress, I trembled almost as if I should disarticulate.

"'I guess your need is greater than mine. The toad is yours,' said the professor, gravely. 'Only don't mutilate the body, I want to keep it as a specimen. You'd better hurry; there isn't much time to lose. There probably will never be found another one like it in the world.'

"I could have thrown myself at the professor's feet. Instead, I prepared my gelatin. In ten minutes I had everything ready for the cultivation of a colony of microbes, if my fate were at hand. Then I took the antediluvian, toothless toad from its box, and bared my scalpel for its divine use. Taking the cold, unresisting creature in the palm of my left hand, I made a quick incision above the heart. Not a drop of blood flowed from its congealed arteries. I plunged the knife deeper, and looked in vain for the priceless fluid. Ah, but I must cut to the heart! If it had nothing to yield, humanity's hope had died with the death of this immortal.

"I plunged the knife in. Then a frenzy seized me. With an oath I grasped the creature, and squeezed it in both my hands. The professor, my promise, everything was forgotten but the fact that I stood at the side of this expiring creature as sponsor for the life of the world. 'Come!' I cried. 'In the name of God Almighty, one drop of blood!'

"Then there slowly oozed like carmine asphalt one dense globule. This I gathered upon the end of my blade. There was no moment for microscopic investigation. I thrust it into the warm gelatinous ooze, Nature's bed for bacilli. Even as I did so, I felt in my hand an icy quiver. I opened it mechanically! The Carboniferous batrachian was dead."

Doctor Cox's voice was lost in the rhythmic pounding of the screw. He lit his pipe, pulled savagely, following the tenuous smoke with his gaze as it was whiffed over the rail out into the silver sea. By the way he scowled as if in pain, I knew that the tragedy was about to be unfolded, and dared not speak. I could only wait for his errant mood to return to me. It might have been after an hour's pause that I heard a click in his throat. It must have been only through a supreme effort that he went on.

"It was night when I arrived in Vienna. The ladies were at the theater, not expecting me until the next day, and I had slipped upstairs, lighted my fire, and was absorbed in the contemplation of my priceless colony of microbes.

"I looked up from my microscope. Elsa stood at the door, closely followed by Max, whose wagging tail was giving me his best greeting. Careful not to jar the table, I caught the splendid girl in my arms, and my lips met hers in the first real lover's kiss that we had exchanged.

"'It has been so long—so long!' she murmured, clinging convulsively. 'I thought I had died waiting for you, Carl, my love!'

"The foolishness that we were guilty of during those first five minutes of transport, if nothing more than a divine memory, was surely worth a century of life. I then held my fiancée at arms' length. Her face was a little thinner and paler, which gave a new glory to her blonde beauty; but her figure was better molded, and this added dignity and womanliness.

"'Ah, dear heart,' I said, aloud, thinking of my cultures, 'you shall never die. I could not bear it.'

"'I do not want to, now I have you, Carl; but I could not have stood another month. I would have died. And Max, poor Max, he is nearly dead now. I only kept him alive by whispering in his ear that his Uncle Carl was coming. Didn't I, Max, dear?' Elsa stooped, and patted the old dog so lovingly that it brought tears to Max's eyes and mine. 'Now, tell me,' she said, brightening up, 'where is it? There? In that jar? That wonderful discovery? Do you mean to say that what is in that muddy jar can restore youth, and you had to spend a whole year away from me finding it? You shall experiment, sir, immediately on Max. Do you hear?'

"Noting my astonishment, she added: 'Max must be saved. Hurry! He may die any minute.'

"'But, my dearest, I haven't experimented on anything yet.'

"'Then you must begin on Max right away. I shan't leave you until you do; and, if I don't, what will mama say?'

"She looked so irresistibly roguish, and added such a potent argument, that I foolishly consented. At that moment Max uttered a deep growl.

"'It's mama,' said Elsa, with a pout. 'Quick! There! At any rate we have had a few minutes together, haven't we?'

"There was a rustling on the stairs. There was a quick cry.

"'Carl, my dearest son!' Before I realized what had happened, Elsa's mother lay in my arms, considerably closer than her daughter had been a moment before. I do not know what stirred within me, but, stunned and dazed, I strained my mother-in-law to my heart.

"'Mama,' cried Elsa, turning pale, 'you forget that Carl has important experiments to make. It is late, and we must leave him. He is tired.' Madame Von Krakenburg gave me a melting look. I could not meet it. My eyes wandered to Elsa. She evidently did not blame me in the least. She stood tapping her foot with high-spirited impatience upon the floor. Her mother had disengaged herself, and stood trembling.

"'You will not forget your promise,' said Elsa, in a low tone, glancing at the bewildered dog. 'Max, you sleep with Carl, to-night. Carl, dear, won't you kiss me good-night?' She stole a triumphant glance at her mother. Shamefacedly, I kissed my fiancée on the lips. I did not linger there, but I felt the chaste and soothing influence that was balm to my harassed heart. Then I looked at her mother, tall, commanding, dark, magnificent and melting, and I did not know whether I hated her or loved her. Then the two women left me with Max and with my tumultuous meditations.

"But my promised experiment nerved me, and in the careful preparation of a spot above the dog's medulla for inoculation, I quite forgot the two ladies of my life. Max seemed to understand, as dogs do when you try to cure them. He did not interrupt or whine, but cocked his aged ears with interest, and tried to see out of his blind eyes. With infinite pains I injected the vivifying bacilli into his blood, sealed the wound from the air, and turned the dog into the hall to seek his mistress' room.

Then I flung myself on the bed, glad to be at home again, and yet puzzled as to the actual outcome of the amorous confusion in which I found myself snarled. Soon youth and health conquered, and I fell into a troubled sleep, only to be awakened in the morning by joyous barking and the eager scratching of a dog at my door. Wondering what could be there, I cautiously opened the door. This was pushed violently to one side, and a magnificent Newfoundland pup darted in, and, leaping all over me, began to kiss me violently.

"Whose was this creature? What could it mean? Then a mad thought illuminated me.

"'Max,' I cried. 'Max, is that you?' At that name the pup whirled about me in ecstasy. But I could not rebuke his exuberance, for before me danced the first illustration of the vitalizing power of the serum at my command. Old age had been wiped from the face of the earth. Death could only entrap us through accident and illness. Immortal youth was the gift of my pleasure.

"After a few dabs and embraces the hurricane bolted out and down stairs. I locked the door, and threw myself upon the bed, feeling within me the power of a god, and wondering at the vast possibilities of my divine discovery.

"As yet Elsa was my only confidante. Without an exhaustive series of experiments, it would be impossible for me to give to humanity my discovery. A thousand problems of proportion, strength, and number of inoculations must be solved beyond a peradventure of a doubt. For the first time I had become reconciled to animal experimentations, for my laboratory work would consist not in torture but in giving joy, not in vivisecting but in vivifying, and I began to gather all the old and worn-out animals I could find. The resurrection of Max had to be explained to Elsa's mother in a way that bordered on a fairy tale. I was alleged to have brought this young pup with me to take the place of the old dog I had mercifully disposed of; but the strange thing was that the young Max seemed to have his senile antipathy to Madame Von Krakenburg redoubled in his rejuvenescence, to use the appropriate word. This antipathy became so serious that the dog had to be kept chained except when he was in Elsa's room, in mine, or out walking. But the noble beast seemed never so happy as when Elsa and I were together.

"'Dear heart,' I pleaded, about a week after my return, 'why can we not marry at once? I need you so much.' Indeed my need of her was becoming urgent. Whenever Elsa took Max out for a morning walk, her mother would run up to my room, ostensibly to put it in order. I do not dare to think of the wild passion that swept like a sirocco over my nature at those times. My heart would cry out for Elsa, while my lips were snarled in what Madame Von Krakenburg was pleased to call a 'mother's kiss.' I was on fire, and, loathing the dual part that I became willing to play, I longed for the flame on the one side to consume me, and for the sweet peace of Elsa on the other hand to calm and comfort me.

"As yet Elsa could not suspect my disloyalty, nor could I explain it. She was curiously devoted to her mother, for whom her placid nature had no feeling of jealousy except when we three were together and Madame Von Krakenburg overstepped the boundary natural to a future mother-in-law. Was ever a man in such a predicament? As I sat between the two at table, and looked from the one to the other, my heart gave alternate leaps. I adored the one, and I could not live without the other. If Elsa had married me then and there, the future of mankind would have been immeasurably changed.

"It was on a day when I found myself peculiarly distraught by the strange entanglement in which I was placed that Elsa's mother received a call from General Von Fersen. This officer was not only an ardent admirer of Madame Von Krakenburg but was in close touch with the Emperor at whose court Elsa's mother was once a famous maid of honor. It seemed that this general had lately persuaded the Emperor to restore to the heirs of the dead Von Krakenburg some family estates that had once been confiscated, and this meant a fortune and an independence to the beautiful widow and her daughter. Stunned by the happy news, the lady fell into a dead faint. I was hastily called, and together the General and I carried her to her room. Elsa and I were then left together.

"As I was about to employ the common restoratives, Elsa put her hand on mine.

"'Carl,' she said in a low voice, 'I will marry you next week if you will inoculate mama now. She will never know it, dear mama.'

"'Nonsense, Elsa!' I exclaimed. 'Don't talk foolishly. I must bring her to.'

"'Carl, dearest, you do not understand. I declare I will never marry you at all if you do not do this for me. Mama has been so unhappy, and, with this new fortune, youth will mean everything to her. I cannot bear to have her grow old. Will you, Carl? And we will be married next week.'

"'But, my God! Elsa, don't you see?' I exclaimed, madly.

"'What? See what?' Elsa asked, wonderingly. Then she straightened herself.

"'You can choose. Take me or lose me. Now, Carl?' I glanced from the indignant girl to the silent and royal woman who even in her pallor thrilled me with a powerful passion.

"'Elsa! Elsa!' I said. 'You know not what you ask. Anything else. My God! I cannot do it, and I cannot refuse.

"'That or nothing.' She spoke with the icy decision peculiar to the blonde temperament.

"My cultures were always ready.

"'Very well,' I said. 'The result is on your own future. I pressed a kiss to my fiancée's lips, and slowly mounted the stairs to my room, hoping that the faint would pass by, and relieve me of my weak promise. When I returned, the woman was still motionless. Hectic with excitement, Elsa watched the process. It was so simple, so fraught with fateful results! In a moment the bacilli of life were sporting in the mother's veins, warring with age and death.

"'How terribly you look,' cried Elsa, glancing up. Then the unconscious woman moved. With a physician's anxiety I peered into her face as her eyes opened. To my frenzied imagination it seemed as if those crow's-feet, indicators of time, were even now disappearing.

"'Carl!' cried the lady, with outstretched arms. Then a puzzled look stole over her features, and with a deep sigh she sank into profound sleep.

"But I could stand it no longer. 'Tomorrow morning, the living-room as usual, before breakfast,' I whispered to Elsa. Ten minutes later I plunged into the frosty winter air, not knowing where I was going, only intent upon getting away from the terrible complication.

"I did not enter until long after midnight, and then I could not sleep. Brunette and blonde, death and life, seemed warring in insane phantasmagoria within my fevered imagination, but rest was an impossibility. Finally I aroused myself from some weirder vision than the rest, and, after a cold plunge, dressed impatiently. I was cooled and comforted, and my heart cried out to Elsa and her trustful love.

"Early the next morning I stole downstairs to the dining-room, where the little German maid had already lighted an open fire. Its morning cheer made my whole nature smile, and I forgot everything but my promised bride.

"I heard Elsa's familiar rustle on the stair, and boyishly I turned my back so as to appear surprised and thus prolong the joy of the greeting. A few light steps across the room, two arms entwined themselves about my neck, and I felt a glowing cheek pressed to mine, and the breath of a garden of jasmine intoxicated my senses.

I closed my eyes in ecstasy, and turning, took the divine creature in my arms, raining upon her face, her mouth, kisses which were avariciously accepted and returned. Such bliss as this beautiful woman bestowed upon me is reserved for few to experience. I could have fainted in my joy. At the moment when it seemed as if heaven had taken the place of this inhospitable earth, I was brought back by a cold, cutting voice from the doorway.

"'Carl,' it said, 'Carl, what does this mean?' Opening my eyes, I saw Elsa in the doorway. She seemed surprised and indignant. In my arms lay the most beautiful woman I had ever seen—a human Jacqueminot—radiant with love, redolent with passion. Ah, it was a woman for whom a man would commit a thousand crimes, and suffer a thousand deaths for one touch of her crimson lips!

"'Who is this woman?' cried Elsa, in a commanding tone. 'Explain her presence in your arms.' There the two creatures confronted each other. Passion and peace dueled for the mastery.

"'Do you not know me, Elsa?' the stranger asked, with a triumphant smile—such as only comes to the mouth of a successful rival. Elsa and I gave each other a quick, comprehensive look. Her tender, blue eyes expressed forgiveness, horror, self-accusation and hopeless misery. Ah, what had she done? What had I done?

"'Well,' cried the splendid creature, 'is this the way that I am received by my daughter? Carl was more sympathetic in his greeting. Oh, I live, I dance, I sing for joy, and I am so happy! I am just beginning to live. I feel as if I were born again. Carl, tell me, am I really beautiful again—or is it a dream? If it is, I will die. I could not bear to go back. Elsa, Carl, will you not explain?' She stood there glancing from one to the other, for we could not speak, as the success of the experiment burst over our disordered minds. For I had conjured from the past, through the blood of the toad, the most glorious woman that my eyes had ever beheld. There she stood, vibrant with life, glowing with youth, eager with the enthusiasm of girlhood, a poem of passion, an ode to ecstasy, and with a heart that quivered with forty-five years of experience. I looked upon this creature of my microbes with blinded eyes. Who could withstand her? She was the incarnation of love. She was the empress, nay the temptress, of the world. Beside her, Elsa seemed a pale replica; but there was that hovering about the girl's lips which made me wonder that I could ever have wavered.

"'Mama,' said Elsa, her lips dry, her tone quiet. 'Carl did it; I asked him. I promised to marry him if he would. That is his great discovery. He made Max young. Now he has made you young. I—I did not know, I did not realize—' The noble girl swayed, and I bounded to her side. 'It is nothing,' she continued, with great dignity. 'Do not touch me, Carl. It is evident that you have a decision to make. You can make it now.'

"Before her daughter had finished, the young mother had thrown herself at my feet, and was kissing my hand.

"'My benefactor! My god! My creator!' she exclaimed, in increasing vehemence.

"There was a bounding on the stairs. A whirlwind in the shape of a big dog rushed in. It was Max. Seeing the hated woman at my feet, he seized her by the arm, and held her in a growling grip.

"This broke the terrible tension. In an instant I had caught the dog by the muzzle, and forced his reluctant jaws apart, dragging him by the collar.

"'I will chain him up,' I said. At the door I stopped, and looked back. Decide? A Jupiter could not have decided. I loved Elsa—I adored her impetuous mother.

"When I found myself in my laboratory with the dog, I doubly bolted the door. By this time madness had taken possession of my mind. To what impossible end had my impious ambition brought me! How I cursed those jars of jelly filled with life! I raged before the phalanx of glasses, of test-tubes and beakers filled with bacilli, shaking my fist at each in order. The window was unlocked. I threw it open for breath. Outside, the air was crisp, and the snow crunched and creaked under horses and sleighs.

"Ah, what misery had I caused when I dreamed of joy and glory to mankind! Is it possible that God knew better than man?

"The idea had never occurred to me. I thought it man's business to outwit God, and this was the result, this topsyturvydom of love.

"Something stronger than my will impelled me. I took up a jar, and threw it out of the window. It fell with a crash. A. few minutes, and eternal life had frozen to death. 'If one, why not all, old boy?' I cried, turning to Max, who wagged his splendid tail encouragingly. Then followed a mad fusillade of microbes. Ah, how the world would have cried out for mercy if it had known what slaughter I was committing!

"Suddenly I stopped, aghast. The last jar had gone, and the gift of the toad had been irretrievably destroyed. God! how we spend the best of our years in searching for life, and how we cast it away! May I never experience such a horrible conflict again. I blessed, I cursed, I rejoiced, I regretted, I stormed, I prayed, I hated, and I loved. At last overcome, broken of life, lost of ambition, and forever deprived of joy, I threw myself on the bed, and sank into blessed unconsciousness, Nature's calm for the storms that wreck and kill.

"That night I packed my bag, and softly stole away as I had come but a few weeks before. I did not see the two women again, but the fleeting kisses of Max's cold nose are still upon my cheek.

"For two years I have been a wanderer, although I have left with Elsa my address in case I am called; but I never expect to hear from them again."

It was long past midnight. I silently wrung the sufferer's hand, and slipped into my room, leaving him sunk in sleepless reverie. The next morning we were up at six. The fog was lazily lifting as the steamer mowed its way slowly up the motionless channel. It was low tide. A dory defiantly sculled across our bow with a big Newfoundland vigorously pursuing it, yapping the salt water from its mouth. At sight of the animal I gravitated toward Doctor Cox, who was at the extreme bow.

"Why not breakfast together at the Grand?"

"All right," he assented, resuming his hopeless stare, the look of a man searching for that which he knows he can never find. The kindly customs officers did not trouble us, as we had no bicycles or whisky, their bête noire. Half an hour later we were seated in a spacious dining-room, waited on by freckled girls who brought us huckleberries and little else. Both of us were ineffably bored. It seemed so petty compared with the tremendous drama enacted by the silent man with his back to the door. The tourists were shoveling in the berries contentedly like cows. Then there was a hash in the clatter. The young clerk stood in the door, flourishing a yellow envelope.

"Dr. Charles Cox!" he called. "Is Doctor Cox here?"

The doctor turned a ghastly shade.

"You take it," he said, "I dare not."

Mechanically I held out my hand, while the blood leaped within me. Somehow I felt that I was providentially in at the finish.

"Open it," he commanded. "Read it first, Doctor—then tell me."

The message had been forwarded from the Doctor's lawyer in Boston, and read thus:—

> "Mama found dead in bed this morning. Max guarding her. Come.
>
> "Elsa."

As I read this call from another continent, the face of my vis-à-vis became changed as through a potent conjuration. Happiness is, after all, the surest elixir of life. He threw off twenty years in twenty seconds. His face radiated power and manhood, for his joy was sublime.

"My God!" he cried. "I did love Elsa! Quick! There is no time—Good-by, Doctor, good-by. You were very good." Languor and restlessness had vanished like mist. He passed out of the stuffy room like a whirlwind, vital as an electric current, and was gone.

MAX HENSIG: BACTERIOLOGIST AND MURDERER
ALGERNON BLACKWOOD

A STORY OF NEW YORK

I

Besides the departmental men on the New York *Vulture*, there were about twenty reporters for general duty, and Williams had worked his way up till he stood easily among the first half-dozen; for, in addition to being accurate and painstaking, he was able to bring to his reports of common things that touch of imagination and humor which just lifted them out of the rut of mere faithful recording. Moreover, the city editor (*anglice* news editor) appreciated his powers, and always tried to give him assignments that did himself and the paper credit, and he was justified now in expecting to be relieved of the hack jobs that were usually allotted to new men.

He was therefore puzzled and a little disappointed one morning as he saw his inferiors summoned one after another to the news desk to receive the best assignments of the day, and when at length his turn came, and the city editor asked him to cover the "Hensig story," he gave a little start of vexation that almost betrayed him into asking what the devil the "Hensig story" was. For it is the duty of every morning newspaper man—in New York at least—to have made himself familiar with all the news of the day before he shows himself at the office, and though Williams had already done this, he could not recall either the name or the story.

"You can run to a hundred or a hundred and fifty, Mr. Williams. Cover the trial thoroughly, and get good interviews with Hensig and the lawyers. There'll be no night assignment for you till the case is over."

Williams was going to ask if there were any private "tips" from the District Attorney's office but the editor was already speaking with Weekes, who wrote the daily "weather story," and he went back slowly to his desk, angry and disappointed, to read up the Hensig case and lay his plans for the day accordingly. At any rate, he reflected, it looked like "a soft job," and as there was to be no second assignment for him that night, he would get off by eight o'clock, and be able to dine and sleep for once like a civilized man. And that was something.

It took him some time, however, to discover that the Hensig case was only a murder story. And this increased his disgust. It was tucked away in the corners of most of the papers, and little importance was attached to it. A murder trial is not first-class news unless there are very special features connected with it, and Williams had already covered scores of them. There was a heavy sameness about them that made it difficult to report them interestingly, and as a rule they were left to the tender mercies of the "flimsy" men—the Press Associations—and no paper sent a special man unless the case was distinctly out of the usual. Moreover, a hundred and fifty meant a column and a half, and Williams, not being a space man, earned the same money whether he wrote a stickful or a page; so that he felt doubly aggrieved, and walked out into the sunny open spaces opposite Newspaper Row heaving a deep sigh and cursing the boredom of his trade.

Max Hensig, he found, was a German doctor accused of murdering his second wife by injecting arsenic. The woman had been buried several weeks when the suspicious relatives got the body exhumed, and a quantity of the poison had been found in her. Williams recalled something about the arrest, now he came to think of it; but he felt no special interest in it, for ordinary murder trials were no longer his legitimate work, and he scorned them. At first, of course, they had thrilled him horribly, and some of his interviews with the prisoners, especially just before execution, had deeply impressed his imagination and kept him awake o' nights. Even now he could not enter the gloomy Tombs Prison, or cross the Bridge of Sighs leading from it to the courts, without experiencing a real sensation, for its huge Egyptian columns and massive walls closed round him like death; and the first time he walked down Murderers' Row, and came in view of the cell doors, his throat was dry, and he had almost turned and run out of the building.

The first time, too, that he covered the trial of a negro and listened to the man's hysterical speech before sentence was pronounced, he was absorbed with interest, and his heart leaped. The wild appeals to the Deity, the long invented words, the ghastly pallor under the black skin, the rolling eyes, and the torrential sentences all seemed to him to be something tremendous to describe for his sensational sheet; and the stickful that was eventually printed—written by the flimsy man too—had given him quite a new standard of the relative value of news and of the quality of the satiated public palate. He had reported the trials of a Chinaman, stolid as wood; of an Italian who had been too quick with his knife; and of a farm girl who had done both her parents to death in their beds, entering their room stark naked, so that no stains should betray her; and at the beginning these things haunted him for days.

But that was all months ago, when he first came to New York. Since then his work had been steadily in the criminal courts, and he had grown a second skin. An execution in the electric chair at Sing Sing could still unnerve him somewhat, but mere murder no longer thrilled or excited him, and he could be thoroughly depended on to write a good "murder story"—an account that his paper could print without blue pencil.

Accordingly he entered the Tombs Prison with nothing stronger than the feeling or vague oppression that gloomy structure always stirred in him, and certainly with no particular emotion connected with the prisoner he was about to interview; and when he reached the second iron door, where a warder peered at him through a small grating, he heard a voice behind him, and turned to find the *Chronicle* man at his heels.

"Hullo, Senator! What good trail are you following down here?" he cried, for the other got no small assignments, and never had less than a column on the *Chronicle* front page at space rates.

"Same as you, I guess—Hensig," was the reply.

"But there's no space in Hensig," said Williams with surprise. "Are you back on salary again?"

"Not much," laughed the Senator—no one knew his real name, but he was always called Senator. "But Hensig's good for two hundred easy. There's a whole list of murders behind him, we hear, and this is the first time he's been caught."

"Poison?"

The Senator nodded in reply, turning to ask the warder some question about another case, and Williams waited for him in the corridor, impatiently rather, for he loathed the musty prison odor. He watched the Senator as he talked, and was distinctly glad he had come. They were good friends: he had helped Williams when he first joined the small army of newspaper men and was not much welcomed, being an Englishman. Common origin and goodheartedness mixed themselves delightfully in his face, and he always made Williams think of a friendly, honest cart-horse—stolid, strong, with big and simple emotions.

"Get a hustle on, Senator," he said at length impatiently.

The two reporters followed the warder down the flagged corridor, past a row of dark cells, each with its occupant, until the man, swinging his keys in the direction indicated, stopped and pointed:

"Here's your gentleman," he said, and then moved on down the corridor, leaving them staring through the bars at a tall, slim young man, pacing to and fro. He had flaxen hair and very bright blue eyes; his skin was white, and his face wore so open and innocent an expression that one would have said he could not twist a kitten's tail without wincing.

"From the *Chronicle* and *Vulture*," explained Williams, by way of introduction, and the talk at once began in the usual way.

The man in the cell ceased his restless pacing up and down, and stopped opposite the bars to examine them. He stared straight into Williams's eyes for a moment, and the reporter noted a very different expression from the one he had first seen. It actually made him shift his position and stand a little to one side. But the movement was wholly instinctive. He could not have explained why he did it.

"Guess you vish me to say I did it, and then egsplain to you *how* I did it," the young doctor said coolly, with a marked German accent. "But I haf no copy to gif you shust now. You see at the trial it is nothing but spite—and shealosy of another woman. I lofed my vife. I vould not haf gilled her for anything in the vorld—"

"Oh, of course, of course, Dr. Hensig," broke in the Senator, who was more experienced in the ways of difficult interviewing. "We quite understand that. But, you know, in New York the newspapers try a man as much as the courts, and we thought you might like to make a statement to the public which we should be very glad to print for you. It may help your case—"

"Nothing can help my case in this tamned country where shustice is to be pought mit tollars!" cried the prisoner, with a sudden anger and an expression of face still further belying the first one; "nothing except a lot of money. But I tell you now two things you may write for your public: One is, no motive can be shown for the murder, because I lofed Zinka and vished her to live alvays. And the other is—" He stopped a moment and stared steadily at Williams making shorthand notes— "that with my knowledge—my egceptional knowledge—of poisons and pacteriology I could have done it in a dozen ways without pumping arsenic into her body. That is a fool's way of killing. It is clumsy and childish and sure of discofery! See?"

He turned away, as though to signify that the interview was over, and sat down on his wooden bench.

"Seems to have taken a fancy to you," laughed the Senator, as they went off to get further interviews with the lawyers. "He never looked at me once."

"He's got a bad face—the face of a devil. I don't feel complimented," said Williams shortly. "I'd hate to be in his power."

"Same here," returned the other. "Let's go into Silver Dollars and wash the dirty taste out."

So, after the custom of reporters, they made their way up the Bowery and went into a saloon that had gained a certain degree of fame because the Tammany owner had let a silver dollar into each stone of the floor. Here they washed away most of the "dirty taste" left by the Tombs atmosphere and Hensig, and then went on to Steve Brodie's, another saloon a little higher up the same street.

"There'll be others there," said the Senator, meaning drinks as well as reporters, and Williams, still thinking over their interview, silently agreed.

Brodie was a character; there was always something lively going on in his place. He had the reputation of having once jumped from the Brooklyn Bridge and reached the water alive. No one could actually deny it, and no one could prove that it really happened; and anyhow, he had enough imagination and personality to make the myth live and to sell much bad liquor on the strength of it. The walls of his saloon were plastered with lurid oil-paintings of the bridge, the height enormously magnified, and Steve's body in midair, an expression of a happy puppy on his face.

Here, as expected, they found "Whitey" Fife, of the *Recorder*, and Galusha Owen, of the *World*. "Whitey," as his nickname implied, was an albino, and clever. He wrote the daily "weather story" for his paper, and the way he spun a column out of rain, wind, and temperature was the envy of every one except the Weather Clerk, who objected to being described as "Farmer Dunne, cleaning his rat-tail file," and to having his dignified office referred to in the public press as "a down-country farm." But the public liked it, and laughed, and "Whitey" was never really spiteful.

Owen, too, when sober, was a good man who had long passed the rubicon of hack assignments. Yet both these men were also on the Hensig story. And Williams, who had already taken an instinctive dislike to the case, was sorry to see this, for it meant frequent interviewing and the possession, more or less, of his mind and imagination. Clearly, he would have much to do with this German doctor. Already, even at this stage, he began to hate him.

The four reporters spent an hour drinking and talking. They fell at length to discussing the last time they had chanced to meet on the same assignment—a private lunatic asylum owned by an incompetent quack without a license, and where most of the inmates, not mad in the first instance, and all heavily paid for by relatives who wished them out of the way, had gone mad from ill-treatment. The place had been surrounded before dawn by the Board of Health officers, and the quasi-doctor arrested as he opened his front door. It was a splendid newspaper "story," of course.

"My space bill ran to sixty dollars a day for nearly a week," said Whitey Fife thickly, and the others laughed, because Whitey wrote most of his stuff by cribbing it from the evening papers.

"A dead cinch," said Galusha Owen, his dirty flannel collar poking up through his long hair almost to his ears. "I 'faked' the whole of the second day without going down there at all."

He pledged Whitey for the tenth time that morning, and the albino leered happily across the table at him, and passed him a thick compliment before emptying his glass.

"Hensig's going to be good, too," broke in the Senator, ordering a round of gin-fizzes, and Williams gave a little start of annoyance to hear the name brought up again. "He'll make good stuff at the trial. I never saw a cooler hand. You should've heard him talk about poisons and bacteriology, and boasting he could kill in a dozen ways without fear of being caught. I guess he was telling the truth right enough!"

"That so?" cried Galusha and Whitey in the same breath, not having done a stroke of work so far on the case.

"RundowntotheTombshangetaninerview," added Whitey, turning with a sudden burst of enthusiasm to his companion. His white eyebrows and pink eyes fairly shone against the purple of his tipsy face.

"No, no," cried the Senator; "don't spoil a good story. You're both as full as ticks. I'll match with Williams which of us goes. Hensig knows us already, and we'll all 'give up' in this story right along. No 'beats.'"

So they decided to divide news till the case was finished, and to keep no exclusive items to themselves; and Williams, having lost the toss, swallowed his gin-fizz and went back to the Tombs to get a further talk with the prisoner on his knowledge of expert poisoning and bacteriology.

Meanwhile his thoughts were very busy elsewhere. He had taken no part in the noisy conversation in the bar-room, because something lay at the back of his mind, bothering him, and claiming attention with great persistence. Something was at work in his deeper consciousness, something that had impressed him with a vague sense of unpleasantness and nascent fear, reaching below that second skin he had grown.

And, as he walked slowly through the malodorous slum streets that lay between the Bowery and the Tombs, dodging the pullers-in outside the Jew clothing stores, and nibbling at a bag of peanuts he caught up off an Italian push-cart *en route*, this "something" rose a little higher out of its obscurity, and began to play with the roots of the ideas floating higgledy-piggledy on the surface of his mind. He thought he knew what it was, but could not make quite sure. From the roots of his thoughts it rose a little higher, so that he clearly felt it as something disagreeable. Then, with a sudden rush, it came to the surface, and poked its face before him so that he fully recognized it.

The blond visage of Dr. Max Hensig rose before him, cool, smiling, and implacable.

Somehow, he had expected it would prove to be Hensig—this unpleasant thought that was troubling him. He was not really surprised to have labeled it, because the man's personality had made an unwelcome impression upon him at the very start. He stopped nervously in the street, and looked round. He did not expect to see anything out of the way, or to find that he was being followed. It was not that exactly. The act of turning was merely the outward expression of a sudden inner discomfort, and a man with better nerves, or nerves more under control, would not have turned at all.

But what caused this tremor of the nerves? Williams probed and searched within himself. It came, he felt, from some part of his inner being he did not understand; there had been an intrusion, an incongruous intrusion, into the stream of his normal consciousness. Messages from this region always gave him pause; and in this particular case he saw no reason why he should think specially of Dr. Hensig with alarm—this light-haired stripling with blue eyes and drooping moustache. The faces of other murderers had haunted him once or twice because they were more than ordinarily bad, or because their case possessed unusual features of horror. But there was nothing so very much out of the way about Hensig—at least, if there was, the reporter could not seize and analyze it. There seemed no adequate reason to explain his emotion. Certainly, it had nothing to do with the fact that he was merely a murderer, for that stirred no thrill in him at all, except a kind of pity, and a wonder how the man would meet his execution. It must, he argued, be something to do with the *personality* of the man, apart from any particular deed or characteristic.

Puzzled, and still a little nervous, he stood in the road, hesitating. In front of him the dark walls of the Tombs rose in massive steps of granite. Overhead white summer clouds sailed across a deep blue sky; the wind sang cheerfully among the wires and chimney-pots, making him think of fields and trees; and down the street surged the usual cosmopolitan New York crowd of laughing Italians, surly negroes, Hebrews chattering Yiddish, tough-looking hooligans with that fighting lurch of the shoulders peculiar to New York roughs, Chinamen, taking little steps like boys—and every other sort of nondescript imaginable. It was early June, and there were faint odours of the sea and of sea-beaches in the air. Williams caught himself shivering a little with delight at the sight of the sky and scent of the wind.

Then he looked back at the great prison, rightly named the Tombs, and the sudden change of thought from the fields to the cells, from life to death, somehow landed him straight into the discovery of what caused this attack of nervousness:

Hensig was no ordinary murderer! That was it. There was something quite out of the ordinary about him. The man was a horror, pure and simple, standing apart from normal humanity. The knowledge of this rushed over him like a revelation, bringing unalterable conviction in its train. Something of it had reached him in that first brief interview, but without explaining itself sufficiently to be recognized, and since then it had been working in his system, like a poison, and was now causing a disturbance, not having been assimilated. A quicker temperament would have labeled it long before.

Now, Williams knew well that he drank too much, and had more than a passing acquaintance with drugs; his nerves were shaky at the best of times. His life on the newspapers afforded no opportunity of cultivating pleasant social relations, but brought him all the time into contact with the seamy side of life—the criminal, the abnormal, the unwholesome in human nature. He knew, too, that strange thoughts, *idées fixes* and what not, grew readily in such a soil as this, and, not wanting these, he had formed a habit—peculiar to himself—of deliberately sweeping his mind clean once a week of all that had haunted, obsessed, or teased him, of the horrible or unclean, during his work; and his eighth day, his holiday, he invariably spent in the woods, walking, building fires, cooking a meal in the open, and getting all the country air and the exercise he possibly could. He had in this way kept his mind free from many unpleasant pictures that might otherwise have lodged there abidingly, and the habit of thus cleansing his imagination had proved more than once of real value to him.

So now he laughed to himself, and turned on those whizzing brooms of his, trying to forget these first impressions of Hensig, and simply going in, as he did a hundred other times, to get an ordinary interview with an ordinary prisoner. This habit, being nothing more nor less than the practice of suggestion, was more successful sometimes than others. This time—since fear is less susceptible to suggestion than other emotions—it was less so.

Williams got his interview, and came away fairly creeping with horror. Hensig was all that he had felt, and more besides. He belonged, the reporter felt convinced, to that rare type of deliberate murderer, cold-blooded and calculating, who kills for a song, delights in killing, and gives its whole intellect to the consideration of each detail, glorying in evading detection and reveling in the notoriety of the trial, if caught. At first he had answered reluctantly, but as Williams plied his questions intelligently, the young doctor warmed up and became enthusiastic with a sort of cold intellectual enthusiasm, till at last he held forth like a lecturer, pacing his cell, gesticulating, explaining with admirable exposition how easy murder could be to a man who knew his business.

And *he* did know his business! No man, in these days of inquests and post-mortem examination, would inject poisons that might be found weeks afterwards in the viscera of the victim. No man who knew his business!

"What is more easy," he said, holding the bars with his long white fingers and gazing into the reporter's eyes, "than to take a disease germ ['cherm' he pronounced it] of typhus, plague, or any cherm you blease, and make so virulent a culture that no medicine in the vorld could counteract it; a really powerful microbe—and then scratch the skin of your victim with a pin? And who could drace it to you, or accuse you of murder?"

Williams, as he watched and heard, was glad the bars were between them; but, even so, something invisible seemed to pass from the prisoner's atmosphere and lay an icy finger on his heart. He had come into contact with every possible kind of crime and criminal, and had interviewed scores of men who, for jealousy, greed, passion, or other comprehensible emotion, had killed and paid the penalty of killing. He understood that. Any man with strong passions was a potential killer. But never before had he met a man who in cold blood, deliberately, under no emotion greater than boredom, would destroy a human life and then boast of his ability to do it. Yet this, he felt sure, was what Hensig had done, and what his vile words shadowed forth and betrayed. Here was something outside humanity, something terrible, monstrous; and it made him shudder. This young doctor, he felt, was a fiend incarnate, a man who thought less of human life than of the lives of flies in summer, and who would kill with as steady a hand and cool a brain as though he were performing a common operation in the hospital.

Thus the reporter left the prison gates with a vivid impression in his mind, though exactly how his conclusion was reached was more than he could tell. This time the mental brooms failed to act. The horror of it remained.

On the way out into the street he ran against Policeman Dowling of the ninth precinct, with whom he had been fast friends since the day he wrote a glowing account of Dowling's capture of a "green-goods-man," when Dowling had been so drunk that he nearly lost his prisoner altogether. The policeman had never forgotten the good turn; it had promoted him to plain clothes; and he was always ready to give the reporter any news he had.

"Know of anything good to-day?" he asked by way of habit.

"Bet your bottom dollar I do," replied the coarse-faced Irish policeman; "one of the best, too. I've got Hensig!"

Dowling spoke with pride and affection. He was mighty pleased, too, because his name would be in the paper every day for a week or more, and a big case helped the chances of promotion.

Williams cursed inwardly. Apparently there was no escape from this man Hensig.

"Not much of a case, is it?" he asked.

"It's a jim dandy, that's what it is," replied the other, a little offended. "Hensig may miss the Chair because the evidence is weak, but he's the worst I've ever met. Why, he'd poison you as soon as spit in your eye, and if he's got a heart at all he keeps it on ice."

"What makes you think that?"

"Oh, they talk pretty freely to us sometimes," the policeman said, with a significant wink. "Can't be used against them at the trial, and it kind o' relieves their mind, I guess. But I'd just as soon not have heard most of what that guy told me—see? Come in," he added, looking round cautiously; "I'll set 'em up and tell you a bit."

Williams entered the side-door of a saloon with him, but not too willingly.

"A glarss of Scotch for the Englishman," ordered the officer facetiously, "and I'll take a horse's collar with a dash of peach bitters in it—just what you'd notice, no more." He flung down a half-dollar, and the bar-tender winked and pushed it back to him across the counter.

"What's yours, Mike?" he asked him.

"I'll take a cigar," said the bar-tender, pocketing the proffered dime and putting a cheap cigar in his waistcoat pocket, and then moving off to allow the two men elbow-room to talk in.

They talked in low voices with heads close together for fifteen minutes, and then the reporter set up another round of drinks. The bar-tender took *his* money. Then they talked a bit longer, Williams rather white about the gills and the policeman very much in earnest.

"The boys are waiting for me up at Brodie's," said Williams at length. "I must be off."

"That's so," said Dowling, straightening up. "We'll just liquor up again to show there's no ill-feeling. And mind you see me every morning before the case is called. Trial begins to-morrow."

They swallowed their drinks, and again the bartender took a ten-cent piece and pocketed a cheap cigar.

"Don't print what I've told you, and don't give it up to the other reporters," said Dowling as they separated. "And if you want confirmation jest take the cars and run down to Amityville, Long Island, and you'll find what I've said is O.K. every time."

Williams went back to Steve Brodie's, his thoughts whizzing about him like bees in a swarm. What he had heard increased tenfold his horror of the man. Of course, Dowling may have lied or exaggerated, but he thought not. It was probably all true, and the newspaper offices knew something about it when they sent good men to cover the case. Williams wished to Heaven he had nothing to do with the thing; but meanwhile he could not write what he had heard, and all the other reporters wanted was the result of his interview. That was good for half a column, even expurgated.

He found the Senator in the middle of a story to Galusha, while Whitey Fife was knocking cocktail glasses off the edge of the table and catching them just before they reached the floor, pretending they were Steve Brodie jumping from the Brooklyn Bridge. He had promised to set up the drinks for the whole bar if he missed, and just as Williams entered a glass smashed to atoms on the stones, and a roar of laughter went up from the room. Five or six men moved up to the bar and took their liquor, Williams included, and soon after Whitey and Galusha went off to get some lunch and sober up, having first arranged to meet Williams later in the evening and get the "story" from him.

"Get much?" asked the Senator.

"More than I care about," replied the other, and then told his friend the story.

The Senator listened with intense interest, making occasional notes from time to time, and asking a few questions. Then, when Williams had finished, he said quietly:

"I guess Dowling's right. Let's jump on a car and go down to Amityville, and see what they think about him down there."

Amityville was a scattered village some twenty miles away on Long Island, where Dr. Hensig had lived and practiced for the last year or two, and where Mrs. Hensig No. 2 had come to her suspicious death. The neighbors would be sure to have plenty to say, and though it might not prove of great value, it would be certainly interesting. So the two reporters went down there, and interviewed any one and every one they could find, from the man in the drugstore to the parson and the undertaker, and the stories they heard would fill a book.

"Good stuff," said the Senator, as they journeyed back to New York on the steamer, "but nothing we can use, I guess." His face was very grave, and he seemed troubled in his mind.

"Nothing the District Attorney can use either at the trial," observed Williams.

"It's simply a devil—not a man at all," the other continued, as if talking to himself. "Utterly unmoral! I swear I'll make McSweater put me on another job."

For the stories they had heard showed Dr. Hensig as a man who openly boasted that he could kill without detection; that no enemy of his lived long; that, as a doctor, he had, or ought to have, the right over life and death; and that if a person was a nuisance, or a trouble to him, there was no reason he should not put them away, provided he did it without rousing suspicion. Of course he had not shouted these views aloud in the market-place, but he had let people know that he held them, and held them seriously. They had fallen from him in conversation, in unguarded moments, and were clearly the natural expression of his mind and views. And many people in the village evidently had no doubt that he had put them into practice more than once.

"There's nothing to give up to Whitey or Galusha, though," said the Senator decisively, "and there's hardly anything we can use in our story."

"I don't think I should care to use it anyhow," Williams said, with rather a forced laugh.

The Senator looked round sharply by way of question.

"Hensig *may be acquitted and get out*," added Williams.

"Same here. I guess you're dead right," he said slowly, and then added more cheerfully, "Let's go and have dinner in Chinatown, and write our copy together."

So they went down Pell Street, and turned up some dark wooden stairs into a Chinese restaurant, smelling strongly of opium and of cooking not Western. Here at a little table on the sanded floor they ordered chou chop suey and chou om dong in brown bowls, and washed it down with frequent doses of the fiery white whisky, and then moved into a corner and began to cover their paper with pencil writing for the consumption of the great American public in the morning.

"There's not much to choose between Hensig and *that*," said the Senator, as one of the degraded white women who frequent Chinatown entered the room and sat down at an empty table to order whisky. For, with four thousand Chinamen in the quarter, there is not a single Chinese woman.

"All the difference in the world," replied Williams, following his glance across the smoky room. "She's been decent once, and may be again some day, but that damned doctor has never been anything but what he is—a soulless, intellectual devil. He doesn't belong to humanity at all. I've got a horrid idea that—"

"How do you spell 'bacteriology,' two *r*'s or one?" asked the Senator, going on with his scrawly writing of a story that would be read with interest by thousands next day.

"Two *r*'s and one *k*," laughed the other. And they wrote on for another hour, and then went to turn it in to their respective offices in Park Row.

II

The trial of Max Hensig lasted two weeks, for his relations supplied money, and he got good lawyers and all manner of delays. From a newspaper point of view it fell utterly flat, and before the end of the fourth day most of the papers had shunted their big men on to other jobs more worthy of their powers.

From Williams's point of view, however, it did not fall flat, and he was kept on it till the end. A reporter, of course, has no right to indulge in editorial remarks, especially when a case is still *sub judice*, but in New York journalism and the dignity of the law have a standard all their own, and into his daily reports there crept the distinct flavor of his own conclusions. Now that new men, with whom he had no agreement to "give up," were covering the story for the other papers, he felt free to use any special knowledge in his possession, and a good deal of what he had heard at Amityville and from officer Dowling somehow managed to creep into his writing. Something of the horror and loathing he felt for this doctor also betrayed itself, more by inference than actual statement, and no one who read his daily column could come to any other conclusion than that Hensig was a calculating, cool-headed murderer of the most dangerous type.

This was a little awkward for the reporter, because it was his duty every morning to interview the prisoner in his cell, and get his views on the conduct of the case in general and on his chances of escaping the Chair in particular.

Yet Hensig showed no embarrassment. All the newspapers were supplied to him, and he evidently read every word that Williams wrote. He must have known what the reporter thought about him, at least so far as his guilt or innocence was concerned, but he expressed no opinion as to the fairness of the articles, and talked freely of his chances of ultimate escape. The very way in which he glorified in being the central figure of a matter that bulked so large in the public eye seemed to the reporter an additional proof of the man's perversity. His vanity was immense. He made most careful toilets, appearing every day in a clean shirt and a new tie, and never wearing the same suit on two consecutive days. He noted the descriptions of his personal appearance in the Press, and was quite offended if his clothes and bearing in court were not referred to in detail. And he was unusually delighted and pleased when any of the papers stated that he looked smart and self-possessed, or showed great self-control—which some of them did.

"They make a hero of me," he said one morning when Williams went to see him as usual before court opened, "and if I go to the Chair—which I tink I not do, you know—you shall see some thing fine. Berhaps they electrocute a corpse only!"

And then, with dreadful callousness, he began to chaff the reporter about the tone of his articles—for the first time.

"I only report what is said and done in court," stammered Williams, horribly uncomfortable, "and I am always ready to write anything you care to say—"

"I haf no fault to find," answered Hensig, his cold blue eyes fixed on the reporter's face through the bars, "none at all. You tink I haf killed, and you show it in all your sendences. Haf you ever seen a man in the Chair, I ask you?"

Williams was obliged to say he had.

"*Ach was!* You haf indeed!" said the doctor coolly.

"It's instantaneous, though," the other added quickly, "and must be quite painless." This was not exactly what he thought, but what else could he say to the poor devil who might presently be strapped down into it with that horrid band across his shaved head!

Hensig laughed, and turned away to walk up and down the narrow cell. Suddenly he made a quick movement and sprang like a panther close up to the bars, pressing his face between them with an expression that was entirely new. Williams started back a pace in spite of himself.

"There are worse ways of dying than that," he said in a low voice, with a diabolical look in his eyes; "slower ways that are bainful much more. I shall get oudt. I shall not be conficted. I shall get oudt, and then perhaps I come and tell you apout them."

The hatred in his voice and expression was unmistakable, but almost at once the face changed back to the cold pallor it usually wore, and the extraordinary doctor was laughing again and quietly discussing his lawyers and their good or bad points.

After all, then, that skin of indifference was only assumed, and the man really resented bitterly the tone of his articles. He liked the publicity, but was furious with Williams for having come to a conclusion and for letting that conclusion show through his reports.

The reporter was relieved to get out into the fresh air. He walked briskly up the stone steps to the court-room, still haunted by the memory of that odious white face pressing between the bars and the dreadful look in the eyes that had come and gone so swiftly. And what did those words mean exactly? Had he heard them right? Were they a threat?

"There are slower and more painful ways of dying, and if I get out I shall perhaps come and tell you about them."

The work of reporting the evidence helped to chase the disagreeable vision, and the compliments of the city editor on the excellence of his "story," with its suggestion of a possible increase of salary, gave his mind quite a different turn; yet always at the back of his consciousness there remained the vague, unpleasant memory that he had roused the bitter hatred of this man, and, as he thought, of a man who was a veritable monster.

There may have been something hypnotic, a little perhaps, in this obsessing and haunting idea of the man's steely wickedness, intellectual and horribly skilful, moving freely through life with something like a god's power and with a list of unproved and unprovable murders behind him. Certainly it impressed his imagination with very vivid force, and he could not think of this doctor, young, with unusual knowledge and out-of-the-way skill, yet utterly unmoral, free to work his will on men and women who displeased him, and almost safe from detection—he could not think of it all without a shudder and a crawling of the skin. He was exceedingly glad when the last day of the trial was reached and he no longer was obliged to seek the daily interview in the cell, or to sit all day in the crowded court watching the detestable white face of the prisoner in the dock and listening to the web of evidence closing round him, but just failing to hold him tight enough for the Chair. For Hensig was acquitted, though the jury sat up all night to come to a decision, and the final interview Williams had with the man immediately before his release into the street was the pleasantest and yet the most disagreeable of all.

"I knew I get oudt all right," said Hensig with a slight laugh, but without showing the real relief he must have felt. "No one peliefed me guilty but my vife's family and yourself, Mr. *Vulture* reporter. I read efery day your repordts. You chumped to a conglusion too quickly, I tink—"

"Oh, we write what we're told to write—"

"Berhaps some day you write anozzer story, or berhaps you read the story some one else write of your own trial. Then you understand better what you make me feel."

Williams hurried on to ask the doctor for his opinion of the conduct of the trial, and then inquired what his plans were for the future. The answer to the question caused him genuine relief.

"Ach! I return of course to Chermany," he said. "People here are now afraid of me a liddle. The newpapers haf killed me instead of the Chair. Goot-bye, Mr. *Vulture* reporter, goot-bye!"

And Williams wrote out his last interview with as great a relief, probably, as Hensig felt when he heard the foreman of the jury utter the words "Not guilty"; but the line that gave him most pleasure was the one announcing the intended departure of the acquitted man for Germany.

III

The New York public want sensational reading in their daily life, and they get it, for the newspaper that refused to furnish it would fail in a week, and New York newspaper proprietors do not pose as philanthropists. Horror succeeds horror, and the public interest is never for one instant allowed to faint by the way.

Like any other reporter who betrayed the smallest powers of description, Williams realized this fact with his very first week on the *Vulture*. His daily work became simply a series of sensational reports of sensational happenings; he lived in a perpetual whirl of exciting arrests, murder trials, cases of blackmail, divorce, forgery, arson, corruption, and every other kind of wickedness imaginable. Each case thrilled him a little less than the preceding one; excess of sensation had simply numbed him; he became, not callous, but irresponsive, and had long since reached the stage when excitement ceases to betray judgment, as with inexperienced reporters it was apt to do.

The Hensig case, however, for a long time lived in his imagination and haunted him. The bald facts were buried in the police files at Mulberry Street headquarters and in the newspaper office "morgues," while the public, thrilled daily by fresh horrors, forgot the very existence of the evil doctor a couple of days after the acquittal of the central figure.

But for Williams it was otherwise. The personality of the heartless and calculating murderer—the intellectual poisoner, as he called him—had made a deep impression on his imagination, and for many weeks his memory kept him alive as a moving and actual horror in his life. The words he had heard him utter, with their covert threats and ill-concealed animosity, helped, no doubt, to vivify the recollection and to explain why Hensig stayed in his thoughts and haunted his dreams with a persistence that reminded him of his very earliest cases on the paper.

With time, however, even Hensig began to fade away into the confused background of piled up memories of prisoners and prison scenes, and at length the memory became so deeply buried that it no longer troubled him at all.

The summer passed, and Williams came back from his hard-earned holiday of two weeks in the Maine backwoods. New York was at its best, and the thousands who had been forced to stay and face its torrid summer heats were beginning to revive under the spell of the brilliant autumn days. Cool sea breezes swept over its burnt streets from the Lower Bay, and across the splendid flood of the Hudson River the woods on the Palisades of New Jersey had turned to crimson and gold. The air was electric, sharp, sparkling, and the life of the city began to pulse anew with its restless and impetuous energy. Bronzed faces from sea and mountains thronged the streets, health and lighthearted ness showed in every eye, for autumn in New York wields a potent magic not to be denied, and even the East Side slums, where the unfortunates crowd in their squalid thousands, had the appearance of having been swept and cleansed. Along the water-fronts especially the powers of sea and sun and scented winds combined to work an irresistible fever in the hearts of all who chafed within their prison walls.

And in Williams, perhaps more than in most, there was something that responded vigorously to the influences of hope and cheerfulness everywhere abroad. Fresh with the vigor of his holiday and full of good resolutions for the coming winter he felt released from the evil spell of irregular living, and as he crossed one October morning to Staten Island in the big double-ender ferryboat, his heart was light, and his eye wandered to the blue waters and the hazy line of woods beyond with feelings of pure gladness and delight.

He was on his way to Quarantine to meet an incoming liner for the *Vulture*. A Jew-baiting member of the German Reichstag was coming to deliver a series of lectures in New York on his favorite subject, and the newspapers who deemed him worthy of notice at all were sending him fair warning that his mission would be tolerated perhaps, but not welcomed. The Jews were good citizens and America a "free country," and his meetings in the Cooper Union Hall would meet with derision certainly, and violence possibly.

The assignment was a pleasant one, and Williams had instructions to poke fun at the officious and interfering German, and advise him to return to Bremen by the next steamer without venturing among flying eggs and dead cats on the platform. He entered fully into the spirit of the job and was telling the Quarantine doctor about it as they steamed down the bay in the little tug to meet the huge liner just anchoring inside Sandy Hook.

The decks of the ship were crowded with passengers watching the arrival of the puffing tug, and just as they drew alongside in the shadow Williams suddenly felt his eyes drawn away from the swinging rope ladder to some point about halfway down the length of the vessel. There, among the intermediate passengers on the lower deck, he saw a face staring at him with fixed intentness. The eyes were bright blue, and the skin, in that row of bronzed passengers, showed remarkably white. At once, and with a violent rush of blood from the heart, he recognized Hensig.

In a moment everything about him changed: the blue waters of the bay turned black, the light seemed to leave the sun, and all the old sensations of fear and loathing came over him again like the memory of some great pain. He shook himself, and clutched the rope ladder to swing up after the Health Officer, angry, yet genuinely alarmed at the same time, to realize that the return of this man could so affect him. His interview with the Jew-baiter was of the briefest possible description, and he hurried through to catch the Quarantine tug back to Staten Island, instead of steaming up the bay with the great liner into dock, as the other reporters did. He had caught no second glimpse of the hated German, and he even went so far as to harbor a faint hope that he might have been deceived, and that some trick of resemblance in another face had caused a sort of subjective hallucination. At any rate, the days passed into weeks, and October slipped into November, and there was no recurrence of the distressing vision. Perhaps, after all, it was a stranger only; or, if it was Hensig, then he had forgotten all about the reporter, and his return had no connection necessarily with the idea of revenge.

None the less, however, Williams felt uneasy. He told his friend Dowling, the policeman.

"Old news," laughed the Irishman. "Headquarters are keeping an eye on him as a suspect. Berlin wants a man for two murders—goes by the name of Brunner—and from their description we think it's this feller Hensig. Nothing certain yet, but we're on his trail. *I'm* on his trail," he added proudly, "and don't you forget it! I'll let you know anything when the time comes, but mum's the word just now!"

One night, not long after this meeting, Williams and the Senator were covering a big fire on the West Side docks. They were standing on the out skirts of the crowd watching the immense flames that a shouting wind seemed to carry half-way across the river. The surrounding shipping was brilliantly lit up and the roar was magnificent. The Senator, having come out with none of his own, borrowed his friend's overcoat for a moment to protect him from spray and flying cinders while he went inside the fire lines for the latest information obtainable. It was after midnight, and the main story had been telephoned to the office; all they had now to do was to send in the latest details and corrections to be written up at the news desk.

"I'll wait for you over at the corner!" shouted Williams, moving off through a scene of indescribable confusion and taking off his fire badge as he went. This conspicuous brass badge, issued to reporters by the Fire Department, gave them the right to pass within the police cordon in the pursuit of information, and at their own risk. Hardly had he unpinned it from his coat when a hand dashed out of the crowd surging up against him and made a determined grab at it. He turned to trace the owner, but at that instant a great lurching of the mob nearly carried him off his feet, and he only just succeeded in seeing the arm withdrawn, having failed of its object, before he was landed with a violent push upon the pavement he had been aiming for.

The incident did not strike him as particularly odd, for in such a crowd there are many who covet the privilege of getting closer to the blaze. He simply laughed and put the badge safely in his pocket, and then stood to watch the dying flames until his friend came to join him with the latest details.

Yet, though time was pressing and the Senator had little enough to do, it was fully half an hour before he came lumbering up through the darkness. Williams recognized him some distance away by the check ulster he wore—his own.

But *was* it the Senator, after all? The figure moved oddly and with a limp, as though injured. A few feet off it stopped and peered at Williams through the darkness.

"That you, Williams?" asked a gruff voice.

"I thought you were some one else for a moment," answered the reporter, relieved to recognize his friend, and moving forward to meet him. "But what's wrong? Are you hurt?"

The Senator looked ghastly in the lurid glow of the fire. His face was white, and there was a little trickle of blood on the forehead.

"Some fellow nearly did for me," he said; "deliberately pushed me clean off the edge of the dock. If I hadn't fallen on to a broken pile and found a boat, I'd have been drowned sure as God made little apples. Think I know who it was, too. *Think!* I mean I *know*, because I saw his damned white face and heard what he said."

"Who in the world was it? What did he want?" stammered the other.

The Senator took his arm, and lurched into the saloon behind them for some brandy. As he did so he kept looking over his shoulder.

"Quicker we're off from this dirty neighborhood, the better," he said.

Then he turned to Williams, looking oddly at him over the glass, and answering his questions.

"Who was it?—why, it was Hensig! And what did he want?—well, he wanted *you!*"

"Me! Hensig!" gasped the other.

"Guess he mistook me for you," went on the Senator, looking behind him at the door. "The crowd was so thick I cut across by the edge of the dock. It was quite dark. There wasn't a soul near me. I was running. Suddenly what I thought was a stump got up in front of me, and, Gee whiz, man! I tell you it was Hensig, or I'm a drunken Dutchman. I looked bang into his face. 'Good-pye, Mr. *Vulture* reporter,' he said, with a damned laugh, and gave me a push that sent me backwards clean over the edge."

The Senator paused for breath, and to empty his second glass.

"*My* overcoat!" exclaimed Williams faintly.

"Oh, he'd been following you right enough, I guess."

The Senator was not really injured, and the two men walked back towards Broadway to find a telephone, passing through a region of dimly-lighted streets known as Little Africa, where the negroes lived, and where it was safer to keep the middle of the road, thus avoiding sundry dark alley-ways opening off the side. They talked hard all the way.

"He's after you, no doubt," repeated the Senator. "I guess he never forgot your report of his trial. Better keep your eye peeled!" he added with a laugh.

But Williams didn't feel a bit inclined to laugh, and the thought that it certainly was Hensig he had seen on the steamer, and that he was following him so closely as to mark his check ulster and make an attempt on his life, made him feel horribly uncomfortable, to say the least. To be stalked by such a man was terrible. To realize that he was marked down by that white-faced, cruel wretch, merciless and implacable, skilled in the manifold ways of killing by stealth—that somewhere in the crowds of the great city he was watched and waited for, hunted, observed: here was an obsession really to torment and become dangerous. Those light-blue eyes, that keen intelligence, that mind charged with revenge, had been watching him ever since the trial, even from across the sea. The idea terrified him. It brought death into his thoughts for the first time with a vivid sense of nearness and reality—far greater than anything he had experienced when watching others die.

That night, in his dingy little room in the East Nineteenth Street boarding-house, Williams went to bed in a blue funk, and for days afterwards he went about his business in a continuation of the same blue funk. It was useless to deny it. He kept his eyes everywhere, thinking he was being watched and followed. A new face in the office, at the boarding-house table, or anywhere on his usual beat, made him jump. His daily work was haunted; his dreams were all nightmares; he forgot all his good resolutions, and plunged into the old indulgences that helped him to forget his distress. It took twice as much liquor to make him jolly, and four times as much to make him reckless.

Not that he really was a drunkard, or cared to drink for its own sake, but he moved in a thirsty World of reporters, policemen, reckless and loose-living men and women, whose form of greeting was "What'll you take?" and method of reproach "Oh, he's sworn off!"

Only now he was more careful how much he took, counting the cocktails and fizzes poured into him during the course of his day's work, and was anxious never to lose control of himself. He must be on the watch. He changed his eating and drinking haunts, and altered any habits that could give a clue to the devil on his trail. He even went so far as to change his boarding-house. His emotion—the emotion of fear—changed everything. It tinged the outer world with gloom, draping it in darker colors, stealing something from the sunlight, reducing enthusiasm, and acting as a heavy drag, as it were, upon all the normal functions of life.

The effect upon his imagination, already diseased by alcohol and drugs, was, of course, exceedingly strong. The doctor's words about developing a germ until it became too powerful to be touched by any medicine, and then letting it into the victim's system by means of a pin-scratch—this possessed him more than anything else. The idea dominated his thoughts; it seemed so clever, so cruel, so devilish. The "accident" at the fire had been, of course, a real accident, conceived on the spur of the moment—the result of a chance meeting and a foolish mistake. Hensig had no need to resort to such clumsy methods. When the right moment came he would adopt a far simpler, *safer* plan.

Finally, he became so obsessed by the idea that Hensig was following him, waiting for his opportunity, that one day he told the news editor the whole story. His nerves were so shaken that he could not do his work properly.

"That's a good story. Make two hundred of it," said the editor at once. "Fake the name, of course. Mustn't mention Hensig, or there'll be a libel suit."

But Williams was in earnest, and insisted so forcibly that Treherne, though busy as ever, took him aside into his room with the glass door.

"Now, see here, Williams, you're drinking too much," he said; "that's about the size of it. Steady up a bit on the wash, and Hensig's face will disappear." He spoke kindly, but sharply. He was young himself, awfully keen, with much knowledge of human nature and a rare "nose for news." He understood the abilities of his small army of men with intuitive judgment. That they drank was nothing to him, provided they did their work. Everybody in that world drank, and the man who didn't was looked upon with suspicion.

Williams explained rather savagely that the face was no mere symptom of delirium tremens, and the editor spared him another two minutes before rushing out to tackle the crowd of men waiting for him at the news desk.

"That so? You don't say!" he asked, with more interest. "Well, I guess Hensig's simply trying to razzle-dazzle you. You tried to kill him by your reports, and he wants to scare you by way of revenge. But he'll never dare do anything. Throw him a good bluff, and he'll give in like a baby. Everything's pretence in this world. But I rather like the idea of the germs. That's original!"

Williams, a little angry at the other's flippancy, told the story of the Senator's adventure and the changed overcoat.

"May be, may be," replied the hurried editor; "but the Senator drinks Chinese whisky, and a man who does that might imagine anything on God's earth. Take a tip, Williams, from an old hand, and let up a bit on the liquor. Drop cocktails and keep to straight whisky, and never drink on an empty stomach. Above all, *don't mix!*"

He gave him a keen look and was off.

"Next time you see this German," cried Treherne from the door, "go up and ask him for an interview on what it feels like to escape from the Chair—just to show him you don't care a red cent. Talk about having him watched and followed—suspected man—and all that sort of flim-flam. Pretend to warn him. It'll turn the tables and make him digest a bit. See?"

Williams sauntered out into the street to report a meeting of the Rapid Transit Commissioners, and the first person he met as he ran down the office steps was—Max Hensig.

Before he could stop, or swerve aside, they were face to face. His head swam for a moment and he began to tremble. Then some measure of self-possession returned, and he tried instinctively to act on the editor's advice. No other plan was ready, so he drew on the last force that had occupied his mind. It was that—or running.

Hensig, he noticed, looked prosperous; he wore a fur overcoat and cap. His face was whiter than ever, and his blue eyes burned like coals.

"Why! Dr. Hensig, you're back in New York!" he exclaimed. "When did you arrive? I'm glad—I suppose—I mean—er—will you come and have a drink?" he concluded desperately. It was very foolish, but for the life of him he could think of nothing else to say. And the last thing in the world he wished was that his enemy should know that he was afraid.

"I tink not, Mr. *Vulture* reporder, tanks," he answered coolly, "but I sit py and vatch you drink." His self-possession was perfect, as it always was.

But Williams, more himself now, seized on the refusal and moved on, saying something about having a meeting to go to.

"I walk a liddle way with you, berhaps," Hensig said, following him down the pavement.

It was impossible to prevent him, and they started side by side across City Hall Park towards Broad way. It was after four o'clock; the dusk was falling; the little park was thronged with people walking in all directions, every one in a terrific hurry as usual. Only Hensig seemed calm and unmoved among that racing, tearing life about them. He carried an atmosphere of ice about with him: it was his voice and manner that produced this impression; his mind was alert, watchful, determined, always sure of itself

Williams wanted to run. He reviewed swiftly in his mind a dozen ways of getting rid of him quickly, yet knowing well they were all futile. He put his hands in his overcoat pockets—the check ulster—and watched sideways every movement of his companion.

"Living in New York again, aren't you?" he began.

"Not as a doctor any more," was the reply. "I now teach and study. Also I write sciendific books a liddle—"

"What about?"

"Cherms," said the other, looking at him and laughing. "Disease cherms, their culture and development." He put the accent on the "op."

Williams walked more quickly. With a great effort he tried to put Treherne's advice into practice.

"You care to give me an interview any time—on your special subjects?" he asked, as naturally as he could.

"Oh yes; with much bleasure. I lif in Harlem now, if you will call von day—"

"Our office is best," interrupted the reporter. "Paper, desks, library, all handy for use, you know."

"If you're afraid—" began Hensig. Then, without finishing the sentence, he added with a laugh, "I haf no arsenic there. You not tink me any more a pungling boisoner? You haf changed your mind about all dat?"

Williams felt his flesh beginning to creep. How could he speak of such a matter! His own wife, too!

He turned quickly and faced him, standing still for a moment so that the throng of people deflected into two streams past them. He felt it absolutely imperative upon him to say something that should convince the German he was not afraid.

"I suppose you are aware, Dr. Hensig, that the police know you have returned, and that you are being watched probably?" he said in a low voice, forcing himself to meet the odious blue eyes.

"And why not, bray?" he asked imperturbably.

"They may suspect something—"

"Susbected—already again? *Ach was!*" said the German.

"I only wished to warn you—" stammered Williams, who always found it difficult to remain self-possessed under the other's dreadful stare.

"No boliceman see what I do—or catch me again," he laughed quite horribly. "But I tank you all the same."

Williams turned to catch a Broadway car going at full speed. He could not stand another minute with this man, who affected him so disagreeably.

"I call at the office one day to gif you interview!" Hensig shouted as he dashed off, and the next minute he was swallowed up in the crowd, and Williams, with mixed feelings and a strange inner trembling, went to cover the meeting of the Rapid Transit Board.

But, while he reported the proceedings mechanically, his mind was busy with quite other thoughts. Hensig was at his side the whole time. He felt quite sure, however unlikely it seemed, that there was no fancy in his fears, and that he had judged the German correctly. Hensig hated him, and would put him out of the way if he could. He would do it in such a way that detection would be almost impossible. He would not shoot or poison in the ordinary way, or resort to any clumsy method. He would simply follow, watch, wait his opportunity, and then act with utter callousness and remorseless determination. And Williams already felt pretty certain of the means that would be employed: "*Cherms!*"

This meant proximity. He must watch every one who came close to him in trains, cars, restaurants—anywhere and everywhere. It could be done in a second: only a slight scratch would be necessary, and the disease would be in his blood with such strength that the chances of recovery would be slight. And what could he do? He could not have Hensig watched or arrested. He had no story to tell to a magistrate, or to the police, for no one would listen to such a tale. And, if he were stricken down by sudden illness, what was more likely than to say he had caught the fever in the ordinary course of his work, since he was always frequenting noisome dens and the haunts of the very poor, the foreign and filthy slums of the East Side, and the hospitals, morgues, and cells of all sorts and conditions of men? No; it was a disagreeable situation, and Williams, young, shaken in nerve, and easily impressionable as he was, could not prevent its obsession of his mind and imagination.

"If I get suddenly ill," he told the Senator, his only friend in the whole city, "and send for you, look carefully for a scratch on my body. Tell Dowling, and tell the doctor the story."

"You think Hensig goes about with a little bottle of plague germs in his vest pocket," laughed the other reporter, "ready to scratch you with a pin?"

"Some damned scheme like that, I'm sure."

"Nothing could be proved anyway. He wouldn't keep the evidence in his pocket till he was arrested, would he?"

During the next week or two Williams ran against Hensig twice—accidentally. The first time it happened just outside his own boarding-house—the *new one*. Hensig had his foot on the stone steps as if just about to come up, but quick as a flash he turned his face away and moved on down the street. This was about eight o'clock in the evening, and the hall light fell through the opened door upon his face. The second time it was not so clear: the reporter was covering a case in the courts, a case of suspicious death in which a woman was chief prisoner, and he thought he saw the doctor's white visage watching him from among the crowd at the back of the court-room. When he looked a second time, however, the face had disappeared, and there was no sign afterwards of its owner in the lobby or corridor.

That same day he met Dowling in the building; he was promoted now, and was always in plain clothes. The detective drew him aside into a corner. The talk at once turned upon the German.

"We're watching him too," he said. "Nothing you can use yet, but he's changed his name again, and never stops at the same address for more than a week or two. I guess he's Brunner right enough, the man Berlin's looking for. He's a holy terror if ever there was one."

Dowling was happy as a schoolboy to be in touch with such a promising case.

"What's he up to now in particular?" asked the other.

"Something pretty black," said the detective. "But I can't tell you yet awhile. He calls himself Schmidt now, and he's dropped the 'Doctor.' We may take him any day—just waiting for advices from Germany."

Williams told his story of the overcoat adventure with the Senator, and his belief that Hensig was waiting for a suitable opportunity to catch him alone.

"That's dead likely too," said Dowling, and added carelessly, "I guess we'll have to make some kind of a case against him anyway, just to get him out of the way. He's too dangerous to be around huntin' on the loose."

IV

So gradual sometimes are the approaches of fear that the processes by which it takes possession of a man's soul are often too insidious to be recognized, much less to be dealt with, until their object has been finally accomplished and the victim has lost the power to act. And by this time the reporter, who had again plunged into excess, felt so nerveless that, if he met Hensig face to face, he could not answer for what he might do. He might assault his tormentor violently—one result of terror—or he might find himself powerless to do anything at all but yield, like a bird fascinated before a snake.

He was always thinking now of the moment when they would meet, and of what would happen; for he was just as certain that they must meet eventually, and that Hensig would try to kill him, as that his next birthday would find him twenty-five years old. That meeting, he well knew, could be delayed only, not prevented, and his changing again to another boarding-house, or moving altogether to a different city, could only postpone the final accounting between them. It was bound to come.

A reporter on a New York newspaper has one day in seven to himself. Williams's day off was Monday, and he was always glad when it came. Sunday was especially arduous for him, because in addition to the unsatisfactory nature of the day's assignments, involving private interviewing which the citizens pretended to resent on their day of rest, he had the task in the evening of reporting a difficult sermon in a Brooklyn church. Having only a column and a half at his disposal, he had to condense as he went along, and the speaker was so rapid, and so fond of lengthy quotations, that the reporter found his shorthand only just equal to the task. It was usually after half-past nine o'clock when he left the church, and there was still the labour of transcribing his notes in the office against time.

The Sunday following the glimpse of his tormentor's face in the court-room he was busily condensing the wearisome periods of the preacher, sitting at a little table immediately under the pulpit, when he glanced up during a brief pause and let his eye wander over the congregation and up to the crowded galleries. Nothing was farther at the moment from his much-occupied brain than the doctor of Amityville, and it was such an unexpected shock to encounter his fixed stare up there among the occupants of the front row, watching him with an evil smile, that his senses temporarily deserted him. The next sentence of the preacher was wholly lost, and his shorthand during the brief remainder of the sermon was quite illegible, he found, when he came to transcribe it at the office.

It was after one o'clock in the morning when he finished, and he went out feeling exhausted and rather shaky. In the all-night drug store at the corner he indulged accordingly in several more glasses of whisky than usual, and talked a long time with the man who guarded the back room and served liquor to the few who knew the password, since the shop had really no license at all. The true reason for this delay he recognized quite plainly: he was afraid of the journey home along the dark and emptying streets. The lower end of New York is practically deserted after ten o'clock: it has no residences, no theatres, no *cafés*, and only a few travelers from late ferries share it with reporters, a sprinkling of policemen, and the ubiquitous ne'erdo-wells who haunt the saloon doors. The newspaper world of Park Row was, of course, alive with light and movement, but once outside that narrow zone and the night descended with an effect of general darkness.

Williams thought of spending three dollars on a cab, but dismissed the idea because of its extravagance. Presently Galusha Owens came in—too drunk to be of any use, though, as a companion. Besides, he lived in Harlem, which was miles beyond Nineteenth Street, where Williams had to go. He took another rye whisky—his fourth—and looked cautiously through the coloured glass windows into the street. No one was visible. Then he screwed up his nerves another twist or two, and made a bolt for it, taking the steps in a sort of flying leap—and running full tilt into a man whose figure seemed almost to have risen out of the very pavement.

He gave a cry and raised his fists to strike.

"Where's your hurry?" laughed a familiar voice. "Is the Prince of Wales dead?" It was the Senator, most welcome of all possible appearances.

"Come in and have a horn," said Williams, "and then I'll walk home with you." He was immensely glad to see him, for only a few streets separated their respective boarding-houses.

"But he'd never sit out a long sermon just for the pleasure of watching you," observed the Senator after hearing his friend's excited account.

"That man'll take any trouble in the world to gain his end," said the other with conviction. "He's making a study of all my movements and habits. He's not the sort to take chances when it's a matter of life and death. I'll bet he's not far away at this moment."

"Rats!" exclaimed the Senator, laughing in rather a forced way. "You're getting the jumps with your Hensig and death. Have another rye."

They finished their drinks and went out together, crossing City Hall Park diagonally towards Broadway, and then turning north. They crossed Canal and Grand Streets, deserted and badly lighted. Only a few drunken loiterers passed them. Occasionally a policeman on the corner, always close to the side-door of a saloon, of course, recognized one or other of them and called good-night. Otherwise there was no one, and they seemed to have this part of Manhattan Island pretty well to themselves. The presence of the Senator, ever cheery and kind, keeping close to his friend all the way, the effect of the half-dozen whiskies, and the sight of the guardians of the law, combined to raise the reporter's spirits somewhat; and when they reached Fourteenth Street, with its better light and greater traffic, and saw Union Square lying just beyond, close to his own street, he felt a distinct increase of courage and no objection to going on alone.

"Good-night!" cried the Senator cheerily. "Get home safe; I turn off here anyway." He hesitated a moment before turning down the street, and then added, "You feel O.K., don't you?"

"You may get double rates for an exclusive bit of news if you come on and see me assaulted," Williams replied, laughing aloud, and then waiting to see the last of his friend.

But the moment the Senator was gone the laughter disappeared. He went on alone, crossing the square among the trees and walking very quickly. Once or twice he turned to see if anybody were following him, and his eyes scanned carefully as he passed every occupant of the park benches where a certain number of homeless loafers always find their night's lodging. But there was nothing apparently to cause him alarm, and in a few minutes more he would be safe in the little back bedroom of his own house. Over the way he saw the lights of Burbacher's saloon, where respectable Germans drank Rhine wine and played chess till all hours. He thought of going in for a night-cap, hesitating for a moment, but finally going on. When he got to the end of the square, however, and saw the dark opening of East Eighteenth Street, he thought after all he would go back and have another drink. He hovered for a moment on the kerbstone and then turned; his will often slipped a cog now in this way.

It was only when he was on his way back that he realized the truth: that his real reason for turning back and avoiding the dark open mouth of the street was because he was afraid of something its shadows might conceal. This dawned upon him quite suddenly. If there had been a light at the corner of the street he would never have turned back at all. And as this passed through his mind, already somewhat fuddled with what he had drunk, he became aware that the figure of a man had slipped forward out of the dark space he had just refused to enter, and was following him down the street. The man was pressing, too, close into the houses, using any protection of shadow or railing that would enable him to move unseen.

But the moment Williams entered the bright section of pavement opposite the wine-room windows he knew that this man had come close up behind him, with a little silent run, and he turned at once to face him. He saw a slim man with dark hair and blue eyes, and recognized him instantly.

"It's very late to be coming home," said the man at once. "I thought I recognized my reporder friend from the *Vulture.*" These were the actual words, and the voice was meant to be pleasant, but what Williams thought he heard, spoken in tones of ice, was something like, "At last I've caught you! You are in a state of collapse nervously, and you are exhausted. I can do what I please with you." For the face and the voice were those of Hensig the Tormentor, and the dyed hair only served to emphasize rather grotesquely the man's features and make the pallor of the skin greater by contrast.

His first instinct was to turn and run, his second to fly at the man and strike him. A terror beyond death seized him. A pistol held to his head, or a waving bludgeon, he could easily have faced; but this odious creature, slim, limp, and white of face, with his terrible suggestion of cruelty, literally appalled him so that he could think of nothing intelligent to do or to say. This accurate knowledge of his movements, too, added to his distress—this waiting for him at night when he was tired and foolish from excess. At that moment he knew all the sensations of the criminal a few hours before his execution: the bursts of hysterical terror, the inability to realize his position, to hold his thoughts steady, the helplessness of it all. Yet, in the end, the reporter heard his own voice speaking with a rather weak and unnatural kind of tone and accompanied by a gulp of forced laughter—heard himself stammering the ever-ready formula: "I was going to have a drink before turning in—will you join me?"

The invitation, he realized afterwards, was prompted by the one fact that stood forth clearly in his mind at the moment—the thought, namely, that whatever he did or said, he must never let Hensig for one instant imagine that he felt afraid and was so helpless a victim.

Side by side they moved down the street, for Hensig had acquiesced in the suggestion, and Williams already felt dazed by the strong, persistent will of his companion. His thoughts seemed to be flying about somewhere outside his brain, beyond control, scattering wildly. He could think of nothing further to say, and had the smallest diversion furnished the opportunity he would have turned and run for his life through the deserted streets.

"A glass of lager," he heard the German say, "I take berhaps that with you. You know me in spite of—" he added, indicating by a movement the changed colour of his hair and moustache. "Also, I gif you now the interview you asked for, if you like."

The reporter agreed feebly, finding nothing adequate to reply. He turned helplessly and looked into his face with something of the sensations a bird may feel when it runs at last straight into the jaws of the reptile that has fascinated it. The fear of weeks settled down upon him, focusing about his heart. It was, of course, an effect of hypnotism, he remembered thinking vaguely through the befuddlement of his drink—this culminating effect of an evil and remorseless personality acting upon one that was diseased and extra receptive. And while he made the suggestion and heard the other's acceptance of it, he knew perfectly well that he was falling in with the plan of the doctor's own making, a plan that would end in an assault upon his person, perhaps a technical assault only—a mere touch—still, an assault that would be at the same time an attempt at murder. The alcohol buzzed in his ears. He felt strangely powerless. He walked steadily to his doom, side by side with his executioner.

Any attempt to analyze the psychology of the situation was utterly beyond him. But, amid the whirl of emotion and the excitement of the whisky, he dimly grasped the importance of *two fundamental things*.

And the first was that, though he was now muddled and frantic, yet a moment would come when his will would be capable of one supreme effort to escape, and that therefore it would be wiser for the present to waste no atom of volition on temporary half-measures. He would play dead dog. The fear that now paralyzed him would accumulate till it reached the point of saturation: that would be the time to strike for his life. For just as the coward may reach a stage where he is capable of a sort of frenzied heroism that no ordinarily brave man could compass, so the victim of fear, at a point varying with his balance of imagination and physical vigor, will reach a state where fear leaves him and he becomes numb to its effect from sheer excess of feeling it. It is the point of saturation. He may then turn suddenly calm and act with a judgment and precision that simply bewilder the object of the attack. It is, of course, the inevitable swing of the pendulum, the law of equal action and reaction.

Hazily, tipsily perhaps, Williams was conscious of this potential power deep within him, below the superficial layers of smaller emotions—could he but be *sufficiently terrified to reach it* and bring it to the surface where it must result in action.

And, as a consequence of this foresight of his sober subliminal self, he offered no opposition to the least suggestion of his tormentor, but made up his mind instinctively to agree to all that he proposed. Thus he lost no atom of the force he might eventually call upon, by friction over details which in any case he would yield in the end. And at the same time he felt intuitively that his utter weakness might even deceive his enemy a little and increase the chances of his single effort to escape when the right moment arrived.

That Williams was able to "imagine" this true psychology, yet wholly unable to analyze it, simply showed that on occasion he could be psychically active. His deeper subliminal self, stirred by the alcohol and the stress of emotion, was guiding him, and would continue to guide him in proportion as he let his fuddled normal self slip into the background without attempt to interfere.

And the second fundamental thing he grasped—due even more than the first to psychic intuition—was the certainty that he could drink more, up to a certain point, with distinct advantage to his power and lucidity—but up to a given point only. After that would come unconsciousness, a single sip too much and he would cross the frontier—a very narrow one. It was as though he knew intuitively that "the drunken consciousness is one bit of the mystic consciousness." At present he was only fuddled and fearful, but additional stimulant would inhibit the effects of the other emotions, give him unbounded confidence, clarify his judgment and increase his capacity to a stage far beyond the normal. Only—he must stop in time.

His chances of escape, therefore, so far as he could understand, depended on these two things: he must drink till he became self-confident and arrived at the abnormally clear-minded stage of drunkenness; and he must wait for the moment when Hensig had so filled him up with fear that he no longer could react to it. Then would be the time to strike. Then his will would be free and have judgment behind it.

These were the two things standing up clearly somewhere behind that great confused turmoil of mingled fear and alcohol.

Thus for the moment, though with scattered forces and rather wildly feeble thoughts, he moved down the street beside the man who hated him and meant to kill him. He had no purpose at all but to agree and to wait. Any attempt he made now could end only in failure.

They talked a little as they went, the German calm, chatting as though he were merely an agreeable acquaintance, but behaving with the obvious knowledge that he held his victim secure, and that his struggles would prove simply rather amusing. He even laughed about his dyed hair, saying by way of explanation that he had done it to please a woman who told him it would make him look younger. Williams knew this was a lie, and that the police had more to do with the change than a woman; but the man's vanity showed through the explanation, and was a vivid little self-revelation.

He objected to entering Burbacher's, saying that he (Burbacher) paid no blackmail to the police, and might be raided for keeping open after hours.

"I know a nice quiet blace on T'ird Avenue. We go there," he said.

Williams, walking unsteadily and shaking inwardly, still groping, too, feebly after a way of escape, turned down the side street with him. He thought of the men he had watched walking down the short corridor from the cell to the "Chair" at Sing Sing, and wondered if they felt as he did. It was just like going to his own execution.

"I haf a new disgovery in bacteriology—in cherms," the doctor went on, "and it will make me famous, for it is very imbortant. I gif it you egsclusive for the *Vulture*, as you are a friend." He became technical, and the reporter's mind lost itself among such words as "toxins," "alkaloids," and the like. But he realized clearly enough that Hensig was playing with him and felt absolutely sure of his victim. When he lurched badly, as he did more than once, the German took his arm by way of support, and at the vile touch of the man it was all Williams could do not to scream or strike out blindly.

They turned up Third Avenue and stopped at the side door of a cheap saloon. He noticed the name of Schumacher over the porch, but all lights were out except a feeble glow that came through the glass fanlight. A man pushed his face cautiously round the half-opened door, and after a brief examination let them in with a whispered remark to be quiet. It was the usual formula of the Tammany saloon-keeper, who paid so much a month to the police to be allowed to keep open all night, provided there was no noise or fighting. It was now well after one o'clock in the morning, and the streets were deserted.

The reporter was quite at home in the sort of place they had entered; otherwise the sinister aspect of a drinking "joint" after hours, with its gloom and general air of suspicion, might have caused him some extra alarm A dozen men, unpleasant of countenance, were standing at the bar, where a single lamp gave just enough light to enable them to see their glasses. The bar-tender gave Hensig a swift glance of recognition as they walked along the sanded floor.

"Come," whispered the German; "we go to the back room. I know the bass-word," he laughed, leading the way.

They walked to the far end of the bar and opened a door into a brightly lit room with about a dozen tables in it, at most of which men sat drinking with highly painted women, talking loudly, quarrelling, singing, and the air thick with smoke. No one took any notice of them as they went down the room to a table in the corner farthest from the door—Hensig chose it; and when the single waiter came up with "Was nehmen die Herren?" and a moment later brought the rye whisky they both asked for, Williams swallowed his own without the "chaser" of soda water, and ordered another on the spot.

"It'sh awfully watered," he said rather thickly to his companion, "and I'm tired."

"Cocaine, under the circumstances, would help you quicker, berhaps!" replied the German with an expression of amusement. Good God! was there nothing about him the man had not found out? He must have been shadowing him for days; it was at least a week since Williams had been to the First Avenue drug store to get the wicked bottle refilled. Had he been on his trail every night when he left the office to go home? This idea of remorseless persistence made him shudder.

"Then we finish quickly if you are tired," the doctor continued, "and to-morrow you can show me your repordt for gorrections if you make any misdakes berhaps. I gif you the address to-night pefore we leave."

The increased ugliness of his speech and accent betrayed his growing excitement. Williams drank his whisky, again without water, and called for yet another, clinking glasses with the murderer opposite, and swallowing half of this last glass, too, while Hensig merely tasted his own, looking straight at him over the performance with his evil eyes.

"I can write shorthand," began the reporter, trying to appear at his ease.

"*Ach*, I know, of course."

There was a mirror behind the table, and he took a quick glance round the room while the other began searching in his coat pocket for the papers he had with him. Williams lost no single detail of his movements, but at the same time managed swiftly to get the "note" of the other occupants of the tables. Degraded and besotted faces he saw, almost without exception, and not one to whom he could appeal for help with any prospect of success. It was a further shock, too, to realize that he preferred the more or less bestial countenances round him to the intellectual and ascetic face opposite. They were at least human, whereas *he* was something quite outside the pale; and this preference for the low creatures, otherwise loathsome to him, brought his mind by sharp contrast to a new and vivid realization of the personality before him. He gulped down his drink, and again ordered it to be refilled.

But meanwhile the alcohol was beginning to key him up out of the dazed and negative state into which his first libations and his accumulations of fear had plunged him. His brain became a shade clearer. There was even a faint stirring of the will. He had already drunk enough under normal circumstances to be simply reeling, but to-night the emotion of fear inhibited the effects of the alcohol, keeping him singularly steady. Provided he did not exceed a given point, he could go on drinking till he reached the moment of high power when he could combine all his forces into the single consummate act of cleverly calculated escape. If he missed this psychological moment he would collapse.

A sudden crash made him jump. It was behind him against the other wall. In the mirror he saw that a middle-aged man had lost his balance and fallen off his chair, foolishly intoxicated, and that two women were ostensibly trying to lift him up, but really were going swiftly through his pockets as he lay in a heap on the floor. A big man who had been asleep the whole evening in the corner stopped snoring and woke up to look and laugh, but no one interfered. A man must take care of himself in such a place and with such company, or accept the consequences. The big man composed himself again for sleep, sipping his glass a little first, and the noise of the room continued as before. It was a case of "knock-out drops" in the whisky, put in by the women, however, rather than by the saloon-keeper. Williams remembered thinking he had nothing to fear of that kind. Hensig's method would be far more subtle and clever—*cherms!* A scratch with a pin and a germ!

"I haf zome notes here of my disgovery," he went on, smiling significantly at the interruption, and taking some papers out of an inner pocket. "But they are written in Cherman, so I dranslate for you. You haf paper and benzil?"

The reporter produced the sheaf of office copy paper he always carried about with him, and prepared to write. The rattle of the elevated trains outside and the noisy buzz of drunken conversation inside formed the background against which he heard the German's steely insistent voice going on ceaselessly with the "dranslation and egsplanation." From time to time people left the room, and new customers reeled in. When the clatter of incipient fighting and smashed glasses became too loud, Hensig waited till it was quiet again. He watched every new arrival keenly. They were very few now, for the night had passed into early morning and the room was gradually emptying. The waiter took snatches of sleep in his chair by the door; the big man still snored heavily in the angle of the wall and window. When he was the only one left, the proprietor would certainly close up. He had not ordered a drink for an hour at least. Williams, however, drank on steadily, always aiming at the point when he would be at the top of his power, full of confidence and decision. That moment was undoubtedly coming nearer all the time. Yes, but so was the moment Hensig was waiting for. He, too, felt absolutely confident, encouraging his companion to drink more, and watching his gradual collapse with unmasked glee. He betrayed his gloating quite plainly now: he held his victim too securely to feel anxious; when the big man reeled out they would be alone for a brief minute or two unobserved—and meanwhile he allowed himself to become a little too careless from over-confidence. And Williams noted that too.

For slowly the will of the reporter began to assert itself, and with this increase of intelligence he of course appreciated his awful position more keenly, and therefore, *felt more fear*. The two main things he was waiting for were coming perceptibly within reach: to reach the saturation point of terror and the culminating moment of the alcohol. Then, action and escape!

Gradually, thus, as he listened and wrote, he passed from the stage of stupid, negative terror into that of active, positive terror. The alcohol kept driving hotly at those hidden centres of imagination within, which, once touched, begin to reveal; in other words, he became observant, critical, alert. Swiftly the power grew. His lucidity increased till he became almost conscious of the workings of the other man's mind, and it was like sitting opposite a clock whose wheels and needles he could just hear clicking. His eyes seemed to spread their power of vision all over his skin; he could see what was going on without actually looking. In the same way he heard all that passed in the room without turning his head. Every moment he became clearer in mind. He almost touched clairvoyance. The presentiment earlier in the evening that this stage would come was at last being actually fulfilled.

From time to time he sipped his whisky, but more cautiously than at first, for he knew that this keen psychical activity was the forerunner of helpless collapse. Only for a minute or two would he be at the top of his power. The frontier was a dreadfully narrow one, and already he had lost control of his fingers, and was scrawling a shorthand that bore no resemblance to the original system of its inventor.

As the white light of this abnormal perceptiveness increased, the horror of his position became likewise more and more vivid. He knew that he was fighting for his life with a soulless and malefic being who was next door to a devil. The sense of fear was being magnified now with every minute that passed. Presently the power of *perceiving* would pass into *doing*; he would strike the blow for his life, whatever form that blow might take.

Already he was sufficiently master of himself to act—to act in the sense of deceiving. He exaggerated his drunken writing and thickness of speech, his general condition of collapse; and this power of *hearing* the workings of the other man's mind showed him that he was successful. Hensig was a little deceived. He proved this by increased carelessness, and by allowing the expression of his face to become plainly exultant.

Williams's faculties were so concentrated upon the causes operating in the terrible personality opposite to him, that he could spare no part of his brain for the explanations and sentences that came from his lips. He did not hear or understand a hundredth part of what the doctor was saying, but occasionally he caught up the end of a phrase and managed to ask a blundering question out of it; and Hensig, obviously pleased with his increasing obfuscation, always answered at some length, quietly watching with pleasure the reporter's foolish hieroglyphics upon the paper.

The whole thing, of course, was an utter blind. Hensig had no discovery at all. He was talking scientific jargon, knowing full well that those shorthand notes would never be transcribed, and that he himself would be out of harm's way long before his victim's senses had cleared sufficiently to tell him that he was in the grasp of a deadly sickness which no medicines could prevent ending in death.

Williams saw and felt all this clearly. It somehow came to him, rising up in that clear depth of his mind that was stirred by the alcohol, and yet beyond the reach, so far, of its deadly confusion. He understood perfectly well that Hensig was waiting for a moment to act; that he would do nothing violent, but would carry out his murderous intention in such an innocent way that the victim would have no suspicions at the moment, and would only realize later that he had been poisoned and—

Hark! What was that? There was a change. Something had happened. It was like the sound of a gong, and the reporter's fear suddenly doubled. Hensig's scheme had moved forward a step. There was no sound actually, but his senses seemed grouped together into one, and for some reason his perception of the change came by way of audition. Fear brimmed up perilously near the breaking point. But the moment for action had not quite come yet, and he luckily saved himself by the help of another and contrary emotion. He emptied his glass, spilling half of it purposely over his coat, and burst out laughing in Hensig's face. The vivid picture rose before him of Whitey Fife catching cocktail glasses off the edge of Steve Brodie's table.

The laugh was admirably careless and drunken, but the German was startled and looked up suspiciously. He had not expected this, and through lowered eyelids Williams observed an expression of momentary uncertainty on his features, as though he felt he was not absolutely master of the situation after all, as he imagined.

"Su'nly thought of Whitey Fife knocking Stevebrodie off'sh Brooklyn Bridsh in a co—cock'tail glashh—" Williams explained in a voice hopelessly out of control. "You know Whhhiteyfife, of coursh, don't you?—ha, ha, ha!"

Nothing could have helped him more in putting Hensig off the scent. His face resumed its expression of certainty and cold purpose. The waiter, wakened by the noise, stirred uneasily in his chair, and the big man in the corner indulged in a gulp that threatened to choke him as he sat with his head sunk upon his chest. But otherwise the empty room became quiet again. The German resumed his confident command of the situation. Williams, he saw, was drunk enough to bring him easily into his net.

None the less, the reporter's perception had not been at fault. There *was* a change. Hensig was about to do something, and his mind was buzzing with preparations.

The victim, now within measuring distance of his supreme moment—the point where terror would release his will, and alcohol would inspire him beyond possibility of error—saw everything as in the clear light of day. Small things led him to the climax: the emptied room; the knowledge that shortly the saloon would close; the grey light of day stealing under the chinks of door and shutter; the increased vileness of the face gleaming at him opposite in the paling gas glare. Ugh! how the air reeked of stale spirits, the fumes of cigar smoke, and the cheap scents of the vanished women. The floor was strewn with sheets of paper, absurdly scrawled over. The table had patches of wet, and cigarette ashes lay over everything. His hands and feet were icy, his eyes burning hot. His heart thumped like a soft hammer.

Hensig was speaking in quite a changed voice now. He had been leading up to this point for hours. No one was there to see, even if anything was to be seen—which was unlikely. The big man still snored; the waiter was asleep too. There was silence in the outer room, and between the walls of the inner there was—*Death.*

"Now, Mr. *Vulture* reporder, I *show* you what I mean all this time to egsplain," he was saying in his most metallic voice.

He drew a blank sheet of the reporter's paper towards him across the little table, avoiding carefully the wet splashes.

"Lend me your bencil von moment, please. Yes?"

Williams, simulating almost total collapse, dropped the pencil and shoved it over the polished wood as though the movement was about all he could manage. With his head sunk forward upon his chest he watched stupidly. Hensig began to draw some kind of outline; his touch was firm, and there was a smile on his lips.

"Here, you see, is the human arm," he said, sketching rapidly; "and here are the main nerves, and here the artery. Now, my discovery, as I haf peen egsplaining to you, is simply—" He dropped into a torrent of meaningless scientific phrases, during which the other purposely allowed his hand to lie relaxed upon the table, knowing perfectly well that in a moment Hensig would seize it—for the purposes of illustration.

His terror was so intense that, for the first time this awful night, he was within an ace of action. The point of saturation had been almost reached. Though apparently sodden drunk, his mind was really at the highest degree of clear perception and judgment, and in another moment—the moment Hensig actually began his final assault—the terror would provide the reporter with the extra vigor and decision necessary to strike his one blow. Exactly how he would do it, or what precise form it would take, he had no idea; that could be left to the inspiration of the moment; he only knew that his strength would last just long enough to bring this about, and that then he would collapse in utter intoxication upon the floor.

Hensig dropped the pencil suddenly: it clattered away to a corner of the room, showing it had been propelled with force, not merely allowed to fall, and he made no attempt to pick it up. Williams, to test his intention, made a pretended movement to stoop after it, and the other, as he imagined he would, stopped him in a second.

"I haf another," he said quickly, diving into his inner pocket and producing a long dark pencil. Williams saw in a flash, through his half-closed eyes, that it was sharpened at one end, while the other end was covered by a little protective cap of transparent substance like glass, a third of an inch long. He heard it click as it struck a button of the coat, and also saw that by a very swift motion of the fingers, impossible to be observed by a drunken man, Hensig removed the cap so that the end was free. Something gleamed there for a moment, something like a point of shining metal—the point of a pin.

"Gif me your hand von minute and I drace the nerve up the arm I speak apout," the doctor continued in that steely voice that showed no sign of nervousness, though he was on the edge of murder. "So, I show you much petter vot I mean."

Without a second's hesitation—for the moment for action had not quite come—he lurched forward and stretched his arm clumsily across the table. Hensig seized the fingers in his own and turned the palm uppermost. With his other hand he pointed the pencil at the wrist, and began moving it a little up towards the elbow, pushing the sleeve back for the purpose. His touch was the touch of death. On the point of the black pin, engrafted into the other end of the pencil, Williams knew there clung the germs of some deadly disease, germs unusually powerful from special culture; and that within the next few seconds the pencil would turn and the pin would *accidentally* scratch his wrist and let the virulent poison into his blood.

He knew this, yet at the same time he managed to remain master of himself. For he also realized that at last, just in the nick of time, the moment he had been waiting for all through these terrible hours had actually arrived, and he was ready to act.

And the little unimportant detail that furnished the extra quota of fear necessary to bring him to this point was—*touch*. It was the touch of Hensig's hand that did it, setting every nerve a-quiver to its utmost capacity, filling him with a black horror that reached the limits of sensation.

In that moment Williams regained his self-control and became absolutely sober. Terror removed its paralyzing inhibitions, having led him to the point where numbness succeeds upon excess, and sensation ceases to register in the brain. The emotion of fear was dead, and he was ready to act with all the force of his being—that force, too, raised to a higher power after long repression.

Moreover, he could make no mistake, for at the same time he had reached the culminating effect of the alcohol, and a sort of white light filled his mind, showing him clearly what to do and how to do it. He felt master of himself, confident, capable of anything. He followed blindly that inner guidance he had been dimly conscious of the whole night, and what he did he did instinctively, as it were, without deliberate plan.

He was *waiting for the pencil to turn* so that the pin pointed at his vein. Then, when Hensig was wholly concentrated upon the act of murder, and thus oblivious of all else, he would find his opportunity. For at this supreme moment the German's mind would be focused on the one thing. He would notice nothing else round him. He would be open to successful attack. But this supreme moment would hardly last more than five seconds at most!

The reporter raised his eyes and stared for the first time steadily into his opponent's eyes, till the room faded out and he saw only the white skin in a blaze of its own light. Thus staring, he caught in himself the full stream of venom, hatred, and revenge that had been pouring at him across the table for so long—caught and held it for one instant, and then returned it into the other's brain with all its original force and the added impetus of his own recovered will behind it.

Hensig felt this, and for a moment seemed to waver; he was surprised out of himself by the sudden change in his victim's attitude. The same instant, availing himself of a diversion caused by the big man in the corner waking noisily and trying to rise, he slowly *turned the pencil round* so that the point of the pin was directed at the hand lying in his. The sleepy waiter was helping the drunken man to cross to the door, and the diversion was all in his favor.

But Williams knew what he was doing. He did not even tremble.

"When that pin scratches me," he said aloud in a firm, sober voice, "it means—death."

The German could not conceal his surprise on hearing the change of voice, but he still felt sure of his victim, and clearly wished to enjoy his revenge thoroughly. After a moment's hesitation he replied, speaking very low:

"You tried, I tink, to get me conficted, and now I punish you, dat is all."

His fingers moved, and the point of the pin descended a little lower. Williams felt the faintest imaginable prick on his skin—or thought he did. The German had lowered his head again to direct the movement of the pin properly. But the moment of Hensig's concentration was also the moment of his own attack. And it had come.

"But the alcohol will counteract it!" he burst out, with a loud and startling laugh that threw the other completely off his guard. The doctor lifted his face in amazement. That same instant the hand that lay so helplessly and tipsily in his turned like a flash of lightning, and, before he knew what had happened, their positions were reversed. Williams held his wrist, pencil and all, in a grasp of iron. And from the reporter's other hand the German received a terrific smashing blow in the face that broke his glasses and dashed him back with a howl of pain against the wall.

There was a brief passage of scramble and wild blows, during which both table and chairs were sent flying, and then Williams was aware that a figure behind him had stretched forth an arm and was holding a bright silvery thing close to Hensig's bleeding face. Another glance showed him that it was a pistol, and that the man holding it was the big drunken man who had apparently slept all night in the corner of the room. Then, in a flash, he recognized him as Dowling's partner—a headquarters detective.

The reporter stepped back, his head swimming again. He was very unsteady on his feet.

"I've been watching your game all the evening," he heard the headquarters man saying as he slipped the handcuffs over the German's unresisting wrists. "We have been on your trail for weeks, and I might jest as soon have taken you when you left the Brooklyn church a few hours ago, only I wanted to see what you were up to—see? You're wanted in Berlin for one or two little dirty tricks, but our advices only came last night. Come along now."

"You'll get nozzing," Hensig replied very quietly, wiping his bloody face with the corner of his sleeve. "See, I have scratched myself!"

The detective took no notice of this remark, not understanding it, probably, but Williams noticed the direction of the eyes, and saw a scratch on his wrist, slightly bleeding. Then he understood that in the struggle the pin had accidentally found another destination than the one intended for it.

But he remembered nothing more after that, for the reaction set in with a rush. The strain of that awful night left him utterly limp, and the accumulated effect of the alcohol, now that all was past, overwhelmed him like a wave, and he sank in a heap upon the floor, unconscious.

* * *

The illness that followed was simply "nerves," and he got over it in a week or two, and returned to his work on the paper. He at once made inquiries, and found that Hensig's arrest had hardly been noticed by the papers. There was no interesting feature about it, and New York was already in the throes of a new horror.

But Dowling, that enterprising Irishman—always with an eye to promotion and the main chance—Dowling had something to say about it.

"No luck, Mr. English," he said ruefully, "no luck at all. It would have been a mighty good story, but it never got in the papers. That damned German, Schmidt, alias Brunner, alias Hensig, died in the prison hospital before we could even get him remanded for further inquiries"

"What did he die of?" interrupted the reporter quickly.

"Black typhus, I think they call it. But it was terribly swift, and he was dead in four days. The doctor said he'd never known such a case."

"I'm glad he's out of the way," observed Williams.

"Well, yes," Dowling said hesitatingly; "but it was a jim dandy of a story, an' he might have waited a little bit longer jest so as I got something out of it for meself."

THE GOLDEN RAT

ALEXANDER HARVEY

What secret of her troubled soul could the youthful and lovely wife of old Gerald Lancaster be concealing now from me? She was decidedly the most baffling of all my patients. I was comparatively young, as men in the professions reckon age, yet I had devoted eleven arduous years to the practice of that department of psychology which goes by the name of psycho-analysis. It seemed obvious, from the very first appearance of the lady in my consultation room, that she suffered from the shock of an underlying emotional disturbance. Mrs. Lancaster, that is to say, had passed through a painful experience. She had striven to banish it from her consciousness.

Now what had been the emotional disturbance in her case? I could but conjecture vaguely. Her experience, whatever it had been, was not extinguished. It remained latent in her sub-consciousness, buried below the level of her waking mentality. The case of Mrs. Lancaster was, to use the technical phraseology one of repression, the experience or emotion which she strove to put out of her mind and her life being what we psychologists call a "complex."

As I concentrated my gaze upon the large but troubled eyes of Mrs. Lancaster, it dawned upon me that the "complex"—the idea or sorrow she strove to annihilate—was emotional, sentimental. Had she formed some unhappy attachment which the fiercest efforts of her will failed to subdue? I made the suggestion which seemed to me the best possible under the circumstances.

"I shall have to hypnotize you."

Speaking in the fluted accents which made her voice harmonize so perfectly with the sweetness of her face, Mrs. Lancaster objected to the very idea. She declined to be hypnotized because she feared the process might undermine the strength of her will. It was not difficult to reassure her on this point. To my surprise, however, I found my patient absolutely unhypnotizable. There remained only the alternative of imploring her to tell me frankly all that was in her mind, all that might be below the level of her consciousness, all that she would hide even from herself.

"I fear," I remarked, as considerately as I could— "I fear you are concealing something from me something of which you do not perhaps realize the importance or even the nature."

She searched her memory in vain. I had, on the occasion of our last interview in my study, forborne to press her. It was my hope that in the course of a subsequent consultation I should elicit the mysterious cause of her nervous state.

How well I remember that summer afternoon! The wife of old Lancaster had taken her departure, and I stood absorbed in baffling reflections with reference to this most mysterious patient. Slowly, at last, I opened the door that afforded access to the garden stretching from my study window quite to the stables. The garden, like the stables themselves, was a luxury, a whim of mine. The value of improved real estate in my native city made the taxes upon my cultivated acres, anything but a trifle. I might have kept a motor car, but my love of horseflesh made it impossible to give up the stables for a garage.

"More rats, doctor."

It was Boggs, the grim coachman. I found him rubbing down the most spirited of the steeds behind which it pleased me to spin through the streets of the city. Boggs indicated a pail near one of the stalls.

I gazed vacantly at the nestful of tiny young rats. My mind was still absorbed by the repressed "complex" of the puzzling Mrs. Lancaster. I still stared at the seven blind, feeble creatures, too young for even a growth of hair to be manifest upon their hides.

Boggs had stepped over to my side by this time. He clutched the nozzle of a streaming line of hose.

"I'll drown 'em, drat 'em!"

He would have flooded the wriggling nestful in a trice had I not stayed his hand.

"That little fellow there," I remarked— "he looks different—lighter than the others."

Boggs peered down into the bottom of the pail.

"Yes, doctor," he conceded, his voice thick with the disgust and annoyance the sight of rats in the stables invariably caused him. "One there is yellow-like."

To the amazement of the honest Boggs, I plunged my hand among the young rats and picked up the specimen that had caught my eye. There he lay now, in the palm of my hand, blind, weak, helpless. The hairs upon his odd little frame were sparse. They were sufficiently thick, none the less, to impart an aspect of fluffy gold to his coat. I was half inclined to drop him to his doom among his brothers when his tiny tail waved vaguely. It was covered nearly to the tip with a growth of down that made it look like a golden wand. Before Boggs had closed his mouth from sheer wonder at my behavior, I had slipped the baby rat into a pocket of my coat.

Slowly I retraced my steps across the grass from the stables to the study door. I was in some perplexity. Should I risk an experiment with the tiny thing breathing still in my pocket? The query vexed me as I paced from the desk in my little study to the door of the laboratory beyond. In this laboratory were stored the test tubes, the culture mediums, the beef broth and the apparatus for clarifying and sterilizing through the medium of which I enlarged the range of my biological knowledge by artificial cultivation of bacteria. Here, too, were the cages in which, at one time, I had bred three generations of white mice. The creatures were all dead long since. I was quite an adept, however, in the care of these rodents. Many a specimen had been inoculated in this laboratory with "cultures" of my own.

Lifting the little rat from my pocket, I laid him, seemingly more dead than alive, in one of my small cages. A spirit lamp had next to be set aflame. With its aid I soon heated enough milk to fill a small bottle, from the corked neck of which protruded a tiny quill. The little rat absorbed the first meal I gave him greedily enough. I had the satisfaction of seeing him curled snugly in sleep upon a litter of scrapped rags before the milk was half consumed.

Many days had not elapsed before I saw the hair upon his coat grow sleek and plentiful. To my surprise, the yellowish tint which had first attracted my attention to the young rat deepened into one of fine gold before I possessed him a week. In a fortnight he was strong enough to climb the side of the box which was his home in my laboratory. He ran about the floor so recklessly that I was forced to keep a careful lookout for stray cats and dogs. My original fear that he would prefer the freedom of the open air or of the cellarage to my laboratory proved groundless. He seemed to be destitute of the quality of timidity. Never in my experience of pets had I acquired one so recklessly tame. It was a source of perennial delight to him to spring from my shoe to the hem of my trousers and climb up to my shoulder. There he remained perched contentedly while I read or wrote or even walked about. As day succeeded day, the exquisite golden color of his coat grew richer. I discovered his tastes in edibles, especially for roasted chestnuts, and gratified it to the full. He seemed to tire of bread and milk as he grew fatter and more golden of hue. I fed him upon cake and nuts. His place of refuge, when pressed for one, was the pocket of my coat. Again and again have I felt him stirring about there while I received a patient in my study. When we were left at last alone, he would peep forth prettily and give a little shriek of delight while returning to my shoulder.

Never was quadruped more careful of its personal appearance. The golden rat balanced itself on its hind legs to lick its belly clean, and it had a trick of wiping itself all over with its forepaws. One of these paws would be passed over the head and the ears and licked into an immaculate cleanliness at each wipe. Philander, for that was the name I bestowed upon the golden rat, was a dazzling spectacle when the light from my study lamp fell upon him. He slept for an hour at a time on the desk before which I sat to read, seeming motionless, a gleaming ornament that might have come in perfect beauty from the cunning of the hand of Benvenuto Cellini.

Philander was washing his golden coat as he sat on my shoulder one morning, when we were interrupted by the unexpected arrival of a patient. The rat—he was a good-sized animal now—took refuge in my pocket the instant old Pawkins was announced. Pawkins, I should explain, was one of the prominent bankers of the city, who had long been under my care because of his neurasthenia. It had not been easy for me in the beginning to trace the source of his disorder. It seemed due primarily to an idea implanted in his mind by the physician who first treated his symptoms. Pawkins had been told that he was threatened with Bright's disease. He had seized this diagnosis eagerly. His ailment was, on its physical side, solely due to a false suggestion. Unfortunately, however, I found it no easy matter to win my way to his confidence. There was in his mind, latent and unconquerable, a suppressed "complex," an idea he would not avow, a thought that held him prisoner. No effort of mine could bring it to the surface. In accordance with my practice, I did not force the revelation I sought from old Pawkins. I was content to bide my time, as I was biding my time with the wife of Lancaster.

The elderly financier had barely seated himself in a chair facing me when I got a sudden fright. It seemed as if he had brought a dog with him. I thought of Philander in my pocket and had difficulty in suppressing an impulse of alarm. A closer inspection of the crouching figure at the feet of old Pawkins sufficed to correct my blunder. It was no dog that sat so near him. It was rather a shadowy outline than a reality, a suggestion of a shape. As I gazed the thing seemed to be a wolf—or shall I say the wraith of a wolf? A minute or two elapsed before I could withdraw my gaze from what I felt now must be a spectre. I had seen what was too evidently a ghost, for when I dropped my eyes once more to the floor the thing had disappeared.

It was easy enough to get rid of old Pawkins after a few perfunctory questions. When he had taken his departure, I gave myself up to a profound reverie. Philander had emerged from his retreat and was gorging himself on the floor with roasted chestnuts. It was borne in upon me at this moment, for the first time, that some connection must exist between the golden rat and a series of emotional and physical experiences and sensations in myself. I asked myself if the golden rat had not communicated to me the symptoms of that fevered state in which I now so often found myself. The state was one of exhilaration—like the first effects of some delightful stimulant. It was an exhilaration which wore away. It left, unlike the thrills that go with opium, no baneful consequences. It brought me a singular capacity to verify with my own eye—at intervals—the fact that practically all sources of illumination emit an ultraviolet light playing no part in ordinary vision. This is the result of the circumstance that the eye is sensitive only to a small proportion of the radiation reaching it. There were times, however, when my eyes became more than ever camera-like, detecting and measuring the intensity of what physicists call the infrared rays. I could see at such times by the aid of a light which physicists have pronounced invisible or at least discernible only through photography.

It occurred to me, after the departure of old Pawkins, that the wolf I had seen at his feet was an optical eccentricity in me. I recalled just then a fit of trembling in Philander while he lay concealed in my pocket. I recalled, too, the peculiarities of his conduct when certain other patients were in my study. The golden rat was subject to an inexplicable panic whenever the wife of a certain clergyman poured the tale of her neurosis into my ear. Philander took refuge under a bookcase or in the remotest recesses of a drawer in my desk. My eye chanced to light upon his frolicking form as I pondered these things. He held a walnut in his forepaws and, perched upon his hind limbs like an educated poodle, was devouring the morsel greedily. I waited until he had satisfied his appetite and then called him by his name. In a trice he was upon my shoulder.

The exigencies of a laboratory experiment that day required the use of a pair of black silk gloves. These were in my lap. The rat was creeping around my neck as I drew one of these gloves over my left hand, fitting it snugly and carefully from force of habit, although my mind was engaged solely with the mystery of the Pawkins wolf. On a sudden I saw a minute speck moving against the blackness of the glove. It was a mere mite of a speck, but it shone in golden luster as it flitted and fluttered.

The darting and dancing mite in the palm of my gloved hand was a flea.

A flood of light was let into every nook and cranny of my mind the moment I had caught the golden insect on the tip of my finger with the aid of a dab of vaseline. Philander, then, was infested with fleas. They were like himself in their peculiarly golden aspect. I brought the rat from his place of rest on my shoulder down to my knee. The critical inspection of his fur to which I abandoned myself—not neglecting a microscope in the process—revealed a quantity of golden fleas. I was unable to identify the species. It is true that the varieties of flea already classified are infinite. I had studied a few in my student days. Here was a species as new as it was strange. There could be no doubt that the fleas on Philander had been the agents of the spread of some infection to me. My symptoms of late had been very puzzling.

I was quite certain that Philander could not have imparted to me the bacillus of any infection so dire as plague. That dread disease appears only in fleas which have bitten affected rats or persons at least twelve hours prior to death. The organism causing the disease itself must exist for a certain interval in the body of Philander, there to undergo a definite alteration, before it could induce an infection in me by transmission through the flea. And there was no known case of plague affecting a human being sufficiently near to involve Philander in the slightest suspicion.

The dilemma of my situation seemed greater on the following morning. I found my fever slightly higher, although the exhilaration was quite pleasant. I observed an accentuation of the eccentricity of my vision. I detected ultra-violet light without the aid of an instrument. There was one close friend to whom I could turn in this crisis. Having ascertained over the telephone that Thorburn, the renowned specialist, who had been my classmate at the medical school, could receive me at once, I hastened to his office.

My brilliant friend, whose researches in microbiology fill the world with his fame, had a touch or two of gray at the temples, I noticed. He received me most effusively, for we had not met in a long time. My eye was held for a minute, as we shook hands, by the large stork standing gravely at Thorburn's side.

"Are you fond of storks?"

I asked the question smilingly. He looked at me in some surprise.

"Not particularly," he replied. "Why?"

It flashed through my mind at once that this bird by Thorburn's side was no more real than the wolf at Pawkins' feet.

"Why?" I repeated, a flash of inspiration rescuing me from the dilemma. "You have been married six years and you have no children."

His face clouded at once.

"You are a great psychologist," I heard him murmur, as if he were talking to himself. "You have guessed the longing that fills my heart, the preoccupation of my life."

I saw now what the stork meant. It was the symbol of the desire in my friend's heart, the thought that would not leave him, the longing he had put out of his mind. His wish for a child to bless his union with Florella had been put from the upper level of his consciousness into that lower level of forgetfulness where his "repressed complex" lay buried. All men living, I knew, bore in their minds the wishes, the aspirations, they had buried in the well of the subconsciousness. Not until this moment did I suspect that the longing buried in the mind, the fond wish one dare not avow but over which one gloated inwardly, was a wraith, a ghost. Thorburn's buried wish was haunting him. The stork at his side was its ghost.

Not a word of all this escaped me; no hint of the presence of the grave bird passed my lips. I laid my case before him to the extent of avowing my fear of some infection. He examined me from head to foot. He made every laboratory test possible in the circumstances. As he came and went, now peering into my eyes, again holding a tube aloft in the bright electric light of his laboratory, I saw the stork follow him, sit at his feet, flap noiseless wings or prepare for some wild flight that was never even attempted.

"There is no organic disorder," was Thorburn's report at last. "I see no evidence yet of the presence of any infection. I can let you know definitely in a week."

The stork, invisible to Thorburn, eyed me gravely as I took my leave. In much perplexity I walked slowly to my home, letting myself in with my own key and repairing to my study with a profound problem on my mind. The first thing was to find Philander. He had a trick of fashioning a nest for himself out of old newspapers under a corner of my desk. I called him by name.

There was no response. At first I suspected him of hiding from me by design, a thing he was very prone to when he feared being shut up in his cage for the night. He had a great affection for the chimney. The soot in that retreat begrimed his coat most sadly, although he never failed to wash himself clean the moment he emerged. There had been no fire in my study since the spring. I thrust my head into the empty grate and called his name loudly. There was again no response.

I was not in any great alarm. He had a way of disappearing now and then, sometimes for as long as twenty-four hours. My one dread was that a stray cat or dog might pounce upon my pet. There was now nothing for it but to compose myself in my easy chair and ponder the events of this day.

My eye wandered vacantly over the papers and test tubes forming a litter in front of me until a gleam of something like light, a flash like the twinkle of a distant star, enchained my glance. The shimmer and slash were a series of stains upon a handkerchief. I picked up the silken article in some bewilderment at first. It looked like some fantastic flag with suns in gold designed upon its center. My own initials worked in a corner of the piece of silk brought back to my recollection a slight bleeding of the nose which had troubled me that morning. I had applied this silk handkerchief to my face. The slight hemorrhage ceased. I had given the matter no further thought. Now I saw spots of shining gold where in the morning my blood had stained this piece of silk a bright red.

In my bewilderment I took the handkerchief over to the window. There could be no doubt now of the brightness of the gold. Never in my experience had I heard of man or woman who bled gold. I resolved to despatch the handkerchief to Thorburn for an immediate analysis. The ringing of the bell, a voice at the door and the entrance of a visitor postponed the execution of this purpose.

"And how is our rising young psychoanalyst?" cried a cheery voice, as a burly form broke rather than appeared through the door. "Upon my word, that last talk of yours upon the mental mechanism of the banished idea has made you famous."

My visitor carried with him, I saw now, a late number of the official organ of a psychological society. One of my studies was given a very prominent place in the periodical. I glanced at the printed page and then rose to greet old Graham. I dearly loved this man, for he had been one of my most honored preceptors in my student days.

"My dear Graham!" I cried.

A silvery dove fluttered about his head, but I was accustomed by this time to my capacity for this species of visualization and I betrayed by neither word nor glance the effect of the sight upon me. The dove, I could see, corresponded to the system of ideas making up the "complex" of this good and generous man. What a contract to the predatory old Pawkins, whose repressed ideas emerged in spite of himself under the guise of a wolf—at least to my vision! It has been well said that in the psychical sphere complexes have an action resembling that of energy in the physical sphere. A system of ideas may lie latent in a man's mind for a long time, becoming active only when stimulated. This explained, no doubt, why the dove hovering over old Doctor Graham flitted out of sight now and then.

"My boy," said the old man, looking somewhat anxiously about him before he sank into the chair I brought, "are we alone?"

I nodded. There was an anxiety on his mind which became more manifest as he proceeded:

"You may have heard that one or two well-defined cases of plague came recently to the notice of the board."

I recalled such a report. I had first heard of the matter at a gathering of physicians some time before. Graham who was in the service of the Board of Health, had taken the matter seriously at the time, but the affair had dropped out of my thoughts long since. The old man leaned forward to impress me with what he had now to say:

"The cases have been increasing. We have made up our minds to make war on the rats."

"The rats!"

I spoke in a tone of some consternation. The words brought the missing Philander back to my memory.

"The rats," repeated Graham solemnly. "We have actually discovered the bacillus in the bodies of no less than three rats."

"Were they rats caught in the city?"

"In this very neighborhood. We have been quietly trapping here and there. We don't want to start a plague panic until we are sure of our facts."

I watched the dove flitting above his head and I thought of Philander. Had they trapped the golden rat? I had to steady my voice with an effort before I could put my question:

"These rats—they are the ordinary gray variety?"

The elderly physician looked troubled.

"Yes—and no," said he slowly. "Our traps have contained gray rats as a rule. But in two instances we have captured a very peculiar variety of the animal—gray rats with a spot of gold on the breast."

He drew from his pocket as he spoke a small leather casket. It opened at the touch of a spring. I saw the stuffed skin of a gray rat, splashed in the spot indicated with gleaming gold.

"This rat," explained old Graham, lifting the stuffed object up for my inspection, "was trapped in the house next door. It is one of six marked in this very extraordinary manner a species never seen before by any authority I have consulted."

I took the stuffed rat from the grasp of my elderly friend and examined its aspect critically. Those who have never studied at first hand the habits of a rodent of such sinister fame can form no idea of the natural cleanliness of the little animal. Apart from the tendency of the flea to infest the rat, it is one of the daintiest of quadrupeds, not, indeed, without a beauty of its own. The spot of gold between the forepaws of this specimen set off its gray coat effectively.

"Although we have trapped rats all over the city," proceeded old Graham earnestly, "they are all of the usual gray type except those few caught next door. I have just been setting traps in your cellar."

The thought of Philander made my blood run cold at these words. I gazed in blank dismay at the physician. What had become of the golden rat?

"Have you"—I faltered before I could speak the question completely— "caught anything here?"

"My dear lad, the traps have just been set—two of them. I can let you know the result in a few days."

"You spoke just now," I resumed, in as natural a voice as I could command, "of having isolated the bacillus in the blood of some of your rats. How about these?"

Graham took the stuffed rat from me and looked it over.

"We have isolated a most curious organism in the blood stream of this little creature," he observed. "A golden microbe."

"What disease does it cause?"

I tried again to speak naturally, but I remembered the golden blood I had shed and felt faint. What if I had acquired a new and strange leprosy from the bite of the golden fleas of Philander!

"Strange as it must seem," I now heard Graham aver, "the microbe—it is really a bacillus with its nucleus and protoplasm—gives rise to no discoverable disease in the rat infected by it. Perhaps it is responsible for the gold spot."

He touched the flaming breast of the stuffed creature.

"The remarkable thing," the old doctor added, "is the golden element in the rod-like process of these organisms. One might almost say the blood of this rat was golden."

My mind reverted to the analysis of my own blood cells which Thorburn was at that moment engaged upon.

"You don't mean to say," I rejoined, smiling, "that you have discovered a form of bacteria that is beneficial to the invaded organism?"

"I'll know more about that when I have trapped more of these rats," the old man told me. "I expect to get some here by the end of the week."

The moment he had taken his leave, which he did almost immediately, the dove fluttering out with him, I rang up Thorburn.

"Come over at once, if you can," he said at the other end of the wire. "I have news for you."

I put on my hat and paced the streets hurriedly. I caught sight of a policeman at the corner taking a prisoner to the lockup. The man in the toils of the law was obviously a beggar. At his heels trotted a snow-white lamb. The policeman was followed by a hawk. I turned and gazed after the pair until both had disappeared around a corner. Was I doomed to see at the heels of every fellow creature the symbol of his suppressed idea, the ghost of his complex? I fairly raced to Thorburn's door.

"There is something very remarkable here," was his first utterance, as he led the way to his laboratory. "What do you make of that?"

He held up a glass slide of the sort used in experimental biology. It was stained with a golden spot.

"Your blood," said he. "It has yielded a pure gold bacterium of the strangest character. Your blood is like the stream in which King Midas bathed—filled with golden sands."

He had scarcely said the words when a movement of flapping wings behind him drew my eyes to the stork. It stood for a moment erect and then retreated to the remotest corner of the laboratory, where it regarded both of us with all its characteristic solemnity. Thorburn was unaware of the ghostly presence. He sat me down in a great chair and questioned me most minutely regarding my symptoms.

"You must have contracted a disease of some sort," was his final verdict.

"Fatal?"

"I am using the word in a technical sense," he laughed, seeing my sober visage. "Disease is, in one aspect, the invasion of one organism by another. Your organism has been invaded by a new and strange bacterium, all gold. You say it does not debilitate you?"

"I never felt better in my life."

I glanced unshrinkingly into his puzzled face. I had carefully concealed from him the fact that I had acquired the novel faculty of beholding the repressed complexes of my fellow creatures.

"Your disease," he went on, "whatever it may be, is the effect of the interaction of two different organisms, just as plague is such an effect, or malaria."

"A new idea?"

"Not at all," retorted Thorburn. "It is not generally disseminated, of course, yet. Since disease is but the effect of one organism upon another, there is necessarily such a thing as an evolution in disease. A disease that has long been among men is a very different thing from the same disease when it first appeared on earth. The lizard is but the survivor of a far more powerful and far more intelligent creature."

I had caught the idea in his mind. The sudden appearance of a new organism is a possible thing, as the mutation theory of evolution has convinced the world. May not a totally new disease make its appearance among men, thanks to the emergence of a fresh form among the bacteria? Has not Burbank evolved new forms of vegetable life by a seeming miracle of metamorphosis? But this was by no means all that Thorburn meant. May it not be that the bacteria which cause disease are prejudicial only because they represent types of degeneracy? They have been corrupted, that is to say, by passing in and out of the blood streams of a fallen human race. It is we who have poisoned the bacteria, not the bacteria which have poisoned us. In that event, science is on the wrong track. We must purify ourselves, in order that the microbe may regain its pristine purity and become the blessing it may have been to our prehistoric ancestors.

I remained in a profound reverie long after Thorburn had finished his elucidation. If what he told me was true, I had acquired an infection, but it was a benevolent process, a source of strength. The flea had transferred to me from the body of Philander an organism that endowed me with a more wonderful power than had been possessed before by any mortal man.

"By the way," remarked Thorburn, suddenly changing the subject, "shall you be at Mrs. Lancaster's dance to-morrow night?"

I started at mention of that name. It had been weeks since I had given a thought to my patient. I replied vaguely that I expected to dine at her house. My mind was running on Philander once more, and I bade him adieu with some abruptness.

There was not the least trace of the presence of the golden rat when I arrived breathless once more in my study. I called him by name more than once. In vain. I thought of the trap set by old Graham. Before visiting the cellars I resolved to peer up the fire-place.

"Philander!" I called. "Philander!" There was a faint sound up the chimney. In a trice I had thrust my arm up the sooty embrasure. Philander descended, clinging to the sleeve of my coat. What a begrimed and blackened aspect his body now wore! I set him upon my desk, where he fell to an assiduous licking and washing of his fur. I had the satisfaction of seeing him restored to his original color before he had completed his toilet. Then he frisked his way to my shoulder, upon which he perched with all his familiar sauciness.

It was vitally important to keep Philander out of reach of the trap set for him. I might have ordered the stableman to remove the horrid instrument, to be sure. Yet that might inspire too much wonder in the mind of old Graham. On the other hand, I must not let the golden rat out of my sight. He spent the night securely locked in his cage. He was not released during the entire next day. His squeaks of protest were incessant. I would have no mercy on him.

After some reflection, I resolved to attend the dinner and dance at the house of Mrs. Lancaster. It seemed the surest method of providing for the safety of Philander. It would be no difficult thing to take him with me, concealed in the pocket of my coat. The golden rat was always shy when strangers were about. I knew that nothing could lure him from the refuge my clothes afforded him if there seemed the least prospect that he might be handled by an unfamiliar acquaintance.

The hour appointed for the dinner at the house of Mrs. Lancaster was already chiming when I entered the dining-room. The guests were barely a dozen. I was already familiar with their faces. Philander was snugly ensconced in a breast pocket of my dress coat. He was fast asleep.

"What a stranger you are, doctor!"

The words were uttered by my fair hostess. I had never seen a more pensive melancholy upon her exquisite features: She sat at some distance from me at the foot of the table. I made my very best bow and smiled before I sat down to the oysters.

"Ha!" exclaimed Thorburn, who chanced to be seated directly opposite me. "You are looking very well—still."

There was a meaning smile upon his kindly features, and I was at no loss to interpret it. The silent stork at his side peered myopically into my face and flapped a pair of wings. I saw the hideous wolf peering greedily from beneath the chair of old Pawkins, who absorbed champagne moodily. Old Lancaster had a fierce ferret on his shoulder, a circumstance to which I was inclined to attribute the restlessness of Philander, who stirred now and then in his sleep. The most interesting object at the dinner table to me was a hyena, which chafed and fretted at the back of a distinguished member of the judiciary. One old lady, whom I had met before, and who was a notorious gambler, revealed to my secret vision as her repressed complex a gigantic pike. The fish literally swam in the air over the dame's head, darting every now and then ferociously at prey invisible to me.

"I hear," observed Pawkins at last, "that there is a case of plague in quarantine."

The wolf leered over his shoulder and licked its hideous jaw. The introduction of so dire a theme at that crisis in my life spoiled the dinner for me. I listened to the flow of talk about me, hearing much speculation regarding such things as fleas and the bacilli. Mrs. Lancaster seemed only half aware of what was transpiring around her. My attention was drawn particularly to her by the suggestion of a wraith upon her shoulder. I had looked eagerly in her direction more than once, hoping to descry the symbolized embodiment of her complex. That there was a form of some description outlined upon her shoulder seemed clear. I thought at first it might be a bird. Later it wore the aspect of a fish. At last, I had to abandon the effort to define to myself the shadowy thing moving from her right arm around her shoulders to her left. The secret of my patient's repressed complex was almost mine. Again and again it eluded me. The vexation of that circumstance made the end of the dinner a welcome relief. I strolled into the smoking room, listening vaguely to the din of the violins, tuning for the dance.

Finding myself alone, I peered into my pocket. Philander was fast asleep. I hated to disturb the repose of the golden creature, and for that reason remained with my cigar alone to the last possible minute. In the end I was obliged to make my appearance in the ballroom.

There was not a dancer on the whole vast floor without his or her attendant creature. A member of the United States Senate was closely followed in the mazes of a waltz by an opossum, while his partner, a lady with some fame as a landscape painter, kept a porcupine in her train. The pastor of a church led a vampire in its flight among the dancers, above whom it poised itself, fanning sundry individuals with its wings. There was one gigantic crocodile in a corner which every now and then abandoned the shelter of the wall to cavort and caper after the founder of fifteen hospitals. In short, wherever I looked I beheld specimens of a zoology unsuspected by those who danced in and about among pelicans, pumas, guinea pigs and polar bears. One gigantic creature, symbolizing the repressed complex of the most famous lawyer in the country, was evidently an antediluvian monster. It appeared to my astonished gaze somewhat like a lepidosiren. These creatures were like the men and women they all haunted in turning, twisting and waltzing to the music. Now and then there were collisions of a significant sort. I beheld a fierce fight between two bantam roosters, one being the repressed complex of a well known novelist and the other that of a successful merchant. The repressed complex of the merchant's wife—a lily white hen—watched the struggle complacently. When the bird symbolizing her husband was routed from the field, I saw the lady begin a fresh dance with the novelist.

It occurred to me to seek my hostess. She had not appeared on the floor for some time. I felt an uneasy movement in the pocket of my coat. For the sake of Philander rather than to secure any repose for myself, I sought the shelter of the Japanese room. I was quite alone when I sank back wearily upon a sofa and looked at my watch. It would soon be time to go.

I was opening my cigarette case when Mrs. Lancaster appeared in the doorway. Her exquisite features wore an unusual gravity, even for her, as she advanced. I divined that she had a revelation to make. Whatever I might have said remained unspoken, however, in the shock of discovering a golden rat perched upon her shoulder. For a moment the idea entered my head that Philander must have escaped from my pocket. I perceived, as soon as I had looked at the creature again, that I could not implicate Philander. The golden rat on the shoulder of Mrs. Lancaster was smaller than my pet. It was of less robust physique, softer in outline, more graceful.

I had placed my hand in Mrs. Lancaster's outstretched fingers, when a flashing form sprang from the pocket of my coat. There was a tiny shriek of joy. I saw Philander capering and shrieking on the floor with the diminutive creature that followed him from the shoulders of the lady who had so long been my most baffling patient.

"I think," I managed to say, my eyes riveted upon the gamboling creatures on the floor— "I think I have the key to your case."

I saw a flush spread from her cheek to her brow. She bowed her head and, still holding my hand, sank upon the chair from which I had just risen. It seems odd to me, as I look back upon all this, that I never suspected the mutual infatuation out of which our repressed complexes were built up. She loved me. I saw the avowal in the eyes she turned up to my face as I bent over her. As our lips met, I felt a convulsive shudder at my breast. I put my hand in my coat. There lay Philander.

To my profound amazement, the rat bit me. With an effort, I repressed an exclamation of pain. Thrusting the little creature, who seemed disposed to escape, back into my pocket, I literally fled the place.

There was no one stirring as I entered my dark study and turned on the light. How long I sat absorbed in my reflections I knew not. There was a patch of crimson in the sky when at last I got up from my desk and walked over to the window.

How long had this woman loved me? Through what circumstance had it become possible for her to identify me with the golden rat? I was, evidently, her repressed complex. As I stood at the window pondering these things, a figure moved across the lawn.

"Boggs!" I called.

It was that honest hostler. He had just set about the business of the stables.

"Have you seen Mrs. Lancaster?"

"She was here to see you last month, sir."

"Why was I not told?"

"Why, sir, I thought the girl would tell you. She waited for you here an hour. She saw the golden rat."

"You mean," I interrupted, "that you showed it to her."

"I told her how fond of it you had grown, sir."

Here then was the explanation I sought. The mention of the golden rat reminded me at once of Philander. I had quite forgotten, in the bewilderment resulting from my experience with Mrs. Lancaster, to shut him up for the night in his cage.

"Philander!"

I called him again and again without effect.

"Boggs," I remarked, "do you remember when Doctor Graham was here to set his traps?"

The stableman scratched his head with a most aggravating stupidity. Yes, he remembered the visit of the physician. He recalled the setting of the traps. He had not seen them placed. He did not know where they were. I lost no time in getting to the stables with a lantern. The search was fruitless. There were no traps that I could discover. Boggs remembered that the old doctor had talked of the cellar. Thither we repaired. I found no traps. The failure to discover the devices did not console me in the least. I knew the old doctor to be a cunning and experienced rat catcher. He might have hidden his deadly devices under a loose plank or in a remote closet.

The full dawn of that morning brought no Philander. I ransacked the house without avail. Neither trap nor rat resulted. The day following was but a repetition of the disappointment. I discovered to my dismay that Doctor Graham had left the city for a few days. The official of the Board of Health to whom I telephoned offered to send an inspector to my house at once. The doctor had left at headquarters a list of every domicile in which a trap was set. I closed with the offer immediately. The result was another vain search of my premises.

The despair to which I was reduced by the continued disappearance of Philander led me to overlook, at the time, a curious circumstance connected with Thorburn. I saw him for a brief interval on the street. He was not accompanied by the ghostly stork. The detail made no impression upon my mind for an hour or more after I had-parted from him. Then I hurried to the street. A week before, I would have beheld the repressed complex of any passerby. Now I saw dozens of pedestrians. No beast or bird attended any.

Turning back into the house with a strange giddiness in my head, I was halted by the arrival before my door of a motor car. Out stepped old Graham.

"The trap!" I shouted. "Where did you set it?"

I observed that no dove fluttered about him now.

"The trap?" he echoed. "In your study, of course."

I staggered after him. He led the way to a corner of a bookcase into which I had not once dreamed of peering. With loud triumph, the old doctor lifted a trap on high. It held Philander, cold and dead.

"Very, very remarkable," he observed. "Wouldn't you say this rat has a golden color?"

His face reflected a grave anxiety. I spoke up savagely:

"It's a golden rat. Are you afraid of it—it is dead."

"I hear you've been looking for me," he said, wiping his eyes with a handkerchief. "I was called out of town by the case of Mrs. Lancaster."

"Is she ill?"

He lifted the dead form of Philander from the trap before replying:

"Her people had her committed to a sanitarium. She insists that she is followed everywhere by a golden rat."

THE SHERIFF OF KONA

JACK LONDON

"You cannot escape liking the climate," Cudworth said, in reply to my panegyric on the Kona coast. "I was a young fellow, just out of college, when I came here eighteen years ago. I never went back, except, of course, to visit. And I warn you, if you have some spot dear to you on earth, not to linger here too long, else you will find this dearer."

We had finished dinner, which had been served on the big *lanai*, the one with a northerly exposure, though *exposure* is indeed a misnomer in so delectable a climate.

The candles had been put out, and a slim, white-clad Japanese slipped, like a ghost through the silvery moonlight, presented us with cigars, and faded away into the darkness of the bungalow. I looked through a screen of banana and lehua trees, and down across the guava scrub to the quiet sea a thousand feet beneath. For a week, ever since I had landed from the tiny coasting-steamer, I had been stopping with Cudworth, and during that time no wind had ruffled that unvexed sea. True, there had been breezes, but they were the gentlest zephyrs that ever blew through summer isles. They were not winds; they were sighs—long, balmy sighs of a world at rest.

"A lotus land," I said.

"Where each day is like every day, and every day is a paradise of days," he answered. "Nothing ever happens. It is not too hot. It is not too cold. It is always just right. Have you noticed how the land and the sea breathe turn and turn about?"

Indeed I had noticed that delicious, rhythmic, breathing. Each morning I had watched the sea-breeze begin at the shore and slowly extend seaward as it blew the mildest, softest whiff of ozone to the land. It played over the sea, just faintly darkening its surface, with here and there and everywhere long lanes of calm, shifting, changing, drifting, according to the capricious kisses of the breeze. And each evening I had watched the sea breath die away to heavenly calm, and heard the land breath softly make its way through the coffee trees and monkey-pods.

"It is a land of perpetual calm," I said. "Does it ever blow here?—ever really blow? You know what I mean."

Cudworth shook his head and pointed eastward.

"How can it blow, with a barrier like that to stop it?"

Far above towered the huge bulks of Mauna Kea and Mauna Loa, seeming to blot out half the starry sky. Two miles and a half above our heads they reared their own heads, white with snow that the tropic sun had failed to melt.

"Thirty miles away, right now, I'll wager, it is blowing forty miles an hour. "

I smiled incredulously.

Cudworth stepped to the *lanai* telephone. He called up, in succession, Waimea, Kohala, and Hamakua. Snatches of his conversation told me that the wind was blowing: "Rip-snorting and back-jumping, eh? . . . How long? . . . Only a week? . . . Hello, Abe, is that you? . . . . Yes, yes . . . You *will* plant coffee on the Hamakua coast . . . . Hang your wind-breaks! You should see *my* trees."

"Blowing a gale," he said to me, turning from hanging up the receiver. "I always have to joke Abe on his coffee. He has five hundred acres, and he's done marvels in wind-breaking, but how he keeps the roots in the ground is beyond me. Blow? It always blows on the Hamakua side. Kohala reports a schooner under double reefs beating up the channel between Hawaii and Maui, and making heavy weather of it."

"It is hard to realize," I said lamely. "Doesn't a little whiff of it ever eddy around somehow, and get down here?"

"Not a whiff. Our land-breeze is absolutely of no kin, for it begins this side of Mauna Kea and Mauna Loa. You see, the land radiates its heat quicker than the sea, and so, at night, the land breathes over the sea. In the day the land becomes warmer than the sea, and the sea breathes over the land . . . . Listen! Here comes the land-breath now, the mountain wind."

I could hear it coming, rustling softly through the coffee trees, stirring the monkey-pods, and sighing through the sugar-cane. On the *lanai* the hush still reigned. Then it came, the first feel of the mountain wind, faintly balmy, fragrant and spicy, and cool, deliciously cool, a silken coolness, a wine-like coolness—cool as only the mountain wind of Kona can be cool.

"Do you wonder that I lost my heart to Kona eighteen years ago?" he demanded. "I could never leave it now. I think I should die. It would be terrible. There was another man who loved it, even as I. I think he loved it more, for he was born here on the Kona coast. He was a great man, my best friend, my more than brother. But he left it, and he did not die."

"Love?" I queried. "A woman?"

Cudworth shook his head.

"Nor will he ever come back, though his heart will be here until he dies."

He paused and gazed down upon the beachlights of Kailua. I smoked silently and waited.

"He was already in love . . . with his wife. Also, he had three children, and he loved them. They are in Honolulu now. The boy is going to college."

"Some rash act?" I questioned, after a time, impatiently.

He shook his head. "Neither guilty of anything criminal, nor charged with anything criminal. He was the sheriff of Kona."

"You choose to be paradoxical," I said.

"I suppose it does sound that way," he admitted, "and that is the perfect hell of it."

He looked at me searchingly for a moment, and then abruptly took up the tale.

"He was a leper. No, he was not born with it—no one is born with it; it came upon him. This man—what does it matter? Lyte Gregory was his name. Every *kamaina* knows the story. He was straight American stock, but he was built like the chieftains of old Hawaii. He stood six feet three. His stripped weight was two hundred and twenty pounds, not an ounce of which was not clean muscle or bone. He was the strongest man I have ever seen. He was an athlete and a giant. He was a god. He was my friend. And his heart and his soul were as big and as fine as his body.

"I wonder what you would do if you saw your friend, your brother, on the slippery lip of a precipice, slipping, slipping, and you were able to do nothing. That was just it. I could do nothing. I saw it coming, and I could do nothing. My God, man! what could I do ? There it was, malignant and incontestable, the mark of the thing on his brow. No one else saw it. It was because I loved him so, I do believe, that I alone saw it. I could not credit the testimony of my senses. It was too incredibly horrible. Yet there it was, on his brow, on his ears. I had seen it, the slight puff of the earlobes—oh, so imperceptibly slight. I watched it for months. Then, next, hoping against hope, the darkening of the skin above both eyebrows—oh, so faint, just like the dimmest touch of sunburn. I should have thought it sunburn but that there was a shine to it, such an invisible shine, like a little highlight seen for a moment and gone the next. I tried to believe it was sunburn, only I could not. I knew better. No one noticed it but me. No one ever noticed it except Stephen Kaluna, and I did not know that till afterward. But I saw it coming, the whole damnable, unnamable awfulness of it; but I refused to think about the future. I was afraid. I could not. And of nights I cried over it.

"He was my friend. We fished sharks on Niihau together. We hunted wild cattle on Mauna Kea and Mauna Loa. We broke horses and branded steers on the Carter Ranch. We hunted goats through Haleakala. He taught me diving and surfing until I was nearly as clever as he, and he was cleverer than the average Kanaka. I have seen him dive in fifteen fathoms, and he could stay down two minutes.

He was an amphibian and a mountaineer. He could climb wherever a goat dared climb. He was afraid of nothing. He was on the wrecked *Luga,* and he swam thirty miles in thirty-six hours in a heavy sea. He could fight his way out through breaking combers that would batter you and me to a jelly. He was a great, glorious man-god. We went through the Revolution together. We were both romantic loyalists. He was shot twice and sentenced to death. But he was too great a man for the republicans to kill. He laughed at them. Later, they gave him honor and made him sheriff of Kona. He was a simple man, a boy that never grew up. His was no intricate brain pattern. He had no twists nor quirks in his mental processes. He went straight to the point, and his points were always simple.

"And he was sanguine. Never have I known so confident a man, nor a man so satisfied and happy. He did not ask anything from life. There was nothing left to be desired. For him life had no arrears. He had been paid in full, cash down, and in advance. What more could he possibly desire than that magnificent body, that iron constitution, that immunity from all ordinary ills, and that lowly wholesomeness of soul? Physically he was perfect. He had never been sick in his life. He did not know what a headache was. When I was so afflicted he used to look at me in wonder, and make me laugh with his clumsy attempts at sympathy. He did not understand such a thing as a headache. He could not understand. Sanguine? No wonder. How could he be otherwise with that tremendous vitality and incredible health?

"Just to show you what faith he had in his glorious star, and, also, what sanction he had for that faith. He was a youngster at the time—I had just met him—when he went into a poker game at Wailuku. There was a big German in it, Schultz his name was, and he played a brutal, domineering game. He had had a run of luck as well, and he was quite insufferable, when Lyte Gregory dropped in and took a hand. The very first hand it was Schultz's blind. Lyte came in, as well as the others, and Schultz raised them out—all except Lyte. He did not like the German's tone, and he raised him back. Schultz raised in turn, and in turn Lyte raised Schultz. So they went, back and forth. The stakes were big. And do you know what Lyte held? A pair of kings and three little clubs. It wasn't poker. Lyte wasn't playing poker. He was playing his optimism. He didn't know what Schultz held, but he raised and raised until he made Schultz squeal, and Schultz held three aces all the time. Think of it! A man with a pair of kings compelling three aces to see before the draw!

"Well, Schultz called for two cards. Another German was dealing, Schultz's friend at that. Lyte knew then that he was up against three of a kind. Now what did he do? What would you have done? Drawn three cards and held up the kings, of course. Not Lyte, He was playing optimism. He threw the kings away, held up the three little clubs, and drew two cards. He never looked at them. He looked across at Schultz to bet, and Schultz did bet, big. Since he himself held three aces he knew he had Lyte, because he played Lyte for threes, and, necessarily, they would have to be smaller threes. Poor Schultz! He was perfectly correct under the premises. His mistake was that he thought Lyte was playing poker. They bet back and forth for five minutes, until Schultz's certainty began to ooze out. And all the time Lyte had never looked at his two cards, and Schultz knew it. I could see Schultz think, and revive, and splurge with his bets again. But the strain was too much for him.

"'Hold on, Gregory,' he said at last. 'I've got you beaten from the start. I don't want any of your money. I've got—'

"'Never mind what you've got,' Lyte interrupted. 'You don't know what I've got. I guess I'll take a look.'

"He looked, and raised the German a hundred dollars. Then they went at it again, back and forth and back and forth, until Schultz weakened and called, and laid down his three aces. Lyte faced his five cards. They were all black. He had drawn two more clubs. Do you know, he just about broke Schultz's nerve as a poker player. He never played in the same form again. He lacked confidence after that, and was a bit wobbly.

"'But how could you do it?' I asked Lyte afterward. 'You knew he had you beaten when he drew two cards. Besides, you never looked at your own draw.'

"'I didn't have to look,' was Lyte's answer. 'I knew they were two clubs all the time. They just had to be two clubs. Do you think I was going to let that big Dutchman beat me? It was impossible that he should beat me. It is not my way to be beaten. I just have to win. Why, I'd have been the most surprised man in this world if they hadn't been all clubs.'

"That was Lyte's way, and maybe it will help you to appreciate his colossal optimism. As he put it, he just had to succeed, to fare well, to prosper. And in that same incident, as in ten thousand others, he found his sanction. The thing was that he did succeed, did prosper. That was why he was afraid of nothing. Nothing could ever happen to him. He knew it, because nothing had ever happened to him. That time the *Luga* was lost and he swam thirty miles, he was in the water two whole nights and a day. And during all that terrible stretch of time he never lost hope once, never once doubted the outcome. He just knew he was going to make the land. He told me so himself, and I know it was the truth.

"Well, that is the kind of a man Lyte Gregory was. He was of a different race from ordinary, ailing mortals. He was a lordly being, untouched by common ills and misfortunes. Whatever he wanted he got. He won his wife—one of the Caruthers, a little beauty—from a dozen rivals. And she settled down and made him the finest wife in the world. He wanted a boy. He got it. He wanted a girl and another boy. He got them. And they were just right, without spot or blemish, with chests like little barrels, and with all the inheritance of his own health and strength.

"And then it happened. The mark of the beast was laid upon him. I watched it for a year. It broke my heart. But he did not know it, nor did anybody else guess it except that cursed *hapa-haole,* Stephen Kaluna. He knew it, but I did not know that he did. And—yes—Doc Strowbridge knew it. He was the federal physician, and he had developed the leper eye. You see, part of his business was to examine suspects and order them to the receiving station at Honolulu. And Stephen Kaluna had developed the leper eye. The disease ran strong in his family, and four or five of his relatives were already on Molokai.

"The trouble arose over Stephen Kaluna's sister. When she became suspect, and before Doc Strowbridge could get hold of her, her brother spirited her away to some hiding place. Lyte was sheriff of Kona, and it was his business to find her.

"We were all over at Hilo that night, in Ned Austin's. Stephen Kaluna was there when we came in, by himself, in his cups, and quarrelsome. Lyte was laughing over some joke—that huge, happy laugh of a giant boy. Kaluna spat contemptuously on the floor. Lyte noticed, so did everybody; but he ignored the fellow. Kaluna was looking for trouble. He took it as a personal grudge that Lyte was trying to apprehend his sister. In half a dozen ways he advertised his displeasure at Lyte's presence, but Lyte ignored him. I imagined Lyte was a bit sorry for him, for the hardest duty of his office was the apprehension of lepers. It is not a nice thing to go into a man's house and tear away a father, mother, or child, who has done no wrong, and to send such a one to perpetual banishment on Molokai. Of course, it is necessary as a protection to society, and Lyte, I do believe, would have been the first to apprehend his own father did he become suspect.

"Finally, Kaluna blurted out: 'Look here, Gregory, you think you're going to find Kalaniweo, but you're not.'

"Kalaniweo was his sister. Lyte glanced at him when his name was called, but he made no answer. Kaluna was furious. He was working himself up all the time.

"'I'll tell you one thing,' he shouted. 'You'll be on Molokai yourself before ever you get Kalaniweo there. I'll tell you what you are. You've no right to be in the company of honest men. You've made a terrible fuss talking about your duty, haven't you? You've sent many lepers to Molokai, and knowing all the time you belonged there yourself.'

"I'd seen Lyte angry more than once, but never quite so angry as at that moment. Leprosy with us, you know, is not a thing to jest about. He made one leap across the floor, dragging Kaluna out of his chair with a clutch on his neck. He shook him back and forth savagely, till you could hear the half-caste's teeth rattling.

"'What do you mean?' Lyte was demanding. 'Spit it out, man, or I'll choke it out of you!'

"You know, in the West there is a certain phrase that a man must smile while uttering. So with us of the islands, only our phrase is related to leprosy. No matter what Kaluna was, he was no coward. As soon as Lyte eased the grip on his throat he answered:—

"'I'll tell you what I mean. You are a leper yourself.'

"Lyte suddenly flung the half-caste sidewise into a chair, letting him down easily enough. Then Lyte broke out into honest, hearty laughter. But he laughed alone, and when he discovered it he looked around at our faces. I had reached his side and was trying to get him to come away, but he took no notice of me. He was gazing, fascinated, at Kaluna, who was brushing at his own throat in a flurried, nervous way, as if to brush off the contamination of the fingers that had clutched him. The action was unreasoned, genuine.

"Lyte looked around at us, slowly passing from face to face.

"'My God, fellows! My God!' he said.

"He did not speak it. It was more a hoarse whisper of fright and horror. It was fear that fluttered in his throat, and I don't think that ever in his life before he had known fear.

"Then his colossal optimism asserted itself, and he laughed again.

"'A good joke—whoever put it up,' he said. 'The drinks are on me. I had a scare for a moment. But, fellows, don't do it again, to anybody. It's too serious. I tell you I died a thousand deaths in that moment. I thought of my wife and the kids, and . . .'

"His voice broke, and the half-caste, still throat-brushing, drew his eyes. He was puzzled and worried.

"'John,' he said, turning toward me.

"His jovial, rotund voice rang in my ears. But I could not answer. I was swallowing hard at that moment, and besides, I knew my face didn't look just right.

"'John,' he called again, taking a step nearer.

"He called timidly, and of all nightmares of horrors the most frightful was to hear timidity in Lyte Gregory's voice.

"'John, John, what does it mean?' he went on, still more timidly. 'It's a joke, isn't it? John, here's my hand. If I were a leper would I offer you my hand? Am I a leper, John?'

"He held out his hand, and what in high heaven or hell did I care? He was my friend. I took his hand, though it cut me to the heart to see the way his face brightened.

"'It was only a joke, Lyte,' I said. 'We fixed it up on you. But you're right. It's too serious. We won't do it again.'

"He did not laugh this time. He smiled, as a man awakened from a bad dream and still oppressed by the substance of the dream.

"'All right, then,' he said. 'Don't do it again, and I'll stand for the drinks. But I may as well confess that you fellows had me going south for a moment. Look at the way I've been sweating.'

"He sighed and wiped the sweat from his forehead as he started to step toward the bar.

"'It is no joke,' Kaluna said abruptly.

"I looked murder at him, and I felt murder, too. But I dared not speak or strike. That would have precipitated the catastrophe which I somehow had a mad hope of still averting.

"'It is no joke,' Kaluna repeated. 'You are a leper, Lyte Gregory, and you've no right putting your hands on honest men's flesh—on the clean flesh of honest men.'

"Then Gregory flared up.

"'The joke has gone far enough! Quit it! Quit it, I say, Kaluna, or I'll give you a beating!'

"'You undergo a bacteriological examination,' Kaluna answered, 'and then you can beat me—to death, if you want to. Why, man, look at yourself there in the glass. You can see it. Anybody can see it. You're developing the lion face. See where the skin is darkened there over your eyes.'

"Lyte peered and peered, and I saw his hands trembling.

"'I can see nothing,' he said finally, then turned on the *hapa-haole*. 'You have a black heart, Kaluna. And I am not ashamed to say that you have given me a scare that no man has a right to give another. I take you at your word. I am going to settle this thing now. I am going straight to Doc Strowbridge. And when I come back, watch out.'

"He never looked at us, but started for the door.

"'You wait here, John,' he said, waving me back from accompanying him.

"We stood around like a group of ghosts.

"'It is the truth,' Kaluna said. 'You could see it for yourselves.'

"They looked at me, and I nodded. Harry Burnley lifted his glass to his lips, but lowered it untasted. He spilled half of it over the bar. His lips were trembling like a child that is about to cry. Ned Austin made a clatter in the ice-chest. He wasn't looking for anything. I don't think he knew what he was doing. Nobody spoke. Harry Burnley's lips were trembling harder than ever. Suddenly, with a most horrible, malignant expression he drove his fist into Kaluna's face. He followed it up. We made no attempt to separate them. We didn't care if he killed the half-caste. It was a terrible beating. We weren't interested. I don't even remember when Burnley ceased and let the poor devil crawl away. We were all too dazed.

"Doe Strowbridge told me about it afterward. He was working late over a report when Lyte came into his office. Lyte had already recovered his optimism, and came swinging in, a trifle angry with Kaluna to be sure, but very certain of himself. 'What could I do?' Doc asked me. 'I knew he had it. I had seen it coming on for months. I couldn't answer him. I couldn't say yes. I don't mind telling you I broke down and cried. He pleaded for the bacteriological test. "Snip out a piece, Doc," he said, over and over. "Snip out a piece of skin and make the test."'

"The way Doc Strowbridge cried must have convinced Lyte. The *Claudine* was leaving next morning for Honolulu. We caught him when he was going aboard. You see, he was headed for Honolulu to give himself up to the Board of Health. We could do nothing with him. He had sent too many to Molokai to hang back himself. We argued for Japan. But he wouldn't hear of it. 'I've got to take my medicine, fellows,' was all he would say, and he said it over and over. He was obsessed with the idea.

"He wound up all his affairs from the Receiving Station at Honolulu, and went down to Molokai. He didn't get on well there. The resident physician wrote us that he was a shadow of his old self. You see he was grieving about his wife and the kids. He knew we were taking care of them, but it hurt him just the same. After six months or so I went down to Molokai. I sat on one side a plate-glass window, and he on the other. We looked at each other through the glass, and talked through what might be called a speaking tube. But it was hopeless. He had made up his mind to remain. Four mortal hours I argued. I was exhausted at the end. My steamer was whistling for me, too.

"But we couldn't stand for it. Three months later we chartered the schooner *Halcyon*. She was an opium smuggler, and she sailed like a witch. Her master was a squarehead who would do anything for money, and we made a charter to China worth his while. He sailed from San Francisco, and a few days later we took out Landhouse's sloop for a cruise. She was only a five-ton yacht, but we slammed her fifty miles to windward into the northeast trade. Seasick? I never suffered so in my life. Out of sight of land we picked up the *Halcyon,* and Burnley and I went aboard.

"We ran down to Molokai, arriving about eleven at night. The schooner hove to and we landed through the surf in a whale-boat at Kalawao—the place, you know, where Father Damien died. That squarehead was game. With a couple of revolvers strapped on him he came right along. The three of us crossed the peninsula to Kalaupapa, something like two miles. Just imagine hunting in the dead of night for a man in a settlement of over a thousand lepers. You see, if the alarm was given, it was all off with us. It was strange ground, and pitch dark. The lepers' dogs came out and bayed at us, and we stumbled around till we got lost.

"The squarehead solved it. He led the way into the first detached house. We shut the door after us and struck a light. There were six lepers. We routed them up, and I talked in native. What I wanted was a *kokua*. A *kokua* is, literally, a helper, a native who is clean that lives in the settlement and is paid by the Board of Health to nurse the lepers, dress their sores, and such things. We stayed in the house to keep track of the inmates, while the squarehead led one of them off to find a *kokua*. He got him, and he brought him along at the point of his revolver. But the *kokua* was all right. While the squarehead guarded the house, Burnley and I were guided by the *kokua* to Lyte's house. He was all alone.

"'I thought you fellows would come,' Lyte said. 'Don't touch me, John. How's Ned, and Charley, and all the crowd? Never mind, tell me afterward. I am ready to go now. I've had nine months of it. Where's the boat?'

"We started back for the other house to pick up the squarehead. But the alarm had got out. Lights were showing in the houses, and doors were slamming. We had agreed that there was to be no shooting unless absolutely necessary, and when we were halted we went at it with our fists and the butts of our revolvers. I found myself tangled up with a big man. I couldn't keep him off of me, though twice I smashed him fairly in the face with my fist. He grappled with me, and we went down, rolling and scrambling and struggling for grips. He was getting away with me, when some one came running up with a lantern. Then I saw his face. How shall I describe the horror of it! It was not a face—only wasted or wasting features—a living ravage, noseless, lipless, with one ear swollen and distorted, hanging down to the shoulder. I was frantic. In a clinch he hugged me close to him until that ear flapped in my face. Then I guess I went insane. It was too terrible. I began striking him with my revolver. How it happened I don't know, but just as I was getting clear he fastened upon me with his teeth. The whole side of my hand was in that lipless mouth. Then I struck him with the revolver butt squarely between the eyes, and his teeth relaxed."

Cudworth held his hand to me in the moonlight, and I could see the scars. It looked as if it had been mangled by a dog.

"Weren't you afraid?" I asked.

"I was. Seven years I waited. You know, it takes that long for the disease to incubate. Here in Kona I waited, and it did not come. But there was never a day of those seven years, and never a night, that I did not look out on . . . on all this . . . ." His voice broke as he swept his eyes from the moon-bathed sea beneath to the snowy summits above. "I could not bear to think of losing it, of never again beholding Kona. Seven years! I stayed clean. But that is why I am single. I was engaged. I could not dare to marry while I was in doubt. She did not understand. She went away to the States, and married. I have never seen her since.

"Just at the moment I got free of the leper policeman there was rush and clatter of hoofs like a cavalry charge. It was the squarehead. He had been afraid of a rumpus and he had improved his time by making those blessed lepers he was guarding saddle up four horses. We were ready for him. Lyte had accounted for three *kokuas,* and between us we untangled Burnley from a couple more. The whole settlement was in an uproar by that time, and as we dashed away somebody opened up on us with a Winchester. It must have been Jack McVeigh, the superintendent of Molokai.

"That was a ride! Leper horses, leper saddles, leper bridles, pitch-black darkness, whistling bullets, and a road none of the best. And the squarehead's horse was a mule, and he didn't know how to ride, either. But we made the whale-boat, and as we shoved off through the surf we could hear the horses coming down the hill from Kalaupapa.

"You're going to Shanghai. You look Lyte Gregory up. He is employed in a German firm there. Take him out to dinner. Open up wine. Give him everything of the best, but don't let him pay for anything. Send the bill to me. His wife and the kids are in Honolulu, and he needs the money for them. I know. He sends most of his salary, and lives like an anchorite. And tell him about Kona. There's where his heart is. Tell him all you can about Kona."

THE SCARLET PLAGUE
JACK LONDON

I

The way led along upon what had once been the embankment of a railroad. But no train had run upon it for many years. The forest on either side swelled up the slopes of the embankment and crested across it in a green wave of trees and bushes. The trail was as narrow as a man's body, and was no more than a wild-animal runway. Occasionally, a piece of rusty iron, showing through the forest-mould, advertised that the rail and the ties still remained. In one place, a ten-inch tree, bursting through at a connection, had lifted the end of a rail clearly into view. The tie had evidently followed the rail, held to it by the spike long enough for its bed to be filled with gravel and rotten leaves, so that now the crumbling, rotten timber thrust itself up at a curious slant. Old as the road was, it was manifest that it had been of the monorail type.

An old man and a boy travelled along this runway. They moved slowly, for the old man was very old, a touch of palsy made his movements tremulous, and he leaned heavily upon his staff. A rude skull-cap of goat-skin protected his head from the sun. From beneath this fell a scant fringe of stained and dirty-white hair. A visor, ingeniously made from a large leaf, shielded his eyes, and from under this he peered at the way of his feet on the trail. His beard, which should have been snow-white but which showed the same weather-wear and camp-stain as his hair, fell nearly to his waist in a great tangled mass. About his chest and shoulders hung a single, mangy garment of goat-skin. His arms and legs, withered and skinny, betokened extreme age, as well as did their sunburn and scars and scratches betoken long years of exposure to the elements.

The boy, who led the way, checking the eagerness of his muscles to the slow progress of the elder, likewise wore a single garment—a ragged-edged piece of bear-skin, with a hole in the middle through which he had thrust his head. He could not have been more than twelve years old. Tucked coquettishly over one ear was the freshly severed tail of a pig. In one hand he carried a medium-sized bow and an arrow.

On his back was a quiverful of arrows. From a sheath hanging about his neck on a thong, projected the battered handle of a hunting knife. He was as brown as a berry, and walked softly, with almost a catlike tread. In marked contrast with his sunburned skin were his eyes—blue, deep blue, but keen and sharp as a pair of gimlets. They seemed to bore into aft about him in a way that was habitual. As he went along he smelled things, as well, his distended, quivering nostrils carrying to his brain an endless series of messages from the outside world. Also, his hearing was acute, and had been so trained that it operated automatically. Without conscious effort, he heard all the slight sounds in the apparent quiet—heard, and differentiated, and classified these sounds—whether they were of the wind rustling the leaves, of the humming of bees and gnats, of the distant rumble of the sea that drifted to him only in lulls, or of the gopher, just under his foot, shoving a pouchful of earth into the entrance of his hole.

Suddenly he became alertly tense. Sound, sight, and odor had given him a simultaneous warning. His hand went back to the old man, touching him, and the pair stood still. Ahead, at one side of the top of the embankment, arose a crackling sound, and the boy's gaze was fixed on the tops of the agitated bushes. Then a large bear, a grizzly, crashed into view, and likewise stopped abruptly, at sight of the humans. He did not like them, and growled querulously. Slowly the boy fitted the arrow to the bow, and slowly he pulled the bowstring taut. But he never removed his eyes from the bear.

The old man peered from under his green leaf at the danger, and stood as quietly as the boy. For a few seconds this mutual scrutinizing went on; then, the bear betraying a growing irritability, the boy, with a movement of his head, indicated that the old man must step aside from the trail and go down the embankment. The boy followed, going backward, still holding the bow taut and ready. They waited till a crashing among the bushes from the opposite side of the embankment told them the bear had gone on. The boy grinned as he led back to the trail.

"A big un, Granser," he chuckled.

The old man shook his head.

"They get thicker every day," he complained in a thin, undependable falsetto. "Who'd have thought I'd live to see the time when a man would be afraid of his life on the way to the Cliff House. When I was a boy, Edwin, men and women and little babies used to come out here from San Francisco by tens of thousands on a nice day. And there weren't any bears then. No, sir. They used to pay money to look at them in cages, they were that rare."

"What is money, Granser?"

Before the old man could answer, the boy recollected and triumphantly shoved his hand into a pouch under his bear-skin and pulled forth a battered and tarnished silver dollar. The old man's eyes glistened, as he held the coin close to them.

"I can't see," he muttered. "You look and see if you can make out the date, Edwin."

The boy laughed.

"You're a great Granser," he cried delightedly, "always making believe them little marks mean something."

The old man manifested an accustomed chagrin as he brought the coin back again close to his own eyes.

"2012," he shrilled, and then fell to cackling grotesquely. "That was the year Morgan the Fifth was appointed President of the United States by the Board of Magnates. It must have been one of the last coins minted, for the Scarlet Death came in 2013. Lord! Lord!—think of it! Sixty years ago, and I am the only person alive to-day that lived in those times. Where did you find it, Edwin?"

The boy, who had been regarding him with the tolerant curiousness one accords to the prattlings of the feeble-minded, answered promptly.

"I got it off of Hoo-Hoo. He found it when we was herdin' goats down near San José last spring. Hoo-Hoo said it was *money*. Ain't you hungry, Granser?"

The ancient caught his staff in a tighter grip and urged along the trail, his old eyes shining greedily.

"I hope Hare-Lip's found a crab . . . or two," he mumbled. "They're good eating, crabs, mighty good eating when you've no more teeth and you've got grandsons that love their old grandsire and make a point of catching crabs for him. When I was a boy—"

But Edwin, suddenly stopped by what he saw, was drawing the bowstring on a fitted arrow. He had paused on the brink of a crevasse in the embankment. An ancient culvert had here washed out, and the stream, no longer confined, had cut a passage through the fill. On the opposite side, the end of a rail projected and overhung. It showed rustily through the creeping vines which overran it. Beyond, crouching by a bush, a rabbit looked across at him in trembling hesitancy. Fully fifty feet was the distance, but the arrow flashed true; and the transfixed rabbit, crying out in sudden fright and hurt, struggled painfully away into the brush. The boy himself was a flash of brown skin and flying fur as he bounded down the steep wall of the gap and up the other side. His lean muscles were springs of steel that released into graceful and efficient action. A hundred feet beyond, in a tangle of bushes, he overtook the wounded creature, knocked its head on a convenient tree-trunk, and turned it over to Granser to carry.

"Rabbit is good, very good," the ancient quavered, "but when it comes to a toothsome delicacy I prefer crab. When I was a boy—"

"Why do you say so much that ain't got no sense?" Edwin impatiently interrupted the other's threatened garrulousness.

The boy did not exactly utter these words, but something that remotely resembled them and that was more guttural and explosive and economical of qualifying phrases. His speech showed distant kinship with that of the old man, and the latter's speech was approximately an English that had gone through a bath of corrupt usage.

"What I want to know," Edwin continued, "is why you call crab 'toothsome delicacy'? Crab is crab, ain't it? No one I never heard calls it such funny things."

The old man sighed but did not answer, and they moved on in silence. The surf grew suddenly louder, as they emerged from the forest upon a stretch of sand dunes bordering the sea. A few goats were browsing among the sandy hillocks, and a skin-clad boy, aided by a wolfish-looking dog that was only faintly reminiscent of a collie, was watching them. Mingled with the roar of the surf was a continuous, deep-throated barking or bellowing, which came from a cluster of jagged rocks a hundred yards out from shore. Here huge sea-lions hauled themselves up to lie in the sun or battle with one another. In the immediate foreground arose the smoke of a fire, tended by a third savage-looking boy. Crouched near him were several wolfish dogs similar to the one that guarded the goats.

The old man accelerated his pace, sniffing eagerly as he neared the fire.

"Mussels!" he muttered ecstatically. "Mussels! And ain't that a crab, Hoo-Hoo? Ain't that a crab? My, my, you boys are good to your old grandsire."

Hoo-Hoo, who was apparently of the same age as Edwin, grinned.

"All you want, Granser. I got four."

The old man's palsied eagerness was pitiful. Sitting down in the sand as quickly as his stiff limbs would let him, he poked a large rock-mussel from out of the coals. The heat had forced its shells apart, and the meat, salmon-colored, was thoroughly cooked. Between thumb and forefinger, in trembling haste, he caught the morsel and carried it to his mouth. But it was too hot, and the next moment was violently ejected. The old man spluttered with the pain, and tears ran out of his eyes and down his cheeks.

The boys were true savages, possessing only the cruel humor of the savage. To them the incident was excruciatingly funny, and they burst into loud laughter. Hoo-Hoo danced up and down, while Edwin rolled gleefully on the ground. The boy with the goats came running to join in the fun.

"Set 'em to cool, Edwin, set 'em to cool," the old man besought, in the midst of his grief, making no attempt to wipe away the tears that still flowed from his eyes. "And cool a crab, Edwin, too. You know your grandsire likes crabs."

From the coals arose a great sizzling, which proceeded from the many mussels bursting open their shells and exuding their moisture. They were large shellfish, running from three to six inches in length. The boys raked them out with sticks and placed them on a large piece of driftwood to cool.

"When I was a boy, we did not laugh at our elders; we respected them."

The boys took no notice, and Granser continued to babble an incoherent flow of complaint and censure. But this time he was more careful, and did not burn his mouth. All began to eat, using nothing but their hands and making loud mouth-noises and lip-smackings. The third boy, who was called Hare-Lip, slyly deposited a pinch of sand on a mussel the ancient was carrying to his mouth; and when the grit of it bit into the old fellow's mucous membrane and gums, the laughter was again uproarious. He was unaware that a joke had been played on him, and spluttered and spat until Edwin, relenting, gave him a gourd of fresh water with which to wash out his mouth.

"Where's them crabs, Hoo-Hoo?" Edwin demanded. "Granser's set upon having a snack."

Again Granser's eyes burned with greediness as a large crab was handed to him. It was a shell with legs and all complete, but the meat had long since departed. With shaky fingers and babblings of anticipation, the old man broke off a leg and found it filled with emptiness.

"The crabs, Hoo-Hoo?" he wailed. "The crabs?"

"I was fooling Granser. They ain't no crabs! I never found one."

The boys were overwhelmed with delight at sight of the tears of senile disappointment that dribbled down the old man's cheeks. Then, unnoticed, Hoo-Hoo replaced the empty shell with a fresh-cooked crab. Already dismembered, from the cracked legs the white meat sent forth a small cloud of savory steam. This attracted the old man's nostrils, and he looked down in amazement.

The change of his mood to one of joy was immediate. He snuffled and muttered and mumbled, making almost a croon of delight, as he began to eat. Of this the boys took little notice, for it was an accustomed spectacle. Nor did they notice his occasional exclamations and utterances of phrases which meant nothing to them, as, for instance, when he smacked his lips and champed his gums while muttering: “Mayonnaise! Just think—mayonnaise! And it’s sixty years since the last was ever made! Two generations and never a smell of it! Why, in those days it was served in every restaurant with crab.”

When he could eat no more, the old man sighed, wiped his hands on his naked legs, and gazed out over the sea. With the content of a full stomach, he waxed reminiscent.

“To think of it! I’ve seen this beach alive with men, women, and children on a pleasant Sunday. And there weren’t any bears to eat them up, either. And right up there on the cliff was a big restaurant where you could get anything you wanted to eat. Four million people lived in San Francisco then. And now, in the whole city and county there aren’t forty all told. And out there on the sea were ships and ships always to be seen, going in for the Golden Gate or coming out. And airships in the air—dirigibles and flying machines. They could travel two hundred miles an hour. The mail contracts with the New York and San Francisco Limited demanded that for the minimum. There was a chap, a Frenchman, I forget his name, who succeeded in making three hundred; but the thing was risky, too risky for conservative persons. But he was on the right clew, and he would have managed it if it hadn’t been for the Great Plague. When I was a boy, there were men alive who remembered the coming of the first aeroplanes, and now I have lived to see the last of them, and that sixty years ago.”

The old man babbled on, unheeded by the boys, who were long accustomed to his garrulousness, and whose vocabularies, besides, lacked the greater portion of the words he used. It was noticeable that in these rambling soliloquies his English seemed to recrudesce into better construction and phraseology. But when he talked directly with the boys it lapsed, largely, into their own uncouth and simpler forms.

"But there weren't many crabs in those days," the old man wandered on. "They were fished out, and they were great delicacies. The open season was only a month long, too. And now crabs are accessible the whole year around. Think of it—catching all the crabs you want, any time you want, in the surf of the Cliff House beach!"

A sudden commotion among the goats brought the boys to their feet. The dogs about the fire rushed to join their snarling fellow who guarded the goats, while the goats themselves stampeded in the direction of their human protectors. A half dozen forms, lean and gray, glided about on the sand hillocks and faced the bristling dogs. Edwin arched an arrow that fell short. But Hare-Lip, with a sling such as David carried into battle against Goliath, hurled a stone through the air that whistled from the speed of its flight. It fell squarely among the wolves and caused them to slink away toward the dark depths of the eucalyptus forest.

The boys laughed and lay down again in the sand, while Granser sighed ponderously. He had eaten too much, and, with hands clasped on his paunch, the fingers interlaced, he resumed his maunderings.

"'The fleeting systems lapse like foam,'" he mumbled what was evidently a quotation. "That's it—foam, and fleeting. All man's toil upon the planet was just so much foam. He domesticated the serviceable animals, destroyed the hostile ones, and cleared the land of its wild vegetation. And then he passed, and the flood of primordial life rolled back again, sweeping his handiwork away—the weeds and the forest inundated his fields, the beasts of prey swept over his flocks, and now there are wolves on the Cliff House beach." He was appalled by the thought. "Where four million people disported themselves, the wild wolves roam to-day, and the savage progeny of our loins, with prehistoric weapons, defend themselves against the fanged despoilers. Think of it! And all because of the Scarlet Death—"

The adjective had caught Hare-Lip's ear.

"He's always saying that," he said to Edwin. "What is *scarlet?*"

"'The scarlet of the maples can shake me like the cry of bugles going by,'" the old man quoted.

"It's red," Edwin answered the question. "And you don't know it because you come from the Chauffeur Tribe. They never did know nothing, none of them. Scarlet is red—I know that."

"Red is red, ain't it?" Hare-Lip grumbled. "Then what's the good of gettin' cocky and calling it scarlet?"

"Granser, what for do you always say so much what nobody knows?" he asked. "Scarlet ain't anything, but red is red. Why don't you say red, then?"

"Red is not the right word," was the reply. "The plague was scarlet. The whole face and body turned scarlet in an hour's time. Don't I know? Didn't I see enough of it? And I am telling you it was scarlet because—well, because it *was* scarlet. There is no other word for it."

"Red is good enough for me," Hare-Lip muttered obstinately. "My dad calls red red, and he ought to know. He says everybody died of the Red Death."

"Your dad is a common fellow, descended from a common fellow," Granser retorted heatedly. "Don't I know the beginnings of the Chauffeurs? Your grandsire was a chauffeur, a servant, and without education. He worked for other persons. But your grandmother was of good stock, only the children did not take after her. Don't I remember when I first met them, catching fish at Lake Temescal?"

"What is *education?*" Edwin asked.

"Calling red scarlet," Hare-Lip sneered, then returned to the attack on Granser. "My dad told me, an' he got it from his dad afore he croaked, that your wife was a Santa Rosan, an' that she was sure no account. He said she was a *hash-slinger* before the Red Death, though I don't know what a *hash-slinger* is. You can tell me, Edwin."

But Edwin shook his head in token of ignorance.

"It is true, she was a waitress," Granser acknowledged. "But she was a good woman, and your mother was her daughter. Women were very scarce in the days after the Plague. She was the only wife I could find, even if she was a *hash-slinger*, as your father calls it. But it is not nice to talk about our progenitors that way."

"Dad says that the wife of the first Chauffeur was a *lady*—"

"What's a *lady?*" Hoo-Hoo demanded.

"A *lady* 'sa Chauffeur squaw," was the quick reply of Hare-Lip.

"The first Chauffeur was Bill, a common fellow, as I said before," the old man expounded; "but his wife was a lady, a great lady. Before the Scarlet Death she was the wife of Van Worden. He was President of the Board of Industrial Magnates, and was one of the dozen men who ruled America. He was worth one billion, eight hundred millions of dollars—coins like you have there in your pouch, Edwin. And then came the Scarlet Death, and his wife became the wife of Bill, the first Chauffeur. He used to beat her, too. I have seen it myself."

Hoo-Hoo, lying on his stomach and idly digging his toes in the sand, cried out and investigated, first, his toe-nail, and next, the small hole he had dug. The other two boys joined him, excavating the sand rapidly with their hands till there lay three skeletons exposed. Two were of adults, the third being that of a part-grown child. The old man hudged along on the ground and peered at the find.

"Plague victims," he announced. "That's the way they died everywhere in the last days. This must have been a family, running away from the contagion and perishing here on the Cliff House beach. They—what are you doing, Edwin?"

This question was asked in sudden dismay, as Edwin, using the back of his hunting knife, began to knock out the teeth from the jaws of one of the skulls.

"Going to string 'em," was the response.

The three boys were now hard at it; and quite a knocking and hammering arose, in which Granser babbled on unnoticed.

"You are truc savages. Already has begun the custom of wearing human teeth. In another generation you will be perforating your noses and ears and wearing ornaments of bone and shell. I know. The human race is doomed to sink back farther and farther into the primitive night ere again it begins its bloody climb upward to civilization. When we increase and feel the lack of room, we will proceed to kill one another. And then I suppose you will wear human scalp-locks at your waist, as well—as you, Edwin, who are the gentlest of my grandsons, have already begun with that vile pigtail. Throw it away, Edwin, boy; throw it away."

"What a gabble the old geezer makes," Hare-Lip remarked, when, the teeth all extracted, they began an attempt at equal division.

They were very quick and abrupt in their actions, and their speech, in moments of hot discussion over the allotment of the choicer teeth, was truly a gabble. They spoke in monosyllables and short jerky sentences that was more a gibberish than a language. And yet, through it ran hints of grammatical construction, and appeared vestiges of the conjugation of some superior culture. Even the speech of Granser was so corrupt that were it put down literally it would be almost so much nonsense to the reader. This, however, was when he talked with the boys.

When he got into the full swing of babbling to himself, it slowly purged itself into pure English. The sentences grew longer and were enunciated with a rhythm and ease that was reminiscent of the lecture platform.

"Tell us about the Red Death, Granser," Hare-Lip demanded, when the teeth affair had been satisfactorily concluded.

"The Scarlet Death," Edwin corrected.

"An' don't work all that funny lingo on us," Hare-Lip went on. "Talk sensible, Granser, like a Santa Rosan ought to talk. Other Santa Rosans don't talk like you."

II

The old man showed pleasure in being thus called upon. He cleared his throat and began.

"Twenty or thirty years ago my story was in great demand. But in these days nobody seems interested—"

"There you go!" Hare-Lip cried hotly. "Cut out the funny stuff and talk sensible. What's *interested?* You talk like a baby that don't know how."

"Let him alone," Edwin urged, "or he'll get mad and won't talk at all. Skip the funny places. We'll catch on to some of what he tells us."

"Let her go, Granser," Hoo-Hoo encouraged; for the old man was already maundering about the disrespect for elders and the reversion to cruelty of all humans that fell from high culture to primitive conditions.

The tale began.

"There were very many people in the world in those days. San Francisco alone held four millions—"

"What is millions?" Edwin interrupted.

Granser looked at him kindly.

"I know you cannot count beyond ten, so I will tell you. Hold up your two hands. On both of them you have altogether ten fingers and thumbs. Very well. I now take this grain of sand—you hold it, Hoo-Hoo." He dropped the grain of sand into the lad's palm and went on. "Now that grain of sand stands for the ten fingers of Edwin. I add another grain. That's ten more fingers. And I add another, and another, and another, until I have added as many grains as Edwin has fingers and thumbs. That makes what I call one hundred. Remember that word—one hundred. Now I put this pebble in Hare-Lip's hand. It stands for ten grains of sand, or ten tens of fingers, or one hundred fingers. I put in ten pebbles. They stand for a thousand fingers. I take a mussel-shell, and it stands for ten pebbles, or one hundred grains of sand, or one thousand fingers. . . ." And so on, laboriously, and with much reiteration, he strove to build up in their minds a crude conception of numbers. As the quantities increased, he had the boys holding different magnitudes in each of their hands. For still higher sums, he laid the symbols on the log of driftwood; and for symbols he was hard put, being compelled to use the teeth from the skulls for millions, and the crab-shells for billions. It was here that he stopped, for the boys were showing signs of becoming tired.

"There were four million people in San Francisco—four teeth."

The boys' eyes ranged along from the teeth and from hand to hand, down through the pebbles and sand-grains to Edwin's fingers. And back again they ranged along the ascending series in the effort to grasp such inconceivable numbers.

"That was a lot of folks, Granser," Edwin at last hazarded.

"Like sand on the beach here, like sand on the beach, each grain of sand a man, or woman, or child. Yes, my boy, all those people lived right here in San Francisco. And at one time or another all those people came out on this very beach—more people than there are grains of sand. More—more—more. And San Francisco was a noble city. And across the bay—where we camped last year, even more people lived, clear from Point Richmond, on the level ground and on the hills, all the way around to San Leandro—one great city of seven million people.—Seven teeth . . . there, that's it, seven millions."

Again the boys' eyes ranged up and down from Edwin's fingers to the teeth on the log.

"The world was full of people. The census of 2010 gave eight billions for the whole world—eight crab-shells, yes, eight billions. It was not like to-day. Mankind knew a great deal more about getting food. And the more food there was, the more people there were. In the year 1800, there were one hundred and seventy millions in Europe alone. One hundred years later—a grain of sand, Hoo-Hoo—one hundred years later, at 1900, there were five hundred millions in Europe—five grains of sand, Hoo-Hoo, and this one tooth. This shows how easy was the getting of food, and how men increased. And in the year 2000, there were fifteen hundred millions in Europe. And it was the same all over the rest of the world. Eight crab-shells there, yes, eight billion people were alive on the earth when the Scarlet Death began.

"I was a young man when the Plague came—twenty-seven years old; and I lived on the other side of San Francisco Bay, in Berkeley. You remember those great stone houses, Edwin, when we came down the hills from Contra Costa? That was where I lived, in those stone houses. I was a professor of English literature."

Much of this was over the heads of the boys, but they strove to comprehend dimly this tale of the past.

"What was them stone houses for?" Hare-Lip queried.

"You remember when your dad taught you to swim?" The boy nodded. "Well, in the University of California—that is the name we had for the houses—we taught young men and women how to think, just as I have taught you now, by sand and pebbles and shells, to know how many people lived in those days. There was very much to teach. The young men and women we taught were called students. We had large rooms in which we taught. I talked to them, forty or fifty at a time, just as I am talking to you now. I told them about the books other men had written before their time, and even, sometimes, in their time—"

"Was that all you did?—just talk, talk, talk?" Hoo-Hoo demanded. "Who hunted your meat for you? and milked the goats? and caught the fish?"

"A sensible question, Hoo-Hoo, a sensible question. As I have told you, in those days food-getting was easy. We were very wise. A few men got the food for many men. The other men did other things. As you say, I talked. I talked all the time, and for this food was given me—much food, fine food, beautiful food, food that I have not tasted in sixty years and shall never taste again. I sometimes think the most wonderful achievement of our tremendous civilization was food—its inconceivable abundance, its infinite variety, its marvellous delicacy. O my grandsons, life was life in those days, when we had such wonderful things to eat."

This was beyond the boys, and they let it slip by, words and thoughts, as a mere senile wandering in the narrative.

"Our food-getters were called *freemen*. This was a joke. We of the ruling classes owned all the land, all the machines, everything. These food-getters were our slaves. We took almost all the food they got, and left them a little so that they might eat, and work, and get us more food—"

"I'd have gone into the forest and got food for myself," Hare-Lip announced; "and if any man tried to take it away from me, I'd have killed him."

The old man laughed.

"Did I not tell you that we of the ruling class owned all the land, all the forest, everything? Any food-getter who would not get food for us, him we punished or compelled to starve to death. And very few did that. They preferred to get food for us, and make clothes for us, and prepare and administer to us a thousand—a mussel-shell, Hoo-Hoo—a thousand satisfactions and delights. And I was Professor Smith in those days—Professor James Howard Smith. And my lecture courses were very popular—that is, very many of the young men and women liked to hear me talk about the books other men had written.

"And I was very happy, and I had beautiful things to eat. And my hands were soft, because I did no work with them, and my body was clean all over and dressed in the softest garments—

"He surveyed his mangy goat-skin with disgust.

"We did not wear such things in those days. Even the slaves had better garments. And we were most clean. We washed our faces and hands often every day. You boys never wash unless you fall into the water or go swimming."

"Neither do you Granzer," Hoo-Hoo retorted.

"I know, I know, I am a filthy old man, but times have changed. Nobody washes these days, there are no conveniences. It is sixty years since I have seen a piece of soap.

"You do not know what soap is, and I shall not tell you, for I am telling the story of the Scarlet Death. You know what sickness is. We called it a disease. Very many of the diseases came from what we called germs. Remember that word—germs. A germ is a very small thing. It is like a woodtick, such as you find on the dogs in the spring of the year when they run in the forest. Only the germ is very small. It is so small that you cannot see it—"

Hoo-Hoo began to laugh.

"You're a queer un, Granser, talking about things you can't see. If you can't see 'em, how do you know they are? That's what I want to know. How do you know anything you can't see?"

"A good question, a very good question, Hoo-Hoo. But we did see—some of them. We had what we called microscopes and ultramicroscopes, and we put them to our eyes and looked through them, so that we saw things larger than they really were, and many things we could not see without the microscopes at all. Our best ultramicroscopes could make a germ look forty thousand times larger. A mussel-shell is a thousand fingers like Edwin's. Take forty mussel-shells, and by as many times larger was the germ when we looked at it through a microscope. And after that, we had other ways, by using what we called moving pictures, of making the forty-thousand-times germ many, many thousand times larger still. And thus we saw all these things which our eyes of themselves could not see. Take a grain of sand. Break it into ten pieces. Take one piece and break it into ten. Break one of those pieces into ten, and one of those into ten, and one of those into ten, and one of those into ten, and do it all day, and maybe, by sunset, you will have a piece as small as one of the germs." The boys were openly incredulous. Hare-Lip sniffed and sneered and Hoo-Hoo snickered, until Edwin nudged them to be silent.

"The woodtick sucks the blood of the dog, but the germ, being so very small, goes right into the blood of the body, and there it has many children. In those days there would be as many as a billion—a crab-shell, please—as many as that crab-shell in one man's body. We called germs micro-organisms. When a few million, or a billion, of them were in a man, in all the blood of a man, he was sick. These germs were a disease. There were many different kinds of them—more different kinds than there are grains of sand on this beach. We knew only a few of the kinds. The micro-organic world was an invisible world, a world we could not see, and we knew very little about it. Yet we did know something. There was the *bacillus anthracis*; there was the *micrococcus*; there was the *Bacterium termo*, and the *Bacterium lactis*—that's what turns the goat milk sour even to this day, Hare-Lip; and there were *Schizomycetes* without end. And there were many others. . . ."

Here the old man launched into a disquisition on germs and their natures, using words and phrases of such extraordinary length and meaninglessness, that the boys grinned at one another and looked out over the deserted ocean till they forgot the old man was babbling on.

"But the Scarlet Death, Granser," Edwin at last suggested.

Granser recollected himself, and with a start tore himself away from the rostrum of the lecture-hall, where, to another world audience, he had been expounding the latest theory, sixty years gone, of germs and germ-diseases.

"Yes, yes, Edwin; I had forgotten. Sometimes the memory of the past is very strong upon me, and I forget that I am a dirty old man, clad in goat-skin, wandering with my savage grandsons who are goatherds in the primeval wilderness. 'The fleeting systems lapse like foam,' and so lapsed our glorious, colossal civilization. I am Granser, a tired old man. I belong to the tribe of Santa Rosans. I married into that tribe. My sons and daughters married into the Chauffeurs, the Sacramentos, and the Palo-Altos. You, Hare-Lip, are of the Chauffeurs. You, Edwin, are of the Sacramentos. And you, Hoo-Hoo, are of the Palo-Altos. Your tribe takes its name from a town that was near the seat of another great institution of learning. It was called Stanford University. Yes, I remember now. It is perfectly clear. I was telling you of the Scarlet Death. Where was I in my story?"

"You was telling about germs, the things you can't see but which make men sick," Edwin prompted.

"Yes, that's where I was. A man did not notice at first when only a few of these germs got into his body. But each germ broke in half and became two germs, and they kept doing this very rapidly so that in a short time there were many millions of them in the body. Then the man was sick. He had a disease, and the disease was named after the kind of a germ that was in him. It might be measles, it might be influenza, it might be yellow fever; it might be any of thousands and thousands of kinds of diseases.

"Now this is the strange thing about these germs. There were always new ones coming to live in men's bodies. Long and long and long ago, when there were only a few men in the world, there were few diseases. But as men increased and lived closely together in great cities and civilizations, new diseases arose, new kinds of germs entered their bodies. Thus were countless millions and billions of human beings killed. And the more thickly men packed together, the more terrible were the new diseases that came to be. Long before my time, in the middle ages, there was the Black Plague that swept across Europe. It swept across Europe many times. There was tuberculosis, that entered into men wherever they were thickly packed. A hundred years before my time there was the bubonic plague. And in Africa was the sleeping sickness. The bacteriologists fought all these sicknesses and destroyed them, just as you boys fight the wolves away from your goats, or squash the mosquitoes that light on you. The bacteriologists—"

"But, Granser, what is a what-you-call-it?" Edwin interrupted.

"You, Edwin, are a goatherd. Your task is to watch the goats. You know a great deal about goats. A bacteriologist watches germs. That's his task, and he knows a great deal about them. So, as I was saying, the bacteriologists fought with the germs and destroyed them—sometimes. There was leprosy, a horrible disease. A hundred years before I was born, the bacteriologists discovered the germ of leprosy. They knew all about it. They made pictures of it. I have seen those pictures. But they never found a way to kill it. But in 1984, there was the Pantoblast Plague, a disease that broke out in a country called Brazil and that killed millions of people. But the bacteriologists found it out, and found the way to kill it, so that the Pantoblast Plague went no farther. They made what they called a serum, which they put into a man's body and which killed the pantoblast germs without killing the man. And in 1910, there was Pellagra, and also the hookworm. These were easily killed by the bacteriologists. But in 1947 there arose a new disease that had never been seen before. It got into the bodies of babies of only ten months old or less, and it made them unable to move their hands and feet, or to eat, or anything; and the bacteriologists were eleven years in discovering how to kill that particular germ and save the babies.

"In spite of all these diseases, and of all the new ones that continued to arise, there were more and more men in the world. This was because it was easy to get food. The easier it was to get food, the more men there were; the more men there were, the more thickly were they packed together on the earth; and the more thickly they were packed, the more new kinds of germs became diseases. There were warnings. Soldervetzsky, as early as 1929, told the bacteriologists that they had no guaranty against some new disease, a thousand times more deadly than any they knew, arising and killing by the hundreds of millions and even by the billion. You see, the micro-organic world remained a mystery to the end. They knew there was such a world, and that from time to time armies of new germs emerged from it to kill men.

"And that was all they knew about it. For all they knew, in that invisible micro-organic world there might be as many different kinds of germs as there are grains of sand on this beach. And also, in that same invisible world it might well be that new kinds of germs came to be. It might be there that life originated—the 'abysmal fecundity,' Soldervetzsky called it, applying the words of other men who had written before him. . . ."

It was at this point that Hare-Lip rose to his feet, an expression of huge contempt on his face.

"Granser," he announced, "you make me sick with your gabble. Why don't you tell about the Red Death? If you ain't going to, say so, an' we'll start back for camp."

The old man looked at him and silently began to cry. The weak tears of age rolled down his cheeks and all the feebleness of his eighty-seven years showed in his grief-stricken countenance.

"Sit down," Edwin counselled soothingly. "Granser's all right. He's just gettin' to the Scarlet Death, ain't you, Granser? He's just goin' to tell us about it right now. Sit down, Hare-Lip. Go ahead, Granser."

III

The old man wiped the tears away on his grimy knuckles and took up the tale in a tremulous, piping voice that soon strengthened as he got the swing of the narrative.

"It was in the summer of 2013 that the Plague came. I was twenty-seven years old, and well do I remember it. Wireless despatches—"

Hare-Lip spat loudly his disgust, and Granser hastened to make amends.

"We talked through the air in those days, thousands and thousands of miles. And the word came of a strange disease that had broken out in New York. There were seventeen millions of people living then in that noblest city of America. Nobody thought anything about the news. It was only a small thing. There had been only a few deaths. It seemed, though, that they had died very quickly, and that one of the first signs of the disease was the turning red of the face and all the body. Within twenty-four hours came the report of the first case in Chicago. And on the same day, it was made public that London, the greatest city in the world, next to Chicago, had been secretly fighting the plague for two weeks and censoring the news despatches—that is, not permitting the word to go forth to the rest of the world that London had the plague.

"It looked serious, but we in California, like everywhere else, were not alarmed. We were sure that the bacteriologists would find a way to overcome this new germ, just as they had overcome other germs in the past. But the trouble was the astonishing quickness with which this germ destroyed human beings, and the fact that it inevitably killed any human body it entered. No one ever recovered. There was the old Asiatic cholera, when you might eat dinner with a well man in the evening, and the next morning, if you got up early enough, you would see him being hauled by your window in the death-cart. But this new plague was quicker than that—much quicker.

"From the moment of the first signs of it, a man would be dead in an hour. Some lasted for several hours. Many died within ten or fifteen minutes of the appearance of the first signs.

"The heart began to beat faster and the heat of the body to increase. Then came the scarlet rash, spreading like wildfire over the face and body. Most persons never noticed the increase in heat and heart-beat, and the first they knew was when the scarlet rash came out. Usually, they had convulsions at the time of the appearance of the rash. But these convulsions did not last long and were not very severe. If one lived through them, he became perfectly quiet, and only did he feel a numbness swiftly creeping up his body from the feet. The heels became numb first, then the legs, and hips, and when the numbness reached as high as his heart he died. They did not rave or sleep. Their minds always remained cool and calm up to the moment their heart numbed and stopped. And another strange thing was the rapidity of decomposition. No sooner was a person dead than the body seemed to fall to pieces, to fly apart, to melt away even as you looked at it. That was one of the reasons the plague spread so rapidly. All the billions of germs in a corpse were so immediately released.

"And it was because of all this that the bacteriologists had so little chance in fighting the germs. They were killed in their laboratories even as they studied the germ of the Scarlet Death. They were heroes. As fast as they perished, others stepped forth and took their places. It was in London that they first isolated it. The news was telegraphed everywhere. Trask was the name of the man who succeeded in this, but within thirty hours he was dead. Then came the struggle in all the laboratories to find something that would kill the plague germs. All drugs failed. You see, the problem was to get a drug, or serum, that would kill the germs in the body and not kill the body. They tried to fight it with other germs, to put into the body of a sick man germs that were the enemies of the plague germs—"

"And you can't see these germ-things, Granser," Hare-Lip objected, "and here you gabble, gabble, gabble about them as if they was anything, when they're nothing at all. Anything you can't see, ain't, that's what. Fighting things that ain't with things that ain't! They must have been all fools in them days. That's why they croaked. I ain't goin' to believe in such rot, I tell you that."

Granser promptly began to weep, while Edwin hotly took up his defence.

"Look here, Hare-Lip, you believe in lots of things you can't see."

Hare-Lip shook his head.

"You believe in dead men walking about. You never seen one dead man walk about."

"I tell you I seen 'em, last winter, when I was wolf-hunting with dad."

"Well, you always spit when you cross running water," Edwin challenged.

"That's to keep off bad luck," was Hare-Lip's defence.

"You believe in bad luck?"

"Sure."

"An' you ain't never seen bad luck," Edwin concluded triumphantly. "You're just as bad as Granser and his germs. You believe in what you don't see. Go on, Granser."

Hare-Lip, crushed by this metaphysical defeat, remained silent, and the old man went on. Often and often, though this narrative must not be clogged by the details, was Granser's tale interrupted while the boys squabbled among themselves. Also, among themselves they kept up a constant, low-voiced exchange of explanation and conjecture, as they strove to follow the old man into his unknown and vanished world.

"The Scarlet Death broke out in San Francisco. The first death came on a Monday morning. By Thursday they were dying like flies in Oakland and San Francisco. They died everywhere—in their beds, at their work, walking along the street. It was on Tuesday that I saw my first death—Miss Collbran, one of my students, sitting right there before my eyes, in my lecture-room. I noticed her face while I was talking. It had suddenly turned scarlet. I ceased speaking and could only look at her, for the first fear of the plague was already on all of us and we knew that it had come. The young women screamed and ran out of the room. So did the young men run out, all but two. Miss Collbran's convulsions were very mild and lasted less than a minute. One of the young men fetched her a glass of water. She drank only a little of it, and cried out:

"'My feet! All sensation has left them.'

"After a minute she said, 'I have no feet. I am unaware that I have any feet. And my knees are cold. I can scarcely feel that I have knees.'

"She lay on the floor, a bundle of notebooks under her head. And we could do nothing. The coldness and the numbness crept up past her hips to her heart, and when it reached her heart she was dead. In fifteen minutes, by the clock—I timed it—she was dead, there, in my own classroom, dead. And she was a very beautiful, strong, healthy young woman. And from the first sign of the plague to her death only fifteen minutes elapsed. That will show you how swift was the Scarlet Death.

"Yet in those few minutes I remained with the dying woman in my classroom, the alarm had spread over the university; and the students, by thousands, all of them, had deserted the lecture-room and laboratories. When I emerged, on my way to make report to the President of the Faculty, I found the university deserted. Across the campus were several stragglers hurrying for their homes. Two of them were running.

"President Hoag, I found in his office, all alone, looking very old and very gray, with a multitude of wrinkles in his face that I had never seen before. At the sight of me, he pulled himself to his feet and tottered away to the inner office, banging the door after him and locking it. You see, he knew I had been exposed, and he was afraid. He shouted to me through the door to go away. I shall never forget my feelings as I walked down the silent corridors and out across that deserted campus. I was not afraid. I had been exposed, and I looked upon myself as already dead. It was not that, but a feeling of awful depression that impressed me. Everything had stopped. It was like the end of the world to me—my world. I had been born within sight and sound of the university. It had been my predestined career. My father had been a professor there before me, and his father before him. For a century and a half had this university, like a splendid machine, been running steadily on. And now, in an instant, it had stopped. It was like seeing the sacred flame die down on some thrice-sacred altar. I was shocked, unutterably shocked.

"When I arrived home, my housekeeper screamed as I entered, and fled away. And when I rang, I found the housemaid had likewise fled. I investigated. In the kitchen I found the cook on the point of departure. But she screamed, too, and in her haste dropped a suitcase of her personal belongings and ran out of the house and across the grounds, still screaming. I can hear her scream to this day. You see, we did not act in this way when ordinary diseases smote us. We were always calm over such things, and sent for the doctors and nurses who knew just what to do. But this was different. It struck so suddenly, and killed so swiftly, and never missed a stroke. When the scarlet rash appeared on a person's face, that person was marked by death. There was never a known case of a recovery.

"I was alone in my big house. As I have told you often before, in those days we could talk with one another over wires or through the air. The telephone bell rang, and I found my brother talking to me. He told me that he was not coming home for fear of catching the plague from me, and that he had taken our two sisters to stop at Professor Bacon's home. He advised me to remain where I was, and wait to find out whether or not I had caught the plague.

"To all of this I agreed, staying in my house and for the first time in my life attempting to cook. And the plague did not come out on me. By means of the telephone I could talk with whomsoever I pleased and get the news. Also, there were the newspapers, and I ordered all of them to be thrown up to my door so that I could know what was happening with the rest of the world.

"New York City and Chicago were in chaos. And what happened with them was happening in all the large cities. A third of the New York police were dead. Their chief was also dead, likewise the mayor. All law and order had ceased. The bodies were lying in the streets un-buried. All railroads and vessels carrying food and such things into the great city had ceased runnings and mobs of the hungry poor were pillaging the stores and warehouses. Murder and robbery and drunkenness were everywhere. Already the people had fled from the city by millions—at first the rich, in their private motor-cars and dirigibles, and then the great mass of the population, on foot, carrying the plague with them, themselves starving and pillaging the farmers and all the towns and villages on the way.

"The man who sent this news, the wireless operator, was alone with his instrument on the top of a lofty building. The people remaining in the city—he estimated them at several hundred thousand—had gone mad from fear and drink, and on all sides of him great fires were raging. He was a hero, that man who staid by his post—an obscure newspaperman, most likely.

"For twenty-four hours, he said, no transatlantic airships had arrived, and no more messages were coming from England. He did state, though, that a message from Berlin—that's in Germany—announced that Hoffmeyer, a bacteriologist of the Metchnikoff School, had discovered the serum for the plague. That was the last word, to this day, that we of America ever received from Europe. If Hoffmeyer discovered the serum, it was too late, or otherwise, long ere this, explorers from Europe would have come looking for us. We can only conclude that what happened in America happened in Europe, and that, at the best, some several score may have survived the Scarlet Death on that whole continent.

"For one day longer the despatches continued to come from New York. Then they, too, ceased. The man who had sent them, perched in his lofty building, had either died of the plague or been consumed in the great conflagrations he had described as raging around him. And what had occurred in New York had been duplicated in all the other cities. It was the same in San Francisco, and Oakland, and Berkeley. By Thursday the people were dying so rapidly that their corpses could not be handled, and dead bodies lay everywhere. Thursday night the panic outrush for the country began. Imagine, my grandsons, people, thicker than the salmon-run you have seen on the Sacramento river, pouring out of the cities by millions, madly over the country, in vain attempt to escape the ubiquitous death. You see, they carried the germs with them. Even the airships of the rich, fleeing for mountain and desert fastnesses, carried the germs.

"Hundreds of these airships escaped to Hawaii, and not only did they bring the plague with them, but they found the plague already there before them. This we learned, by the despatches, until all order in San Francisco vanished, and there were no operators left at their posts to receive or send. It was amazing, astounding, this loss of communication with the world. It was exactly as if the world had ceased, been blotted out. For sixty years that world has no longer existed for me. I know there must be such places as New York, Europe, Asia, and Africa; but not one word has been heard of them—not in sixty years. With the coming of the Scarlet Death the world fell apart, absolutely, irretrievably. Ten thousand years of culture and civilization passed in the twinkling of an eye, 'lapsed like foam.'

"I was telling about the airships of the rich. They carried the plague with them and no matter where they fled, they died. I never encountered but one survivor of any of them—Mungerson. He was afterwards a Santa Rosan, and he married my eldest daughter. He came into the tribe eight years after the plague. He was then nineteen years old, and he was compelled to wait twelve years more before he could marry. You see, there were no unmarried women, and some of the older daughters of the Santa Rosans were already bespoken. So he was forced to wait until my Mary had grown to sixteen years. It was his son, Gimp-Leg, who was killed last year by the mountain lion.

"Mungerson was eleven years old at the time of the plague. His father was one of the Industrial Magnates, a very wealthy, powerful man. It was on his airship, the Condor, that they were fleeing, with all the family, for the wilds of British Columbia, which is far to the north of here. But there was some accident, and they were wrecked near Mount Shasta. You have heard of that mountain. It is far to the north. The plague broke out amongst them, and this boy of eleven was the only survivor. For eight years he was alone, wandering over a deserted land and looking vainly for his own kind. And at last, travelling south, he picked up with us, the Santa Rosans.

"But I am ahead of my story. When the great exodus from the cities around San Francisco Bay began, and while the telephones were still working, I talked with my brother. I told him this flight from the cities was insanity, that there were no symptoms of the plague in me, and that the thing for us to do was to isolate ourselves and our relatives in some safe place. We decided on the Chemistry Building, at the university, and we planned to lay in a supply of provisions, and by force of arms to prevent any other persons from forcing their presence upon us after we had retired to our refuge.

"All this being arranged, my brother begged me to stay in my own house for at least twenty-four hours more, on the chance of the plague developing in me. To this I agreed, and he promised to come for me next day. We talked on over the details of the provisioning and the defending of the Chemistry Building until the telephone died. It died in the midst of our conversation. That evening there were no electric lights, and I was alone in my house in the darkness. No more newspapers were being printed, so I had no knowledge of what was taking place outside.

"I heard sounds of rioting and of pistol shots, and from my windows I could see the glare of the sky of some conflagration in the direction of Oakland. It was a night of terror. I did not sleep a wink. A man—why and how I do not know—was killed on the sidewalk in front of the house. I heard the rapid reports of an automatic pistol, and a few minutes later the wounded wretch crawled up to my door, moaning and crying out for help. Arming myself with two automatics, I went to him. By the light of a match I ascertained that while he was dying of the bullet wounds, at the same time the plague was on him. I fled indoors, whence I heard him moan and cry out for half an hour longer.

"In the morning, my brother came to me. I had gathered into a handbag what things of value I purposed taking, but when I saw his face I knew that he would never accompany me to the Chemistry Building. The plague was on him. He intended shaking my hand, but I went back hurriedly before him.

"'Look at yourself in the mirror,' I commanded.

"He did so, and at sight of his scarlet face, the color deepening as he looked at it, he sank down nervelessly in a chair.

"'My God!' he said. 'I've got it. Don't come near me. I am a dead man.'

"Then the convulsions seized him. He was two hours in dying, and he was conscious to the last, complaining about the coldness and loss of sensation in his feet, his calves, his thighs, until at last it was his heart and he was dead.

"That was the way the Scarlet Death slew. I caught up my handbag and fled. The sights in the streets were terrible. One stumbled on bodies everywhere. Some were not yet dead. And even as you looked, you saw men sink down with the death fastened upon them. There were numerous fires burning in Berkeley, while Oakland and San Francisco were apparently being swept by vast conflagrations. The smoke of the burning filled the heavens, so that the midday was as a gloomy twilight, and, in the shifts of wind, sometimes the sun shone through dimly, a dull red orb. Truly, my grandsons, it was like the last days of the end of the world.

"There were numerous stalled motor cars, showing that the gasoline and the engine supplies of the garages had given out. I remember one such car. A man and a woman lay back dead in the seats, and on the pavement near it were two more women and a child. Strange and terrible sights there were on every hand. People slipped by silently, furtively, like ghosts—white-faced women carrying infants in their arms; fathers leading children by the hand; singly, and in couples, and in families—all fleeing out of the city of death. Some carried supplies of food, others blankets and valuables, and there were many who carried nothing.

"There was a grocery store—a place where food was sold. The man to whom it belonged—I knew him well—a quiet, sober, but stupid and obstinate fellow, was defending it. The windows and doors had been broken in, but he, inside, hiding behind a counter, was discharging his pistol at a number of men on the sidewalk who were breaking in. In the entrance were several bodies—of men, I decided, whom he had killed earlier in the day. Even as I looked on from a distance, I saw one of the robbers break the windows of the adjoining store, a place where shoes were sold, and deliberately set fire to it. I did not go to the groceryman's assistance. The time for such acts had already passed. Civilization was crumbling, and it was each for himself."

IV

"I went away hastily, down a cross-street, and at the first corner I saw another tragedy. Two men of the working class had caught a man and a woman with two children, and were robbing them. I knew the man by sight, though I had never been introduced to him. He was a poet whose verses I had long admired. Yet I did not go to his help, for at the moment I came upon the scene there was a pistol shot, and I saw him sinking to the ground. The woman screamed, and she was felled with a fist-blow by one of the brutes. I cried out threateningly, whereupon they discharged their pistols at me and I ran away around the corner. Here I was blocked by an advancing conflagration. The buildings on both sides were burning, and the street was filled with smoke and flame. From somewhere in that murk came a woman's voice calling shrilly for help. But I did not go to her. A man's heart turned to iron amid such scenes, and one heard all too many appeals for help.

"Returning to the corner, I found the two robbers were gone. The poet and his wife lay dead on the pavement. It was a shocking sight. The two children had vanished—whither I could not tell. And I knew, now, why it was that the fleeing persons I encountered slipped along so furtively and with such white faces. In the midst of our civilization, down in our slums and labor-ghettos, we had bred a race of barbarians, of savages; and now, in the time of our calamity, they turned upon us like the wild beasts they were and destroyed us. And they destroyed themselves as well.

"They inflamed themselves with strong drink and committed a thousand atrocities, quarreling and killing one another in the general madness. One group of workingmen I saw, of the better sort, who had banded together, and, with their women and children in their midst, the sick and aged in litters and being carried, and with a number of horses pulling a truck-load of provisions, they were fighting their way out of the city. They made a fine spectacle as they came down the street through the drifting smoke, though they nearly shot me when I first appeared in their path. As they went by, one of their leaders shouted out to me in apologetic explanation. He said they were killing the robbers and looters on sight, and that they had thus banded together as the only means by which to escape the prowlers.

"It was here that I saw for the first time what I was soon to see so often. One of the marching men had suddenly shown the unmistakable mark of the plague. Immediately those about him drew away, and he, without a remonstrance, stepped out of his place to let them pass on. A woman, most probably his wife, attempted to follow him. She was leading a little boy by the hand. But the husband commanded her sternly to go on, while others laid hands on her and restrained her from following him. This I saw, and I saw the man also, with his scarlet blaze of face, step into a doorway on the opposite side of the street. I heard the report of his pistol, and saw him sink lifeless to the ground.

"After being turned aside twice again by advancing fires, I succeeded in getting through to the university. On the edge of the campus I came upon a party of university folk who were going in the direction of the Chemistry Building. They were all family men, and their families were with them, including the nurses and the servants. Professor Badminton greeted me, and I had difficulty in recognizing him. Somewhere he had gone through flames, and his beard was singed off. About his head was a bloody bandage, and his clothes were filthy. He told me he had prowlers, and that his brother had been killed the previous night, in the defence of their dwelling.

"Midway across the campus, he pointed suddenly to Mrs. Swinton's face. The unmistakable scarlet was there. Immediately all the other women set up a screaming and began to run away from her. Her two children were with a nurse, and these also ran with the women. But her husband, Doctor Swinton, remained with her.

"'Go on, Smith,' he told me. 'Keep an eye on the children. As for me, I shall stay with my wife. I know she is as already dead, but I can't leave her. Afterwards, if I escape, I shall come to the Chemistry Building, and do you watch for me and let me in.'

"I left him bending over his wife and soothing her last moments, while I ran to overtake the party. We were the last to be admitted to the Chemistry Building. After that, with our automatic rifles we maintained our isolation. By our plans, we had arranged for a company of sixty to be in this refuge. Instead, every one of the number originally planned had added relatives and friends and whole families until there were over four hundred souls. But the Chemistry Building was large, and, standing by itself, was in no danger of being burned by the great fires that raged everywhere in the city.

"A large quantity of provisions had been gathered, and a food committee took charge of it, issuing rations daily to the various families and groups that arranged themselves into messes. A number of committees were appointed, and we developed a very efficient organization. I was on the committee of defence, though for the first day no prowlers came near. We could see them in the distance, however, and by the smoke of their fires knew that several camps of them were occupying the far edge of the campus. Drunkenness was rife, and often we heard them singing ribald songs or insanely shouting. While the world crashed to ruin about them and all the air was filled with the smoke of its burning, these low creatures gave rein to their bestiality and fought and drank and died. And after all, what did it matter? Everybody died anyway, the good and the bad, the efficients and the weaklings, those that loved to live and those that scorned to live. They passed. Everything passed.

"When twenty-four hours had gone by and no signs of the plague were apparent, we congratulated ourselves and set about digging a well. You have seen the great iron pipes which in those days carried water to all the city-dwellers. We feared that the fires in the city would burst the pipes and empty the reservoirs. So we tore up the cement floor of the central court of the Chemistry Building and dug a well. There were many young men, undergraduates, with us, and we worked night and day on the well. And our fears were confirmed. Three hours before we reached water, the pipes went dry.

"A second twenty-four hours passed, and still the plague did not appear among us. We thought we were saved. But we did not know what I afterwards decided to be true, namely, that the period of the incubation of the plague germs in a human's body was a matter of a number of days. It slew so swiftly when once it manifested itself, that we were led to believe that the period of incubation was equally swift. So, when two days had left us unscathed, we were elated with the idea that we were free of the contagion.

"But the third day disillusioned us. I can never forget the night preceding it. I had charge of the night guards from eight to twelve, and from the roof of the building I watched the passing of all man's glorious works. So terrible were the local conflagrations that all the sky was lighted up. One could read the finest print in the red glare. All the world seemed wrapped in flames. San Francisco spouted smoke and fire from a score of vast conflagrations that were like so many active volcanoes. Oakland, San Leandro, Haywards—all were burning; and to the northward, clear to Point Richmond, other fires were at work. It was an awe-inspiring spectacle. Civilization, my grandsons, civilization was passing in a sheet of flame and a breath of death. At ten o'clock that night, the great powder magazines at Point Pinole exploded in rapid succession. So terrific were the concussions that the strong building rocked as in an earthquake, while every pane of glass was broken. It was then that I left the roof and went down the long corridors, from room to room, quieting the alarmed women and telling them what had happened.

"An hour later, at a window on the ground floor, I heard pandemonium break out in the camps of the prowlers. There were cries and screams, and shots from many pistols. As we afterward conjectured, this fight had been precipitated by an attempt on the part of those that were well to drive out those that were sick. At any rate, a number of the plague-stricken prowlers escaped across the campus and drifted against our doors. We warned them back, but they cursed us and discharged a fusillade from their pistols. Professor Merryweather, at one of the windows, was instantly killed, the bullet striking him squarely between the eyes. We opened fire in turn, and all the prowlers fled away with the exception of three. One was a woman. The plague was on them and they were reckless. Like foul fiends, there in the red glare from the skies, with faces blazing, they continued to curse us and fire at us. One of the men I shot with my own hand. After that the other man and the woman, still cursing us, lay down under our windows, where we were compelled to watch them die of the plague.

"The situation was critical. The explosions of the powder magazines had broken all the windows of the Chemistry Building, so that we were exposed to the germs from the corpses. The sanitary committee was called upon to act, and it responded nobly. Two men were required to go out and remove the corpses, and this meant the probable sacrifice of their own lives, for, having performed the task, they were not to be permitted to reenter the building. One of the professors, who was a bachelor, and one of the undergraduates volunteered. They bade good-bye to us and went forth. They were heroes. They gave up their lives that four hundred others might live. After they had performed their work, they stood for a moment, at a distance, looking at us wistfully. Then they waved their hands in farewell and went away slowly across the campus toward the burning city.

"And yet it was all useless. The next morning the first one of us was smitten with the plague—a little nurse-girl in the family of Professor Stout. It was no time for weak-kneed, sentimental policies. On the chance that she might be the only one, we thrust her forth from the building and commanded her to be gone.

"She went away slowly across the campus, wringing her hands and crying pitifully. We felt like brutes, but what were we to do? There were four hundred of us, and individuals had to be sacrificed.

"In one of the laboratories three families had domiciled themselves, and that afternoon we found among them no less than four corpses and seven cases of the plague in all its different stages.

"Then it was that the horror began. Leaving the dead lie, we forced the living ones to segregate themselves in another room. The plague began to break out among the rest of us, and as fast as the symptoms appeared, we sent the stricken ones to these segregated rooms. We compelled them to walk there by themselves, so as to avoid laying hands on them. It was heartrending. But still the plague raged among us, and room after room was filled with the dead and dying. And so we who were yet clean retreated to the next floor and to the next, before this sea of the dead, that, room by room and floor by floor, inundated the building.

"The place became a charnel house, and in the middle of the night the survivors fled forth, taking nothing with them except arms and ammunition and a heavy store of tinned foods. We camped on the opposite side of the campus from the prowlers, and, while some stood guard, others of us volunteered to scout into the city in quest of horses, motor cars, carts, and wagons, or anything that would carry our provisions and enable us to emulate the banded workingmen I had seen fighting their way out to the open country.

"I was one of these scouts; and Doctor Hoyle, remembering that his motor car had been left behind in his home garage, told me to look for it. We scouted in pairs, and Dombey, a young undergraduate, accompanied me. We had to cross half a mile of the residence portion of the city to get to Doctor Hoyle's home. Here the buildings stood apart, in the midst of trees and grassy lawns, and here the fires had played freaks, burning whole blocks, skipping blocks and often skipping a single house in a block. And here, too, the prowlers were still at their work. We carried our automatic pistols openly in our hands, and looked desperate enough, forsooth, to keep them from attacking us. But at Doctor Hoyle's house the thing happened. Untouched by fire, even as we came to it the smoke of flames burst forth.

"The miscreant who had set fire to it staggered down the steps and out along the driveway. Sticking out of his coat pockets were bottles of whiskey, and he was very drunk. My first impulse was to shoot him, and I have never ceased regretting that I did not. Staggering and maundering to himself, with bloodshot eyes, and a raw and bleeding slash down one side of his bewhiskered face, he was altogether the most nauseating specimen of degradation and filth I had ever encountered. I did not shoot him, and he leaned against a tree on the lawn to let us go by. It was the most absolute, wanton act. Just as we were opposite him, he suddenly drew a pistol and shot Dombey through the head. The next instant I shot him. But it was too late. Dombey expired without a groan, immediately. I doubt if he even knew what had happened to him.

"Leaving the two corpses, I hurried on past the burning house to the garage, and there found Doctor Hoyle's motor car. The tanks were filled with gasoline, and it was ready for use. And it was in this car that I threaded the streets of the ruined city and came back to the survivors on the campus. The other scouts returned, but none had been so fortunate. Professor Fairmead had found a Shetland pony, but the poor creature, tied in a stable and abandoned for days, was so weak from want of food and water that it could carry no burden at all. Some of the men were for turning it loose, but I insisted that we should lead it along with us, so that, if we got out of food, we would have it to eat.

"There were forty-seven of us when we started, many being women and children. The President of the Faculty, an old man to begin with, and now hopelessly broken by the awful happenings of the past week, rode in the motor car with several young children and the aged mother of Professor Fairmead. Wathope, a young professor of English, who had a grievous bullet-wound in his leg, drove the car. The rest of us walked, Professor Fairmead leading the pony.

"It was what should have been a bright summer day, but the smoke from the burning world filled the sky, through which the sun shone murkily, a dull and lifeless orb, blood-red and ominous. But we had grown accustomed to that blood-red sun. With the smoke it was different. It bit into our nostrils and eyes, and there was not one of us whose eyes were not bloodshot. We directed our course to the southeast through the endless miles of suburban residences, travelling along where the first swells of low hills rose from the flat of the central city. It was by this way, only, that we could expect to gain the country.

"Our progress was painfully slow. The women and children could not walk fast. They did not dream of walking, my grandsons, in the way all people walk to-day. In truth, none of us knew how to walk. It was not until after the plague that I learned really to walk. So it was that the pace of the slowest was the pace of all, for we dared not separate on account of the prowlers. There were not so many now of these human beasts of prey. The plague had already well diminished their numbers, but enough still lived to be a constant menace to us. Many of the beautiful residences were untouched by fire, yet smoking ruins were everywhere. The prowlers, too, seemed to have got over their insensate desire to burn, and it was more rarely that we saw houses freshly on fire.

"Several of us scouted among the private garages in search of motor cars and gasoline. But in this we were unsuccessful. The first great flights from the cities had swept all such utilities away. Calgan, a fine young man, was lost in this work. He was shot by prowlers while crossing a lawn. Yet this was our only casualty, though, once, a drunken brute deliberately opened fire on all of us. Luckily, he fired wildly, and we shot him before he had done any hurt.

"At Fruitvale, still in the heart of the magnificent residence section of the city, the plague again smote us. Professor Fairmead was the victim. Making signs to us that his mother was not to know, he turned aside into the grounds of a beautiful mansion. He sat down forlornly on the steps of the front veranda, and I, having lingered, waved him a last farewell. That night, several miles beyond Fruitvale and still in the city, we made camp. And that night we shifted camp twice to get away from our dead. In the morning there were thirty of us. I shall never forget the President of the Faculty. During the morning's march his wife, who was walking, betrayed the fatal symptoms, and when she drew aside to let us go on, he insisted on leaving the motor car and remaining with her. There was quite a discussion about this, but in the end we gave in. It was just as well, for we knew not which ones of us, if any, might ultimately escape.

"That night, the second of our march, we camped beyond Haywards in the first stretches of country. And in the morning there were eleven of us that lived. Also, during the night, Wathope, the professor with the wounded leg, deserted us in the motor car. He took with him his sister and his mother and most of our tinned provisions. It was that day, in the afternoon, while resting by the wayside, that I saw the last airship I shall ever see. The smoke was much thinner here in the country, and I first sighted the ship drifting and veering helplessly at an elevation of two thousand feet. What had happened I could not conjecture, but even as we looked we saw her bow dip down lower and lower. Then the bulkheads of the various gas-chambers must have burst, for, quite perpendicular, she fell like a plummet to the earth.

"And from that day to this I have not seen another airship. Often and often, during the next few years, I scanned the sky for them, hoping against hope that somewhere in the world civilization had survived. But it was not to be. What happened with us in California must have happened with everybody everywhere.

"Another day, and at Niles there were three of us. Beyond Niles, in the middle of the highway, we found Wathope. The motor car had broken down, and there, on the rugs which they had spread on the ground, lay the bodies of his sister, his mother, and himself.

"Wearied by the unusual exercise of continual walking, that night I slept heavily. In the morning I was alone in the world. Canfield and Parsons, my last companions, were dead of the plague. Of the four hundred that sought shelter in the Chemistry Building, and of the forty-seven that began the march, I alone remained—I and the Shetland pony. Why this should be so there is no explaining. I did not catch the plague, that is all. I was immune. I was merely the one lucky man in a million—just as every survivor was one in a million, or, rather, in several millions, for the proportion was at least that."

V

"For two days I sheltered in a pleasant grove where there had been no deaths. In those two days, while badly depressed and believing that my turn would come at any moment, nevertheless I rested and recuperated. So did the pony. And on the third day, putting what small store of tinned provisions I possessed on the pony's back, I started on across a very lonely land. Not a live man, woman, or child, did I encounter, though the dead were everywhere. Food, however, was abundant. The land then was not as it is now. It was all cleared of trees and brush, and it was cultivated.

The food for millions of mouths was growing, ripening, and going to waste. From the fields and orchards I gathered vegetables, fruits, and berries. Around the deserted farmhouses I got eggs and caught chickens. And frequently I found supplies of tinned provisions in the store-rooms.

"A strange thing was what was taking place with all the domestic animals. Everywhere they were going wild and preying on one another. The chickens and ducks were the first to be destroyed, while the pigs were the first to go wild, followed by the cats. Nor were the dogs long in adapting themselves to the changed conditions. There was a veritable plague of dogs. They devoured the corpses, barked and howled during the nights, and in the daytime slunk about in the distance. As the time went by, I noticed a change in their behavior. At first they were apart from one another, very suspicious and very prone to fight. But after a not very long while they began to come together and run in packs. The dog, you see, always was a social animal, and this was true before ever he came to be domesticated by man. In the last days of the world before the plague, there were many many very different kinds of dogs—dogs without hair and dogs with warm fur, dogs so small that they would make scarcely a mouthful for other dogs that were as large as mountain lions. Well, all the small dogs, and the weak types, were killed by their fellows. Also, the very large ones were not adapted for the wild life and bred out. As a result, the many different kinds of dogs disappeared, and there remained, running in packs, the medium-sized wolfish dogs that you know to-day."

"But the cats don't run in packs, Granser," Hoo-Hoo objected.

"The cat was never a social animal. As one writer in the nineteenth century said, the cat walks by himself. He always walked by himself, from before the time he was tamed by man, down through the long ages of domestication, to to-day when once more he is wild.

"The horses also went wild, and all the fine breeds we had degenerated into the small mustang horse you know to-day. The cows likewise went wild, as did the pigeons and the sheep. And that a few of the chickens survived you know yourself. But the wild chicken of to-day is quite a different thing from the chickens we had in those days.

"But I must go on with my story. I travelled through a deserted land. As the time went by I began to yearn more and more for human beings. But I never found one, and I grew lonelier and lonelier. I crossed Livermore Valley and the mountains between it and the great valley of the San Joaquin. You have never seen that valley, but it is very large and it is the home of the wild horse. There are great droves there, thousands and tens of thousands. I revisited it thirty years after, so I know. You think there are lots of wild horses down here in the coast valleys, but they are as nothing compared with those of the San Joaquin. Strange to say, the cows, when they went wild, went back into the lower mountains. Evidently they were better able to protect themselves there.

"In the country districts the ghouls and prowlers had been less in evidence, for I found many villages and towns untouched by fire. But they were filled by the pestilential dead, and I passed by without exploring them. It was near Lathrop that, out of my loneliness, I picked up a pair of collie dogs that were so newly free that they were urgently willing to return to their allegiance to man. These collies accompanied me for many years, and the strains of them are in those very dogs there that you boys have to-day. But in sixty years the collie strain has worked out. These brutes are more like domesticated wolves than anything else."

Hare-Lip rose to his feet, glanced to see that the goats were safe, and looked at the sun's position in the afternoon sky, advertising impatience at the prolixity of the old man's tale. Urged to hurry by Edwin, Granser went on.

"There is little more to tell. With my two dogs and my pony, and riding a horse I had managed to capture, I crossed the San Joaquin and went on to a wonderful valley in the Sierras called Yosemite. In the great hotel there I found a prodigious supply of tinned provisions. The pasture was abundant, as was the game, and the river that ran through the valley was full of trout. I remained there three years in an utter loneliness that none but a man who has once been highly civilized can understand. Then I could stand it no more. I felt that I was going crazy. Like the dog, I was a social animal and I needed my kind. I reasoned that since I had survived the plague, there was a possibility that others had survived. Also, I reasoned that after three years the plague germs must all be gone and the land be clean again.

"With my horse and dogs and pony, I set out. Again I crossed the San Joaquin Valley, the mountains beyond, and came down into Livermore Valley. The change in those three years was amazing. All the land had been splendidly tilled, and now I could scarcely recognize it, such was the sea of rank vegetation that had overrun the agricultural handiwork of man. You see, the wheat, the vegetables, and orchard trees had always been cared for and nursed by man, so that they were soft and tender. The weeds and wild bushes and such things, on the contrary, had always been fought by man, so that they were tough and resistant. As a result, when the hand of man was removed, the wild vegetation smothered and destroyed practically all the domesticated vegetation. The coyotes were greatly increased, and it was at this time that I first encountered wolves, straying in twos and threes and small packs down from the regions where they had always persisted.

"It was at Lake Temescal, not far from the one-time city of Oakland, that I came upon the first live human beings. Oh, my grandsons, how can I describe to you my emotion, when, astride my horse and dropping down the hillside to the lake, I saw the smoke of a campfire rising through the trees. Almost did my heart stop beating. I felt that I was going crazy. Then I heard the cry of a babe—a human babe. And dogs barked, and my dogs answered. I did not know but what I was the one human alive in the whole world. It could not be true that here were others—smoke, and the cry of a babe.

"Emerging on the lake, there, before my eyes, not a hundred yards away, I saw a man, a large man. He was standing on an outjutting rock and fishing. I was overcome. I stopped my horse. I tried to call out but could not. I waved my hand. It seemed to me that the man looked at me, but he did not appear to wave. Then I laid my head on my arms there in the saddle. I was afraid to look again, for I knew it was an hallucination, and I knew that if I looked the man would be gone. And so precious was the hallucination, that I wanted it to persist yet a little while. I knew, too, that as long as I did not look it would persist.

"Thus I remained, until I heard my dogs snarling, and a man's voice. What do you think the voice said? I will tell you. It said: '*Where in hell did you come from??*'

"Those were the words, the exact words. That was what your other grandfather said to me, Hare-Lip, when he greeted me there on the shore of Lake Temescal fifty-seven years ago. And they were the most ineffable words I have ever heard. I opened my eyes, and there he stood before me, a large, dark, hairy man, heavy-jawed, slant-browed, fierce-eyed. How I got off my horse I do not know. But it seemed that the next I knew I was clasping his hand with both of mine and crying. I would have embraced him, but he was ever a narrow-minded, suspicious man, and he drew away from me. Yet did I cling to his hand and cry."

Granser's voice faltered and broke at the recollection, and the weak tears streamed down his cheeks while the boys looked on and giggled.

"Yet did I cry," he continued, "and desire to embrace him, though the Chauffeur was a brute, a perfect brute—the most abhorrent man I have ever known. His name was . . . strange, how I have forgotten his name. Everybody called him Chauffeur—it was the name of his occupation, and it stuck. That is how, to this day, the tribe he founded is called the Chauffeur Tribe.

"He was a violent, unjust man. Why the plague germs spared him I can never understand. It would seem, in spite of our old metaphysical notions about absolute justice, that there is no justice in the universe. Why did he live?—an iniquitous, moral monster, a blot on the face of nature, a cruel, relentless, bestial cheat as well. All he could talk about was motor cars, machinery, gasoline, and garages—and especially, and with huge delight, of his mean pilferings and sordid swindlings of the persons who had employed him in the days before the coming of the plague. And yet he was spared, while hundreds of millions, yea, billions, of better men were destroyed.

"I went on with him to his camp, and there I saw her, Vesta, the one woman. It was glorious and . . . pitiful. There she was, Vesta Van Warden, the young wife of John Van Warden, clad in rags, with marred and scarred and toil-calloused hands, bending over the campfire and doing scullion work—she, Vesta, who had been born to the purple of the greatest baronage of wealth the world had ever known. John Van Warden, her husband, worth one billion, eight hundred millions and President of the Board of Industrial Magnates, had been the ruler of America. Also, sitting on the International Board of Control, he had been one of the seven men who ruled the world. And she herself had come of equally noble stock. Her father, Philip Saxon, had been President of the Board of Industrial Magnates up to the time of his death. This office was in process of becoming hereditary, and had Philip Saxon had a son that son would have succeeded him. But his only child was Vesta, the perfect flower of generations of the highest culture this planet has ever produced. It was not until the engagement between Vesta and Van Warden took place, that Saxon indicated the latter as his successor. It was, I am sure, a political marriage. I have reason to believe that Vesta never really loved her husband in the mad passionate way of which the poets used to sing. It was more like the marriages that obtained among crowned heads in the days before they were displaced by the Magnates.

"And there she was, boiling fish-chowder in a soot-covered pot, her glorious eyes inflamed by the acrid smoke of the open fire. Hers was a sad story. She was the one survivor in a million, as I had been, as the Chauffeur had been. On a crowning eminence of the Alameda Hills, overlooking San Francisco Bay, Van Warden had built a vast summer palace. It was surrounded by a park of a thousand acres. When the plague broke out, Van Warden sent her there. Armed guards patrolled the boundaries of the park, and nothing entered in the way of provisions or even mail matter that was not first fumigated. And yet did the plague enter, killing the guards at their posts, the servants at their tasks, sweeping away the whole army of retainers—or, at least, all of them who did not flee to die elsewhere. So it was that Vesta found herself the sole living person in the palace that had become a charnel house.

"Now the Chauffeur had been one of the servants that ran away. Returning, two months afterward, he discovered Vesta in a little summer pavilion where there had been no deaths and where she had established herself. He was a brute. She was afraid, and she ran away and hid among the trees. That night, on foot, she fled into the mountains—she, whose tender feet and delicate body had never known the bruise of stones nor the scratch of briars. He followed, and that night he caught her. He struck her. Do you understand? He beat her with those terrible fists of his and made her his slave. It was she who had to gather the firewood, build the fires, cook, and do all the degrading camp-labor—she, who had never performed a menial act in her life. These things he compelled her to do, while he, a proper savage, elected to lie around camp and look on. He did nothing, absolutely nothing, except on occasion to hunt meat or catch fish."

"Good for Chauffeur," Hare-Lip commented in an undertone to the other boys. "I remember him before he died. He was a corker. But he did things, and he made things go. You know, Dad married his daughter, an' you ought to see the way he knocked the spots outa Dad. The Chauffeur was a son-of-a-gun. He made us kids stand around. Even when he was croaking he reached out for me, once, an' laid my head open with that long stick he kept always beside him."

Hare-Lip rubbed his bullet head reminiscently, and the boys returned to the old man, who was maundering ecstatically about Vesta, the squaw of the founder of the Chauffeur Tribe.

"And so I say to you that you cannot understand the awfulness of the situation. The Chauffeur was a servant, understand, a servant. And he cringed, with bowed head, to such as she. She was a lord of life, both by birth and by marriage. The destinies of millions, such as he, she carried in the hollow of her pink-white hand. And, in the days before the plague, the slightest contact with such as he would have been pollution. Oh, I have seen it. Once, I remember, there was Mrs. Goldwin, wife of one of the great magnates. It was on a landing stage, just as she was embarking in her private dirigible, that she dropped her parasol. A servant picked it up and made the mistake of handing it to her—to her, one of the greatest royal ladies of the land! She shrank back, as though he were a leper, and indicated her secretary to receive it. Also, she ordered her secretary to ascertain the creature's name and to see that he was immediately discharged from service. And such a woman was Vesta Van Warden. And her the Chauffeur beat and made his slave.

"—Bill—that was it; Bill, the Chauffeur. That was his name. He was a wretched, primitive man, wholly devoid of the finer instincts and chivalrous promptings of a cultured soul. No, there is no absolute justice, for to him fell that wonder of womanhood, Vesta Van Warden. The grievous-ness of this you will never understand, my grandsons; for you are yourselves primitive little savages, unaware of aught else but savagery. Why should Vesta not have been mine? I was a man of culture and refinement, a professor in a great university. Even so, in the time before the plague, such was her exalted position, she would not have deigned to know that I existed. Mark, then, the abysmal degradation to which she fell at the hands of the Chauffeur. Nothing less than the destruction of all mankind had made it possible that I should know her, look in her eyes, converse with her, touch her hand—ay, and love her and know that her feelings toward me were very kindly. I have reason to believe that she, even she, would have loved me, there being no other man in the world except the Chauffeur. Why, when it destroyed eight billions of souls, did not the plague destroy just one more man, and that man the Chauffeur?

"Once, when the Chauffeur was away fishing, she begged me to kill him. With tears in her eyes she begged me to kill him. But he was a strong and violent man, and I was afraid. Afterwards, I talked with him. I offered him my horse, my pony, my dogs, all that I possessed, if he would give Vesta to me. And he grinned in my face and shook his head. He was very insulting. He said that in the old days he had been a servant, had been dirt under the feet of men like me and of women like Vesta, and that now he had the greatest lady in the land to be servant to him and cook his food and nurse his brats. 'You had your day before the plague,' he said; 'but this is my day, and a damned good day it is. I wouldn't trade back to the old times for anything.' Such words he spoke, but they are not his words. He was a vulgar, low-minded man, and vile oaths fell continually from his lips.

"Also, he told me that if he caught me making eyes at his woman he'd wring my neck and give her a beating as well. What was I to do? I was afraid. He was a brute. That first night, when I discovered the camp, Vesta and I had great talk about the things of our vanished world. We talked of art, and books, and poetry; and the Chauffeur listened and grinned and sneered. He was bored and angered by our way of speech which he did not comprehend, and finally he spoke up and said: 'And this is Vesta Van Warden, one-time wife of Van Warden the Magnate—a high and stuck-up beauty, who is now my squaw. Eh, Professor Smith, times is changed, times is changed. Here, you, woman, take off my moccasins, and lively about it. I want Professor Smith to see how well I have you trained.'

"I saw her clench her teeth, and the flame of revolt rise in her face. He drew back his gnarled fist to strike, and I was afraid, and sick at heart. I could do nothing to prevail against him. So I got up to go, and not be witness to such indignity. But the Chauffeur laughed and threatened me with a beating if I did not stay and behold. And I sat there, perforce, by the campfire on the shore of Lake Temescal, and saw Vesta, Vesta Van Warden, kneel and remove the moccasins of that grinning, hairy, apelike human brute.

"—Oh, you do not understand, my grandsons. You have never known anything else, and you do not understand.

"'Halter-broke and bridle-wise,' the Chauffeur gloated, while she performed that dreadful, menial task. 'A trifle balky at times, Professor, a trifle balky; but a clout alongside the jaw makes her as meek and gentle as a lamb.'

"And another time he said: 'We've got to start all over and replenish the earth and multiply. You're handicapped, Professor. You ain't got no wife, and we're up against a regular Garden-of-Eden proposition. But I ain't proud. I'll tell you what, Professor.' He pointed at their little infant, barely a year old. 'There's your wife, though you'll have to wait till she grows up. It's rich, ain't it? We're all equals here, and I'm the biggest toad in the splash. But I ain't stuck up—not I. I do you the honor, Professor Smith, the very great honor of betrothing to you my and Vesta Van Warden's daughter. Ain't it cussed bad that Van Warden ain't here to see?'"

VI

"I lived three weeks of infinite torment there in the Chauffeur's camp. And then, one day, tiring of me, or of what to him was my bad effect on Vesta, he told me that the year before, wandering through the Contra Costa Hills to the Straits of Carquinez, across the Straits he had seen a smoke. This meant that there were still other human beings, and that for three weeks he had kept this inestimably precious information from me. I departed at once, with my dogs and horses, and journeyed across the Contra Costa Hills to the Straits. I saw no smoke on the other side, but at Port Costa discovered a small steel barge on which I was able to embark my animals. Old canvas which I found served me for a sail, and a southerly breeze fanned me across the Straits and up to the ruins of Vallejo. Here, on the outskirts of the city, I found evidences of a recently occupied camp.

"Many clam-shells showed me why these humans had come to the shores of the Bay. This was the Santa Rosa Tribe, and I followed its track along the old railroad right of way across the salt marshes to Sonoma Valley. Here, at the old brickyard at Glen Ellen, I came upon the camp. There were eighteen souls all told. Two were old men, one of whom was Jones, a banker. The other was Harrison, a retired pawnbroker, who had taken for wife the matron of the State Hospital for the Insane at Napa. Of all the persons of the city of Napa, and of all the other towns and villages in that rich and populous valley, she had been the only survivor. Next, there were the three young men—Cardiff and Hale, who had been farmers, and Wainwright, a common day-laborer. All three had found wives. To Hale, a crude, illiterate farmer, had fallen Isadore, the greatest prize, next to Vesta, of the women who came through the plague. She was one of the world's most noted singers, and the plague had caught her at San Francisco. She has talked with me for hours at a time, telling me of her adventures, until, at last, rescued by Hale in the Mendocino Forest Reserve, there had remained nothing for her to do but become his wife. But Hale was a good fellow, in spite of his illiteracy. He had a keen sense of justice and right-dealing, and she was far happier with him than was Vesta with the Chauffeur.

"The wives of Cardiff and Wainwright were ordinary women, accustomed to toil with strong constitutions—just the type for the wild new life which they were compelled to live. In addition were two adult idiots from the feeble-minded home at Eldredge, and five or six young children and infants born after the formation of the Santa Rosa Tribe. Also, there was Bertha. She was a good woman, Hare-Lip, in spite of the sneers of your father. Her I took for wife. She was the mother of your father, Edwin, and of yours, Hoo-Hoo. And it was our daughter, Vera, who married your father, Hare-Lip—your father, Sandow, who was the oldest son of Vesta Van Warden and the Chauffeur.

"And so it was that I became the nineteenth member of the Santa Rosa Tribe. There were only two outsiders added after me. One was Mungerson, descended from the Magnates, who wandered alone in the wilds of Northern California for eight years before he came south and joined us. He it was who waited twelve years more before he married my daughter, Mary. The other was Johnson, the man who founded the Utah Tribe. That was where he came from, Utah, a country that lies very far away from here, across the great deserts, to the east. It was not until twenty-seven years after the plague that Johnson reached California. In all that Utah region he reported but three survivors, himself one, and all men. For many years these three men lived and hunted together, until, at last, desperate, fearing that with them the human race would perish utterly from the planet, they headed westward on the possibility of finding women survivors in California. Johnson alone came through the great desert, where his two companions died. He was forty-six years old when he joined us, and he married the fourth daughter of Isadore and Hale, and his eldest son married your aunt, Hare-Lip, who was the third daughter of Vesta and the Chauffeur. Johnson was a strong man, with a will of his own. And it was because of this that he seceded from the Santa Rosans and formed the Utah Tribe at San José. It is a small tribe—there are only nine in it; but, though he is dead, such was his influence and the strength of his breed, that it will grow into a strong tribe and play a leading part in the recivilization of the planet.

"There are only two other tribes that we know of—the Los Angelitos and the Carmelitos. The latter started from one man and woman. He was called Lopez, and he was descended from the ancient Mexicans and was very black. He was a cowherd in the ranges beyond Carmel, and his wife was a maidservant in the great Del Monte Hotel. It was seven years before we first got in touch with the Los Angelitos. They have a good country down there, but it is too warm. I estimate the present population of the world at between three hundred and fifty and four hundred—provided, of course, that there are no scattered little tribes elsewhere in the world. If there be such, we have not heard from them. Since Johnson crossed the desert from Utah, no word nor sign has come from the East or anywhere else. The great world which I knew in my boyhood and early manhood is gone. It has ceased to be. I am the last man who was alive in the days of the plague and who knows the wonders of that far-off time. We, who mastered the planet—its earth, and sea, and sky—and who were as very gods, now live in primitive savagery along the water courses of this California country.

"But we are increasing rapidly—your sister, Hare-Lip, already has four children. We are increasing rapidly and making ready for a new climb toward civilization. In time, pressure of population will compel us to spread out, and a hundred generations from now we may expect our descendants to start across the Sierras, oozing slowly along, generation by generation, over the great continent to the colonization of the East—a new Aryan drift around the world.

"But it will be slow, very slow; we have so far to climb. We fell so hopelessly far. If only one physicist or one chemist had survived! But it was not to be, and we have forgotten everything. The Chauffeur started working in iron. He made the forge which we use to this day. But he was a lazy man, and when he died he took with him all he knew of metals and machinery. What was I to know of such things? I was a classical scholar, not a chemist.. The other men who survived were not educated. Only two things did the Chauffeur accomplish—the brewing of strong drink and the growing of tobacco. It was while he was drunk, once, that he killed Vesta. I firmly believe that he killed Vesta in a fit of drunken cruelty though he always maintained that she fell into the lake and was drowned.

"And, my grandsons, let me warn you against the medicine-men. They call themselves *doctors*, travestying what was once a noble profession, but in reality they are medicine-men, devil-devil men, and they make for superstition and darkness. They are cheats and liars. But so debased and degraded are we, that we believe their lies. They, too, will increase in numbers as we increase, and they will strive to rule us. Yet are they liars and charlatans. Look at young Cross-Eyes, posing as a doctor, selling charms against sickness, giving good hunting, exchanging promises of fair weather for good meat and skins, sending the death-stick, performing a thousand abominations. Yet I say to you, that when he says he can do these things, he lies. I, Professor Smith, Professor James Howard Smith, say that he lies. I have told him so to his teeth. Why has he not sent me the death-stick? Because he knows that with me it is without avail. But you, Hare-Lip, so deeply are you sunk in black superstition that did you awake this night and find the death-stick beside you, you would surely die. And you would die, not because of any virtues in the stick, but because you are a savage with the dark and clouded mind of a savage.

"The doctors must be destroyed, and all that was lost must be discovered over again. Wherefore, earnestly, I repeat unto you certain things which you must remember and tell to your children after you. You must tell them that when water is made hot by fire, there resides in it a wonderful thing called steam, which is stronger than ten thousand men and which can do all man's work for him. There are other very useful things. In the lightning flash resides a similarly strong servant of man, which was of old his slave and which some day will be his slave again.

"Quite a different thing is the alphabet. It is what enables me to know the meaning of fine markings, whereas you boys know only rude picture-writing. In that dry cave on Telegraph Hill, where you see me often go when the tribe is down by the sea, I have stored many books. In them is great wisdom. Also, with them, I have placed a key to the alphabet, so that one who knows picture-writing may also know print. Some day men will read again; and then, if no accident has befallen my cave, they will know that Professor James Howard Smith once lived and saved for them the knowledge of the ancients.

"There is another little device that men inevitably will rediscover. It is called gunpowder. It was what enabled us to kill surely and at long distances. Certain things which are found in the ground, when combined in the right proportions, will make this gunpowder. What these things are, I have forgotten, or else I never knew. But I wish I did know. Then would I make powder, and then would I certainly kill Cross-Eyes and rid the land of superstition—"

"After I am man-grown I am going to give Cross-Eyes all the goats, and meat, and skins I can get, so that he'll teach me to be a doctor," Hoo-Hoo asserted. "And when I know, I'll make everybody else sit up and take notice. They'll get down in the dirt to me, you bet."

The old man nodded his head solemnly, and murmured:

"Strange it is to hear the vestiges and remnants of the complicated Aryan speech falling from the lips of a filthy little skin-clad savage. All the world is topsy-turvy. And it has been topsy-turvy ever since the plague."

"You won't make me sit up," Hare-Lip boasted to the would-be medicine-man. "If I paid you for a sending of the death-stick and it didn't work, I'd bust in your head—understand, you Hoo-Hoo, you?"

"I'm going to get Granser to remember this here gunpowder stuff," Edwin said softly, "and then I'll have you all on the run. You, Hare-Lip, will do my fighting for me and get my meat for me, and you, Hoo-Hoo, will send the death-stick for me and make everybody afraid. And if I catch Hare-Lip trying to bust your head, Hoo-Hoo, I'll fix him with that same gunpowder. Granser ain't such a fool as you think, and I'm going to listen to him and some day I'll be boss over the whole bunch of you."

The old man shook his head sadly, and said:

"The gunpowder will come. Nothing can stop it—the same old story over and over. Man will increase, and men will fight. The gunpowder will enable men to kill millions of men, and in this way only, by fire and blood, will a new civilization, in some remote day, be evolved. And of what profit will it be? Just as the old civilization passed, so will the new. It may take fifty thousand years to build, but it will pass. All things pass. Only remain cosmic force and matter, ever in flux, ever acting and reacting and realizing the eternal types—the priest, the soldier, and the king. Out of the mouths of babes comes the wisdom of all the ages. Some will fight, some will rule, some will pray; and all the rest will toil and suffer sore while on their bleeding carcasses is reared again, and yet again, without end, the amazing beauty and surpassing wonder of the civilized state. It were just as well that I destroyed those cave-stored books—whether they remain or perish, all their old truths will be discovered, their old lies lived and handed down. What is the profit—"

Hare-Lip leaped to his feet, giving a quick glance at the pasturing goats and the afternoon sun.

"Gee!" he muttered to Edwin, "The old geezer gets more long-winded every day. Let's pull for camp."

While the other two, aided by the dogs, assembled the goats and started them for the trail through the forest, Edwin stayed by the old man and guided him in the same direction. When they reached the old right of way, Edwin stopped suddenly and looked back. Hare-Lip and Hoo-Hoo and the dogs and the goats passed on. Edwin was looking at a small herd of wild horses which had come down on the hard sand. There were at least twenty of them, young colts and yearlings and mares, led by a beautiful stallion which stood in the foam at the edge of the surf, with arched neck and bright wild eyes, sniffing the salt air from off the sea.

"What is it?" Granser queried.

"Horses," was the answer. "First time I ever seen 'em on the beach. It's the mountain lions getting thicker and thicker and driving 'em down."

The low sun shot red shafts of light, fan-shaped, up from a cloud-tumbled horizon. And close at hand, in the white waste of shore-lashed waters, the sea-lions, bellowing their old primeval chant, hauled up out of the sea on the black rocks and fought and loved.

"Come on, Granser," Edwin prompted. And old man and boy, skin-clad and barbaric, turned and went along the right of way into the forest in the wake of the goats.

THE BEAUTIFUL BACILLUS

PATRICK DUTTON

The recent death of my poor friend Erasmus Polen removes whatever restriction I formerly felt on the subject of the disclosures I am about to make. These disclosures involve not only the sad fate of my friend who for the last few months of his life was confined in a mad house, but they cast light also upon the disappearance of Professor Glissop.

In regard to this last mentioned circumstance, indeed, I do not feel justified in longer withholding the facts, completely exonerating as they do the memory of my friend Polen. Nor is my position, as executor of the small estate he left, incompatible with permitting in the interest of Science the publication of the voluminous diary and other papers which have come into my possession, and which record, for the most part in Polen's handwriting, and with all possible technical accuracy, certain startling researchers into the dark and unfathomed domain of the origin of life. Awaiting the editing of which voluminous scientific data at the hands of those better qualified for the task than I am. I shall here outline briefly and so far as I can in untechnical language, the whole matter—a matter that for all its scientific verification seems to soar into the realm of unbelievable fantasy, like a tragedy of daylight fact linked to a weird and incredible dream. And were it all from beginning to end only the record of an insane delusion, it would still be remarkable enough as such to challenge attention.

It will be remembered that the disappearance of Professor Glissop some six months ago caused a sensation in the world of scholars and was not altogether unnoticed at the time by the public journals. There was a good deal of speculation rife at the time. But beyond casting undeserved suspicion upon the man Polen, who was the companion of the Professor's solitary labors, the news side of the story has died a natural death from want of material to speculate about. Indeed the chief element in the whole occurrence was the eminence of Andrew Glissop. Outside of this the facts were simple. Known to be deeply immersed in his studies, the Professor gradually withdrew from what slight social acquaintance he possessed, spending all his time in that laboratory of his in his back garden, at last even having his meals brought out to him from the house by a servant, and sleeping there, alone save for the company of Erasmus Polen his assistant, and finally was seen no more. Nor did all this occasion undue comment until later.

It is probable that Glissop was last seen by his housekeeper somewhere about the middle of July 1927. He happened to be crossing his yard to go into his laboratory. The woman exchanged a few remarks with him of a commonplace character, and remembered afterwards having noticed on that occasion, as indeed she had on other occasions immediately preceding it, the man's haggard look, and his shrunken appearance, as though his clothes were too large for him. This laboratory of his was a brick building two stories in height. It had originally been a stable belonging to the house. The Professor's dwelling was an old frame structure facing on the little tree-shaded lane known as Hilliard Place, in the city of Cambridge, Mass.—an isolated remnant of an earlier Colonial period, surrounded and hemmed in by buildings of a newer type which had supplanted the original ones. The house stood, and still stands, back from the street, in a recess of its own, its yard running through the block, and this yard containing a small garden, much neglected. At the foot of the garden was the door, by which the Professor in going from his house was accustomed to enter the stable building which faced on another street. The interior of this latter building had been transformed into a laboratory, containing the most modern appliances, at first for biological and later for bacteriological research.

Here it was that Professor Glissop, having in his sixtieth year or thereabout severed the last remaining link of his connection with the University by the abandonment of his post-graduate courses in evolutionary biology, devoted his whole time to experimental work. It is not generally known outside a certain narrow University circle that Glissop began his career as an instructor in Greek, though it, is known that he was a man of wide interests and attainments, whose works on various subjects, from mining geology to the chemistry of foods, have had their day as the last word of their time in text books in their respective fields. But as is the case with many scholars and men of science, he appears in later life to have narrowed his field, until at last the master of so much erudition concentrated the whole of his genius upon one particular line of experiment in the wide range of the field of biology, namely, the attempt to solve the riddle of the origin of the lower forms of life, or rather, it would be more in character with the Professor him self to say, the attempt to add some considerable data to results already attained in that direction.

Beyond this it is to be noticed simply that, having no family ties, it was easy for him to drop in the end all social duties, and appear to the world of men only in a semi-occasional address before some learned body. The last of these—to mention a single instance—was a paper read in Philadelphia about three years ago on "The bacterium of Davaino's septicæmia in rabbits," which strangely enough, because of its conservative tone drew but little attention even from those to whose intelligence it was directly addressed. And so Professor Glissop by degrees became completely immersed and absorbed in his chosen work, shut off from all human intercourse except that of his sole companion and assistant, my friend Erasmus Polen.

Polen and I used sometimes to play chess together of an evening. I mention this circumstance, though it has no particular bearing on my narrative, because it was in this connection that I first realized a certain change in Polen.

I think it was a little over a year ago that, dropping in at Polen's lodgings one evening on Walker Street, I found he had given them up and had gone to live with Glissop at Hilliard Place. A few days later I ran across him taking a late afternoon stroll and was struck by a strange, melancholy look in his eyes. Polen's eyes were ordinarily large and dark, and possessed a direct and challenging keenness, an expression at once daring and sensitive, a kind of wistful fearlessness often seen in the eyes of scholars. I noticed now that they wore a look of drugged steadiness. They were like the eyes of one who has been brought face to face with a realization of some terrible nature and cannot shake himself free of its spell. That is as near as I can come to a description of the look he wore. I stopped him and spoke to him, and we went to dinner together at the nearby Hotel Commander. After dinner we strolled around to my rooms, and as I got out the chess board and started to set up the pieces, I rallied him on his melancholy appearance.

"I don't know," he said, "what is the matter with me. Overwork—I guess. These experiments—" He broke off there with his sentence unfinished, heaved a sigh and stared darkly ahead of him, his eyes glistening with that unnatural light I had noticed.

"Why don't you bring your violin around and let us try some duets together?" I suggested.

He looked vacantly at me. "What's that? Oh, my violin. I haven't touched it for months."

I should have said that Erasmus Polen was something of a musician, his particular devotion being the violin, and that for a short period he had actually supported himself as a member of a Boston orchestra before he became Glissop's assistant.

We were soon deep in a chess game and I now noticed a peculiar circumstance. Whereas formerly I had invariably won from Polen something like four games out of five, he now beat me from the start with provoking ease. After three straight defeats, I am afraid I showed a little irritation, but Polen set up the pieces again without appearing to notice anything out of the way in my manner. In fact, he played the game in a queerly abstracted way, which dawned on me as something quite odd. Instead of studying the board before making his moves, he took a single swift glance at it and then leaned back with his eyes shut as though to impress on his retina the picture of the various chess pieces and their location and inter-relation. And then, after some moments of thought, he looked down again with that same expression of drugged steadiness and made his move. It seemed to me as I watched him with a growing curiosity that long devotion to the microscopic work in bacteriology, in which I knew him to be engaged, instead of bringing about the weakening of his eyesight, had perhaps trained it and developed his powers of visualization to an abnormal extent. At least, so I put it down at the time.

We were in the middle of this fourth game and I had gained, as I supposed, a slight advantage in the exchange of a knight for a bishop when he suddenly rose, seized his hat and took his departure without a word.

The next time my friend dropped in to see me, I noticed with alarm that he looked fairly sick. His eyes now glared in an unhealthy way. I tried to cheer him up and suggested our unfinished game. He looked blank and unresponsive until I brought out the board and showed him the pieces as we had left them.

"Oh, yes—the game," he observed absently. "Why, you've won," he said with a quick glance at the board. "See here—"

"Hold on," I interrupted. "I'm white, not black."

"Oh," he said, "I'm black, am I? Well then you've lost and I've won. Don't you see? I'll show you." And he proceeded to demonstrate what he called a complex, tactical plan by which my queen was lost in four moves, resulting in a strategic plan, which indicated by the sacrifice of a rook and queen on his part, a final check mate in some seven to ten moves more It was almost too intricate for me to follow. Certainly it was too deep for me to have discovered alone. And this, I thought, is the man I used to beat at chess.

"What book on the game have you been boning up on recently?" I asked him.

"Nothing," he replied in his jerky way. "Too busy—and besides I'm not well. Can't touch anything outside my work. My work—"

Then he broke off and sat down and stared at the mantelpiece with that unnatural, fixed glare.

"I advise you to knock off work then," I rejoined. "You look pretty sick. Why don't you try your violin for a relaxation?" But indeed, sick as he looked, his faculties appeared in some way to have been amazingly quickened.

Polen must have taken my advice at last about the violin, for, some time after, hurrying along the street upon which Professor Glissop's laboratory faced, I heard sounds issuing thence. It was late on a dreary, rainy evening. Pausing in my walk and standing still a moment, I detected a low soft music blending with the monotonous swish of the rain—a kind of fugue with strophe and antistrophe repeated. Hardly at first did the tones seem those of a violin, so low and flute-like were they. I cannot describe this weird music. I can only say I stood there in the rain and drizzle, fascinated, for quite a long while, until the sounds ceased, and then, looking at my watch, hurried on. And this, strange to say, was the last time I ever sensibly heard from my poor friend. It was in fact his farewell to me—though both of us were unaware of it at the time, and he, shut up inside that brick building, was unaware even of my presence in the damp and cold outside, as listening to his music, I shrank under the eaves close to the wall to escape the drip from the roof above. For I had to leave town on business early that summer, and later went abroad.

When I returned one of the first things I undertook was to look up Erasmus Polen. I went around to Professor Glissop's house on Hilliard Place. To be exact, it was the Second of last May—a Wednesday afternoon. I found the housekeeper in a state of fearful and hysterical trepidation. She had sent for several gentlemen living in Cambridge—former friends of her master. I was to learn that for months the two men—Glissop and Polen—had shut themselves up in the laboratory. That she had been bringing their meals out there to them. That for the last two days Polen, who usually came to the door to meet her, had refused to answer her knock, though she had caught a glimpse of him through an upper window. And that the door of the laboratory was locked. After some discussion, we all adjourned to the yard, crossed the garden and knocked upon the door without receiving any answer. We then forced the door and went in. The lower floor was deserted. It still gave evidence of its former use as a stable. The stalls for horses were swept clean and bare. I called up the stairs. As if for answer, all at once on the still air there floated down the soft wonderful sounds of Polen's violin. Enchanted for the moment and held spellbound, we all of us remained standing there at the foot of the stairs. Then I started to tip-toe part way up. I think the others followed close on my heels. The music meanwhile seemed to grow faster and louder. A rhapsodical abandon carried it almost to the point of screeching. Then came a crash.

We sprang up, all together, threw open the door of the laboratory and came upon Erasmus Polen, his hands pressed to his eyes, pacing the floor, a veritable mad man, as it was soon ascertained. And the broken violin with its bow was lying upon a table, whereon beside it lay also a great open notebook or diary in which Polen, as we afterwards discovered, had been for a long time past writing.

But there was no sign anywhere of the Professor. Careful search revealed nothing save a suit of his clothing with some underwear and shoes cast to one side in the sleeping apartment and covered with the dust of several months. Nor indeed could even my poor demented friend's broken ejaculations—crazed as he appeared to be with the pain of his eyes—furnish the slightest hint in regard to this mysterious and complete disappearance of Professor Andrew Glissop.

But it is this diary of Polen's to which I have just alluded, whose acid-stiffened and soiled pages have made clear what I heard and saw on that fateful Wednesday afternoon on the Second of May, 1928—have unfolded indeed a tale so strange and fascinating, that far as it delves into dark and hitherto unexplored regions of scientific hypothesis, so far does it also wander into the region of pure imagination. For never a weird, uncanny tragedy could be more unbelievable or more grotesquely big with atrabiliar symbolism than this one which played itself out unnoticed of mankind in that dingy little brick stable belonging to the house on Hilliard Place.

Technical as the whole matter is in its details, I can here give but a sketchy outline which shall nevertheless perhaps furnish to the lay mind a clearer picture than would a faithful scientific critique, were I qualified to compose such. Nor am I qualified either to venture a determination as to how far Polen's insanity may have reached back into the record he kept, or at what point that change from fact to delusion took place, if indeed it occurred at all. I must leave that to others.

It was, as I have said, inquiries into the causative phenomena of life, which in his later years, and to the exclusion of everything else, attracted Andrew Glissop. Familiar as he must have been with previous work in that direction—such as experiments on the lower forms of life in sea-water—he seems to have begun his search for the origin of life from a unique standpoint, to wit, investigations into the realm of disease. That is about as succinctly as I can put the matter. And here, at the very start, appears evidence of a certain surprising originality and untramelled quality of the man's mind, something surprising indeed, I am led to infer, even to his former associates in the University. For, whereas all of Glissop's predecessors have studied and isolated the germs of various diseases with the sole object of discovering an antitoxin, he himself abandoned this so to say hostile method as "too humanly self-centered," to use his own words as reported in Polen's diary, and adopted in its place an attitude of approach, the most truly scientific it is possible for anyone to conceive.

There is to be observed in this connection, the general truth that the majority of thinkers and investigators pursue their work fettered by an inherited fringe of folkways. It is only the few who can cast off a garment of tradition, which restricts every movement of the intellect and let their souls soar naked and unconfined in the awful realms of pure spirit. Of this rare company of the great was Glissop, in the light of whole achievement, we can now look back and realize the narrow and so-to-speak provincial quality of those minds, however acute as compared to the average, whose sole object in the study of bacteria has been benefit to man and persistent harm, nay death and obliteration, to the bacteria! For Professor Glissop, with an intellectual honesty so great as to be almost beyond appreciation, cast from him in his search for truth the very remembrance of his own connection with the human race and approached the phenomena of disease, so-called, free of any possible enmity, temporal or eternal. And thus did he accomplish naught else, he did for Bacteriology what Kant did for Metaphysics, Einstein for Space, Nietzsche for Ethics and Spangler for History—established a Critique of Pure Investigation.

Glissop's extraordinary clearness of vision seems to have led him very early to thus abandon the field of toxins, a field in which he felt himself as absurdly confined as would, for instance, an historian of the Life of the German People who should be forced to stake his entire thesis upon the somewhat foreign proposition of resistance to an Invasion of France! Glissop took up at the start the question of living tissues considered as food for the disease germs, trying throughout to discover what these germs actually were in themselves under the utmost favorable circumstances for the development of their life histories. His experiments covered a period of years and were productive of an encyclopedic mass of data, enlarged photographs, tabulated charts and mathematical and chemical formulas. He also, in the course of this work, succeeded in detecting and isolating several new forms of schizomycetes or bacteria. One of the results obtained incidental to the general mass of the work of these years and small compared to his later results, has yet a certain interest as bearing upon those results. It appeared that given a colony of germs in living tissue, the germs in some rare cases, by a gradual infusion of mineral substance, can be weaned from the living tissue and made to generate themselves in a medium of saline solution, being wholly artificial and dead in the ordinary accepted sense. To this extent the Professor did bridge over the supposed chasm between live and dead matter, a chasm which appears such at a distance but which to use his own words "upon approach is seen to be a beautiful valley over grown with the flowers of significant truths, connecting two noble mountains, easy of descent and passage."

And here I must ask the reader's patience to dwell a moment on a somewhat theoretical aspect of the Professor's work. I feel I must at least attempt to convey something of that aspect of it, since it is so intimately related to the strange facts which later took place.

For, at this point—the isolation of certain living germs in dead mineral matter—as it happened, the Professor conceived a rather novel and inventive application to his experiment of two simple truths and thus applying them, attained a result hitherto unknown to Science. The first of these truths is one which impinges especially, upon the imagination of the student of geology and astronomy. "The gradual transformations, the casting of mountains into the sea, nay the moulding and spinning of planets, are but the matters of a moment. Compared to the great infinity of the Time Sense mirrored in the human soul, they are as rapid as the interlocking of atoms in a chemical reaction."

The second truth is taken from the domain of Speculative Mechanics and is stated by Glissop to be the "actual existence independent of the Time-Space Category of an unchangeable norm of size." So far as I can make out, the Professor here is thinking of the familiar relation of linears and solids by which an increase in length of 2 involves an increase in size not of 2 but of 8. For he goes on to say in elucidation, "What is to prevent the world and the entire Universe from shrinking suddenly or at a given rate to one half or one millionth of its size, or from expanding in the same manner? Or if such a thing happened, how would I, changing with it, be able to know the fact—how feel different from a man, whose back turned to an observer, walks away from that observer absolutely unconscious of his own various changes in size on the perspective of the observer's picture, himself bearing with him ever the actuality of the unchangeable norm of size? Or why could not this observed man with equal ease and unconsciousness remain stationary and shrink? The answer is that the illusion of relative size may be kept indistinguishably constant, as for instance in a photographic enlargement or reduction. But the slightest alteration of the actual size of reality itself would mean a disarrangement of gravitational movement, so that the system of things would crack apart at once." Whatever this may mean I leave to the reader. Glissop seems to hint, further, in discussing planets and atoms, that chemical affinity may be nothing other than "gravity in a different relation to this unchangeable norm of size." I And still further on he drifts into the identification of Space and Time as one thing and thus attains, as he himself admits, much the same result as Kant did by his external negation and Einstein by his relativity.

But even with these brief extracts, I am afraid I am following the Professor's search for truth into realms too abstruse and mathematical for either myself or the reader to exist in comfortably. Consequently I will leave them as they stand and abandon once for all this metaphysical accompaniment of Glissop's experiments, an accompaniment which runs through his entire work like an harmonious diapason supporting and rounding out a melody, and having already gotten beyond my own depth, will return straightway to a simple narrative of the facts.

The idea came to Glissop then, to put the matter in simple language, while pondering on the suggestive contrast exhibited in the life of germs, of men and animals and of stars and planets, to combine in an unusual way these two general truths concerning size and rapidity I have so lamely presented above. And however that novel and original combination was worked out in theory and experiment—a matter too deep and intricate for any attempt to summarize—the facts resulted as I shall show. For it occurred to Glissop in view of the often commented on brevity of human life compared to the demands of scientific observation that inasmuch as the period of a single individual existence like his own could not be sensibly prolonged, it might be a useful thing if could devise a means of outside interference which compress within that period more of the process of evolution, as one might alter the speed of a film of moving pictures. In other words, if he could not prolong the time allotted to himself as observer, he might hasten the speed of the events observed. Accordingly, by concentrating on the task all the powers of his creative intellect, all the resources of his genius, he attempted this vast feat of scientific ingenuity, an attempt which, in its application to the microscopic handling under various conditions of time and space, size and rapidity, of those minute forms of life, both individual and group, known as bacteria, was successful even beyond his hopes.

It often happens with the greatest of discoveries that while looking for one thing the seeker has chanced upon something entirely different. And so this thing also came to pass in the case of Andrew Glissop, who after long years of patient labor in this one avenue of approach to the origin of life, by pure accident fell upon a discovery both startling and tragic. Its tragic results so far as concerned himself he would have been the first to disregard, the last to deplore. But his discovery was in great part at variance with his preconceived metaphysical and scientific hypotheses, even though it grew out of them. So that the long, slowly gestating labors of a lifetime, gradually culminating upon the phenomena of the origin of life, were suddenly, in a few months, torn completely away from their moorings by a dimly realizable and awfully suggestive discovery, which, like an explosion lit up for an instant the mysterious teleological domain of the future of Life and Evolution, and then, carrying with it as two specks of ashes the identity of the one man and the reason of the other whose efforts had blindly lit the fuse, went out in the horror and finality of darkness!

It is here that I must take up again the connection which my friend Erasmus Polen had with these experiments. Polen was for many years an assistant to Professor Glissop in biological work in the University laboratory and when the latter retired from that activity and devoted his time solely to special work with bacteria, Polen, of his own choice, followed him in it. This relation of the two men persisted for a number of years during which Polen was treated more as an equal by his great master than as a paid helper.

The two together must have worked with an almost fanatic devotion and a complete absorption which cut them off from the world of their friends and practically isolated them in that garden laboratory and work shop in the centre of the busy, academic atmosphere of a University town, as much as if they had been alone together on the topmost peak of some unexplored mountain range. And indeed, metaphorically speaking, they were on such a peak—on the heights of scientific attainment unknown to and apart from their fellow men. And there in that loneliness they committed a strange and untraceable mistake which brought them unheralded into the presence of the discovery I am about to relate.

In Professor Glissop's endeavor to increase *the speed of the phenomena of evolution* by means of instruments registering on a sensitive film the exact rate of motion and reproduction of these colonies of bacteria kept alive artificially, he was able to determine the laws of their health and longevity, taking the words in their comparative sense, and to devise chemical and thermal combinations which should produce the most rapid changes in the shortest possible time. It was found that after periods of enforced ill health in conditions of colder temperature, many of the bacilli exhibited increased activity on the renewal of heat. And devices were introduced to cause ever quicker changes of alternating heat and cold in a series of rhythmic pulses. One of these complicated, electrically controlled machines reached the point of increasing the pulses of alternating temperatures to an almost incredible rate of speed, such speed as might be likened best to the vibrations of a violin string in producing a tone.

It was during the latter part of this period of effort in the direction of increasing the rapidity of life that the Professor ventured a hypothesis which, jotted down in Polen's note book, is vividly suggestive, to say the least. Stated in rough form, it is that, Evolution being infinite in time and possibility, the war of the human race and higher mammals with the forces of disease is at the present day probably only in its earliest stages—that the great battles are to come—that the spores of bacilli being the most difficult of all forms of life to destroy, such other forms of life as man, mammals, birds, reptiles and even insects are doomed to perish from any given habitable planet, overcome in turn through long ages of warfare by the indomitable armies of Disease. And these germs, with their life forces of almost indestructible grandeur, are destined millions of aeons in the future to develop on this earth into a race of beings, more and more intelligent, of a size microscopic indeed it may be but thus small enough to be the prey to no smaller forms of life. Along with the gigantic prehistoric animals already extinct, all other species will have perished until these smallest and strongest and least subject to the relentless centripedal pull of nature known as gravitation, will alone survive and unhindered dominate the earth, an earth to them many times larger and more habitable. In consequence they will develop intelligences as superior to ours as they are remote from us by aeons of geologic ages. But as to what these conquerors of men and bees will look like, imagination falters.

It was about this time, which appears in Polen's record to have been away back in August 1926, that the experimenters, aiming to decrease the size of the bacilli until facts bearing on the ultimate cause of their life should be arrived at, found their solutions working unaccountably in the other direction. For the smallest were found to produce in some cases the largest offspring. This was the miscalculation to which I have alluded. There appears to be no explanation of it now available. For, rather than devote their time to the discovery of the cause of their mistake, the two men quickly seized the clue of circumstance thus given them and abandoning previous hypotheses, content to record only new facts in the search for truth wherever they might lead, concentrated their attention entirely for the time upon increasing the size of some of the bacilli, the history of whose colonies had been recorded with the most voluminous painstaking during years of observation. And here sudden and remarkable results awaited them.

One particular culture of the bacillus known as *Spirochæta Glissopi*, transformed already through millions of generations, began to take on a peculiar behavior. Several of the infant spores were weak, but here and there one appeared so much larger and stronger than the parent stem as to give the effect under the microscope of unnaturally gigantic offspring. Also, and strangely enough, reproduction now began to take place through a rudimentary form of sex activity. Isolation of these favored ones, with a view to increasing their size still further, however, invariably brought about death, until the idea of a gradual return to living tissue as the medium of nourishment was put in practice. Whereupon the giants, so-called, began to flourish, and under the application of the rhythmic temperature machine, already mentioned, they produced with amazing rapidity still larger descendants. These were then, some of them, weaned back again as their ancestors countless generations before had been to sustenance upon inorganic chemical solutions. It was found now, that upon isolation of further selected individuals, death did not ensue.

One of these selected individuals, of an ancestry dating back to the original spirochæta, developed more rapidly than the others, but lost the power of reproduction. This bacillus was kept carefully by itself. Within a month it had attained to incredible dimensions. It was actually visible to the naked eye!

A certain laziness of action was now noticeable on the part of the bacillus. In a bowl of solution it swam about but slowly. But it kept on increasing astonishingly in size from day to day, like some wonderful plant growth, and finally—I am now passing over detailed observations of day after day and night after night for a period of nearly a year, and giving in gross the outcome of experiments of such a voluminously complex nature as to stagger the imagination of any but the greatest of scientists—finally the bacillus grew to such proportions that it could be carried downstairs and placed in one of the stalls where formerly horses had been stabled and there, its roots floating in a solution in a glass bowl and its branches clinging to the wall, it was kept in the dark. Sunlight and even indirect rays of any great magnitude, it was noticed, caused it to shrivel. The bacillus was observed henceforth under a dim violet electric light, and photographed from time to time by a flashlight.

There it began to grow like an ivy over the sides of the wall, and one, day, June 14th 1927, Polen discovered its roots drawn up completely out of the bowl containing the saline solution, which had hitherto afforded its sustenance, and called Glissop to witness the fact.

Henceforth, so far as could be known, the strange creature lived upon air. Another unlooked for fact made its appearance before long in this wise. One morning, Polen, entering the laboratory earlier than usual, discovered that the transformed bacillus was missing. He was no sooner joined by Professor Glissop than he communicated this startling news and the two men instituted a search. They finally came upon the fugitive bacillus in a far corner of the lower story of the building, clinging to the wall. One tendril had found its way over the ledge of a little window that was cut high up in the wall of that part of the building. The sunlight outside fell upon the fragile length of the curving tendril. Marvelling greatly at this power of locomotion so displayed by the strange plant-like being, they marveled the more to discover that the tendril exposed to the sunlight had blossomed into a flower of the most wonderfully iridescent and beautiful hues. The blossom was bell-shaped, something like a morning glory, and was joined to the rest of the plant by a slender, fragile neck. But it emitted a strange perfume as of some compound of sulphur.

The Professor at length came to the conclusion that the creature was not only alive but conscious. He drew this amazing inference from certain details connected with the behavior of the tendrils and branches which involved a suggestive resemblance to ganglionic neurons and graded synaptic resistances belonging to a complete nervous system, an array of details too abstruse to be set down here. The stem, unlike the flower, seemed, when exposed to the sunlight, to writhe as though in pain, and always, upon the slightest touch, it shrank away. The creature moved that day back again to its old place in the stall, having as it were deliberately put itself to the pain and agony of giving birth to its blossom in the nearest available sunlight. It regained its former location in darkness with a slow, gradual, creeping motion over the walls. The two scientists watched it, fascinated.

A few days later Polen thought that he observed from time to time a certain rhythmical motion in the bell-shaped flower. And once coming closer, his ears detected a low hum issuing, it seemed, from the inside. This low hum was repeated in certain rhythms. At last, inspired by a sudden revelation, Polen got out his violin and copying thereon the rhythms he heard coming from the flower, produced the most wonderful effect in the creature. Its stalk bristled with a kind of ecstacy, its answering tones came forth louder and with a delicate, flute-like and penetrating quality, and Polen, by a series of experiments of this nature, at last actually established a means of communication between himself and the bacillus, or at least so it seemed. A sort of rhythmical alphabet made of musical phrases, as exquisitely intelligible as it was incapable of translation into the words of any human language. In all this Professor Glissop took now a secondary place. Not being a musician, as was Polen, his ear could not detect and recognize the harmonic relations and meanings of these musical phrases. By comparison of the dates in Polen's record with my own memory, I am able to state that one of the times upon which this process of communication was taking place, coincided with the evening I had stood outside in the rain and listened in spellbound silence to the soft music which had seemed to me to be a kind of fugue, with its repeated strophe and antistrophe.

But it seemed that the Professor, having first put forward the theory of the creature's consciousness and having had it so well corroborated, now went a step further and declared to Polen his opinion that plant-like as it appeared in form, it represented with its visible nerve-like construction, a type of being as much above the human race as the highest pinnacle of the human race is above the lowest sea animal.—A daring hypothesis indeed and one entirely characteristic of Glissop. The bacillus was, he maintained, the realization through artificial stimulation of the forces of Evolution, aeons ahead of its time of that race of bacilli destined finally to overcome all other forms of life on the globe and then to expand into creatures of a sublime intelligence. Glissop further conjectured that the strange creature so recently endowed with consciousness, and which had doubtless passed through certain quasi-embryonic and infant stages of being under their observation, was now in turn observing them, but in a degree a thousand times more severely scientific. And it was also the Professor's opinion that the creature possessing, as he believed, attributes of a keener self-consciousness and a superior intelligence, must of necessity also possess beneficence and the sense of humor to a degree undreamed of by even the most advanced individuals of the human race. As to its beneficence, his conjecture remains unverified. But the sense of humor possessed by the bacillus became once fatally apparent.

For I must now chronicle that tragic accident, which, more serious even than the first mistake in regard to the saline solutions, came to change utterly by a swift and unlooked for interruption the course of Glissop's and Polen's experiment, and eventuated in plunging the whole matter into a horror of inconceivable proportions. As may be imagined, the Professor had been reduced all this time to the necessity of taking Polen's communications with the bacillus at second hand, trying in a helpless way to attach some meaning in words to the harmonies uttered by the bell-shaped blossom. And there is no telling how far this strange intercommunication might have proceeded and to what rare and undreamed-of levels of consciousness beyond thought—if the matter may be so expressed—the minds of the two scientists eventually might have been brought. But it so happened that Glissop, after some reflection, came to a decision to attempt the training of his own ear. The first time he took the violin in his hands under the direction of his assistant, he produced, as might have been expected, tones badly out of tune.

In this absorption, as of a music teacher and pupil at their first lesson, the attention of the two men was momentarily taken away from the strange creature that watched them. Then Polen, happening to glance toward the bacillus, noticed that it was rocking back and forth on its stalk in a paroxysm of what his awakened mind, sensitive from long training to every shade of meaning in phenomena coming before his eyes, recognized immediately to be laughter. Low musical sounds, but choked, were emitted from the flower. The tendrils alternately grasped and let go of the wall of the stall, and once the creature was in imminent danger of falling off altogether and saved itself by a spasmodic clutch. And all this time the Professor, old and bald, standing there in a posture of awkward dignity, unconscious of the flower, his face contracted with a look of extreme and solemn effort, clutching the bow with a certain delicacy but with utter lack of feeling for the proper stress, produced the most exquisitely ludicrous scraping. So that Polen himself at last burst into a paroxysm of uncontrollable merriment. He stepped forward to take the violin away from the Professor. "Here," he cried, "let me have it before both of us die laughing." But he was too late, and his lightly spoken word came, in the case of the bacillus, close upon the awful truth. With one final convulsive heave the bell-shaped flower broke off at the neck, its color faded in an instant, and like a grey piece of gossamer it floated before the eyes of the two awe-stricken beholders carried along on some gentle current of air and disappeared out through the window, while the remaining tendrils of the plant-like creature relaxed their hold upon the side of the stall and slipped to the ground.

The poor beautiful bacillus, advance guard of a far distant race of undreamed of beings, had suffered the realization suddenly forced upon it of the limited, one-sided development of even the highest type of academic and scholarly excellence. Unable to endure longer the sight of a University professor it had, literally, died of laughing!

I come now to the final turn of these events, and how to depict adequately the horror of the situation which gradually closed in upon Erasmus Polen, I do not know. It began shortly after the death of the bacillus, and Professor Glissop, while yet retaining to the full the powers of mind which were destined later to leave him, attributed the change directly to that—to the fact that he and not Polen had reached down to grasp the fallen lifeless vine which crumbled to dust in his hand. Some deadly quality in it, some humanly speaking poisonous emanation, must have entered Glissop's body with his respiration and so produced in him the change which he was to exhibit later, a change which did not come to Polen. And yet from the start Polen's situation was the more horrible of the two. The Professor could but meet an untimely end. His poor assistant, on the other hand, was doomed with all his faculties alert and sympathetic to watch a gradual loss of identity, an awful fate never before meted out to one human being, the observation of it never before offered to the eyes of another.

As nearly as can be ascertained from Polen's records made at the time, it must have been a week after the death of the bacillus, and during a period devoted to a resumption of experiments with the colonies of bacteria whose existence had been in great measure neglected for the study and tabulation of results concerning the one strange individual that had emerged therefrom, experiments now carried on with a view to the production of another, that Polen was made aware of an alteration in the Professor's appearance. Glissop seemed to have shrunk into himself and to have lost an inch or two in height. Absorbed in work as Polen was, this rather extraneous matter was forced finally upon his attention. At first the Professor scouted the idea that anything was the matter with him. But on finding that day by day his shirt collar became too large and his clothes swung more and more loosely about him, he at last admitted the seriousness of the matter and agreed with Polen that something was happening to him. Accordingly at Polen's suggestion both men at once proceeded to place themselves under their own observation. By means of accurate and careful measurements they discovered in a few days, and registered the fact, that Glissop was shrinking at the startling average of 16.64 millimeters or .655 inches per day in height and 46.7 ounces avoirdupois in weight. Polen's weight and measurements remained stationary. That is to say they suffered a slight normal variation in a period of twenty four hours but always returned to an approximate maximum. But Glissop was beyond all question losing in an alarming manner. The thing finally became so pronounced in Glissop's case that it was deemed not only advisable but absolutely necessary for him to avoid notice and to live constantly in the laboratory attended by Polen. Meals were brought to the door by the housekeeper. The young assistant turned his whole attention to observing the strange unidentified disease which had attacked his master, who also devoted his efforts likewise to arranging and classifying these data. Nor did the latter feel the worse for the change, nor worry over his personal safety or what in the end would befall him. Indeed, his sole care at this time seems to have been to make the data of his case as full as possible, his sole fear that some important fact might be overlooked.

It must have been with mingled feelings of horror and interest that Polen watched his master working over these notes from day to day. Several tentative theories were put forward by the great scientist to account for the rapid and yet seemingly unreal because painless changes that came over him. But he admitted frankly from the start that the matter was beyond any safe or reasonable scientific conjecture and lay, so far as he could see, within the realm of the unexplained which is mistakenly denominated the supernatural. And yet every possible medical and scientific test was called into requisition—blood tests, blood pressure, respiration, temperature, fluid analyses, and so on—with the result that so far as the Professor, himself an eminent specialist in diseases of the blood, could ascertain, there was no functional or organic departure from the normal. During this period a fanciful thought came to Polen, and he even went so far as to set it down in his note book. He suggests that the Professor was following the line of his own illustrative reasoning in respect to the norm of size and was simply walking away, his image becoming unconsciously and painlessly smaller in the observer's—Polen's—retinal picture at each succeeding moment of time as he proceeded ever on toward the unknown and the distant. This digression is one of the very few departures from strict recording of fact of which Polen's notes are guilty. There are one or two others which I shall quote later.

At one time, for a period of a month or so, Polen records the fact that he practically deserted his friend, leaving him alone at the work locked up in his laboratory safe from intrusion, and returning only to bring him food. During this period the younger man haunted the stacks of the nearby University library. But it appears that exhaustive examination of the files to date, of medical periodicals and monographs in several languages, failed to reveal anything like the extraordinary case of Professor Glissop, which now bid fair in its early stages to go on record some day as Glissop's disease, had not even more extraordinary events intervened. And so Polen gave up that end of the matter and returned to join forces with Glissop in the observation of this strange disease.

It was four months after the first evidence of shrinking that any abnormal symptom other than shrinkage appeared. The Professor had long since discarded the clothes he had worn up on what was to be his last entrance into the laboratory, which had been the scene of his life's work and where his fate, as yet wholly unrealized, awaited him. He now wore a small wrapper which was part of a bath robe cut down to fit him and tied with a cord, inasmuch as his height had diminished to an incredible extent and was less than four feet, and his weight had gone below fifty pounds. His face hardly retained a trace of that noble expression formerly characteristic of the thinker and scientist. Only the eyes kept their look of penetrating intelligence and almost superhuman concentration. It was, I say, about this time that the first abnormal symptom—abnormal in an evolutionary sense—made its appearance. On the end phalange of Glissop's right forefinger, Polen, with the naked eye detected soft downy hairs which the day before had not been noticed under the microscope This growth increased and spread until in a week unmistakable hairs appeared on the first joint of every finger of both hands. The Professor's mind at once grasped the significance of this marked Simian characteristic. "I suspect," he said, his shrunken features irradiated as with a smile of triumph, so great was the man's absorption in the strange eventuation of the deep task which had engaged the ardor of his life, "I suspect that I am about to undergo some mutation, whether temporary or permanent I do not know, which may involve a lowering of my mental vitality equally with physical changes in a direction exactly contrary to the known laws of Evolution. The changes might be called involution or even degradation. It may be sudden. And I consider Science fortunate that, thus isolated as we are from extraneous interference, the minute stages of this interesting process are to be under the observation of one like yourself, my dear friend and helper, so well qualified to observe."

The Professor then followed with directions covering many points in respect to the observation of the phenomena of the evolution of species, all of which Polen faithfully set down in his book and as faithfully carried out. It was also decided, in view of that threat of a possible weakening of the powers of Glissop's mind, that the two begin by spending as much time in mutual converse as possible. Accordingly they sat for six days and nights under the influence of stimulants. Polen has left a record of these talks. Apparently he made his transcription as full as he could under the circumstances. And while it is not necessary here to reproduce this intensely significant material, one may yet imagine the quality of the conversation of the two doomed scientists, one of them a great man, a world thinker, on the eve of a strange departure which he had every reason to feel might be permanent and irrevocable, looking forward, for all his learning along a path leading into an inferno of the unknown. In these six days and nights he outlined to Polen theories on many subjects, such as the Evolution of Matter, the Future, the Origin and Destiny of Life. And all this while, during these late autumn days of 1927, a city full of the *gens humana* was going about its business, eating, drinking and sleeping, as unconscious as any similarly occupied colony of bacteria of what awful and unbelievable revelation reaching into eternity and chaos lay before these two men self-imprisoned at their task in the little brick stable in the weed-grown garden belonging to an old house on Hilliard Place.

At the end of the sixth day their endurance finally gave way under the strain and they fell side by side into a sleep, before which they clasped hands in farewell, as men cast upon an unknown shore not knowing what the morrow might hold.

Polen awoke first. The Professor lay on the bed still asleep and remained so for two days longer. At the end of that time he awoke also and sat up. It was midafternoon of a bright sunshiny day, Saturday, December 17th, 1927. He started to talk to Polen and the latter at once felt a change. The blow had fallen. There was a lack of consecutiveness amounting to incoherence in Glissop's words as though the man had lost the power of concentration. The fine balance of his mind was gone forever. He could only chatter aimlessly. Polen averted his face in dismay, and tried to conceal his discovery from his friend, in spite of which Glissop noticed it himself after a little while and for the first time in the whole grewsome experience, a rush of emotion overcame him. He sprang across the room, becoming suddenly frantic, raving and uttering hideous, meaningless animal cries, tearing the clothing he wore from his withered body upon which a thick growth of hair was now apparent, and altogether becoming unmanageable until Polen was able to seize and hold him and administer a hyperdermic sedative. The next day, with the Professor's consent, fearing insanity, Polen procured a collar and a chain and chained Glissop to the wall.

I spare the reader as far as possible the painful details of what followed. Enough that from the day he chained his friend, Erasmus Polen knew that thenceforth it was his doom to tread the path alone. Nor can I describe what his feelings must have been, nor the sublimity of courage necessary to hold a grasp of his own mentality and to perform heroically his daily appointed labors of minute observation, measurement and experiment, recording everything with the cold exactness of one whose very soul was not seared with the horror of his task and the awful wonder of it. I despair of conveying to the reader the pangs of a loneliness more terrible because now at last, foreseen and realized in all its graded clarity, as his companion slipped ever farther away in the early stages of the awful metamorphosis which had come upon one of the foremost minds of this or any age. And though he nowhere mentions such a circumstance in his record, one may suppose that it must have seemed to Polen in those days that the tragic, flutelike laughter of the bacillus—that creature of disease brought into being by Andrew Glissop to attain an intelligence so vastly surpassing his own—echoed still within the walls of the laboratory like the laughter of some strange and heartless god from a dim future age.

Nor can any but the pen of Erasmus Polen himself, the original records and tabulations with their running commentary, severely scientific and yet written as it were in the blood of the man's heart, do justice to the further facts of the end of his friend and master. In advance of, the publication *in toto* of these memoirs, capably revised and edited as I have every reason to believe they will be, it must be sufficient to outline in a few words the course of the six months during which Polen, chained to his task as was Glissop chained to the wall, became the insane wreck of a man that we afterwards found. The shrinking process on the part of Glissop, horrible as it had been, was to be even more unspeakably awful. It continued, until having lost all human semblance, his own safety as well as Polen's required that he be imprisoned in a cage.

One day this diminutive creature, which was now all that was left of Andrew Glissop, escaped by squeezing through the bars of the cage. Fortunately the season was winter and the windows of the laboratory were closed. Polen, who had let himself drop upon the bed for a few hours of deferred sleep, woke to find it swimming in a basin of the solution which had been used in the earlier experiments as an artificial sustenance for the disease germs. Thereafter Polen kept it confined in a large glass jar. Rapidly in the space of several weeks, the creature, still constantly dwindling in size, retrograded through the series of reptilian stages of Evolution, changes on this strange backward journey which are carefully preserved in the amazing records of these days. And strangest of all to relate, it became at last so small as to require transference to a specially prepared saline solution in a tiny glass tube. This was finally altered to a delicate arrangement of glass slides, which could be placed under a microscope! And there Polen proceeded to examine it with the aid of an oil-immersion lens.

From now on I indicate the progress of the case leading up to the final swift catastrophe by a few excerpts, taken at somewhat extended intervals during the last month or two from the commentary inscribed in Polen's note book.

"March 10, 1928. This morning at 7 resumed microscopic observations. Change which I suspected and noted in record of

February 26 (q. v.) already beginning to be evident. Photographic enlarged film No. 82361 shows marked modification of the filaments. Have decided not to introduce living tissue as yet, but will keep temperature as formerly in order to avoid introduction of factor of reproduction. So long as I can keep the creature barely alive, unless it sinks below visibility of micro scope, I shall not complicate problem by addition of other possible individuals."

"March 11, 3 P. M. It is true! My diagnosis has been followed and verified to the last iota. The creature is in every possible way a veritable *Spirochæta Glissopi!* Proved now beyond question by observation detailed March 5, 6. See also February 26. I must continue yet a while longer to observe before I try effect of extraneous change or resumption of rhythmic temperature experiment. My friend, if he could speak, would so command."

"March 16th. At 8 P. M. no change! For five successive days now, as my records show, absolutely no new fact to record. I shall continue observations three days longer, at the end of which period I shall remove the artificial saline stimulant and begin the introduction of living tissue at a temperature favorable to development of a culture of *Spirochæta Glissopi.*"

"March 20th. After noting final observation last night with still no change in the bacillus, I lay down for a long sleep. Today, on waking, have decide to postpone living tissue experiment, and to rest in order to regain strength and power of attention for work which I shall begin tomorrow. Have rested all day. This evening, taking advantage of enforced idleness, a thing unusual with me, who have trained my mind rather to meet the severe demands of observational method, allowed my mind to travel back idly over the long arduous course of these almost unbelievable experiments, and the strange thought comes to me now that I have been perhaps too close to see them all in a just perspective of their significance. Perhaps the mind sees some things better without the microscope. The strange notion bothers me. I recall a simple remark Andrew Glissop once made. It was at the time we sat up for six nights when the knowledge of his fate first dimly dawned upon us. I cannot forget that wonderful discussion wherein my master poured out the treasures of his intellect upon an unworthy helper. A farewell gift of exceeding richness. This particular remark of his I did not set down then in my diary. It seemed to me at the time so simple and unimportant, so far beneath the scientific and metaphysical level of the deductions connected with our work. And yet the memory of it clings.

"What he said was this: '*Whenever we observe anything closely enough to discover the workings of law therein, that thing, even though, it be repulsive, becomes to us beautiful.*' And to this he added, '*A man who devotes his life to one thing should beware of his choice, for the end is that he shall become that thing.*'

"Is this then the meaning of it all? And if it is, what is to become of me? God knows."

"March 1. Today I feel a slight pain in one side of my face, having left window next to bed open too far. Fear I have caught cold. Necessary that I begin new experiments under favorable circumstances. Postpone till tomorrow. My left eye and cheek slightly inflamed."

"March 23. I hardly know how to put in words the tragedy which happened this morning. It would be a terrible thing for the cause of Science to break off these experiments before their utmost possibilities had been exhausted. I woke early and, feeling better of my slight cold, I began at once to prepare for work. But on focusing the microscope I discovered that the bacillus has gone! It is no longer visible between the slides. It has escaped. Yet how could it have slipped away since the shrinking process has long since stopped? Did that process recommence, and if so, is the bacillus present but below the power of the lenses to reveal, or has it in fact slipped from between the slides and floated away on a current of air? There is now but one chance, a chance in a million, that if the creature has in fact escaped, it has fastened itself to some tiny exposed particle of organic matter in the room, in which case it will increase and multiply until it becomes recoverable. Yet I incline to the belief that it is still in the fluid between the slides but too small to be revealed by the microscope. On the whole it is a negligible possibility that it could have gotten away. But what a tragedy all this is!"

"April 8. Have now minutely searched and tested every square millimeter of walls and floor—a gigantic task. No trace of the bacillus inorganic matter anywhere in the room. I fear the worst—that these experiments are at an end. I shall nevertheless remain."

"April 23. The last week of suffering has been horrible. Both eyes now inflamed and I am practically prohibited from using the microscope even were the bacillus to be found. I must wait for the cold to run its course."

"May 1. 6 A. M. Have eaten no food since day before yesterday. Did not even go to the door to speak to housekeeper when she knocked. Last night a recurrence of the same dream described April 17 and April 26, Second recurrence. Query—What relation this dream, if any, to my own psychology? Professor Glissop, as I recall him just before the great change—looking straight into my eyes—awaking after it with vivid recollection of the dream, and eyes smarting severely. But this morning an added circumstance. Closed my eyes again after waking and looking at watch. It was then 5.07 A. M. And on the red, inflamed, greatly enlarged interior surface of eyelids, I saw clearly depicted Professor's face. Same face as in dream but wearing a horrible leer. Hallucinations and their relation to pain. Am acquainted only superficially with subject. Wish I knew more about it, for every time I now close my eyes I see reappearance of that horrible image, sometimes multiplied into several images.

442 P. M. Since writing above another knock on door. I must not be seen for fear of being forcibly removed to be put under physician's care. Duty demands my presence here at whatever cost of temporary pain. Cold, which has settled in face and neck, should loosen soon.

"5 P. M. The agony is terrible but I think I can survive it by holding on a littlc longer and then return to experiments. I have not given up hope of recovering the missing bacillus. But would I had the courage of a Glissop. I seem to need it at this juncture."

"May 2.4 A. M. Pain frightful. 6 A. M. Pain lessen.

8.30 A. M. In spite of handicap of lowered power of vision in my eyes, I have made the test suggested in my notes of April 25, and I have, with the utmost care, checked up my results. The infection of my eyes is now beyond all question caused by the *Spirochæta Glissopi.* My God! Can I bear to write down deliberately the horrible truth, which for weeks I have not suspected and which now dawns on me in an agony of mind and body? The missing bacillus has found its living tissue. *It is in my eye! The Professor, Professor Glissop, my friend, is in my eye, millions and millions of him!* I cannot write further.

"The pain is returning. Severe. I am doomed. Yet the observations I have made on my own eyes will be valuable to science and I am thankful for the strength to have written them down. I do not know the time. It is somewhere about noon I should say, judging from temperature of room. I am in darkness, cannot see, dead now to the world, except for what takes place in the agony of my eyes and which I must continue to write down while life and reason last. I fear that reason will go first. I dare not lay down pencil for fear it will fall and I lose it—

"Since writing above have lived in hell for it seems the space of two days. Variations of heat and cold are all I have to tell the movement of time from day to night. Probably less in actual fact. Pacing room and clutching pencil—at last fell unconscious and on coming to rose and felt my way to shelves N. E. corner of room, found hyperdermic, something which in my distress of mind I had strangely neglected to think of before. Am out of pain now, though unable to see—pain returns—bottle fallen and broken—I brushed it aside in my blindness, reaching for it. I still am clutching pencil—but I fear my reason is going now and the end has come. I hardly know as I feel these pages under my hands if what I write—Hark! I hear knocking sounds on the door. No, they are building a gallows—hammering—hammering—to build a gallows outside in the garden—to hang me—for your murder, Andrew Glissop! Look not at me with that hideous leer of accusation. I am guiltless—I did but follow you. Ah, had I my violin instead of this pencil traveling in the darkness, I should play that I might forget the pain of my eyes. Have I not been faithful, Master, to the search for Truth? I am even now—in my dark agony—writing my observations in the Cause of Science. Observations of all that is real! They are still hammering on the gallows outside. They will hang me—yes—by the eyelids! The pain is too great. I shall take my violin and play once more—play for the little images to dance in my eyelids. Ah, little red images of terror you have led me a dance—now you shall dance—you shall dance—I can but play for you—my work is done. I have been faithful to Science—followed the vision—believed in it with my soul—to the end—and I am blind—blind—"

NOEKKEN OF NORWAY

BOB OLSEN

The Tarn of Peril

"Whatever you do, laddy of mine, you must keep away from Bjerke Tjern!"

This warning, uttered in a squeaky voice by the wrinkled lips of Borghild Bjornsdatter, was my first introduction to that pool of mystery and death which the Norwegian country-folk called "Birch Tarn."

"Why do you say that, Granny?" I asked in my labored and somewhat broken Norwegian, "What's the matter with Bjerke Tjern?"

"Matter enough," she whined. "Anybody but a fool would know that Bjerke Tjern is the place where Nœkken abides. That ought to mean something to you, laddy mine, because it was Nœkken who slew all of your uncles."

It was true that my father's three elder brothers had all disappeared under very mysterious circumstances and that neither their bodies nor any other traces of them had ever been found. I had also heard rumors that their deaths had been accomplished by supernatural influences; but naturally I had given no credence to this superstitious nonsense. It was because of this complete and sudden eradication of my Norwegian relatives that I, the last male descendent of the Lungaard clan, had been sent from America to take over the management of the family estate requiring supervision.

"Are you sure that Bjerke Tjern is haunted, Granny Borghild?" I laughed. "If that is true, it makes me all that more eager to visit that interesting spot. I'd love to meet a huge Trold or a band of tiny Nissen. Perhaps I might be lucky enough to run into one of those beautiful golden-haired Huldren and have a dance with her."

"Scoff all you please," the old lady grumbled, "but if you have an ounce of brains in that noddle of yours, you will keep away from Bjerke Tjern, *especially at night*."

Stubbornness is a typically Norse trait. Some call it determination and class it as virtue. Others regard it as stupid, mulish perversity. Take your choice. For my own part, I must have inherited some of this Scandinavian obstinacy from my ancestors, for I had hardly finished supper that twilight summer evening, when I became obsessed with an overpowering desire to visit the very place which I had been warned to avoid

Outside, near the ponderous log stable I found one of the Lungaard farm hands.

"How do I get to Bjerke Tjern?" I asked him.

For a minute or so, he just stared at me fearfully, his eyes bulging, his lower lip sagging.

Somewhat impatiently I repeated the question.

Finally he found his voice and stammered, "You'd better not go up there, Sir."

"Never mind the advice," I snapped. "Are you going to tell me how to get up to Bjerke Tjern, or—"

"It's up there," he muttered, pointing to a cleft in the mountains just north of our farm.

For a few hundred yards the trail was plainly marked; but it wasn't long before I had to force my way through a dense growth of weeds and underbrush which choked the remainder of the path. It was quite clear that the way to Bjerke Tjern had not been traversed for some time.

Crawling, climbing, stumbling over branches and creepers, I finally worked my way up to the gap in the hills, which the farm hand had pointed out to me.

When I reached the highest point in the path and looked down into the bowl-like depression on the other side of the ridge, the sight of which met my eyes made me gasp with delight. Below me lay a small lake, almost perfectly circular in outline, with the loveliest little toy island set in its exact center. Never in my life have I seen a body of water so clear and so still. Not even the tiniest of ripples disturbed its placid surface. It might have been frozen over, except that even the smoothest of ice could not possibly have reflected the surroundings with such perfect faithfulness. Like an image in a flawless plate glass mirror, the mountain peaks, the clouds, the gaunt white birch trees, the toy island and the lily pads were counterfeited within that magic circle of water.

It was about nine o'clock of a summer evening, although the sun was still visible. Like a great crimson ball it hung just over the hill to the southwest. With incredible speed it rolled downward. By the time I reached the ridge it had slid out of sight behind the horizon. Down in that cupped amphitheater in which the tarn lay sleeping, the direct light of the sun must have vanished some time previously. Strange to say, however, it seemed to be illuminated much clearer by the mysterious Norse twilight than by the glare of a noonday sun.

One thing that heightened this illusion was the total lack of shadows. Like fluid light, the ghastly, crepuscular glow seemed to flow into every nook and cranny, bringing out all the details with startling clearness.

The light was not the only thing which had been transformed. There were equally drastic changes in the sounds which reached—or rather railed to reach my ears. A few minutes earlier the woods had been teeming with life. Numberless birds had been twittering and chattering in the branches. Twigs had crackled beneath the steps of small animals. The leaves had rustled continuously as they were whipped about by the brisk west wind.

But now, after sun-down, all these sounds had been suddenly hushed. Not a breath of air was stirring. Not a bird chirped. Not a branch creaked. It was as if Mother Nature was angry with her children and put them all to bed before their time.

In that deathly, sepulchral silence, I found myself treading on tip toes, almost holding my breath for fear that I might miss hearing some slight sound to tell me there were other living creatures besides myself in that place of mystery.

Carefully and stealthily I clambered down the slope which led to the pond. Cautious as I was I couldn't help making a lot of noise. Each time a twig snapped or a pebble rolled down the hill ahead of me, the sound seemed to be magnified and repeated again and again by the echoing hills which guarded the tarn.

When I reached the grassy shore my nostrils were greeted by a delightful perfume. Clearly it originated from a fleet of water lilies which rode at anchor a dozen yards beyond my reach. The waxy blossoms, nestling among the oval leaves and spear-shaped buds, were as beautiful as they were fragrant. I had an intense yearning to pluck them.

Searching for a way to accomplish this purpose without exposing myself to the frigid waters of the lake, I stumbled upon a weather-beaten rowboat. It was an ancient pram, exactly like the small boats which the Vikings used in olden days for making short trips across the fjords. Staunchly built of oaken planks it had obviously rested there, embedded in the mud, for many years.

Despite its age, the skiff looked quite sound and seaworthy, except that it was half full of rainwater. I tried to empty it by tipping it over on its side, but it was too heavy for me alone to handle. Then, a few feet away I discovered another mysterious object. It was a silver-mounted drinking horn, such as the Norsemen of yore used for quaffing their mead.

Using it as a bailer, I soon had most of the water out of the boat. I expected to have a job loosening the craft from its muddy bed, but it slid out easily at the first push I gave it.

Tossing the drinking horn into the bottom of the boat, I looked around, half expecting to find a pair of ancient oars conveniently laid out for me, but in this I was disappointed. So I opened my jack-knife and cut down a birch sapling. Amputating the top and lopping off the branches, I fashioned a stout pole about fifteen feet long. Equipped with this, I stepped into the pram and shoved off.

As the prow of the craft nosed in among the moored lily pads, I leaned over the stern and thrusting my hand far down into the water caught hold of one of the wiry stems and jerked the blossom loose.

Hardly had I plucked the water lily when I felt a jar which made me almost loose my balance.

The boat began to move!

Straight for the center of the lake it headed, gliding silently along as if it were being towed by an underwater cable. I peered into the water on both sides of the pram but could see nothing but the lily stems and the angular furrows which the nose of the boat was plowing in the clear, transparent water.

Halfway to the island the skiff stopped abruptly. I heard a cracking sound and was horrified to see the thick, oaken sides of the boat bend inward as if they were being crushed between the jaws of a powerful, hydraulic press. Along the seams in the bottom of the craft two large cracks yawned. Water, cold as a glacier stream, began to gush against my legs.

Grabbing the drinking horn, I started to bail in frantic haste.

THEN I SAW *IT!*

Between me and the island, another smaller isle reared itself above the surface of the water. At first it looked like some floating, inanimate object, so formless and so lifeless did it seem to be.

Slowly—so slowly that it didn't stir up a single ripple in that glassy surface, the Thing swelled upward until two bulging emerald eyes came into new just above the water level. How can I hope to describe what I saw in those unspeakable eyes? Hunger, lust, ferocity, wickedness, cruelty, and devilish, murderous *hate* were all written there.

In my terror I forgot to bail, but it wouldn't have made any difference anyway for the gunwales of the pram were already awash. The frigid water made my legs feel as if they were frozen in a solid block of ice.

Then the fish, or animal, or whatever it was, began to move leisurely toward me.

I waited no longer. Pulling myself out of the damnable spell of fear which had taken possession of me, I stood up, placed my feet against the high stern of the pram and with a mighty kick, dove into the icy water. Luckily for me I had done a lot of swimming in my youth. Apparently Nœkken (I suppose I may as well refer to that Thing by its Norse name) had never before had to deal with a swimmer who knew the Australian crawl stroke. Otherwise I am sure it would not have permitted me to get such a start. I must have broken a record for the twenty-yard dash in the sprint I made that day. Nevertheless, I had barely scrambled up on the bank when I heard Nœkken slithering out of the water behind me. Without turning around I ran toward the path with all the speed I could muster. I hadn't taken more than a few steps when I stumbled over an exposed root and fell flat on my face.

Something heavy and cold and slimy flowed over my foot and wrapped itself around my left leg. Then I felt myself being dragged, slowly and relentlessly toward the water. I managed to twist my body around so that I was in a sitting position. Glaring at me, only a few feet away were those horrible, fiendish eyes. They were embedded in a loathesome mass of translucent glair, resembling the body of a colossal, shapeless jelly-fish.

One edge of this preposterous monster had wrapped itself about my leg. The opposite side of it was still in the water, six or seven yards away. Apparently without effort, the creature seemed to flow along the ground, dragging me along with it. Frantically, clutching for something to hang to, my hand closed over the top of the birch sapling which I had dropped there a few minutes before. Using it as a whip, I struck again and again at the part of the beast which gripped my leg.

Against such a formidable foe my improvised weapon seemed ridiculously puny; yet it proved to be far more effective than I could reasonably have expected. Beneath the stinging blows of the switch, the jelly-like substance cringed and drew back. Jerking my leg free from that dire embrace, I leaped to my feet and dashed madly up that tangled trail which (in my hopes at least) led to safety.

As I crashed down through the underbrush on the southerly slope of the ridge, I saw, looming up before me, the figure of a man. It was Lars Thorvaldsen, Borghild Bjornsdatter's grandson.

Tall, broad-shouldered and blond, with prominent cheekbones and a firm, determined mouth, Lars was a typical Nordic farmer lad. Of all the men and women who made their home at Lundgaard, Thorvaldsen was the only one who had been educated beyond the rudimentary requirements of the local country schools. Having displayed unusual interest in scholarly attainments, Lars had been awarded a stipendium and a scholarship at the University of Oslo. He spoke perfect English, with the meticulous inflection of an Oxford graduate.

"Hi, there, George!" he greeted me. "Where the devil have you been? I've hunted for you endlessly."

"I've been to Bjerke Tjern," I panted. "There's a—there's a—"

As I paused to catch my breath, Lars suddenly grasped me by the arm and cried, "What's the matter with you man? You look like you've seen a ghost!"

"I have!" was my excited response. "I've seen Nœkken!"

"You've seen what?"

"Nœkken," I whispered. "Granny Borghild was right. There is something — something horrible, something supernatural up there in Bjerke Tjern!"

I half expected him to make fun of me. Instead he put his arm around my shoulder and said in a kind, soothing voice, "You're all excited, my boy. Here, sit down on this log and tell me what happened."

After first casting a furtive glance behind me to make sure that I had not been followed, I sat down and, in short, jerky sentences related to him my encounter with the monster of Bjerke Tjern.

In concluding my narrative I said, "I know, Lars, that you are not superstitious like the rest of the folks around here. You probably think I've been seeing things. But I'm telling you that I saw Nœkken just as clearly as I see you now. It caught hold of me and tried to drag me into the water. I'm sure it wasn't imagination on my part."

"Of course it wasn't," he conceded.

"Then you really believe me—you think that Nœkken actually exists?"

"Certainly."

Without waiting for me to finish my sentence, Lars went on: "I've made quite a study of Norse folk lore. It's a very interesting subject. Most so-called educated people are inclined to dismiss these stories lightly—regarding them purely as myths, which they think are based solely on ignorance and superstition. My investigations have led me to the conclusion that, after due allowances have been made for exaggerations which may naturally be expected when narratives of this sort are retold again and again, all of these familiar stories originated in actual, true experiences of sane, sober human beings."

"Do you really believe that?" I asked in astonishment.

"Most certainly," he assured me. "There isn't one of these so-called supernatural beings, mentioned in folk lore, that cannot be explained in accordance with well recognized scientific facts."

"For; instance?" I prompted him.

"Well, suppose we start with Trolds. They were nothing but giants. Real giants are not at all uncommon, even today."

"True enough," I corroborated him. "And one of the best known of the modern giants is a motion picture actor and was born in Norway."

"There are plenty of other giants, besides those who exhibit themselves in shows," Lars rejoined. "Science explains them as eases of overdeveloped pituitary glands. Most of these giants are sensitive about their abnormal size. Consequently they prefer to live apart from other people. That trait ties in with the stories about Trolds, who were supposed to lead solitary lives."

"Sounds reasonable," I commented. "But you could hardly say that Nœkken—"

He interrupted me with, "Giants are not the only freaks that can be accounted for by endocrinology. Take for example the little people who are called Nissen. They were nothing more nor less than midgets, of which there are thousands in existence today. Every biologist knows that midgets result from deficiency in the secretion of the thyroid gland. This hormone, you know, has been isolated and has been given the name of *Thyroxine*. Analysis shows that this substance contains iodine. It is a well known fact that midgets are prevalent in places where people drink water from melted snow and which consequently contains no iodine. Hence we would naturally expect to find many dwarfs, or Nissen, if you want to call them that, in the mountainous sections of Norway."

"To be sure," I agreed. "But the Trolds and Nissen were at least shaped like human beings. You could hardly attribute a monster like Nœkken to glandular disturbances of animal beings."

"Don't be so positive about that," he contradicted me.

"You mean?"

"Just this. Nœkken of course is not human in origin—at least one would hardly suppose so, to judge from the generally accepted descriptions of the being, with which your account seems to agree remarkably."

"Then in the name of creation, what is it?"

"My theory is that Nœkken is an abnormal development of some simple, extremely low type of organism."

"For instance," I persisted.

"Well it might be an over-developed amœba."

"Amœba?" I questioned. "What in the dickens is an amœba?"

"It's a microscopic organism. You know what protoplasm is don't you?"

I didn't know, but I nodded nevertheless.

"That's all there is to an amœba." He went on, "It's just a single-celled blob of protoplasm. It can change its shape at will. That's how it got its name. Amœba comes from a Greek word meaning change. The amœba obtains its food by wrapping itself around other microbes and digesting them."

"Do you mean to infer that Nœkken mistook me for a microbe?"

"It probably wasn't particularly choosey about its diet," Lars laughed. "To a monster such as that, almost anything living would be acceptable food."

By this time I had recovered sufficiently from my fright so that I could appreciate the ludicrous aspects of the adventure; so I came back with, "Is that so? By the way that baby went for me, I am sure it regarded me as an especially delicious morsel."

"Maybe so," Lars conceded.

"And, furthermore," I continued, "I don't think that thing I saw at Bjerke Tjern was anything like an amœba."

"According to your description it was very much like a gigantic amœba," Lars disagreed.

"But I thought you said an amœba is just a single cell."

"Correct. What of it?"

"Oh nothing," I said sarcastically, "Except that a single cell is always microscopic in size."

"Not necessarily," he contradicted me. "The yolk of an ostrich egg is a single cell and you could hardly call that microscopic. Nevertheless you are right when you infer that amœbas and other protozoa are usually minutely small. When one of them reaches maturity it divides forming two daughter amœbas. Sometimes two amœbas fuse together to form one organism."

"What of it?" I challenged.

"Just this: It is quite conceivable that, under certain conditions, which may happen to exist in Bjerke Tjern, an amœba might continue to grow without dividing until it reached gigantic proportions."

"And if that happened would it still be a single cell?" I asked.

"Possibly. Why?"

"I don't see how it could be possible for a single cell to be so large."

"Why not? After all, size is relative. The yolk of an egg is probably millions of times as large as a microbe. Yet each of them is a single cell. And surely it wouldn't take more than a few million yolks to make a creature the size of Nœkken."

"All right," I said. "Suppose we assume that the Thing in Bjerke Tjern *is* an overgrown amœba. What then?"

"Nothing except that I think it is your duty to exterminate it."

"What?" I yelled.

"I said it is your duty to exterminate Nœkken before it kills any more people."

"No thanks," was my emphatic response. "I've had one bout with it. That's plenty."

As if to express his contempt, Lars cleared his throat and spat at a cluster of caraway stalks which grew beside the path.

"So you're afraid, are you?" he sneered.

"Not exactly afraid. But what's the use of borrowing trouble?"

"I just told you why. A monster like that is a constant menace to human life. It ought to be stamped out before it kills any more people."

"Granted," I agreed. "But why should I do the dirty work?"

Speaking in a disdainful tone, Lars said, "Because Nœkken has already killed three of your father's brothers. You are the only one of the Lundgaards who is left here now. Aren't you man enough to understand that you are the one who should avenge the deaths of your kinsmen?"

"I guess I'm man enough to assume any responsibilities that rightfully fall on my shoulders," I retorted angrily.

"Spoken like a true Norseman!" Lars exclaimed. "What do you say we go for Nœkken this very night?"

"We?" I echoed. "You mean that you will help me kill Nœkken?"

"Certainly I will help you. That is if you want me to."

"I'll be grateful for your assistance," I assured him. "Never having hunted for giant amœbas, I'll probably need coaching. Just what is the proper procedure in a case like this?"

"I have a dandy Krag-Jörgensen rifle," he told me. "And I'm sure I can scare up some kind of gun for you. I'll go and fetch them."

"What's the hurry?" I hedged. "Why do you want to go after it to-night?"

"Because it is evidently out hunting for food to-night. If it finds something to eat and returns to its lair it may not show up again for a long, long while."

"But it's getting late." Showing him my wrist watch I protested, "Look it's nearly eleven. In a few minutes there won't even be enough twilight to see by. Why can't we wait until to-morrow morning?"

"They say Nœkken never makes his appearance by daylight," Lars reminded me.

"Then let's make it to-morrow evening."

Lars agreed.

After a sleepless night, pregnant with dread and worry, I arose early and went to the huge room which served as kitchen, refectory and assembly room at Lundgaard.

Early as I was, Granny Bjornsdatter had risen ahead of me. She had finished her breakfast and was sitting by the stone hearth embroidering a wonderful Hardanger tablecloth.

After we had exchanged greetings I said, "Please tell me more about Nœkken, little Grandmother."

"What do you want to know about it, laddy of mine?" she mumbled through her toothless lips.

"I'd like to know what Nœkken looks like and how it behaves." I suggested.

"Nœkken takes many forms," Borghild began.

I was somewhat startled to hear that. It tailed so closely with what Lars had said about the proclivity of amœbas for constantly changing their shapes. However, Granny's next statement was not nearly so scientific. It was, "Sometimes it takes the form of a dog or wolf. At other times it makes itself look like an oaken chest with copper bands. When some nosey dunce goes to investigate—opi! Out jumps Nœkken and the dunce is in his power!"

"Nœkken must be a clever fellow," I remarked.

"You have said it. But its favorite trick is to take the shape of a big, black horse. When he catches sight of his victim he snuggles right up to him and coaxes the fellow to climb up on his back. If he is fool enough to do it, opi! Nœkken gives one big leap out into the tarn and devours the dunce with one big gulp."

"But doesn't Nœkken stay in the water most of the time?" I asked.

"Yes. It's only when he is very hungry that he starts hunting on land. Generally he is content to lie in wait, floating quietly on the surface of the tarn like a stump or a log. Sometimes he contrives to have a pram handy, by the shore of the tarn. If any man is fool enough to get into that boat, he may as well say his prayers."

I was becoming more and more interested in Borghild's dissertation.

"What happens to the dunce if he gets into the boat?" I asked eagerly.

"First Nœkken sneaks up under the water and grabs hold of the bottom of the pram. Then he gives it a tug and tows it out into deep water."

"And then?" I prompted.

"Sometimes he tips the boat over. But his favorite stunt is to squeeze the pram until it cracks open."

Reaching out she picked up a small match box and held it up in her bony fingers as she went on, "Nœkken is so strong that he can crack the stoutest boat just like this," and she crushed the flimsy box, scattering the matches all over the floor.

"What happens next?" I said with a shudder.

"Naturally the boat sinks and the dunce is at the mercy of Nœkken. It doesn't matter whether he can swim or not, Nœkken is sure to get him. Sometimes he gobbles him up with the first gulp. But if he isn't very hungry and the man is a good swimmer, Nœkken loves to play with his victim, like a cat with a mouse. Still another clever trick of Nœkken is to—"

"Excuse me Granny," I interrupted her. "Do you mind if I ask you a question?"

"Certainly not, laddy of mine. What is it?"

"Suppose one wanted to do away with Nœkken. Isn't there some way one could kill it or exorcise it?"

"There is only one way I know to slay Nœkken, and that is with an arrow made of mistletoe wood."

"How about a silver bullet? Wouldn't that be a good thing to kill Nœkken with?"

"Of course not, you dunce. Silver bullets are for were-wolves. Any fool knows that!"

"But how should one of these mistletoe arrows be made? Are there any special rules to be observed?"

"Naturally. In the first place it must have neither a metal nor a stone head. The point must be sharpened with a dirk that has killed a man and must be hardened by heating it over a fire made of caraway stalks. Crow feathers are best for the end."

"How about the bow? Does that have to be made in any special way?"

"Of course not. Any bow will do. One can even throw the arrow if one is strong enough."

What happened after I left Granny Bjornsdatter I hesitate to tell. Even to-day I can't help feeling a bit ashamed of the way in which I permitted my supposedly educated mind to be swayed by atavistic superstitions. I excused myself by reflecting that Granny Bjorndatter's descriptions of the Thing at Bjerke Tjern had been amazingly accurate. Naturally I did not give any credence to the parts about the creature assuming the shapes of wolves and horses, but I had to admit that the account of what Nœkken did, to a dunce who embarked in a boat, coincided remarkably with my own experience. I began to think that Borghild knew more about Nœkken than Lars, with all his scientific training.

As far as the mistletoe myth was concerned, perhaps there was as much science as magic behind that idea. Who could tell us that the sap of this weird parasitic plant might not be poisonous to the thing that Granny called Nœkken?

I located a few sprigs of mistletoe in an old, run-down orchard belonging to one of our neighbors. From Lundgaard's stocked armory I selected a wicked-looking dagger with brownish stains on the blade. With it I fashioned two short arrows according to Granny's instructions. I also made a bow from a spruce sapling and spent a few hours practicing with it. Though I got so I could hit the end of a cask providing I got close enough to it, I certainly was no rival of Robin Hood or William Tell.

That evening Lars and I slipped away from the farm shortly after supper. I concealed my bow and my mistletoe arrows by rolling them up in a blanket of homespun wool which I lugged under my arm. In the other hand I carried a rifle. Lars was similarly armed.

When we reached the tarn, twilight had overtaken us, yet the natural amphitheater was illuminated with incomparable clearness. Taking up positions a few feet from each other, we sat on the grass with our backs against a couple of birch trees.

We decided it was best not to talk to each other. After all, what was there to say? Gradually almost imperceptibly, the weird ghostly light faded. After what seemed at least ten hours of breathless suspense, I heard a rhythmic series of snores from the place where Lars was sitting. My eyes had become blurred from gazing at the glassy surface of the lake and I had just started to nod myself when I saw Nœkken. Only five or six inches of its body protruded above the surface in the midst of the fleet of lily pads which were moored about twenty yards from the shore. I would never have seen it had it not been for the luminous gleam in its baleful eyes.

Crawling softly to where Lars was reclining, I slapped him gently on the cheek. He awoke with a jump.

"It's there," I whispered. "Out there among the lily pads. You can see it can't you?"

"Like hell I can," he swore softly. "Where the devil is it?"

"Get your gun ready and I'll show you. When I turn my electric torch on him, let him have it. Are you ready?"

"Let her go!"

I pressed the button of my American flashlight and directed its beam straight into the eyes of the creature that lurked among the lily pads. There was a sharp crash followed by deafening reverberations which the echoes repeated and magnified to the proportions of a long peal of thunder.

Like most Norwegians, Lars was a dead shot with a rifle. At that distance he couldn't possibly have missed. In fact I am positive I saw the bullet spatter a tiny jet of spray just a fraction of an inch below one of the monster's eyes.

I expected to see the body sink beneath the surface, but instead it started to swell up like a balloon does when the gas is first turned into it. Then it moved slowly toward us.

There was no need for the flash-light now. Lars, I knew, could see his quarry plainly. He ran to the edge of the water, pumping bullets into that ominous form as fast as he could work the bolt of his gun between repeated loadings of the magazine.

Suddenly I remembered about my bow and arrows and ran back

to my blanket to get them. When I turned around again, the Thing was only a few feet from where Lars was standing. The muzzle of his rifle was almost touching it when Lars fired his last shot and took to his heels.

Moving with amazing speed the monster slid along the ground in pursuit.

With trembling fingers I fitted an arrow to the string of my bow, took quick aim and let fly. The dart hit the earth more than a foot behind the pursuing beast. Before I had time to get a second arrow ready the forward edge of the creature shot out and gave Lars a resounding slap on the back, sending him tumbling to the turf. Then, repeating the same tactics as it had used with me, it wrapped a portion of itself about Lars' legs and started to drag him toward the water.

Screaming with terror, Lars clutched madly at everything that lay in his way. Luckily he managed to throw his arms around a young birch tree, locking his fingers together and hanging on with superhuman strength which fear inspires.

"Help, George!" He shrieked. "Help me or I'm a dead man."

I picked up my rifle and pumped several shots into that horrid mass, taking care to aim at the parts which were farthest away from Lars' body. The bullets seemed to have no effect whatever on Nœkken. It continued to heave and tug at Lars' body until I could hear the joints of his shoulders crack.

When I had fired my last cartridge, I heaved the gun itself, straight at those two unspeakable eyes. It sank out of sight in that plastic mass of flesh, which closed oozingly over it.

Then I thought of my remaining arrow, which was sticking in my belt. I had dropped the bow when I picked up my gun. While I was hunting for it I could hear Lars groaning and screaming in agony. "Heaven help me!" he yelled in Norwegian.

"I can't hold fast any longer!"

Just then a miracle happened. At any rate, to my tortured, fear numbed brain it seemed like a miracle.

Although it was only a few minutes after three o'clock, dawn was beginning to break over the hill to the northeast of us. The spot we had selected for our vigil was near the southwesterly edge of the lake. The first beams of that morning sun which crept down into that wooded bowl seemed to drench both Lars and Nœkken in rosy light.

Aided by this unexpected illumination, I quickly located my discarded bow. Carefully fitting my last mistletoe arrow to the cord, I drew as close to the monster as I dared. As I sighted along the shaft, I saw something which had previously escaped my notice but which was now clearly revealed by the direct sunlight.

In the midst of that translucent mass of jelly-like glair there was a globule of darker hue. It was about the size of a watermelon and it throbbed and squirmed within the outer covering of protoplasm. For all I knew it was the creature's heart—if it had a heart—or it might have been its brain. Whatever it was, it looked like a vital organ and I decided that, if I was ever going to kill Nœkken, that inner spheroid would have to be my target.

Taking careful aim and drawing the cord of my bow back as far as I dared, I let the arrow fly. Straight through that slimy mass it sped, scoring a perfect bull's-eye in its central core.

A terrific shudder ran all through that enormous body. Slowly its grip on Lars relaxed and it sank down as flat as an enormous pancake. Feeling himself free from that terrible embrace, Lars crawled out from under the heavy body, which was now inert and lifeless.

"Are you all right?" I gasped. "Can you walk?"

"Can I walk?" he yelled. "No! I can't walk a step. But just watch me run!" and he dashed up the tangled trail at a pace that would have made Frank Wyckoff turn green with envy. Needless to add, I lost no time in following him.

Remembering somewhat tardily the warnings which Granny Bjornsdatter had given us we waited until high noon before venturing back to the tarn. We found what was left of my gun. The stock was completely missing and the metal parts were corroded as if they had been soaked in nitric acid.

Surrounding the remains of the weapon was a ring of matted

grass, which was seared to a sickly yellow hue. It was covered with a slimy, glistening substance such as one sees on the beach where a jelly fish has melted in the sun.

"That's all that's left of Nœkken!" I announced. "When it was hit by the direct rays of the sun, it just melted away. It looks like your amœba theory is correct."

"You are altogether too modest;" he complimented me. "The sun may have had something to do with Nœkken's demise, but I don't think there is any question but that you killed it when you shot that arrow into its nucleus."

"Nucleus?" I questioned.

"Yes. That's what they call the central, vital portion of an amœba. It was so small in comparison to the size of the whole creature that I must have missed it completely with my bullets."

"Then you really think that the mistletoe arrow did the trick?"

"Yes. But any kind of arrow would have served just as well. The mistletoe had nothing to do with it."

"O, ja?" I said. The inflection I gave to the Norwegian word, sound exactly like the American slang expression, "Oh, yeah?"

I bent down and picked up what looked like the branch of a birch tree.

"Do you see this?" I went on. "It's the switch I used to beat off Nœkken when he tried to drag me into the water the day before yesterday. I guess you know now that it wasn't such an easy task to accomplish. Just take a good look at this branch."

He examined it and then said, in English:

"Well, I'll be a dirty name. If that isn't a sprig of mistletoe growing out of that birch switch, I'll eat what's left of Nœkken!"

THE BLUE GERM
MARTIN SWAYNE

1
BLACK MAGIC

I had just finished breakfast, and deeply perplexed had risen from the table in order to get a box of matches to light a cigarette, when my black cat got between my feet and tripped me up.

I fell forwards, making a clutch at the table-cloth. My forehead struck the corner of the fender and the last thing I remembered was a crash of falling crockery. Then all became darkness. My parlour-maid found me lying face downwards on the hearth-rug ten minutes later. My cat was sitting near my head, blinking contentedly at the fire. A little blood was oozing from a wound above my left eye.

They carried me up to my bedroom and sent for my colleague, Wilfred Hammer, who lived next door. For three days I lay insensible, and Hammer came in continually, whenever he could spare the time from his patients, and brooded over me. On the fourth day I began to move about in my bed, restless and muttering, and Hammer told me afterwards that I seemed to be talking of a black cat. On the night of the fourth day I suddenly opened my eyes. My perplexity had left me. An idea, clear as crystal, was now in my mind.

From that moment my confinement to bed was a source of impatience to me. Hammer, large, fair, square-headed, and imperturbable, insisted on complete rest, and I chafed under the restraint. I had only one desire—to get up, slip down to St. Dane's Hospital in my car, mount the bare stone steps that led up to the laboratory and begin work at once.

"Let me up, Hammer," I implored.

"My dear fellow, you're semi-delirious."

"I must get up," I muttered.

He laughed slowly.

"Not for another week or two, Harden. How is the black cat?"

"That cat is a wizard."

I lay watching him between half-closed eyelids.

"He gave me the idea."

"He gave you a nasty concussion," said Hammer.

"It was probably the only way to the idea," I answered. "I tell you the cat is a wizard. He did it on purpose. He's a black magician."

Hammer laughed again, and went towards the door.

"Then the idea must be black magic," he said.

I smiled painfully, for my head was throbbing. But I was happier then than I had ever been, for I had solved the problem that had haunted my brain for ten years.

"There's no such thing as black magic," I said.

Three weeks later I beheld the miracle. It was wrought on the last day of December, in the laboratory of the hospital, high above the gloom and squalor of the city. The miracle occurred within a brilliant little circle of light, and I saw it with my eye glued to a microscope. It passed off swiftly and quietly, and though I expected it, I was filled with a great wonder and amazement.

To a lay mind the amazement with which I beheld the miracle will require explanation. I had witnessed the transformation of one germ into another; a thing which is similar to a man seeing a flock of sheep on a hill-side change suddenly into a herd of cattle. For many minutes I continued to move the slide in an aimless way with trembling fingers. My temperament is earthy; it had once occurred to me quite seriously that if I saw a miracle I would probably go mad under the strain. Now that I had seen one, after the first flash of realization my mind was listless and dull, and all feeling of surprise had died away. The black rods floated with slow motion in the minute currents of fluid I had introduced. The faint roar of

London came up from far below; the clock ticked steadily and the microscope lamp shone with silent radiance. And I, Richard Harden, sat dangling my short legs on the high stool, thinking and thinking. . . .

That night I wrote to Professor Sarakoff. A month later I was on my way to Russia.

2
SARAKOFF'S MANIFESTO

The recollection of my meeting with Sarakoff remains vividly in my mind. I was shown into a large bare room, heated by an immense stove like an iron pagoda. The floor was of light yellow polished wood; the walls were white-washed, and covered with pencil marks. A big table covered with papers and books stood at one end. At the other, through an open doorway, there was a glimpse of a laboratory. Sarakoff stood in the centre of the room, his hands deep in his pockets, his pipe sending up clouds of smoke, his tall muscular frame tilted back. His eyes were fixed on an extraordinary object that crawled slowly over the polished floor. It was a gigantic tortoise—a specimen of *Testudo elephantopus*—a huge cumbersome brute. Its ancient, scaly head was thrust out and its eyes gleamed with a kind of sharp intelligence. The surface of its vast and massive shell was covered over with scribbles in white chalk—notes made by Sarakoff who was in the habit of jotting down figures and formulæ on anything near at hand.

As there was only one chair in the room, Sarakoff eventually thrust me into it, while he sat down on the great beast—whom he called Belshazzar—and told me over and over again how glad he was to see me. And this warmth of his was pleasant to me.

"Are you experimenting on Belshazzar?" I asked at length.

He nodded, and smiled enigmatically.

"He is two hundred years old," he said. "I want to get at his secret."

That was the first positive proof I got of the line of research Sarakoff was intent upon, although, reading between the lines of his many publications, I had guessed something of it.

In every way, Sarakoff was a complete contrast to me. Tall, lean, black-bearded and deep-voiced, careless of public opinion and prodigal in ideas, he was just my antithesis. He was possessed of immense energy. His tousled black hair, moustaches and beard seemed to bristle with it; it shone in his pale blue eyes. He was full of sudden violence, flinging test-tubes across the laboratory, shouting strange songs, striding about snapping his fingers. There was no repose in him. At first I was a little afraid of him, but the feeling wore off. He spoke English fluently, because when a boy he had been at school in London.

I will not enter upon a detailed account of our conversation that first morning in Russia, when the snow lay thick on the roofs of the city, and the ferns of frost sparkled on the window-panes of the laboratory. Briefly, we found ourselves at one over many problems of human research, and I congratulated myself on the fact that in communicating the account of the miracle at St. Dane's Hospital to Sarakoff alone, I had done wisely. He was wonderfully enthusiastic.

"That discovery of yours has furnished the key to the great riddle I had set myself," he exclaimed, striding to and fro. "We will astonish the world, my friend. It is only a question of time."

"But what is the riddle you speak of?" I asked.

"I will tell you soon. Have patience!" he cried. He came towards me impulsively and shook my hand. "We shall find it beyond a doubt, and we will call it the Sarakoff-Harden Bacillus! What do you think of that?"

I was somewhat mystified. He sat down again on the back of the tortoise, smoking in his ferocious manner and smiling and nodding to himself. I though it best to let him disclose his plans in his own way, and kept back the many eager questions that rose to my lips.

"It seems to me," said Sarakoff suddenly, "that England would be the best place to try the experiment. There's a telegraph everywhere, reporters in every village, and enough newspapers to carpet every square inch of the land. In a word, it's a first-class place to watch the results of an experiment."

"On a large scale?"

"On a gigantic scale—an experiment, ultimately, on the world."

I was puzzled and was anxious to draw him into fuller details.

"It would begin in England?" I asked carelessly.

He nodded.

"But it would spread. You remember how the last big outbreak of influenza, which started in this country, spread like wildfire until the waves, passing east and west, met on the other side of the globe? That was a big experiment."

"Of nature," I added.

He did not reply.

"An experiment of nature, you mean?" I urged. At the time of the last big outburst of influenza which began in Russia, Sarakoff must have been a student. Did he know anything about the origin of the mysterious and fatal visitation?

"Yes, of nature," he replied at last, but not in a tone that satisfied me. His manner intrigued me so much that I felt inclined to pursue the subject, but at that moment we were interrupted in a singular way.

The door burst open, and into the room rushed a motley crowd of men. Most of them were young students, but here and there I saw older men, and at the head of the mob was a white-bearded individual, wearing an astrachan cap, who brandished a copy of some Russian periodical in his hand.

Belshazzar drew in his head with a hiss that I could hear even above the clamour of this intrusion.

A furious colloquy began, which I could not understand, since it was in Russian. Sarakoff stood facing the angry crowd coolly enough, but that he was inwardly roused to a dangerous degree, I could tell from his gestures. The copy of the periodical was much in evidence. Fists were shaken freely. The aged, white-bearded leader worked himself up into a frenzy and finally jumped on the periodical, stamping it under his feet until he was out of breath.

Then this excited band trooped out of the room and left us in peace.

"What is it?" I asked when their steps had died away.

Sarakoff shrugged his shoulders and then laughed. He picked up the battered periodical and pointed to an article in it.

"I published a manifesto this morning—that is all," he remarked airily.

"What sort of manifesto?"

"On the origin of death." He sat down on Belshazzar's broad back and twisted his moustaches. "You see, Harden, I believe that in a few more years death will only exist as an uncertain element, appearing rarely, as an unnatural and exceptional incident. Life will be limitless; and the length of years attained by Belshazzar will seem as nothing."

It is curious how the spirit of a new discovery broods over the world like a capricious being, animating one investigator here, another there; partially revealing itself in this continent, disclosing another of its secrets in that, until all the fragments when fitted together make up the whole wonder. It seems that my discovery, coupled with the results of his own unpublished researches, had led Sarakoff to make that odd manifesto. Our combined work, although carried out independently, had given the firm groundwork of an amazing theory which Sarakoff had been maturing in his excited brain for many long years.

Sarakoff translated the manifesto to me. It was a trifle bombastic, and its composition appeared to me vague. No wonder it had roused hostility among his colleagues, I thought, as Sarakoff walked about, declaiming with outstretched arm. Put as briefly as possible, Sarakoff held all disease as due to germs of one sort or another; and decay of bodily tissue he regarded in the same light. In such a theory I stood beside him.

He continued to translate from the soiled and torn periodical, waving his arm majestically.

"We have only to eliminate all germs from the world to banish disease and decay—and *death*. Such an end can be attained in one way alone; a way which is known only to me, thanks to a magnificent series of profound investigations. I announce, therefore, that the disappearance of death from this planet can be anticipated with the utmost confidence. Let us make preparations. Let us consider our laws. Let us examine our resources. Let us, in short, begin the reconstruction of society."

"Good heavens!" I exclaimed, and sat staring at him.

He twirled his moustaches and observed me with shining eyes.

"What do you think of it?"

I shrugged my shoulders helplessly.

"Surely it is far fetched?"

"Not a bit of it. Now listen to me carefully. I'll give you, step by step, the whole matter." He walked up and down for some minutes and then suddenly stopped beside me and thumped me on the back. "There's not a flaw in it!" he cried. "It's magnificent. My dear fellow, death is only a failure in human perfection. There's nothing mysterious in it. Religion has made a ridiculous fuss about it. There's nothing more mysterious in it than there is in a badly-oiled engine wearing out. Now listen. I'm going to begin. . . ."

I listened, fascinated.

3
THE BUTTERFLIES

Two years passed by after my return to London without special incident, save that my black cat died. My work as a consulting physician occupied most of my time. In the greater world beyond my consulting-room door life went on undisturbed by any thought of the approaching upheaval, full of the old tragedies of ambition and love and sickness. But sometimes as I examined my patients and listened to their tales of suffering and pain, a curious contraction of the heart would come upon me at the thought that perhaps some day, not so very far remote, all the endless cycle of disease and misery would cease, and a new dawn of hope burst with blinding radiance upon weary humanity. And then a mood of unbelief would darken my mind and I would view the creation of the bacillus as an idle and vain dream, an illusion never to be realized. . . .

One evening as I sat alone before my study fire, my servant entered and announced there was a visitor to see me.

"Show him in here," I said, thinking he was probably a late patient who had come on urgent business.

A moment later Professor Sarakoff himself was shown in.

I rose with a cry of welcome and clasped his hand.

"My dear fellow, why didn't you let me know you were coming?" I cried.

He smiled upon me with a mysterious brightness.

"Harden," he said in a low voice, as if afraid of being heard, "I came on a sudden impulse. I wanted to show you something. Wait a moment."

He went out into the hall and returned bearing a square box in his hands. He laid it on the table and then carefully closed the door.

"It is the first big result of my experiments," he whispered. He opened the box and drew out a glass case covered over with white muslin.

He stepped back from the table and looked at me triumphantly.

"What is it?" I asked.

"Lift up the muslin."

I did so. On the wooden floor of the glass case were a great number of dark objects. At first I thought they were some kind of grub, and then on closer inspection I saw what they were.

"Butterflies!" I exclaimed.

He held up a warning finger and tiptoed to the door. He opened it suddenly and seemed relieved to find no one outside.

"Hush!" he said, closing the door again. "Yes, they are butterflies." He came back to the table and gave one of the glass panels a tap with his finger. The butterflies stirred and some spread their wings. They were a brilliant greenish purple shot with pale blue. "Yes, they are butterflies."

I peered at them.

"The specimen is unknown in England as far as I know."

"Quite so. They are peculiar to Russia."

"But what are you doing with them?" I asked.

He continued to smile.

"Do you notice anything remarkable about these butterflies?"

"No," I said after prolonged observation, "I can't say I do . . . save that they are not denizens of this country."

"I think we might christen them," he said. "Let us call them *Lepidoptera Sarakoffii.*" He tapped the glass again and watched the insects move. "But they are very remarkable," he continued. "Do they appear healthy to you?"

"Perfectly."

"You agree, then, that they are in good condition?"

"They seem to be in excellent condition."

"No signs of decay—or disease?"

"None."

He nodded.

"And yet," he said thoughtfully, "they should be, according to natural law, a mass of decayed tissue."

"Ah!" I looked at him with dawning comprehension. "You mean—?"

"I mean that they should have died long ago."

"How long do they live normally?"

"About twenty to thirty hours. At the outside their life is not more than thirty-six hours. These are somewhat older."

I gazed at the little creatures crawling aimlessly about. *Aimless*, did I say? There they were, filling up the floor of the glass case, moving with difficulty, getting in each other's way, sprawling and colliding, apparently without aim or purpose. At that spectacle my thoughts might well have taken a leap into the future and seen, instead of a crowded mass of butterflies, a crowded mass of humanity. I asked Sarakoff a question.

"How old are they?" I expected to hear they had existed perhaps a day or two beyond their normal limit.

"They are almost exactly a year old," was the reply. I stared, marvelling. A year old! I bent down, gazing at the turbulent restless mass of gaudy colour. A year old—and still vital and healthy!

"You mean these insects have lived a whole year?" I exclaimed, still unconvinced.

He nodded.

"But that is a miracle!"

"It is, proportionately, equal to a man living twenty-five thousand years instead of the normal seventy."

"You don't suggest—?"

He replaced the muslin covering and took out his pipe and tobacco pouch. Absurd, outrageous ideas crowded to my mind. Was it, then, possible that our dream was to become reality?

"I don't suppose they'll live much longer," I stammered.

He was silent until he had lit his pipe.

"If you met a man who had lived twenty-five thousand years, would you be inclined to tell me he would not live much longer, simply on general considerations?"

I could not find a satisfactory answer.

As a matter of fact the question scarcely conveyed anything to me. One can realize only by reference to familiar standards. The idea of a man who has lived one hundred and fifty years is to me a more realistic curiosity than the idea of a man twenty-five thousand years old. But I caught a glimpse, as it were, of strange figures, moving about in a colourless background, with calm gestures, slow speeches, silences perhaps a year in length. The familiar outline of London crumbled suddenly away, the blotches of shadow and the coloured shafts of light striking between the gaps in the crowds, the violet-lit tubes, the traffic, faded into the conception of twenty-five thousand years. All this many-angled, many-coloured modern spectacle that was a few thousand years removed from cave dwellings, was rolled flat and level, merging into this grey formless carpet of time.

Next morning Sarakoff returned to Russia, bearing with him the wonderful butterflies, and for many months I heard nothing from him. But before he went he told me that he would return soon.

"I have only one step further to take and the ideal germ will be created, Harden. Then we poor mortals will realize the dream that has haunted us since the beginning of time. We will attain immortality, and the fear of death, round which everything is built, will vanish. We will become gods!"

"Or devils, Sarakoff," I murmured.

4
THE SIX TUBES

One night, just as I entered my house, the telephone bell in the hall rang sharply. I picked up the receiver impatiently, for I was tired with the long day's work.

"Is that Dr. Harden?"

"Yes."

"Can you come down to Charing Cross Station at once? The station-master is speaking."

"An accident?"

"No. We wish you to identify a person who has arrived by the boat-train. The police are detaining him as a suspect. He gave your name as a reference. He is a Russian."

"All right. I'll come at once."

I hung up the receiver and told the servant to whistle for a taxicab. Ten minutes later I was picking my way through the crowds on the platform to the station-master's office. I entered, and found a strange scene being enacted. On one side of a table stood Sarakoff, very flushed, with shining eyes, clasping a black bag tightly to his breast. On the other side stood a group of four men, the station-master, a police officer, a plain clothes man and an elderly gentleman in white spats. The last was pointing an accusing finger at Sarakoff.

"Open that bag and we'll believe you!" he shouted.

Sarakoff glared at him defiantly.

I recognized his accuser at once. It was Lord Alberan, the famous Tory obstructionist.

"Anarchist!" Lord Alberan's voice rang out sharply. He took out a handkerchief and mopped his face.

"Arrest him!" he said to the constable with an air of satisfaction. "I knew he was an anarchist the moment I set eyes on him at Dover. There is an infernal machine in that bag. The man reeks of vodka. He is mad."

"Idiot," exclaimed Sarakoff, with great vehemence. "I drink nothing but water."

"He wishes to destroy London," said Lord Alberan coldly. "There is enough dynamite in that bag to blow the whole of Trafalgar Square into fragments. Arrest him instantly."

I stepped forward from the shadows by the door. Sarakoff uttered a cry of pleasure.

"Ah, Harden, I knew you would come. Get me out of this stupid situation!"

"What is the matter?" I asked, glancing at the station-master. He explained briefly that Lord Alberan and Sarakoff had travelled up in the same compartment from Dover, and that Sarakoff's strange restlessness and excited movements had roused Lord Alberan's suspicions. As a consequence Sarakoff had been detained for examination.

"If he would open his bag we should be satisfied," added the station-master. I looked at my friend significantly.

"Why not open it?" I asked. "It would be simplest."

My words had the effect of quieting the excited professor. He put the bag on the table, and placed his hands on the top of it.

"Very well," he said slowly, "I will open it, since my friend Dr. Harden has requested me to do so."

"Stand back!" cried Lord Alberan, flinging out his arms. "We may be so much dust flying over London in a moment."

Sarakoff took out a key and unlocked the bag. There was silence for a moment, only broken by hurrying footsteps on the platform without. Then Lord Alberan stepped cautiously forward.

He saw the worn canvas lining of the bag. He took a step nearer and saw a wooden rack, fitted in the interior, containing six glass tubes whose mouths were stopped with plugs of cotton wool.

"You see, there is nothing important there," said Sarakoff with a smile. "These objects are of purely scientific interest." He took out one of the tubes and held it up to the light. It was half full of a semi-transparent jelly-like mass, faintly blue in colour. The detective, the policeman and the station official clustered round, their faces turned up to the light and their eyes fixed on the tube. The Russian looked at them narrowly, and reading nothing but dull wonderment in their expressions, began to speak again.

"Yes—the *Bacillus Pyocyaneus*," he said, with a faint mocking smile and a side glance at me. "It is occasionally met with in man and is easily detected by the blue bye-product it gives off while growing." He twisted the tube slowly round. "It is quite an interesting culture," he continued idly. "Do you observe the uniform distribution of the growth and the absence of any sign of liquefaction in the medium?"

Lord Alberan cleared his throat.

"I—er—I think we owe you an apology," he said. "My suspicions were unfounded. However, I did my duty to my country by having you examined. You must admit your conduct was suspicious—highly suspicious, sir!"

Sarakoff replaced the tube and locked the bag. Lord Alberan marched to the door and held it open.

"We need not detain you, sir," said the detective. The policeman squared his shoulders and hitched up his belt. The station official looked nervous.

Dr. Sarakoff, with a gesture of indifference, picked up the bag and, taking me by the arm, passed out on to the brilliantly-lit platform. "*Pyocyaneus*," he muttered in my ear; "*pyocyaneus*, indeed! Confound the fellow. He might have got me into no end of trouble if he had known the truth, Harden."

"But what is it?" I asked. "What have you got in the bag?"

He stopped under a sizzling arc-lamp outside the station.

"The bag," he said touching the worn leather lovingly, "contains six tubes of the Sarakoff-Harden bacillus. Yes, I have added your name to it. I will make your name immortal—by coupling it with mine."

"But what is the Sarakoff-Harden bacillus?" I cried.

He struck an attitude under the viperish glare of the lamp and smiled. He certainly did look like an anarchist at the moment. He loomed over me, huge, satanic, inscrutable.

A thrill, almost of fear, passed over me. I glanced round in some apprehension. Under an archway near by I saw Lord Alberan looking fixedly at us. The expression of suspicion had returned to his face.

"You mean—?" He nodded. I gulped a little. "You really have—?" He continued to nod. "Then we can try the great experiment?" I whispered, dry throated.

"At once!" The detective passed us, brushing against my shoulder. I caught Sarakoff by the arm.

"Look here—we must get away," I muttered. I felt like a criminal. Sarakoff clasped the bag firmly under his free arm. We began to walk hurriedly away. Our manner was furtive. Once I looked back and saw Alberan talking, with excited gestures, to the detective. They were both looking in our direction. The impulse to run possessed me. "Quick," I exclaimed, "there's a taxi. Jump in. Drive to Harley Street—like the devil."

Inside the cab I lay back, my mind in a whirl.

"We begin the experiment to-morrow," said Sarakoff at last. "Have you made plans as I told you?"

"Yes—yes. Of course. Only I never believed it possible." I controlled myself and sat up. "I fixed on Birmingham. It seemed best—but I never dreamed—"

"Good!" he exclaimed. "Birmingham, then!"

"Their water supply comes from Wales."

We spoke no more till I turned the key of my study door behind me. It was in this way that the germ, which made so vast and strange an impression on the course of the world's history, first reached England. It had lain under the very nose of Lord Alberan, who opposed everything new automatically. Yet it, the newest of all things, escaped his vigilance.

We decided to put our plans into action without delay, and next morning we set off, carrying with us the precious tubes of the Sarakoff-Harden bacillus. Throughout the long journey we scarcely spoke to each other. Each of us was absorbed in his picture of the future effects of the germ.

There was one strange fact that Sarakoff had told me the night before, and that I had verified. The bacillus was ultra-microscopical—that is, it could not be seen, even with the highest power, under the microscope. Its presence was only to be detected by the blue stain it gave off during its growth.

5

THE GREAT AQUEDUCT

The Birmingham reservoirs are a chain of lakes artificially produced by damming up the River Elan, a tributary of the Wye. The great aqueduct which carries the water from the Elan, eighty miles across country, travelling through hills and bridging valleys, runs past Ludlow and Cleobury Mortimer, through the Wyre Forest to Kidderminster, and on to Birmingham itself through Frankley, where there is a large storage reservoir from which the water is distributed.

The scenery was bleak and desolate. Before us the sun was sinking in a flood of crimson light. We walked briskly, the long legs of the Russian carrying him swiftly over the uneven ground while I trotted beside him. Before the last rays of the sun had died away we saw the black outline of the Caban Loch dam before us, and caught the sheen of water beyond. On the north lay the river Elan and on the south the steep side of a mountain towered up against the luminous sky. The road runs along the left bank of the river bounded by a series of bold and abrupt crags that rise to a height of some eight hundred feet above the level of the water. Just below the Caban Dam is a house occupied by an inspector in charge of the gauge apparatus that is used to measure the outflow of water from the huge natural reservoirs. The lights from his house twinkled through the growing darkness as we drew near, and we skirted it by a short detour and pressed on.

"How long does water take to get from here to Birmingham?" asked Sarakoff as we climbed up to the edge of the first lake.

"It travels about a couple of miles an hour," I replied. "So that means about a day and a half."

We spoke in low voices, for we were afraid of detection. The presence of two visitors at that hour might well have attracted attention.

"A day and a half! Then the bacillus has a long journey to take." He stopped at the margin of the water and stared across the shadowy lake. "Yes, it has a long journey to take, for it will go round the whole world."

The last glow in the sky tinted the calm sheet of water a deep blood colour. Sarakoff opened his bag and took out a couple of tubes.

He pulled the cotton-wool plugs out of the tubes, and with a long wire, loosened the gelatinous contents. Then, inverting the tubes he flung them into the lake close to the beginning of the huge aqueduct.

I stared as the tubes vanished from sight, feeling that it was too late to regret what had now been done, for nothing could collect those millions of bacilli, that had been set free in the water. Already some of them had perhaps entered the dark cavernous mouth of the first culvert to start on their slow journey to Birmingham. The light faded from the sky and darkness spread swiftly over the lake. Sarakoff emptied the remaining tubes calmly and then turned his footsteps in the direction of Rhayader. I waited a moment longer in the deep silence of that lonely spot; and then with a shiver followed my friend. The bacillus had been let loose on the world.

6

THE ATTITUDE OF MR. THORNDUCK

We reached London next day in the afternoon. I felt exhausted and could scarcely answer Sarakoff, who had talked continuously during the journey.

But his theory had interested me. The Russian had revealed much of his character, under the stress of excitement. He spoke of the coming of Immortality in the light of a *physical* boon to mankind. He seemed to see in his mind's eye a great picture of comfort and physical enjoyment and of a humanity released from the grim spectres of disease and death, and ceaselessly pursuing pleasure.

"I love life," he remarked. "I love fame and success. I love comfort, ease, laughter, and companionship. The whole of Nature is beautiful to me, and a beautiful woman is Nature's best reward. Now that the dawn of Immortality is at hand, Harden, we must set about reorganizing the world so that it may yield the maximum of pleasure."

"But surely there will be some limit to pleasure?" I objected.

"Why? Can't you see that is just what there will not be?" he cried excitedly. "We are going to do away with the confining limits. Your imagination is too cramped! You sit there, huddled up in a corner, as if we had let loose a dreadful plague on Birmingham!"

"It may prove to be so," I muttered. I do not think I had any clear idea as to the future, but there is a natural machinery in the mind that doubts golden ages and universal panaceas. Call it superstition if you will, but man's instinct tells him he cannot have uninterrupted pleasure without paying for it. I said as much to the Russian.

He gave vent to a roar of laughter.

"You have all the caution and timidity of your race," he said. "You are fearful even in your hour of deliverance. My friend, it is impossible to conceive, even faintly, of the change that will come over us towards the meaning of life. Can't you see that, as soon as the idea of Immortality gets hold of people, they will devote all their energies to making their earth a paradise? Why, it is obvious. They will then know that there is no other paradise."

He took out his watch and made a calculation. His face became flushed.

"The bacillus has travelled forty-two miles towards Birmingham," he said, just as our train drew in to the London terminus.

I was busy with patients until dinner-time and did not see anything of Sarakoff. While working, my exhaustion and anxiety wore off, and were replaced by a mild exhilaration. One of my patients was a professor of engineering at a northern university; a brilliant young man, who, but for physical disease, had the promise of a great career before him. He had been sent to me, after having made a round of the consultants, to see if I could give him any hope as to the future. I went into his case carefully, and then addressed him a question.

"What is your own view of your case, Mr. Thornduck?"

He looked surprised. His face relaxed, and he smiled. I suppose he detected a message of hope in my expression.

"I have been told by half-a-dozen doctors that I have not long to live, Dr. Harden," he replied. "But it is very difficult for me to grasp that view. I find that I behave as if nothing were the matter. I still go on working. I still see goals far ahead. Death is just a word—frequently uttered, it is true—but meaningless. What am I to do?"

"Go on working."

"And am I to expect only a short lease of life?"

I rose from my writing-table and walked to the hearth. A surge of power came over me as I thought of the bacillus which was so silently and steadily advancing on Birmingham.

"Do you believe in miracles?" I asked.

"That is an odd question." He reflected for a time. "No, I don't think so. All one is taught now-a-days is in a contrary direction, isn't it?"

"Yes, but our knowledge only covers a very small field—perhaps an artificially isolated one, too."

"Then you think only a miracle will save my life?"

I nodded and gazed at him.

"You seem amused," he remarked quietly.

"I am not amused, Mr. Thornduck. I am very happy."

"Does my case interest you?"

"Extremely. As a case, you are typical. Your malady is invariably fatal. It is only one of the many maladies that we know to be fatal, while we remain ignorant of all else. Under ordinary circumstances, you would have before you about three years of reasonable health and sanity."

"And then?"

"Well, after that you would be somewhat helpless. You would begin to employ that large section of modern civilization that deals with the somewhat helpless."

I began to warm to my theme, and clasped my hands behind my back.

"Yes, you would pass into that class that disproves all theories of a kindly Deity, and you would become an undergraduate in the vast and lamentable University of Suffering, through whose limitless corridors we medical men walk with weary footsteps. Ah, if only an intelligent group of scientists had had the construction of the human body to plan! Think what poor stuff it is! Think how easy it would have been to make it more enduring! The cell—what a useless fragile delicacy! And we are made of millions of these useless fragile delicacies."

To my surprise he laughed with great amusement. He stood there, young, pleasant, and smiling. I stared at him with a curious uneasiness. For the moment I had forgotten what it had been my intention to say. The dawn of Immortality passed out of my mind, and I found myself gazing, as it were, on something strangely mysterious.

"Your religion helps you?" I hazarded.

"Religion?" He mused for a moment. "Don't you think there is some meaning behind our particular inevitable destinies—that we may perhaps have earned them?"

"Nonsense! It is all the cruel caprice of Nature, and nothing else."

"Oh, come, Dr. Harden, you surely take a larger view. Do you think the short existence we have here is all the chance of activity we ever have? That I have a glimpse of engineering, and you have a short phase of doctoring on this planet, and that then we have finished all experience?"

"Certainly. It would not be possible to take any other view—horrible."

"But you believe in some theory of evolution—of slow upward progress?"

"Yes, of course. That is proved beyond all doubt."

"And yet you think it applies only to the body—to the instrument—and not to the immaterial side of us?"

I stared at him in astonishment.

"I do not think there is any immaterial side, Mr. Thornduck."

He smiled.

"A very unsatisfying view, surely?" he remarked.

"Unsatisfying, perhaps, but sound science," I retorted.

"Sound?" He pondered for an instant. "Can a thing be sound and unsatisfying at the same time? When I see a machine that's ugly—that's unsatisfying from the artist's point of view—I always know it's wrongly planned and inefficient. Don't you think it's the same with theories of life?" He took out his watch and glanced at it. "But I must not keep you. Good-bye, Dr. Harden."

He went to the door, nodded, and left the room before I recalled that I meant to hint to him that a miracle was going to happen, and save his life. I remained on the hearth-rug, wondering what on earth he meant.

7
LEONORA

I found a note in the hall from Sarakoff asking me to come round to the Pyramid Restaurant at eight o'clock to meet a friend of his. It was a crisp clear evening, and I decided to walk. There were two problems on my mind. One was the outlook of Sarakoff, which even I deemed to be too materialistic. The other was the attitude of young Thornduck, which was obviously absurd.

In my top hat and solemn frock-coat I paced slowly down Harley Street.

Thornduck talked as if suffering, as if all that side of existence which the Blue Germ was to do away with, were necessary and salutary. Sarakoff spoke as if pleasure was the only aim of life. Now, though sheer physical pleasure had never entered very deeply into my life, I had never denied the fact that it was the only motive of the majority of my patients. For what was all our research for? Simply to mitigate suffering; and that is another way of saying that it was to increase physical well-being. Why, then, did Sarakoff's views appear extreme to me? What was there in my composition that whispered a doubt when I had the doctrine of maximum pleasure painted with glowing enthusiasm by the Russian in the train that afternoon?

I moved into Oxford Street deeply pondering. The streets were crowded, and from shop windows there streamed great wedges of white and yellow light. The roar of traffic was round me. The 'buses were packed with men and women returning late from business, or on the way to seek relaxation in the city's amusements. I passed through the throng as through a coloured mist of phantoms. My eyes fastened on the faces of those who passed by. Who could really doubt the doctrine of pleasure? Which one of those people would hesitate to plunge into the full tide of the senses, did not the limitations of the body prevent him?

I crossed Piccadilly Circus with a brisker step. It was no use worrying over questions which could not be examined scientifically. The only really important question in life was to be a success.

The brilliant entrance of the Pyramid Restaurant was before me, and within, standing on the marble floor, I saw the tall figure of the Russian.

Sarakoff greeted me with enthusiasm. He was wearing evening-dress with a white waistcoat, and the fact perturbed me. I put my hat and stick in the cloakroom.

"Who is coming?" I asked anxiously.

"Leonora," he whispered. "I only found out she was in London this afternoon. I met her when I was strolling in the Park while you were busy with your patients."

"But who is Leonora?" I asked. "And can I meet her in this state?"

"Oh, never mind about your dress. You are a busy doctor and she will understand. Leonora is the most marvellous woman in the world. I intend to make her marry me."

"Is she English?" I stammered.

He laughed.

"Little man, you look terrified, as usual. You are always terrified. It is your habit. No, Leonora is not English. She is European. If you went out into the world of amusement a little more—and it would be good for you—you would know that she has the most exquisite voice in the history of civilization. She transcends the nightingale because her body is beautiful. She transcends the peacock because her voice is beautiful. She is, in fact, worthy of every homage, and you will meet her in a short time. Like all perfect things she is late."

He took out his watch and glanced at the door.

"You are an extraordinary person, Sarakoff," I observed, after watching him a moment. "Will you answer me a rather intimate question?"

"Certainly."

"What precisely do you mean when you say you intend to make the charming lady marry you?"

"Precisely what I say. She loves fame. So far I have been unsuccessful, because she does not think I am famous enough."

"How do you intend to remedy that?"

He stared at me in amazement.

"Do you think that any people have ever been so famous as you and I will be in a few days?"

I looked away and studied the bright throng of visitors in the hall.

"In a few days?" I asked. "Are you not a trifle optimistic? Don't you think that it will take months before the possibilities and meaning of the germ are properly realized?"

"Rubbish," exclaimed Sarakoff. "You are a confirmed pessimist. You are impossible, Harden. You are a mass of doubts and apprehensions. Ah, here is Leonora at last. Is she not marvellous?"

I looked towards the entrance. I saw a woman of medium height, very fair, dressed in some soft clinging material of a pale primrose colour. From a shoulder hung a red satin cloak. Round her neck was a string of large pearls, and in her hair was a jewelled osprey. She presented a striking appearance and I gained the impression of some northern spirit in her that shone out of her eyes with the brilliancy of ice.

Sarakoff strode forward, and the contrast that these two afforded was extraordinary. Tall, dark, warm and animated, he stood beside her, and stooped to kiss her hand. She gazed at him with a smile so slight that it seemed scarcely to disturb the perfect symmetry of her face. He began to talk, moving his whole body constantly and making gestures with his arms, with a play of different expressions in his face. She listened without moving, save that her eyes wandered slowly round the large hall. At length Sarakoff beckoned to me.

I approached somewhat awkwardly and was introduced.

"Leonora," said the Russian, "this is a little English doctor with a very large brain. He was closely connected with the great discovery of which I am going to tell you something to-night at dinner. He is my friend and his name is Richard Harden."

"I like your name," said Leonora, in a clear soft voice.

I took her hand. We passed into the restaurant. It was one of those vast pleasure-palaces of music, scent, colour and food that abounded in London. An orchestra was playing somewhere high aloft. The luxury of these establishments was always sounding a curious warning deep down in my mind. But then, as Sarakoff had said, I am a pessimist, and if I were to say that I have noticed that nature often becomes very prodigal and lavish just before she takes away and destroys, I would be uttering, perhaps, one of the many half-truths in which the pessimistic spirit delights.

Our table was in a corner at an agreeable distance from the orchestra. Sarakoff placed Leonora between him and myself. Attentive waiters hurried to serve us; and the eyes of everyone in our immediate neighbourhood were turned in our direction. Leonora did not appear to be affected by the interest she aroused. She flung her cloak on the back of her chair, put her elbows on the table, and gazed at the Russian intently.

"Tell me of your discovery, Alexis."

He smiled, enchanted.

"I shall be best able to give you some idea of what our discovery means if I begin by telling you that I am going to read your character. Does that interest you?"

She nodded. Then she turned to me and studied me for a moment.

"No, Alexis. Let Richard read my character first."

I blushed successfully.

"Why do you blush?" she asked with some interest.

"He blushed because of your unpardonable familiarity in calling him Richard," laughed Sarakoff.

"I shall be most happy, Leonora," I stammered, making an immense effort, and longing for the waiter to bring the champagne. "But I am not good at the art."

"But you must try."

I saw no way out of the predicament. Sarakoff's eyes were twinkling roguishly, so I began, keeping my gaze on the table.

"You have a well-controlled character, with a considerable power of knowing exactly what you want to do with your life, and you come from the North. I fancy you sleep badly."

"How do you know I sleep badly?" she challenged.

"Your eyes are a clear frosty blue, and you are of rather slight build. I am merely speaking from my own experience as a doctor."

I suppose my words were not particularly gracious or well-spoken. Leonora simply nodded and leaned back from the table.

"Now, Alexis, tell me about myself," she said.

My glass now contained champagne and I decided to allow that wizard to take charge of my affairs for a time.

"Leonora, you are one of those women who visit this dull planet from time to time for reasons best known to themselves. I think you must come from Venus, or one of the asteroids; or it may be from Sirius. From the beginning you knew you were not like ordinary people."

"Alexis," she drawled, "you are boring me."

"Capital!" said Sarakoff. "Now we will descend to facts, as our friend here did. You are the most inordinately vain, ambitious, cold-hearted woman in Europe, Leonora. You value yourself before everything. You think your voice and your beauty cannot be beaten, and you are right. Now if I were to tell you that your voice and your beauty could be preserved, year after year, without any change, what would you think?"

A kind of fierce vitality sprang into her face.

"What do you mean?" she asked quietly. "Have you discovered the elixir of youth?"

He nodded. She laid her hand on his arm.

"How long does its effect last?"

"Well—for a considerable time."

"You are certain?"

"Absolutely."

She leaned towards him.

"You will let no one else have it, Alexis," she asked softly. "Only me?"

Sarakoff glanced at me.

"Leonora, you are very selfish."

"Of course."

"Well, you are not the only person who is going to have the elixir. The whole world is going to have it."

I watched her with absorbed attention. She seemed to accept the idea of an elixir of youth without any incredulity, and did not find anything extraordinary in the fact of its discovery. In that respect, I fancied, she was typical of a large class of women—that class that thinks a doctor is a magician, or should be. But when Sarakoff said that the whole world was going to have the elixir, a spasm of anger showed for a moment in her face. She lowered her eyes.

"This is unkind of you, Alexis. Why should not just you and I have the elixir?" She raised her eyes and turned them directly on Sarakoff. "Why not?" she murmured.

The Russian flushed slightly.

"Leonora, it must either not be, or else the whole world must have it. It can't be confined. It must spread. It's a germ. We have let it loose in Birmingham."

She shuddered.

"A germ? What does he mean?" She turned to me.

"It's a germ that will do away with all disease and decay," I said.

"It will make me younger?"

"Of that I am uncertain. It will more probably fix us where we are."

The Russian nodded in confirmation of my view. Leonora considered for a while. I could see nothing in her appearance that she could have wished altered, but she seemed dissatisfied.

"I should have preferred it to make us all a little younger," she said decidedly. Her total lack of the sense of miracles astonished me. She behaved as if Sarakoff had told her that we had discovered a new kind of soap or a new patent food. "But I am glad you have found it, Alexis," she continued. "It will certainly make you famous. That will be nice, but I am sorry you should have given the elixir to Birmingham first. Birmingham is in no need of an elixir, my friend. You should have put something else in their water-supply." She turned to me and examined me with calm criticism. "What a pity you didn't discover the elixir when you were younger, Richard. Your hair is grey at the temples." A clear laugh suddenly came from her. "What a lot of jealously there will be, Alexis. The old ones will be so envious of the young. Think how Madame Réaour will rage—and Betty, and the Signora—all my friends—oh, I feel quite glad now that it doesn't make people younger. You are sure it won't?"

"I don't think so," said Sarakoff, watching her through half-closed lids. "No, I think you are safe, Leonora."

"And my voice?"

"It will preserve that . . . indefinitely, I think."

She was arrested by the new idea. She looked into the distance and fingered the pearls at her throat.

"Then I shall become the most famous singer in the whole world," she murmured. "And I shall have all the money I want. My friend, you have done me a service. I will not forget it." She looked at him and laughed slightly. "But I do not think you have done the world a service. A great many people will not like the germ. No, they will desire to get rid of it, Alexis."

She shuddered a little. I stared at her.

"I think you are mistaken," said Alexis, gruffly.

She shook her head.

"Come, let us finish dinner quickly and I will take you both to my flat and sing to you a little."

Leonora's flat was in Whitehall Court, and of its luxury I need not speak. I must confess to the fact that, sober and timid as is my nature, I thoroughly enjoyed the atmosphere. Leonora was generous. Her voice was exquisite. I sat on a deep couch of green satin and gazed at a Chinese idol cut in green jade, that stood on a neighbouring table, with all my senses lulled by the charm of her singing. The sense of responsibility fell away from me like severed cords. I became pagan as I lolled there, a creature of sensuous feeling.

Sarakoff lay back in a deep chair in the shadow with his eyes fixed on Leonora. We were both in a kind of delicious drowsiness when the opening of the door roused us.

Leonora stopped abruptly. With some difficulty I removed my gaze from the Chinese figure, which had hypnotized me, and looked round resentfully.

Lord Alberan was standing in the doorway. He seemed surprised to find that Leonora had visitors. I could not help marking a slight air of proprietorship in his manner.

"I am afraid I am interrupting," he said smoothly. He crossed to the piano and leant over Leonora. "You got my telegram?"

"No," she replied; "I did not even know you had returned from France."

"I came the day before yesterday. I had to go down to Maltby Towers. I came up to town to-day and wired you on the way."

He straightened himself and turned towards us. Leonora rose and came down the room. We rose.

"Geoffrey," she said, drawling slightly, "I want to introduce you to two friends of mine. They will soon be very famous—more famous than you are—because they have discovered a germ that is going to keep us all young."

Lord Alberan glanced at me and then looked hard at the Russian. A swiftly passing surprise showed that he recognized Sarakoff. Leonora mentioned our names casually, took up a cigarette and dropped into a chair.

"Yes," she continued, "these gentlemen have put the germ into the water that supplies Birmingham." She struck a match and lit the cigarette. I noticed she actually smoked very little, but seemed to like to watch the burning cigarette. "Do sit down. What are you standing for, Geoffrey?"

Lord Alberan's attitude relaxed. He had evidently decided on his course of action.

"That is very interesting," he observed, as if he had never seen Sarakoff before. "A germ that is going to keep us all young. It reminds me of the Arabian Nights. I should like to see it."

"You've seen it already," replied Sarakoff, imperturbably.

Lord Alberan's cold eyes looked steadily before him. His mouth tightened.

"Really?"

"You saw it at Charing Cross Station the night before last."

"At Charing Cross Station?"

I tried to signal to the Russian, but he seemed determined to proceed.

"Yes—you thought I was an anarchist. You saw the contents of my bag. Six tubes containing a blue-coloured gelatine. Perhaps, Lord Alberan, you remember now."

"I remember perfectly," he exclaimed, smiling slightly. "Yes, I regret my mistake. One has to be careful."

"Did you think my Alexis was an anarchist?" cried Leonora. "You are the stupidest of Englishmen."

It was obvious that Alberan did not like this. He glanced at a thin gold watch that he carried in his waistcoat pocket.

"I will not interrupt you any longer," he remarked gravely. "You are quite occupied, I see, and I much apologize for intruding."

"Don't be still more stupid," she said lazily. "Sit down. Tell me how you like the idea of never dying."

"I am afraid I cannot entertain the idea seriously." He hesitated and then looked firmly at Sarakoff. "Do I understand, sir, that you have actually put some germ into the Birmingham water-supply?"

The Russian nodded.

"You'll hear about it in a day or two," he said quietly.

"You had permission to do this?"

"No, I had no permission."

"Are you aware that you are making a very extraordinary statement, sir?"

"Perfectly."

Lord Alberan became very red. The lower part of his face seemed to expand. His eyes protruded.

"Don't gobble," said Leonora.

"Gobble?" stuttered Alberan, turning upon her. "How dare you say I gobble?"

"But you are gobbling."

"I refuse to stay here another moment. I will leave immediately. As for you, sir, you shall hear from me in course of time. To-morrow I am compelled to go abroad again, but when I return I shall institute a vigorous and detailed enquiry into your movements, which are highly suspicious, sir,—highly suspicious." He moved to the door and then turned. "Mademoiselle, I wish you good-night." He bowed stiffly and went out.

"Thank heaven, I've got rid of him for good," murmured Leonora. "He proposed to me last week, Alexis."

"And what did you say?" asked Sarakoff.

"I said I would see, but things are different now." She turned her eyes straight in his direction. "That is, if you have told me the truth, Alexis. Oh, isn't it wonderful!" She jumped up and threw out her arms. "Suppose that it all comes true, Alexis! Immortality—always to be young and beautiful!"

"It will come true," he said.

She lowered her arms slowly and looked at him.

"I wonder how long love will last?"

8
THE BLUE DISEASE

Next day the first news of the Sarakoff-Harden bacillus appeared in a small paragraph in an evening paper, and immediately I saw it, I hurried back to the house in Harley Street where Sarakoff was writing a record of our researches.

"Listen to this," I cried, bursting excitedly into the room. I laid the paper on the table and pointed to the column. "Curious disease among trout in Wales," I read. "In the Elan reservoirs which have long been famed for their magnificent trout, which have recently increased so enormously in size and number that artificial stocking is entirely unnecessary, a curious disease has made its appearance. Fish caught there this morning are reported to have an unnatural bluish tint, and their flesh, when cooked, retains this hue. It is thought that some disease has broken out. Against this theory is the fact that no dead fish have been observed. The Water Committee of the City Council of Birmingham are investigating this matter."

Sarakoff pushed his chair back and twisted it round towards me. For some moments we stared at each other with almost scared expressions. Then a smile passed over the Russian's face.

"Ah, we had forgotten that. A bluish tint! Of course, it was to be expected."

"Yes," I cried, "and what is more, the bluish tint will show itself in every man, woman or child infected with the bacillus. Good heavens, fancy not thinking of that ourselves!"

Sarakoff picked up the paper and read the paragraph for himself. Then he laid it down. "It is strange that one so persistently neglects the obvious in one's calculations. Of course there will be a bluish tint." He leaned back and pulled at his beard. "I should think it will show itself in the whites of the eyes first, just as jaundice shows itself there. Leonora won't like that—it won't suit her colouring. You see that these fish, when cooked, retained the bluish hue. That is very interesting."

"It's very bad luck on the trout."

"Why?"

"After getting the bacillus into their system, they blunder on to a hook and meet their death straight away."

"The bacillus is not proof against death by violence," replied Sarakoff gravely. "That is a factor that will always remain constant. We are agreed in looking on all disease as eventually due to poisons derived from germ activity, but a bang on the head or asphyxiation or prussic acid or a bullet in the heart are not due to a germ. Yes, these poor trout little knew what a future they forfeited when they took the bait."

"The bacillus is in Birmingham by now," I said suddenly. I passed my hand across my brow nervously, and glanced at the manuscript lying before Sarakoff. "You had better keep those papers locked up. I spent an awful day at the hospital. It dawned on me that the whole medical profession will want to tear us in pieces before the year is out."

"In theory they ought not to."

"Who cares for theory, when it is a question of earning a living? As I walked along the street to-day, I could have shrieked aloud when I saw everybody hurrying about as if nothing were going to happen. This is unnerving me. It is so tremendous."

Sarakoff picked up his pen, and traced out a pattern in the blotting-pad before him.

"The Water Committee of Birmingham are investigating the matter," he observed. "It will be amusing to hear their report. What will they think when they make a bacteriological examination of the water in the reservoir? It will stagger them."

The next morning I was down to breakfast before my friend and stood before the fire eagerly scanning the papers. At first I could find nothing that seemed to indicate any further effects of the bacillus. I was in the act of buttering a piece of toast when my eye fell on one of the newspapers lying beside me. A heading in small type caught my eye.

"*The measles epidemic in Ludlow.*" I picked the paper up.

"The severe epidemic of measles which began last week and seemed likely to spread through the entire town, has mysteriously abated. Not only are no further cases reported, but several doctors report that those already attacked have recovered in an incredibly short space of time. Doubt has been expressed by the municipal authorities as to whether the epidemic was really measles."

I adjusted my glasses to read the paragraph again. Then I got up and went into my study. After rummaging in a drawer I pulled out and unrolled a map of England. The course of the aqueduct from Elan to Birmingham was marked by a thin red line. I followed it slowly with the point of my finger and came on the town of Ludlow about half-way along. I stared at it.

"Of course," I whispered at length, my finger still resting on the position of the town. "All these towns on the way are supplied by the aqueduct. I hadn't thought of that. The bacillus is in Ludlow."

For about a minute I did not move. Then I rolled up the map and went up to Sarakoff's bedroom. I met the Russian on the landing on his way to the bathroom.

"The bacillus is in Ludlow," I said in a curiously small voice. I stood on the top stair, holding on to the bannister, my big glasses aslant on my nose, and the map hanging down in my limp grasp.

I had to repeat the sentence before Sarakoff heard me.

"Where's Ludlow?"

I sank on my knees and unrolled the map on the floor and pointed directly with my finger.

Sarakoff went down on all fours and looked at the spot keenly.

"Ah, on the line of the aqueduct! But how do you know it is there?"

"It has cut short an epidemic of measles. The doctors are puzzled."

Sarakoff nodded. He was looking at the names of the other towns that lay on the course of the aqueduct.

"Cleobury-Mortimer," he spelt out. "No news from there?"

"None."

"And none from Birmingham yet?"

"None."

"We'll have news to-morrow." He raised himself on his knees. "Trout and then measles!" he said, and laughed. "This is only the beginning. No wonder the Ludlow doctors are puzzled."

The same evening there was further news of the progress of the bacillus. From Cleobury-Mortimer, ten miles from Ludlow, and twenty from Birmingham, it was reported that the measles epidemic there had been cut short in the same mysterious manner as noticed in Ludlow. But next morning a paragraph of considerable length appeared which I read out in a trembling voice to Sarakoff.

"It was reported a short time ago that the trout in the Elan reservoirs appeared to be suffering from a singular disease, the effect of which was to tint their scales and flesh a delicate bluish colour. The matter is being investigated. In the meanwhile it has been noticed, both in Ludlow and Cleobury-Mortimer, and also in Knighton, that the peculiar bluish tint has appeared amongst the inhabitants. Our correspondent states that it is most marked in the conjunctivæ, or whites of the eyes. There must undoubtedly be some connection between this phenomenon and the condition of the trout in the Elan reservoirs, as all the above-mentioned towns lie close to, and receive water from, the great aqueduct. The most remarkable thing, however, is that the bluish discolouration does not seem to be accompanied by any symptoms of illness in those whom it has affected. No sickness or fever has been observed. It is perhaps nothing more than a curious coincidence that the abrupt cessation of the measles epidemic in Ludlow and Cleobury-Mortimer, reported in yesterday's issue, should have occurred simultaneously with the appearance of bluish discolouration among the inhabitants."

On the same evening, I was returning from the hospital and saw the following words on a poster:—

"Blue Disease in Birmingham."

I bought a paper and scanned the columns rapidly. In the stop-press news I read:—

"The Blue Disease has appeared in Birmingham. Cases are reported all over the city. The Public Health Department are considering what measures should be adopted. The disease seems to be unaccompanied by any dangerous symptoms."

I stood stock-still in the middle of the pavement. A steady stream of people hurrying from business thronged past me. A newspaper boy was shouting something down the street, and as he drew nearer, I heard his hoarse voice bawling out:—

"Blue Disease in Birmingham."

He passed close to me, still bawling, and his voice died away in the distance. Men jostled me and glanced at me angrily. . . . But I was lost in a dream. The paper dropped from my fingers. In my mind's eye I saw the Sarakoff-Harden bacillus in Birmingham, teeming in every water-pipe in countless billions, swarming in the carafes on dining-room tables, and in every ewer and finger-basin, infecting everything it came in contact with. And the vision of Birmingham and the whole stretch of country up to the Elan watershed passed before me, stained with a vivid blue.

9
THE MAN FROM BIRMINGHAM

The following day while walking to the hospital, I noticed a group of people down a side street, apparently looking intently at something unusual. I turned aside to see what it was. About twenty persons, mostly errand boys, were standing round a sandwich-board man. At the outskirts of the circle, I raised myself on tip-toe and peered over the heads of those in front. The sandwich-board man's back was towards me.

"What's the matter?" I asked of my neighbour.

"One of the blue freaks from Birmingham," was the reply.

My first impulse was to fly. Here I was in close proximity to my handiwork. I turned and made off a few paces. But curiosity overmastered me, and I came back. The man was now facing me, and I could see him distinctly through a gap in the crowd. It was a thin, unshaven face with straightened features and gaunt cheeks. The eyes were deeply sunken and at that moment turned downwards. His complexion was pale, but I could see a faint bluish tinge suffusing the skin, that gave it a strange, dead look. And then the man lifted his eyes and gazed straight at me. I caught my breath, for under the black eye brows, the whites of the eyes were stained a pure sparrow-egg blue.

"I came from Birmingham yesterday," I heard him saying. "There ain't nothing the matter with me."

"You ought to go to a fever hospital," said someone.

"We don't want that blue stuff in London," added another.

"Perhaps it's catching," said the first speaker.

In a flash everyone had drawn back. The sandwich-board man stood in the centre of the road alone looking sharply round him. Suddenly a wave of rage seemed to possess him. He shook his fist in the air, and even as he shook it, his eyes caught the blue sheen of the tense skin over the knuckles. He stopped, staring stupidly, and the rage passed from his face, leaving it blank and incredulous.

"Lor' lumme," he muttered. "If that ain't queer."

He held out his hand, palm downwards. And from the pavement I saw that the man's nails were as blue as pieces of turquoise.

The sun came out from behind a passing cloud and sent a sudden flame of radiance over the scene in the side street—the sandwich-board man, his face still blank and incredulous, staring stupidly at his hands; the crowd standing well back in a wide semicircle; I further forward, peering through my spectacles and clutching my umbrella convulsively. Then a tall man, in morning coat and top-hat, pushed his way through and touched the man from Birmingham on the shoulder.

"Can you come to my house?" he asked in an undertone. "I am a doctor and would like to examine you."

I shifted my gaze and recognized Dr. Symington-Tearle. The man pointed to his boards.

"How about them things?"

"Oh, you can get rid of them. I'll pay you. Here is my card with the address. I'll expect you in half-an-hour, and it will be well worth while your coming."

Symington-Tearle moved away, and a sudden spasm of jealousy affected me as I watched the well-shaped top-hat glittering down the street in the strong sunlight. Why should Symington-Tearle be given an opportunity of impressing a credulous world with some fantastic rubbish of his own devising? I stepped into the road.

"Do you want a five-pound note?" I asked. The man jumped with surprise. "Very well. Come round to this address at once."

I handed him my card. My next move was to telephone to the hospital to say I would be late, and retrace my footsteps homewards.

My visitor arrived in a very short time, after handing over his boards to a comrade on the understanding of suitable compensation, and was shown into my study. Sarakoff was present, and he pored over the man's nails and eyes and skin with rapt attention. At last he enquired how he felt.

"Ain't never felt so well in me life," said the man. "I was saying to a pal this morning 'ow well I felt."

"Do you feel as if you were drunk?" asked Sarakoff tentatively.

"Well, sir, now you put it that way, I feel as if I'd 'ad a good glass of beer. Not drunk, but 'appy."

"Are you naturally cheerful?"

"I carn't say as I am, sir. My profession ain't a very cheery one, not in all sorts and kinds of weather."

"But you are distinctly more cheerful this morning than usual?"

"I am, sir. I don't deny it. I lost my temper sudden like when that crowd drew away from me as if I'd got the leprosy, and I'm usually a mild and forbearin' man."

"Sit down," said Sarakoff. The man obeyed, and Sarakoff began to examine him carefully. He told him once or twice not to speak, but the man seemed in a loquacious mood and was incapable of silence for more than a minute of time.

"And I ain't felt so clear 'eaded not for years," he remarked. "I seem to see twice as many things to what I used to, and everything seems to 'ave a new coat of paint. I was saying to a pal early this morning what a very fine place Trafalgar Square was and 'ow I'd never seemed to notice it before, though I've known it all my life. And up Regent Street I begun to notice all sort o' little things I'd never seen before, though it was my old beat 'afore I went to Birmingham. O' course it may be because I been out o' London a spell. But blest if I ever seed so many fine shop windows in Regent Street before, or so many different colours."

"Headache?"

"Bless you, no, sir. Just the opposite, if you understand." He looked round suddenly. "What's that noise?" he asked. "It's been worryin' me since I came in here."

We listened intently, but neither I nor Sarakoff could hear anything.

"It comes from there." The man pointed to the laboratory door. I went and opened it and stood listening. In a corner by the window a clock-work recording barometer was ticking with a faint rhythm.

"That's the noise," said the man from Birmingham. "I knew it wasn't no clock, 'cause it's too fast."

Sarakoff glanced significantly at me.

"All the senses very acute," he said. "At least, hearing and seeing." He took a bottle from the laboratory and uncorked it in one corner of the study. "Can you smell what this is?"

The man, sitting ten feet away, gave one sniff.

"Ammonia," he said promptly, and sneezed. "This 'ere Blue Disease," said the man after a long pause, "is it dangerous?"

He spread out his fingers, squeezing the turquoise nails to see if the colour faded. He frowned to find it fixed. I was standing at the window, my back to the room and my hands twisting nervously with each other behind me.

"No, it is not dangerous," said Sarakoff. He sat on the edge of the writing-table, swinging his legs and staring meditatively at the floor. "It is not dangerous, is it, Harden?"

I replied only with a jerky, impatient movement.

"What I mean," persisted the man, "is this—supposin' the police arrest me, when I go back to my job. 'Ave they a right? 'Ave people a right to give me the shove—to put me in a 'orspital? That crowd round me in the street—it confused me, like—as if I was a leper." He paused and looked up at Sarakoff enquiringly. "What's the cause of it?"

"A germ—a bacillus."

"Same as what gives consumption?"

Sarakoff nodded. "But this germ is harmless," he added.

"Then I ain't going to die?"

"No. That's just the point. You aren't going to die," said the Russian slowly. "That's what is so strange."

I jumped round from the window.

"How do you know?" I said fiercely. "There's no proof. It's all theory so far. The calculations may be wrong."

The man stared at me wonderingly. He saw me as a man fighting with some strange anxiety, with his forehead damp and shining, his spectacles aslant on his nose and the heavy folds of his frock-coat shaken with a sudden impetuosity.

"How do you know?" I repeated, shaking my fist in the air. "How do you know he isn't going to die?"

Sarakoff fingered his beard in silence, but his eyes shone with a quiet certainty. To the man from Birmingham it must have seemed suddenly strange that we should behave in this manner. His mind was sharpened to perceive things. Yesterday, had he been present at a similar scene, he would probably have sat dully, finding nothing curious in my passionate attitude and the calm, almost insolent, inscrutability of Sarakoff. He forgot his turquoise finger nails, and stared, open-mouthed.

"Ain't going to die?" he said. "What do yer mean?"

"Simply that you aren't going to die," was Sarakoff's soft answer.

"Yer mean, not die of the Blue Disease?"

"Not die at all."

"Garn! Not die at all." He looked at me. "What's he mean, Mister?" He looked almost surprised with himself at catching the drift of Sarakoff's sentence. Inwardly he felt something insistent and imperious, forcing him to grasp words, to blunder into new meanings. Some new force was alive in him and he was carried on by it in spite of himself. He felt strung up to a pitch of nervous irritation. He got up from his chair and came forward, pointing at Sarakoff. "What's this?" he demanded. "Why don't you speak out? Yer cawn't hide it from me." He stopped. His brain, working at unwonted speed, had discovered a fresh suspicion. "Look 'ere, you two know something about this blue disease." He came a step closer, and looking cunningly in my face, said: "That's why you offered me a five-pound note, ain't it?"

I avoided the scrutiny of the sparrow-egg blue orbs close before me.

"I offered you the money because I wished to examine you," I said shortly. "Here it is. You can go now."

I took a note from a safe in the corner of the room, and held it out. The man took it, felt its crispness and stowed it away in a secure pocket. His thoughts were temporarily diverted by the prospect of an immediate future with plenty of money, and he picked up his hat and went to the door. But his turquoise finger nails lying against the rusty black of the hat brought him back to his suspicions. He paused and turned.

"My name's Wain," he said. "I'm telling you, in case you might 'ear of me again. 'Erbert Wain. I know what yours is, remember, because I seed it on the door." He twisted his hat round several times in his hands and drew his brows together, puzzled at the speed of his ideas. Then he remembered the card that Symington-Tearle had given him.

He pulled it out and examined it. "I'm going across to see this gent," he announced. "It's convenient, 'im living so close. Perhaps he'll 'ave a word to say about this 'ere disease. Fair spread over Birmingham, so they say. It would be nasty if any bloke was responsible for it. Good day to yer." He opened the door slowly, and glanced back at us standing in the middle of the room watching him. "Look 'ere," he said swiftly, "what did 'e mean, saying I was never going to die and—" The light from the window was against his eyes, and he could not see the features of Sarakoff's face, but there was something in the outline of his body that checked him. "Guv'ner, it ain't true." The words came hoarsely from his lips. "I ain't never not going to die."

Sarakoff spoke.

"You are never going to die, Mr. Herbert Wain . . . you understand? . . . *Never* going to die, unless you get killed in an accident—or starve."

I jerked up my hand to stop my friend.

Wain stared incredulously. Then he burst into a roar of laughter and smacked his thigh.

"Gor lumme!" he exclaimed, "if that ain't rich. Never going to die! Live for ever! Strike me, if that ain't a notion!" The tears ran down his cheeks and he paused to wipe them away. "If I was to believe what you say," he went on, "it would fair drive me crazy. Live for ever—s'elp me, if that wouldn't be just 'ell. Good-day to yer, gents. I'm obliged to yer."

He went out into the sunlit street still roaring with laughter, a thin, ragged, tattered figure, with the shadow of immortality upon him.

10
THE ILLNESS OF MR. ANNOT

The departure of Mr. Herbert Wain was a relief. I turned to Sarakoff at once and spoke with some heat.

"You were more than imprudent to give that fellow hints that we knew more about the Blue Disease than anybody else," I exclaimed. "This may be the beginning of incalculable trouble."

"Nonsense," replied the Russian. "You are far too apprehensive, Harden. What can he do?"

"What may he not do?" I cried bitterly. "Do you suppose London will welcome the spread of the germ? Do you think that people will be pleased to know that you and I were responsible for its appearance?"

"When they realize that it brings immortality with it, they will hail us as the saviours of humanity."

"Mr. Herbert Wain did not seem to accept the idea of immortality with any pleasure," I muttered. "The suggestion seemed to strike him as terrible."

Sarakoff laughed genially.

"My friend," he said, "Mr. Herbert Wain is not a man of vision. He is a cockney, brought up in the streets of a callous city. To him life is a hard struggle, and immortality naturally appears in a poor light. You must have patience. It will take some time before the significance of this immortality is grasped by the people. But when it is grasped, all the conditions of life will change. Life will become beautiful. We will have reforms that, under ordinary circumstances, would have taken countless ages to bring about. We will anticipate our evolution by thousands of centuries. At one step we will reach the ultimate goal of our destiny."

"And what is that?"

"Immortality, of course. Surely you must see by now that all the activities of modern life are really directed towards one end—towards solving the riddle of prolonging life and at the same time increasing pleasure? Isn't that the inner secret desire that you doctors find in every patient? So far a compromise has only been possible, but now that is all changed."

"I don't agree, Sarakoff. Some people must live for other motives. Take myself . . . I live for science."

"It is merely your form of pleasure."

"That's a quibble," I cried angrily. "Science is aspiration. There's all the difference in the world between aspiration and pleasure. I have scarcely known what pleasure is. I have worked like a slave all my life, with the sole ambition of leaving something permanent behind me when I die."

"But you won't die," interposed the Russian. "That is the charm of the new situation."

"Then why should I work?" The question shaped itself in my mind and I uttered it involuntarily. I sat down and stared at the fire. A kind of dull depression came over me, and for some reason the picture of Sarakoff's butterflies appeared in my mind. I saw them with great distinctness, crawling aimlessly on the floor of their cage. "Why should I work?" I repeated.

Sarakoff merely shrugged his shoulders and turned away. Questions of that kind did not seem to bother him. His was a nature that escaped the necessity of self-analysis. But I was different, and our conversation had aroused a train of odd thought. What, after all, was it that kept my nose to the grindstone? Why had I slaved incessantly all my life, reading when I might have slept, examining patients when I might have been strolling through meadows, hurrying through meals when I might have eaten at leisure? What was the cause behind all the tremendous activity and feverish haste of modern people? When Sarakoff had said that I would not die, and that therein lay the charm of the new situation, it seemed as if scales had momentarily fallen from my eyes. I beheld myself as something ridiculous, comparable to a hare that persists in dashing along a country lane in front of the headlight of a motor car, when a turn one way or another would bring it to safety. A great uneasiness filled me, and with it came a determination to ignore these new fields of thought that loomed round me—a determination that I have seen in old men when they are faced by the new and contradictory—and I began to force my attention elsewhere. I was relieved when the door opened and my servant entered. She handed me a telegram. It was from Miss Annot, asking me to come to Cambridge at once, as her father was seriously ill. I scribbled a reply, saying I would be down that afternoon.

After the servant had left the room, I remained gazing at the fire, but my depression left me. In place of it I felt a quiet elation, and it was not difficult for me to account for it.

"I was wrong in saying that I had scarcely known what pleasure is," I observed at length, looking up at Sarakoff with a smile. "I must confess to you that there is one factor in my life that gives me great pleasure."

Sarakoff placed himself before me, hands in pockets and pipe in mouth, and gazed at me with an answering smile in his dark face.

"A woman?"

I flushed. The Russian seemed amused.

"I thought as much," he remarked. "This year I noticed a change in you. Your fits of abstraction suggested it. Well, may I congratulate you? When are you to be married?"

"That is out of the question at present," I answered hurriedly. "In fact, there is no definite arrangement—just a mutual understanding. . . . She is not free."

Sarakoff raised his shaggy eyebrows.

"Then she is already married?"

This cross-examination was intensely painful to me. Between Miss Annot and myself there was, I hoped, a perfect understanding, and I quite realized the girl's position. She was devoted to her father, who required her constant attention and care, and until she was free there could be no question of marriage, or even an engagement, for fear of wounding the old man's feelings. I quite appreciated her situation and was content to wait.

"No! She has an invalid father, and—"

"Rubbish!" said Sarakoff, with remarkable force. "Rubbish! Marry her, man, and then think of her father. Why, that sort of thing—" He drew a deep breath and checked himself.

I shook my head.

"That is impossible. Here, in England, we cannot do such things. . . . The girl's duty is plain. I am quite prepared to wait."

"To wait for what?"

I looked at him in unthinking surprise.

"Until Mr. Annot dies, of course."

Sarakoff remained motionless. Then he took his pipe out of his mouth, strolled to the window, and began to whistle to himself in subdued tones. A moment later he left the room. I picked up a time-table and looked out a train, a little puzzled by his behaviour.

I reached Cambridge early in the afternoon and took a taxi to the Annots' house. Miss Annot met me at the door.

"It is so good of you to come," she said with a faint smile. "My father behaved very foolishly yesterday. He insisted on inviting the Perrys to lunch, and he talked a great deal and insisted on drinking wine, with the result that in the night he had a return of his gastritis. He is very weak to-day and his mind seems to be wandering a little."

"You should not have allowed him to do that," I remonstrated. "He is in too fragile a state to run any risks."

"Oh, but I couldn't help it. The Perrys are such old friends of father's, and they were only staying one day in Cambridge. Father would have fretted if they had not come."

I had taken off my coat in the hall, and we were now standing in the drawing-room.

"You are tired, Alice," I said.

"I've been up most of the night," she replied, with an effort towards brightness. "But I do feel tired, I admit."

I turned away from her and went to the window. For the first time I felt the awkwardness of our position. I had a strong and natural impulse to comfort her, but what could I do? After a moment's reflection, I made a sudden resolution.

"Alice," I said, "you and I had better become engaged. Don't you think it would be easier for you?"

"Oh, don't," she cried. "Father would never endure the idea that I belonged to another man. He would worry about my leaving him continually. No, please wait. Perhaps it will not be—"

She checked herself. I remained silent, staring at the pattern of the carpet with a frown. To my annoyance, I could not keep Sarakoff's words out of my mind. And yet Alice was right. I felt sure that no one is a free agent in the sense that he or she can be guided solely by love. It is necessary to make a compromise. As these thoughts formed in my mind I again seemed to hear the loud voice of Sarakoff, sounding in derision at my cautious views. A conflict arose in my soul. I raised my eyes and looked at Alice. She was standing by the mantelpiece, staring listlessly at the grate. A wave of emotion passed over me. I took a step towards her.

"Alice!" And then the words stuck in my throat. She turned her head and her eyes questioned me. I tried to continue, but something prevented me, and I became suddenly calm again. "Please take me up to your father," I begged her. She obeyed silently, and I followed her upstairs.

Mr. Annot was lying in a darkened room with his eyes closed. He was a very old man, approaching ninety, with a thin aquiline face and white hair. He lay very still, and at first I thought he was unconscious. But his pulse was surprisingly good, and his breathing deep and regular.

"He is sleeping," I murmured.

She leaned over the bed.

"He scarcely slept during the night," she whispered. "This will do him good."

"His pulse could not be better," I murmured.

She peered at him more closely.

"Isn't he very pale?"

I stooped down, so that my face was close to hers. The old man certainly looked very pale. A marble-like hue lay over his features, and yet the skin was warm to the touch.

"How long has he been asleep?" I asked.

"He was awake over an hour ago, when I looked in last. He said then that he was feeling drowsy."

"I think we'll wake him up."

Alice hesitated.

"Won't you wait for tea?" she whispered. "He would probably be awake by then."

I shook my head.

"I must get back to London by five. Do you mind if we have a little more light?"

She moved to the window and raised the blind half way. I examined the old man attentively. There was no doubt about the curious pallor of his skin. It was like the pallor of extreme collapse, save for the presence of a faint colour in his cheeks which seemed to lie as a bright transparency over a dead background. My fingers again sought his pulse. It was full and steady. As I counted it my eyes rested on his hand.

I stooped down suddenly with an exclamation. Alice hurried to my side.

"Where did those friends of his come from?" I asked swiftly.

"The Perrys? From Birmingham."

"Was there anything wrong with them?"

"What do you mean?"

Before I could reply the old man opened his eyes. The light fell clearly on his face. Alice uttered a cry of horror. I experienced an extraordinary sensation of fear. Out of the marble pallor of Mr. Annot's face, two eyes, stained a sparrow-egg blue, stared keenly at us.

11
THE RESURRECTION

For some moments none of us spoke. Alice recovered herself first.

"What is the matter with him?" she gasped.

I was incapable of finding a suitable reply, and stood, tongue-tied, staring foolishly at the old man. He seemed a little surprised at our behaviour.

"Dr. Harden," he said, "I am glad to see you. My daughter did not tell me you were coming."

His voice startled me. It was strong and clear. On my previous visit to him he had spoken in quavering tones.

"Oh, father, how do you feel?" exclaimed Alice, kneeling beside the bed.

"My dear, I feel extremely well. I have not felt so well for many years." He stretched out his hand and patted his daughter's head. "Yes, my sleep has done me good. I should like to get up for tea."

"But your eyes—" stammered Alice "Can you see, father?"

"See, my dear? What does she mean, Dr. Harden?"

"There is some discolouration of the conjunctivæ," I said hastily. "It is nothing to worry about."

At that moment Alice caught sight of his finger nails.

"Look!" she cried, "they're blue."

The old man raised his hands and looked at them in astonishment.

"How extraordinary," he murmured. "What do you make of that, doctor?"

"It is nothing," I assured him. "It is only pigmentation caused—er—caused by some harmless germ."

"I know what it is," cried Alice suddenly. "It's the Blue Disease. Father, you remember the Perrys were telling us about it yesterday at lunch. They said it was all over Birmingham, and that they had come south partly to escape it. They must have brought the infection with them."

"Yes," I said, "that is certainly the explanation. And now, Mr. Annot, let me assure you that this disease is harmless. It has no ill effects."

Mr. Annot sat up in bed with an exhibition of vigour that was remarkable in a man of his age.

"I can certainly witness to the fact that it causes no ill effects, Dr. Harden," he exclaimed. "This morning I felt extremely weak and was prepared for the end. But now I seem to have been endowed with a fresh lease of life. I feel young again. Do you think this Blue Disease is the cause of it?"

"Possibly. It is difficult to say," I answered in some confusion. "But you must not think of getting up, Mr. Annot. Rest in bed for the next week is essential."

"Humbug!" cried the old man, fixing his brilliant eyes upon me. "I am going to get up this instant."

"Oh, father, please don't be so foolish!"

"Foolish, child? Do you think I'm going to lie here when I feel as if my body and mind had been completely rejuvenated? I repeat I am going to get up. Nothing on earth will keep me in bed."

The old man began to remove the bedclothes. I made an attempt to restrain him, but was met by an outburst of irritation that warned me not to interfere. I motioned Alice to follow me, and together we left the room. As we went downstairs I heard a curious sound proceeding from Mr. Annot's bedroom. We halted on the stairs and listened. The sound became louder and clearer.

"Father is singing," said Alice in a low voice. Then she took out her handkerchief and began to sob.

We continued our way downstairs, Alice endeavouring to stifle her sobs, and I in a dazed condition of mind. I was stunned by the fact that that mad experiment of ours should have had such a sudden and strange result. It produced in me a fear that was far worse to bear than the vague anxiety I had felt ever since those fatal tubes of the Sarakoff-Harden bacillus had been emptied into the lake. I stumbled into the drawing-room and threw myself upon a chair. My legs were weak, and my hands were trembling.

"Alice," I said, "you must not allow this to distress you. The Blue Disease is not dangerous."

She lifted a tear-stained face and looked at me dully.

"Richard, I can't bear it any longer. I've given half my life to looking after father. I simply can't bear it."

I sat up and stared at her. What strange intuition had come to her?

"What do you mean?"

She sobbed afresh.

"I can't endure the sight of him with those blue eyes," she went on, rather wildly. "Richard, I must get away. I've never been from him for more than a few hours at a time for the last fifteen years. Don't think I want him to die."

"I don't."

"I'm glad he's better," she remarked irrelevantly.

"So am I."

"The Perrys were saying that the doctors up in Birmingham think that the Blue Disease cut short other diseases, and made people feel better." She twisted her handkerchief for some moments. "Does it?" she asked, looking at me directly.

"I—er—I have heard it does."

An idea had come into my mind, and I could not get rid of it. Why should I not tell her all that I knew?

"I'm thirty-five," she remarked.

"And I'm forty-two." I tried to smile.

"Life's getting on for us both," she added.

"I know, Alice. I suggested that we should get engaged a short while ago. Now I suggest that we get married—as soon as possible." I got up and paced the room. "Why not?" I demanded passionately.

She shook her head, and appeared confused.

"It's impossible. Who could look after him? I should never be happy, Richard, as long as he was living."

I stopped before her.

"Not with me?"

"No, Richard. I should be left a great deal to myself. A doctor's wife always is. I've thought it out carefully. I would think of him."

After a long silence, I made a proposal that I had refused to entertain before.

"Well, there's no reason why he should not come and live with us. There is plenty of room in my house at Harley Street. Would that do?"

It was a relief to me when she said that she would not consent to an arrangement of that kind. I sat down again.

"Alice," I said quietly, "it is necessary that we should decide our future. There are special reasons."

She glanced at me enquiringly. There was a pause in which I tried to collect my thoughts.

"Your father," I continued, "is suffering from a very peculiar disease. It is wrong, perhaps, to call it a disease. You wouldn't call life a disease, would you?"

"I don't understand."

"No, of course not. Well, to put it as simply as possible, it is likely that your father will live a long time now. When he said he felt as if his mind and body had been rejuvenated he was speaking the truth."

"But he will be ninety next year," she said bluntly.

"I know. But that will make no difference. This germ, that is now in his body, has the power of arresting all further decay. Your father will remain as he is now for an indefinite period."

I met her eyes as steadily as I could, but there was a quality in her gaze that caused me to look elsewhere.

"How do you know this?" she asked after a painful silence.

"I—er—I can't tell you." The colour mounted to my cheeks, and I began to tap the carpet impatiently with the toe of my boot. "You wouldn't understand," I continued in as professional a manner as I could muster. "You would need first to study the factors that bring about old age."

"Where did the Blue Disease come from? Tell me. I can surely understand that!"

"You have read the paper, haven't you?"

"I've read that no one understands what it is, and that the doctors are puzzled."

"How should I know where it comes from?"

She regarded me searchingly.

"You know something about it," she said positively. "Richard, you are keeping it back from me. I have a right to know what it is."

I was silent.

"If you don't tell me, how can I trust you again?" she asked. "Don't you see that there will always be a shadow between us?"

It was not difficult for me to guess that my guilty manner had roused her suspicions. She had seen my agitation, and had found it unaccountable. I resolved to entrust her with the secret of the germ.

"Do you remember that I once told you my friend, Professor Sarakoff, had succeeded in keeping butterflies alive for over a year?"

She nodded.

"He and I have been experimenting on those lines and he has found a germ that has the property of keeping human beings alive in the same way. The germ has escaped . . . into the world . . . and it is the cause of the Blue Disease."

"How did it escape?"

I winced. In her voice I was conscious of a terrible accusation.

"By accident," I stammered.

She jumped to her feet.

"I don't believe it! That is a lie!"

"Alice, you must calm yourself! I am trying to tell you exactly what happened."

"Was it by accident?"

The vision of that secret expedition to the water supply of Birmingham passed before me. I felt like a criminal. I could not raise my eyes; my cheeks were burning. In the silence that followed, the sound of Mr. Annot's voice became audible. Alice stood before me, rigid and implacable.

"It was—by accident," I said. I tried to look at her, and failed. She remained motionless for about a minute. Then she turned and left the room. I heard her go slowly upstairs. A door banged. Actuated by a sudden desire, I stepped into the hall, seized my coat and hat and opened the front door. I was just in time. As I gently closed the door I heard Mr. Annot on the landing above. He was singing some long-forgotten tune in a strange cracked voice.

I stood outside on the doorstep, listening, until, overcome by curiosity, I bent down and lifted the flap of the letter-box. The interior of the hall was plainly visible. Mr. Annot had ceased singing and was now standing before the mirror which hung beside the hatstand. He was a trifle unsteady, and swayed on his frail legs, but he was staring at himself with a kind of savage intensity. At last he turned away and I caught the expression on his face. . . . With a slight shiver, I let down the flap noiselessly. There was something in that expression that for me remains unnamable; and I think now, as I look back into those past times, that of all the signs which showed me that the Sarakoff-Harden bacillus was an offence against humanity, that strange look on the nonagenarian's face was the most terrible and obvious.

12
MR. CLUTTERBUCK'S OPINION

When I reached London it was dusk, and a light mist hung in the darkening air. The lamps were twinkling in the streets. I decided to get some tea in a restaurant adjoining the station. When I entered it was crowded, and the only seat that was empty was at a small table already occupied by another man. I sat down, and gave my order to the waitress, and remained staring moodily at the soiled marble surface of the table. My neighbour was engrossed in his paper.

During my journey from Cambridge I had come to a certain conclusion. Sarakoff was of the opinion that we should publish a statement about the germ of immortality, and now I was in agreement with him. For I had been reflecting upon the capacity of human mind for retaining secrets and had come to the conclusion that it is so constructed that its power of retention is remarkably small. I felt that it would be a matter of extraordinary relief if everyone in that tea-shop knew the secret of the Blue Germ.

I began to study the man who sat opposite me. He was a quietly dressed middle-aged man. The expression on his rather pale, clean-shaven face suggested that he was a clerk or secretary. He looked reliable, unimaginative, careful and methodical. He was reading his newspaper with close attention. A cup of tea and the remains of a toasted muffin were at his elbow. It struck me that here was a very average type of man, and an immense desire seized upon me to find out what opinion he would pronounce if I were to tell him my secret. I waited until he looked up.

"Is there any news?" I asked.

He observed me for a moment as if he resented my question.

"The Blue Disease is spreading in London," he remarked shortly, and returned to his paper. I felt rebuffed, but reflected that this, after all, was how an average man might be expected to behave.

"A curious business," I continued. "I am a doctor, and therefore very much interested in it."

His manner changed. He assumed the attitude of the average man towards a doctor at once, and I was gratified to observe it.

"I was just thinking I'd like to hear what a doctor thinks about it," he said, laying down his paper. "I thought of calling in on Dr. Sykes on my way home to-night; he attends my wife. Do you know Dr. Sykes?"

"Which one?" I asked cautiously, not willing to disappoint him.

"Dr. Sykes of Harlesden," he said, with a look of surprise.

"Oh, yes, I know Dr. Sykes. Why did you think of going to see him?"

He smiled apologetically and pointed to the paper.

"It sounds so queer . . . the disease. They say, up in Birmingham, that it's stopping all diseases in the hospitals . . . everywhere. People getting well all of a sudden. Now I don't believe that."

"Have you seen a case yet?"

"Yes. A woman. In the street this afternoon as I was coming from lunch. The police took her. She was mad, I can tell you. There was a big crowd. She screamed. I think she was drunk." He paused, and glanced at me. "What do you think of it?"

I took a deep breath.

"I don't *think*, I *know*," I said, in as quiet a manner as possible. He stared a moment, and a nervous smile appeared and swiftly vanished. He seemed uncertain what to do.

"You've found out something?" he asked at length, playing with his teaspoon and keeping his eyes on the table. I regarded him carefully. I was not quite certain if he still thought I was a doctor.

"I'm not a lunatic," I said. "I'm merely stating a rather extraordinary fact. I know all about the germ of the Blue Disease."

He raised his eyes for an instant, and then lowered them. His hand had stopped trifling with the teaspoon.

"Yes," he said, "the doctors think it's due to a germ of some sort." He made a sort of effort and continued. "It is funny, some of these germs being invisible through microscopes. Measles and chickenpox and common things like that. They've never seen the germs that cause them, that's what the papers say. It seems odd—having something you can't see." He turned his head, and looked for his hat that hung on a peg behind him.

"One moment," I said. I took out my card-case. "I want you to read this card. Don't think I'm mad. I want to talk to you for a particular reason which I'll explain in a moment." He took the card hesitatingly and read it. Then he looked at me. "The reason why I am speaking to you is this," I said. "I want to find out what a decent citizen like yourself will think of something I know. It concerns the Blue Disease and its origin."

He seemed disturbed, and took out his watch.

"I ought to get home. My wife—"

"Is your wife ill?"

"Yes."

"What's the matter with her?"

He frowned.

"Dr. Sykes thinks it's lung trouble."

"Consumption?"

He nodded, and an expression of anxiety came over his face.

"Good," I exclaimed. "Now listen to what I have to say. Before the week is out your wife will be cured. I swear it."

He said nothing. It was plain that he was still suspicious.

"You read what they say in the papers about the Blue Disease cutting short other diseases? Well, that Blue Disease will be all over London in a day or two. Now do you understand?"

I saw that I had interested him. He settled himself on his chair, and began to examine me. His gaze travelled over my face and clothes, pausing at my cuff-links and my tie and collar. Then he looked at my card again. Inwardly he came to a decision.

"I'm willing to listen to what you've got to say," he remarked, "if you think it's worth saying."

"Thank you. I think it's worth hearing." I leaned my arms on the table in front of me. "This Blue Disease is not an accidental thing. It was deliberately planned, by two scientists. I was one of those scientists."

"You can't plan a disease," he remarked, after a considerable silence.

"You're wrong. We found a way of creating new germs. We worked at the idea of creating a particular kind of germ that would kill all other germs . . . and we were successful. Then we let loose the germ on the world."

"How?"

"We infected the water supply of Birmingham at its origin in Wales."

I watched his expression intently.

"You mean that you did this secretly, without knowing what the result would be?" he asked at last.

"We foresaw the result to a certain extent."

He thought for some time.

"But you had no right to infect a water supply. That's criminal, surely?"

"It's criminal if the infection is dangerous to people. If you put cholera in a reservoir, of course it's criminal."

"But this germ . . . ?"

"This germ does not kill people. It kills the germs in people."

"What's the difference?"

"All the difference in the world! It's like this. . . . By the way, what is your name?"

"Clutterbuck." The word escaped his lips by accident. He looked annoyed. I smiled reassuringly.

"It's like this, Mr. Clutterbuck. If you kill all the germs in a person's body, that person doesn't die. He lives . . . indefinitely. Now do you see?"

"No, I don't see," said Clutterbuck with great frankness. "I don't understand what you're driving at. You tell me that you're a doctor and you give me a card bearing a well-known specialist's name. Then you say you created a germ and put it in the Birmingham water supply and that the result is the Blue Disease. This germ, you say, doesn't kill people, but does something else which I don't follow. Now I was taught that germs are dangerous things, and it seems to me that if your story is true—which I don't believe—you are guilty of a criminal act." He pushed back his chair and reached for his hat. There was a flush on his face.

"Then you don't believe my tale?"

"No, I'm sorry, but I don't."

"Well, Mr. Clutterbuck, will you believe it when you see your wife restored to health in a few days' time?"

He paused and stared at me.

"What you say is impossible," he said slowly. "If you were a doctor you'd know that as well as I do."

"But the reports in the paper?"

"Oh, that's journalistic rubbish."

He picked up his umbrella and beckoned to the waitress. I made a last attempt.

"If I take you to my house will you believe me then?"

"Look here," he said in an angry tone, "I've had enough of this. I can't waste my time. I'm sure of one thing and that is that you're no doctor. You've got somebody's card-case. You don't look like a doctor and you don't speak like one. I should advise you to be careful."

He moved away from the table. Some neighbouring people stared at me for a moment and then went on eating. Mr. Clutterbuck paid at the desk and left the establishment. I had received the verdict of the average man.

13
THE DEAD IMMORTAL

When I reached home, Sarakoff was out. He had left a message to say he would not be in until after midnight, as he was going to hear Leonora sing at the opera, and purposed to take her to supper afterwards. Dinner was therefore a solitary meal for me, and when it was all over I endeavoured to plunge into some medical literature. The hours passed slowly. It was almost impossible to read, for the process, to me, was similar to trying to take an interest in a week-old newspaper.

The thought of the bacillus made the pages seem colourless; it dwarfed all meaning in the words. I gave up the attempt and set myself to smoking and gazing into the fire. What was I to do about Alice?

Midnight came and my mind was still seething. I knew sleep was out of the question and the desire to walk assailed me. I put on a coat and hat and left the house. It was a cold night, clear with stars. Harley Street was silent. My footsteps led me south towards the river. I walked rapidly, oblivious of others. The problem of Alice was beyond solution, for the simple reason that I found it impossible to think of her clearly. She was overshadowed by the wonder of the bacillus. But the picture of her father haunted me. It filled me with strange emotions, and at moments with stranger misgivings.

There are meanings, dimly caught at the time, which remain in the mind like blind creatures, mewing and half alive. They pluck at the brain ceaselessly, seeking birth in thought. Old Annot's face peering into the hall mirror—what was it that photographed the scene so pitilessly in my memory? I hurried along, scarcely noticing where I went, and as I went I argued with myself aloud.

On the Embankment I returned to a full sense of my position in space. The river ran beneath me, cold and dark. I leaned over the stone balustrade and stared at the dark forms of barges. Yes, it was true enough that I had not realized that the germ would keep Mr. Annot alive indefinitely. Sarakoff's significant whistle that morning came to my mind, and I saw that I had been guilty of singular denseness in not understanding its meaning.

And now old Annot would live on and on, year after year. Was I glad? It is impossible to say. It was that expression in the old man's face that dominated me. I tried to think it out. It had been a triumphant look; and more than that . . . a triumphant *toothless* look. Was that the solution? I reflected that triumph is an expression that belongs to youth, to young things, to all that is striving upwards in growth. Surely old people should look only patient and resigned—never triumphant—in this world? Some strong action with regard to Alice's position would be necessary. It was absurd to think that her father should eternally come between her and me. It would be necessary to go down to Cambridge and make a clean confession to Alice. And then, when forgiven, I would insist on an immediate arrangement concerning our marriage. Marriage! The word vibrated in my soul. The solemnity of that ceremony was great enough to mere mortals, but what would it mean to us when we were immortals? Sarakoff had hinted at a new marriage system. Was such a thing possible? On what factors did marriage rest? Was it merely a discipline or was it ultimately selfishness?

My agitation increased, and I hurried eastwards, soon entering an area of riverside London that, had I been calmer, might have given me some alarm. It must have been about two o'clock in the morning when the pressure of thoughts relaxed in my mind. I found myself in the great dock area. The forms of giant cranes rose dimly in the air. A distant glare of light, where nightshifts were at work, illuminated the huge shapes of ocean steamers. The quays were littered with crates and bales. A clanking of buffers and the shrill whistles of locomotives came out of the darkness. For some time I stood transfixed. In my imagination I saw these big ships, laden with cargo, slipping down the Thames and out into the sea, carrying with them an added cargo to every part of the earth. For by them would the Blue Germ travel over the waterways of the world and enter every port. From the ports it would spread swiftly into the towns, and from the towns onwards across plain and prairie until the gift of Immortality had been received by every human being. The vision thrilled me. . . .

A commotion down a side street on my right shattered this glorious picture. Hoarse cries rang out, and a sound of blows. I could make out a small dark struggling mass which seemed to break into separate parts and then coalesce again. A police whistle sounded. The mass again broke up, and some figures came rushing down the street in my direction. They passed me in a flash, and vanished. At the far end of the street two twinkling lights appeared. After a period of hesitation—what doctor goes willingly into the accidents of the streets?—I walked slowly in their direction.

When I reached them I found two policemen bending over the body of a man, which lay in the gutter face downwards.

"Good evening," I said. "Can I be of any service? I am a doctor."

They shone their lamps on me suspiciously. "What are you doing here?"

"Walking," I replied. Exercise had calmed me. I felt cool and collected. "I often walk far at nights. Let me see the body."

I stooped down and turned the body over. The policemen watched me in silence. The body was that of a young, fair-haired sailor man. There was a knife between his ribs. His eyes were screwed up into a rigid state of contraction which death had not yet relaxed. His whole body was rigid. I knew that the knife had pierced his heart. But the most extraordinary thing about him was his expression. I have never looked on a face either in life or death that expressed such terror. Even the policemen were startled. The light of their lamps shone on that monstrous and distorted countenance, and we gazed in horrified silence.

"Is he dead?" asked one at last.

"Quite dead," I replied, "but it is odd to find this rigidity so early." I began to press his eyelids apart. The right eye opened. I uttered a cry of astonishment.

"Look!" I cried.

They stared.

"Blest if that ain't queer," said one. "It's that Blue Disease. He must 'ave come from Birmingham."

"Queer?" I said passionately. "Why, man, it's tragedy—unadulterated tragedy. The man was an Immortal."

They stared at me heavily.

"Immortal?" said one.

"He would have lived for ever," I said. "In his system there is the most marvellous germ that the world has ever known. It was circulating in his blood. It had penetrated to every part of his body. A few minutes ago, as he walked along the dark street, he had before him a future of unnumbered years. And now he lies in the gutter. Can you imagine a greater tragedy?"

The policemen transferred their gaze from me to the dead man. Then, as if moved by a common impulse, they began to laugh. I watched them moodily, plunged in an extraordinary vein of thought. When I moved away they at once stopped me.

"No, you don't," said one. "We'll want you at the police station to give your evidence. Not," he continued with a grin, "to tell that bit of information you just gave us, about him being an angel or something."

"I didn't say he was an angel."

They laughed tolerantly. Like Mr. Clutterbuck, they thought I was mad.

"Let's hope he's an angel," said the other. "But, by his face, he looks more like the other thing. Bill, you go round for the ambulance. I'll stay with the gentleman."

The policeman moved away ponderously and vanished in the darkness.

"What was that you were saying, sir?" asked the policeman who remained with me.

"Never mind," I muttered, "you wouldn't understand."

"I'm interested in religious matters," continued the policeman in a soft voice. "You think that the Blue Disease is something out of the common?"

I am never surprised at London policemen, but I looked at this one closely before I replied.

"You seem a reasonable man," I said. "Let me tell you that what I have told you about the germ—that it confers immortality—is correct. In a day or two you will be immortal."

He seemed to reflect in a calm massive way on the news. His eyes were fixed on the dead man's face.

"An Immortal Policeman?"

"Yes."

"You're asking me to believe a lot, sir."

"I know that. But still, there it is. It's the truth."

"And what about crime?" he continued. "If we were all Immortals, what about crime?"

"Crime will become so horrible in its meaning that it will stop."

"It hasn't stopped yet. . . ."

"Of course not. It won't, till people realize they are immortal."

He shifted his lantern and shone it down the road.

"Well, sir, it seems to me it will be a long time before people realize *that*. In fact, I don't see how anyone could ever realize it."

"Why not?"

"Just think," he said, with a large air. "Supposing crime died out, what would happen to the Sunday papers? Where would those lawyers be? What would we do with policemen? No, you can't realize it. You can't realize the things you exist for all vanishing. It's not human nature." He brooded for a time. "You can't do away with crime," he continued. "What's behind crime? Woman and gold—one or the other, or both. Now you don't mean to tell me, sir, that the Blue Disease is doing away with women and gold in a place like Birmingham? Why, sir, what made Birmingham? What do you suppose life is?"

"I have never been asked the question before by a policeman," I said. "I do not know what made Birmingham, but I will tell you what life is. It is ultimately a cell, containing protoplasm and a nucleus."

A low rumbling noise began somewhere in his vast bulk. It gradually increased to a roar. I became aware that he was laughing. He held his sides. I thought his shining belt would burst. At length his hilarity slowly subsided, and he became sober. He surveyed the dead body at his feet.

"No, sir," he said, "don't you believe it. Life is women and gold. It always was that, and it always will be." He shone his lamp downwards so that the light fell on the terrible features of the dead sailor. "Now this man, sir, was killed because of money, I'll wager. And behind the money I reckon you'll find a woman." He mused for a time. "Not necessarily a pretty woman, but a woman of some sort."

"How do you account for that look of fear on his face?"

"I couldn't say. I've never seen anything like it. I've seen a lot of dead faces, but they are usually quiet enough, as if they were asleep. But I'll tell you one thing, sir, that I have noticed, and that is that money—which includes diamonds and such like, makes a man die worse and more bitter than anything else."

He turned his lantern down the street. A sound of wheels reached us.

"That's the ambulance."

"Will you really require me at the police station?" I asked.

"Yes."

"Will it be necessary to prove who I am?"

He smiled.

"You won't need to prove that you're a doctor, sir," he said genially. "We have a lot to do with doctors. I could tell you were a doctor after talking a minute with you. You are all the same."

"What do you mean?"

"Well—it's the things you say. Now only a doctor could have said what you did—about life being a cell. Do you know, sir, I sometimes believe that doctors is more innocent than parsons. It's the things they say. . . ."

The low rumbling began again in his interior. I waited silently until the ambulance came up. I felt a slight shade of annoyance.

But how could I expect the enormous uneducated bulk beside me to take a really intelligent and scientific view of life? Of course life was a cell. Every educated person knew that—and now that cell was, for the first time in history, about to become immortal—but what did the policeman care? How stupid people were, I reflected. We moved off in a small procession towards the police station. Half an hour later I was on my way west, deeply pondering on the causes of that extraordinary expression of fear in the dead sailor's face. Never in my life before had I seen so agonized a countenance, but I was destined to see others as terrible. As I walked, the strangeness of the dead man's tragedy grew in my mind and filled me with a tremendous wonder, for who had ever seen a dead Immortal?

On reaching home I roused Sarakoff and related to him what I had seen.

14

FIRST IMPRESSIONS OF IMMORTALITY

After two hours of sleep I awoke. My brief rest had been haunted by unpleasant dreams, vague and indefinite, but seeming to centre about the idea of an impending catastrophe. I lay in bed staring at the dimly outlined window. I felt quite rested and very wide awake. For some time I remained motionless, reflecting on my night adventures and idly thinking whether it was worth while getting up and attending to some correspondence that was overdue. The prospect of a chilly study was not attractive. And then I noticed a very peculiar sensation.

There is only one thing that I can compare it with. After a day of exhausting work a glass of champagne produces in me an almost immediate effect. I feel as if the worries of the day are suddenly removed to a great and blessed distance. A happy indifference takes their place. I felt the same effect as I lay in bed on that dreary winter's morning. The idea that I should get up and work retreated swiftly. A pleasant sense of languor came over me. My eyes closed and for some time I lay in a blissful state of peace, such as I had never experienced before so far as my memory could tell.

I do not know how long I lay in this state, but at length a persistent noise made me open my eyes. I looked round. It seemed to be full daylight now. The first thing I noticed was the unusual size of the room. The ceiling seemed far above my head. The walls seemed to have receded many feet. In my astonishment I uttered an exclamation. The result was startling. My voice seemed to reverberate and re-echo as if I had shouted with all my strength.

Considerably startled, I remained in a sitting posture, gazing at my unfamiliar surroundings. The persistent noise that had first roused me continued, and for a long time I could not account for it. It appeared to come from under my bed. I leaned over the edge, but could see nothing. And then, in a flash, I knew what it was. It was the sound of my watch, that lay under my pillow.

I drew it out and stared at it in a state of mystification. Each of its ticks sounded like a small hammer striking sharply against a metal plate. I held it to my ear and was almost deafened. For a moment I wondered whether I were not in the throes of some acute nervous disorder, in which the senses became sharpened to an incredible degree. Such an exultation of perception could only be due to some powerful intoxicant at work on my body. Was I going mad? I laid the watch on the counterpane and in the act of doing it, the explanation burst on my mind. For the recollection of Mr. Herbert Wain and the Clockdrum suddenly came to me. I flung aside the bedclothes, ran to the window and drew the curtains. The radiance of the day almost blinded me. I pressed my hands to my eyes in a kind of agony, feeling that they had been seared and destroyed, and dropped on my knees. I remained in this position for over a minute and then gradually withdrew my hands and gazed at the carpet. I dared not look up yet. The pattern of the carpet glowed in colours more brilliant than I had ever seen before. As I knelt there, in attitude of prayer, it seemed to me that I had never noticed colour before; that all my life had been passed without any consciousness of colour. At last I lifted my sight from the miracle of the carpet to the miracle of the day. High overhead, through the dingy windowpane, was a patch of clear sky, infinitely sweet, remote and inaccessible, framed by golden clouds. As I gazed at it an indescribable reverence and joy filled my mind. In the purity of the morning light, it seemed the most lovely and wonderful thing I had ever beheld. And I, Richard Harden, consulting physician who had hitherto looked on life through a microscope, remained kneeling on my miraculous carpet, gazing upwards at the miraculous heavens. Acting on some strange impulse I stretched out my hands, and then I saw something which turned me into a rigid statue.

It was in this attitude that Sarakoff found me.

He entered my room violently. His hair was tousled and his beard stuck out at a grotesque angle. He was clad in pink pyjamas, and in his hand he carried a silver-backed mirror. My attitude did not seem to cause him any surprise. The door slammed behind him, with a noise of thunder, and he rushed across the room to where I knelt, and stooping, examined my finger nails at which I was staring.

"Good!" he shouted. "Good! Harden, you've got it too!"

He pointed triumphantly. Under the nails there was a faint tinge of blue, and at the nail-bed this was already intense, forming little crescent-shaped areas of vivid turquoise.

Sarakoff sat down on the edge of my bed and studied himself attentively in the hand mirror.

"A slight pallor is perceptible in the skin," he announced as if he was dictating a note for a medical journal, "and this is due, no doubt, to a deposit of the blue pigment in the deeper layers of the epidermis. The hair is at present unaffected save at the roots. God knows what colour blond hair will become. I am anxious about Leonora. The expression—I suppose I can regard myself as a typical case, Harden—is serene, if not animated. Subjectively, one may observe a great sense of exhilaration coupled with an extraordinary increase in the power of perception. You, for example, look to me quite different."

"In what way?" I demanded.

"Well, as you kneel there, I notice in you a kind of angular grandeur, a grotesque touch of the sublime, that was not evident to me before. If I were a sculptor, I would like to model you like that. I cannot explain why—I am just saying what I feel. I have never felt any impulse towards art until this morning." He twisted his moustache. "Yes, you have quite an interesting face, Harden. I can see in it evidence that you have suffered intensely. You have taken life too seriously. You have worked too hard. You are stunted and deformed with work."

I regarded him with some astonishment.

"Work is all very well," he continued, "but this morning I see with singular clarity that it is only a means of development. My dear Harden, if it is overdone, it simply dwarfs the soul. Our generation has not recognized this properly."

"But you were always an apostle of hard work," I remarked irritably.

"May be." He made a gesture of dismissal. "Now, I am an Immortal, and you are an Immortal. The background to life has changed. Formerly, the idea of death lurked constantly in the depths of the unconscious mind, and by its vaguely-felt influences spurred us on to continual exertion. That is all changed. We have, at one stroke, removed this dire spectre. We are free."

He rose suddenly and flung the mirror across the room.

"What do we need mirrors for?" he cried. "It is only when we fear death that we need mirrors to tell us how long we have to live." He strode over to me and halted. "You seem in no hurry to get up from that carpet," he observed. His remark made me realize that I had been kneeling for some minutes. Now this was rather odd. I am restless by nature and rarely remain in one position for any length of time, and to stay like that, kneeling before the window, was indeed curious. I got up and moved to the dressing-table, thinking. Sarakoff must have been thinking in the same direction, for he asked me a question.

"Did you realize you were kneeling?"

"Yes," I replied. "I knew what I was doing. It merely did not occur to me that I should change my position."

"The explanation is simple," said the Russian. "Restlessness, or the idea that we must change our position, or that we should be doing something else, belongs to the anxious side of life; and the anxious side of life is nourished and kept vigorous by the latent fear of death. All that is removed from you, and therefore you see no reason why you should do anything until it pleases you."

I began to study myself in the glass on the dressing-table. The examination interested me immensely. There was certainly a marble-like hue about the skin. The whites of my eyes were distinctly stained, but not so intensely as had been the case with Mr. Herbert Wain, showing that I had not suffered from the Blue Disease as long as he had. But when I began to study my reflection from the æsthetic point of view, I became deeply engrossed.

"I don't agree with you, Sarakoff," I remarked at length. "We still need mirrors. In fact I have never found the mirror so interesting in my life."

"Don't use that absurd phrase," he answered. "It implies that something other than life exists."

"So it does."

"What do you mean?"

"Well, if I stick this pair of scissors into your heart you will die, my dear fellow." He was silent, and a frown began to gather on his brow. "Yes," I continued, "your psychological deductions are not entirely valid. The fear of death still exists, but now limited to a small sphere. In that sphere, it will operate with extreme intensity." I picked up the scissors and made a stealthy movement towards him. To my amazement I obtained an immediate proof of my theory. He sprang up with a loud cry, darted to the door and vanished. For a moment I stood in a state of bewilderment. Was it possible that he, with all his size and strength, was afraid of me? And then a great fit of laughter overcame me and I sank down on my bed with the tears coming from my eyes.

15
THE TERRIBLE FEAR

On coming down to breakfast, I found Sarakoff already seated at the table devouring the morning papers. I picked up a discarded one and stood by the fire, glancing over its contents. There was only one subject of news, and that was the spread of the Blue Disease. From every part of the north cases were reported, and in London it had broken out in several districts.

"So it's all come true," I remarked.

He nodded, and continued reading. I sauntered to the window. A thin driving snow was now falling, and the passers-by were hurrying along in the freezing slush, with collars turned up and heads bowed before the wind.

"This is an ideal day to spend indoors by the fireside," I observed. "I think I'll telephone to the hospital and tell Jones to take my work."

Sarakoff raised his eyes, and then his eyebrows.

"So," he said, "the busy man suddenly thinks work a bother. The power of the germ, Harden, is indeed miraculous."

"Do you think my inclination is due to the germ?"

"Beyond a doubt. You were the most over-conscientious man I ever knew until this morning."

For some reason I found this observation very interesting. I wished to discuss it, and I was about to reply when the door opened and my housemaid announced that Dr. Symington-Tearle was in the hall and would like an immediate interview.

"Show him in," I said equably. Symington-Tearle usually had a most irritating effect upon me, but at the moment I felt totally indifferent to him. He entered in his customary manner, as if the whole of London were feverishly awaiting him. I introduced Sarakoff, but Symington-Tearle hardly noticed him.

"Harden," he exclaimed in his loud dominating tones, "I am convinced that there is no such thing as this Blue Disease. I believe it all to be a colossal plant. Some practical joker has introduced a chemical into the water supply."

"Probably," I murmured, still thinking of Sarakoff's observation.

"I'm going to expose the whole thing in the evening papers; I examined a case yesterday—a man called Wain—and was convinced there was nothing wrong with him. He was really pigmented. And what is it but mere pigmentation?" He passed his hand over his brow and frowned. "Yes, yes," he continued, "that's what it is—a colossal joke. We've all been taken in by it—everyone except me." He sat down by the breakfast table suddenly and once more passed his hand over his brow.

"What was I saying?" he asked.

Sarakoff and I were now watching him intently.

"That the Blue Disease was a joke," I said.

"Ah, yes—a joke." He looked up at Sarakoff and stared for a moment. "Do you know," he said, "I believe it really is a joke."

An expression of intense solemnity came over his face, and he sat motionless gazing in front of him with unblinking eyes. I crossed to where he sat and peered at his face.

"I thought so," I remarked. "You've got it too."

"Got what?"

"The Blue Disease. I suppose you caught it from Wain, as we did." I picked up one of his hands and pointed to the faintly-tinted fingernails. Dr. Symington-Tearle stared at them with an air of such child-like simplicity and gravity that Sarakoff and I broke into loud laughter.

The humour of the situation passed with a peculiar suddenness and we ceased laughing abruptly. I sat down at the table, and for some time the three of us gazed at one another and said nothing. The spirit-lamp that heated the silver dish of bacon upon the table spurted at intervals and I saw Symington-Tearle stare at it in faint surprise.

"Does it sound very loud?" asked Sarakoff at length.

"Extraordinarily loud. And upon my soul your voice nearly deafens me."

"It will pass," I said. "One gets adjusted to the extreme sensitiveness in a short time. How do you feel?"

"I feel," said Symington-Tearle slowly, "as if I were newly constructed from the crown of my head to the soles of my feet. After a Turkish bath and twenty minutes' massage I've experienced a little of the feeling."

He stared at Sarakoff, then at me, and finally at the spirit lamp. We must have presented an odd spectacle. For there we sat, three men who, under ordinary circumstances, were extremely busy and active, lolling round the unfinished breakfast table while the hands of the clock travelled relentlessly onward.

Relentlessly? That was scarcely correct. To me, owing to some mysterious change that I cannot explain, the clock had ceased to be a tyrannous and hateful monster. I did not care how fast it went or to what hour it pointed. Time was no longer precious, any more than the sand of the sea is precious.

"Aren't you going to have any breakfast?" asked Symington-Tearle.

"I'm not in the least hurry," replied Sarakoff. "I think I'll take a sip of coffee. Are you hungry, Harden?"

"No. I don't want anything save coffee. But I'm in no hurry."

My housemaid entered and announced that the gentleman who had been waiting in Dr. Symington-Tearle's car, and was now in the hall, wished to know if the doctor would be long.

"Oh, that is a patient of mine," said Symington-Tearle, "ask him to come in."

A large, stout, red-faced gentleman entered, wrapped in a thick frieze motor coat. He nodded to us briefly.

"Sorry to interrupt," he said, "but time's getting on, Tearle. My consultation with Sir Peverly Salt was for half past nine, if you remember. It's that now."

"Oh, there's plenty of time," said Tearle. "Sit down, Ballard. It's nice and warm in here."

"It may be nice and warm," replied Mr. Ballard loudly, "but I don't want to keep Sir Peverly waiting."

"I don't see why you shouldn't keep him waiting," said Tearle. "In fact I really don't see why you should go to him at all."

Mr. Ballard stared for a moment. Then his eyes travelled round the table and dwelt first on Sarakoff and then on me. I suppose something in our manner rather baffled him, but outwardly he showed no sign of it.

"I don't quite follow you," he said, fixing his gaze upon Tearle again. "If you recollect, you advised me strongly four days ago to consult Sir Peverly Salt about the condition of my heart, and you impressed upon me that his opinion was the best that was obtainable. You rang him up and an appointment was fixed for this morning at half-past nine, and I was told to call on you shortly after nine."

He paused, and once more his eyes dwelt in turn upon each of us. They returned to Tearle. "It is now twenty-five minutes to ten," he said. His face had become redder, and his voice louder. "And I understood that Sir Peverly is a very busy man."

"He certainly is busy," said Tearle. "He's far too busy. It is very interesting to think that business is only necessary in so far—"

"Look here," said Mr. Ballard violently. "I'm a man with a short temper. I'm hanged if I'll stand this nonsense. What the devil do you think you're all doing? Are you playing a joke on me?"

He glared round at us, and then he made a sudden movement towards the table. In a moment we were all on our feet. I felt an acute terror seize me, and without waiting to see what happened, I flung open the door that led into my consulting room, darted to the further door, across the hall and up to my bedroom.

There was a cry and a rush of feet across the hall. Mr. Ballard's voice rang out stormily. A door slammed, and then another door, and then all was silent.

I became aware of a movement behind me, and looking round sharply, I saw my housemaid Lottie staring at me in amazement. She had been engaged in making the bed.

"Whatever is the matter, sir?" she asked.

"Hush!" I whispered. "There's a dangerous man downstairs."

I turned the key in the lock, listened for a moment, and then tip-toed my way across the floor to a chair. My limbs were shaking. It is difficult to describe the intensity of my terror. There was a cold sweat on my forehead. "He might have killed me. Think of that!"

Her eyes were fixed on me.

"Oh, sir, you do look bad," she exclaimed. "Whatever has happened to you?" She came nearer and gazed into my eyes. "They're all blue, sir. It must be that disease you've got."

A sudden irritation flashed over me. "Don't stare at me like that. You'll have it yourself to-morrow," I shouted. "The whole of the blessed city will have it." A loud rap at the door interrupted me. I jumped up, darted across the room and threw myself under the bed. "Don't let anyone in," I whispered. The rap was repeated. Sarakoff's voice sounded without.

"Let me in. It's all right. He's gone. The front door is bolted." I crawled out and unlocked the door. Sarakoff, looking rather pale, was standing in the passage. He carried a poker. "Symington-Tearle's in the coal-cellar," he announced. "He won't come out."

I wiped my brow with a handkerchief.

"Good heavens, Sarakoff," I exclaimed, "this kind of thing will lead to endless trouble. I had no idea the terror would be so uncontrollable."

"I'm glad you feel it as I do," said the Russian. "When you threatened me with a pair of scissors this morning I felt mad with fear."

"It's awful," I murmured. "We can't be too careful." We began to descend the stairs. "Sarakoff, you remember I told you about that dead sailor? I see now why that expression was on his face. It was the terror that he felt."

"Extraordinary!" he muttered. "He couldn't have known. It must have been instinctive."

"Instincts are like that," I said. "I don't suppose an animal knows anything about death, or even thinks of it, yet it behaves from the very first as if it knew. It's odd."

A door opened at the far end of the hall, and Symington-Tearle emerged. There was a patch of coal-dust on his forehead. His hair, usually so flat and smooth that it seemed like a brass mirror, was now disordered.

"Has he gone?" he enquired hoarsely.

We nodded. I pointed to the chain on the door.

"It's bolted," I said. "Come into the study."

I led the way into the room. Tearle walked to the window, then to a chair, and finally took up a position before the fire.

"This is extraordinary!" he exclaimed.

"What do you make of it?" I asked.

"I can make nothing of it. What's the matter with me? I never felt anything like that terror that came over me when Ballard approached me."

Sarakoff took out a large handkerchief and passed it across his face. "It's only the fear of physical violence," he said. "That's the only weak spot. Fear was formerly distributed over a wide variety of possibilities, but now it's all concentrated in one direction."

"Why?" Tearle stared at me questioningly.

"Because the germ is in us," I said. "We're immortal."

"Immortal?"

Sarakoff threw out his hands, and flung back his head. "Immortals!"

I crossed to my writing-table, and picked up a heavy volume.

"Here is the first edition of Buckwell Pink's *System of Medicine*. This book was produced at immense cost and labour, and it is to be published next week. When that book is published no one will buy it."

"Why not?" demanded Tearle. "I wrote an article in it myself."

"So did I," was my reply. "But that won't make any difference. No member of the medical profession will be interested in it."

"Not interested? I can't believe that. It contains all the recent work."

"The medical profession will not be interested in it for a very simple reason. The medical profession will have ceased to exist."

A look of amazement came to Tearle's face. I tapped the volume and continued.

"You are wrong in thinking it contains all the recent work. It does not. The last and greatest achievement of medical science is not recorded in these pages. It is only recorded in ourselves. For that blue pigmentation in your eyes and fingers is due to the Sarakoff-Harden bacillus which closes once and for all the chapter of medicine."

16

THE VISIT OF THE HOME SECRETARY

In a few hours the initial effects of stimulation had worn off. The acuity of hearing was no longer so pronounced and the sense of refreshment, although still present, was not intense. We were already becoming adjusted to the new condition. The feeling of inertia and irresponsibility became gradually replaced by a general sense of calmness. To me, it seemed as if I had entered a world of new perspectives, a larger world in which space and time were widened out immeasurably. I could scarcely recall the nature of those impulses that had once driven me to and fro in endless activities, and in a constant state of anxiety. For now I had no anxiety.

It is difficult to describe fully the extraordinary sense of freedom that came from this change. For anxiety—the great modern emotion—is something that besets a life on all sides so silently and so continuously that it escapes direct detection. But it is there, tightening the muscles, crinkling the skin, quickening the heart and shortening the breath. Though almost imperceptible, it lurks under the most agreeable surroundings, requiring only a word or a look to bring it into the light. To be free from it—ah, that was an experience that no man could ever forget! It was perhaps the nearest approach to that condition of bliss, which many expect in one of the Heavens, that had ever been attained on earth. As long as no physical danger threatened, this bliss-state surrounded me. Its opposite, that condition of violent, agonizing, uncontrollable fear that suddenly surged over one on the approach of bodily danger, was something which passed as swiftly as it came, and left scarcely a trace behind it. But of that I shall have more to say, for it produced the most extraordinary state of affairs and more than anything else threatened to disorganize life completely.

I fancy Sarakoff was more awed by the bliss-state than I was. During the rest of the day he was very quiet and sat gazing before him His boisterousness had vanished. Symington-Tearle had left us—a man deeply amazed and totally incredulous. I noticed that Sarakoff scarcely smoked at all during that morning. As a rule his pipe was never out. He was in the habit of consuming two ounces of tobacco a day, which in my opinion was suicidal. He certainly lit his pipe several times, mechanically, but laid it aside almost immediately. At lunch—we had not moved out of the house yet—we had very little appetite. As a matter of interest I will give exactly what we ate and drank. Sarakoff took some soup and a piece of bread, and then some cheese. I began with some cold beef, and finding it unattractive, pushed it away and ate some biscuits and butter. There was claret on the table. I wish here to call attention to a passing impression that I experienced when sipping that claret. I had recently got in several dozen bottles of it and on that day regretted it because it seemed to me to be extremely poor stuff. It tasted sour and harsh.

We did not talk much. It was not because my mind was devoid of ideas, but rather because I was feeling that I had a prodigious, incalculable amount to think about. Perhaps it was the freedom from anxiety that made thinking easier, for there is little doubt that anxiety, however masked, deflects and disturbs the power of thought more than anything else. Indeed it seemed to me that I had never really thought clearly before. To begin a conversation with Sarakoff seemed utterly artificial. It would have been a useless interruption. I was entirely absorbed.

Sarakoff was similarly absorbed. When, therefore, the servant came in to announce that two gentlemen wished to see us, and were in the waiting-room, we were loth to move. I got up at length and went across the hall. I recollect that before entering the waiting-room I was entirely without curiosity. It was a matter of total indifference to me that two visitors were within. They had no business to interrupt me—that was my feeling. They were intruders and should have known better.

I entered the room. Standing by the fire was Lord Alberan. Beside him was a tall thin man, carefully dressed and something of a dandy, who looked at me sharply as I came across the room. I recognized his face, but failed to recall his name.

Lord Alberan, holding himself very stiffly, cleared his throat.

"Good day, Dr. Harden," he said, without offering his hand. "I have brought Sir Robert Smith to interview you. As you may know he is the Home Secretary." He cleared his throat again, and his face became rather red. "I have reported to the Home Secretary the information that I—er—that I acquired from you and your Russian companion concerning this epidemic that has swept over Birmingham and is now threatening London." He paused and stared at me. His eyes bulged. "Good heavens," he exclaimed, "you've got it yourself."

Sir Robert Smith took a step towards me and examined my face attentively.

"Yes," he said, "there's no doubt you've got it."

I indicated some chairs with a calm gesture.

"Won't you sit down?"

Lord Alberan refused, but Sir Robert lowered himself gracefully into an arm-chair and crossed his legs.

"Dr. Harden," he said, in smooth and pleasant tones, "I wish you to understand that I come here, at this unusual hour, solely in the spirit of one who desires to get all the information possible concerning the malady, called the Blue Disease, which is now sweeping over England. I understand from my friend Lord Alberan, that you know something about it."

"That is true."

"How much do you know?"

"I know all there is to be known."

"Ah!" Sir Robert leaned forward. Lord Alberan nodded violently and glared at me. There was a pause. "What you say is very interesting," said Sir Robert at length, keeping his eyes fixed upon me.

"You understand, of course, that the Blue Disease is causing a lot of anxiety?"

"Anxiety?" I exclaimed. "Surely you are wrong. It has the opposite effect. It abolishes anxiety."

"You mean—?" he queried politely.

"I mean that the germ, when once in the system, produces an atmosphere of extraordinary calm," I returned. "I am aware of that atmosphere at this moment. I have never felt so perfectly tranquil before."

He nodded, without moving his eyes.

"So I see. You struck me, as you came into the room, as a man who is at peace with himself." Lord Alberan snorted, and was about to speak, but Sir Robert held up his hand. "Tell me, Dr. Harden, did you actually contaminate the water of Birmingham?"

"My friend Sarakoff and I introduced the germ that we discovered into the Elan reservoirs."

"With what object?"

"To endow humanity with the gift of immortality."

"Ah!" he nodded gently. "The gift of immortality." He mused for a moment, and never once did his eyes leave my face. "That is interesting," he continued. "I recollect that at the International Congress at Moscow, a few years ago, there was much talk about longevity. Virchow, I fancy, and Nikola Tesla made some suggestive remarks. So you think you have discovered the secret?"

"I am sure."

"Of course you use the term immortality in a relative sense? You mean that the—er—germ that you discovered confers a long life on those it attacks?"

"I mean what I say. It confers immortality."

"Indeed!" His expression remained perfectly polite and interested, but his eyes turned for a brief moment in the direction of Lord Alberan. "So you are now immortal, Dr. Harden?"

"Yes."

"And will you, in such circumstances, go on practicing medicine—indefinitely?"

"No. There will be no medicine to practice."

"Ah!" he nodded. "I see—the germ does away with disease. Quite so." He leaned back in the chair and pressed his finger tips together. "I suppose," he continued, "that you are aware that what you say is very difficult to believe?"

"Why?"

"Well, the artificial prolongation of life is, I believe, a possibility that we are all prepared to accept. By special methods we may live a few extra years, and everything goes to show that we are actually living longer than our ancestors. At least I believe so. But for a man of your position, Dr. Harden, to say that the epidemic is an epidemic of immortality is, in my opinion, an extravagant statement."

"You are entitled to any opinion you like," I replied tranquilly. "It is possible to live with totally erroneous opinions. For all I know you may think the earth is square. It makes no difference to me."

"What do you mean, sir?" exclaimed Lord Alberan. He had become exceedingly red during our conversation and the lower part of his face had begun to swell. "Be careful what you say," he continued violently. "You are in danger of being arrested, sir. Either that, or being locked in an asylum."

The Home Secretary raised a restraining hand.

"One moment, Lord Alberan," he said, "I have not quite finished. Dr. Harden, will you be so good as to ask your friend—his name is Sarakoff, I believe—to come in here?"

I rose without haste and fetched the Russian. He behaved in an extremely quiet manner, nodded to Alberan and bowed to the Home Secretary.

Sir Robert gave a brief outline of the conversation he had had with me, which Sarakoff listened to with an absolutely expressionless face.

"I see that you also suffer from the epidemic," said Sir Robert. "Are you, then, immortal?"

"I am an Immortal," said the Russian, in deep tones. "You will be immortal to-morrow."

"I quite understand that I will probably catch the Blue Disease," said Sir Robert, suavely. "At present there are cases reported all over London, and we are at a loss to know what to do."

"You can do nothing," I said.

"We had thought of forming isolation camps." He stared at us thoughtfully. There was a slightly puzzled look in his face. It was the first time I had noticed it. It must have been due to Sarakoff's profound calm. "How did you gentlemen find the germ?" he asked suddenly.

Sarakoff reflected.

"It would take perhaps a week to explain."

Sir Robert smiled slightly.

"I'm afraid I am too busy," he murmured.

"You are wasting your time," muttered Alberan in his ear. "Arrest them."

The Home Secretary took no notice.

"It is curious that this epidemic seems to cut short other diseases," he said slowly. "That rather supports what you tell me."

His eyes rested searchingly on my face.

"You are foolish to refuse to believe us," I said. "We have told you the truth."

"It would be very strange if it were true." He walked to the window and stood for a moment looking on to the street. Then he turned with a movement of resolution. "I will not trespass on your time," he said. "Lord Alberan, we need not stay. I am satisfied with what these gentlemen have said." He bowed to us and went to the door. Lord Alberan, very fierce and upright, followed him. The Home Secretary paused and looked back. The puzzled looked had returned to his face.

"The matter is to be discussed in the House to-night," he said. "I think that it will be as well for you if I say nothing of what you have told me. People might be angry." We gazed at him unmoved. He took a sudden step towards us and held out his hands. "Come now, gentlemen, tell me the truth. You invented that story, didn't you?" Neither of us spoke. He looked appealingly at me, and with a laugh left the room. He turned, however, in a moment, and stood looking at me. “There is a meeting at the Queen’s Hall to-night,” he said slowly. “It is a medical conference on the Blue Disease. No doubt you know of it. I am going to ask you a question.” He paused and smiled at Sarakoff. “Will you gentlemen make a statement before those doctors to-night?”

“We intended to do so,” said Sarakoff.

“I am delighted to hear it,” said the Home Secretary. “It is a great relief to me. They will know how best to deal with you. Good day.”

He left the room.

I heard the front door close and then brisk footsteps passing the window on the pavement outside.

“There’s no doubt that they’re both a little mad.” Sir Robert’s voice sounded for a moment, and then died away.

17
CLUTTERBUCK'S ODD BEHAVIOUR

Scarcely had the Home Secretary departed when my maid announced that a patient was waiting to see me in my study.

I left Sarakoff sitting tranquilly in the waiting-room and entered the study. A grave, precise, clean-shaven man was standing by the window. He turned as I entered. It was Mr. Clutterbuck.

"So you are Dr. Harden!" he exclaimed.

He stopped and looked confused.

"Yes," I said; "please sit down, Mr. Clutterbuck."

He did so, twisting his hat awkwardly and gazing at the floor.

"I owe you an apology," he said at length. "I came to consult you, little expecting to find that it was you after all—that you were Dr. Harden. I must apologize for my rudeness to you in the tea-shop, but what you said was so extraordinary . . . you could not expect me to believe."

He glanced at me, and then looked away. There was a dull flush on his face.

"Please do not apologize. What did you wish to consult me about?"

"About my wife."

"Is she worse?"

"No." He dropped his hat, recovered it, and finally set it upon a corner of the table. "No, she is not worse. In fact, she is the reverse. She is better."

I waited, feeling only a mild interest in the cause of his agitation.

"She has got the Blue Disease," he continued, speaking with difficulty. "She got it yesterday and since then she has been much better. Her cough has ceased. She—er—she is wonderfully better." He began to drum with his fingers on his knee, and looked with a vacant gaze at the corner of the room. "Yes, she is certainly better. I was wondering if—"

There was a silence.

"Yes?"

He started and looked at me.

"Why, you've got it, too!" he exclaimed. "How extraordinary! I hadn't noticed it." He got to his feet and went to the window. "I suppose I shall get it next," he muttered.

"Certainly, you'll get it."

He nodded, and continued to stare out of the window. At length he spoke.

"My wife is a woman who has suffered a great deal, Dr. Harden. I have never had enough money to send her to health resorts, and she has always refused to avail herself of any institutional help. For the last year she has been confined to a room on the top floor of our house—a nice, pleasant room—and it has been an understood thing between Dr. Sykes and myself that her malady was to be given a convenient name. In fact, we have called it a weak heart. You understand, of course."

"Perfectly."

"I have always been led to expect that the end was inevitable," he continued, speaking with sudden rapidity. "Under such circumstances I made certain plans. I am a careful man, Dr. Harden, and I look ahead and lay my plans." He stopped abruptly and turned to face me. "Is there any truth in what you told me the other day?"

I nodded. A curiously haggard expression came over him. He stepped swiftly towards me and caught my arm.

"Does the germ cure disease?"

"Of course. Your wife is now immortal. You need not be alarmed, Mr. Clutterbuck. She is immortal. Before her lies a future absolutely free from suffering. She will rapidly regain her normal health and strength. Provided she avoids accidents, your wife will live for ever."

"My wife will live forever?" he repeated hoarsely. "Then what will happen to me?"

"You, too, will live for ever," I said calmly. "Please do not grasp my arm so violently."

He drew back. He was extremely pale, and there were beads of perspiration on his brow.

"Are you married?" he asked.

"No."

"Have you any idea what all this means to me if what you say is true?" he exclaimed. He drew his hand across his eyes. "I am mad to believe you for an instant. But she is better—there is no denying that. Good God, if it is true, what a tragedy you have made of human lives!"

He remained standing in the middle of the room, and I, not comprehending, gazed at him. Then, of a sudden, he picked up his hat, and muttering something, dashed out and vanished.

I heard the front door bang. Perfectly calm and undisturbed, I rejoined Sarakoff in the waiting-room. The incident of Mr. Clutterbuck passed totally from my mind, and I began to reflect on certain problems arising out of the visit of the Home Secretary.

18
IMMORTAL LOVE

On the same afternoon Miss Annot paid me a visit. I was still sitting in the waiting-room, and Sarakoff was with me. My mind had been deeply occupied with the question of the larger beliefs that we hold. For it had come to me with peculiar force that law and order, and officials like the Home Secretary, are concerned only with the small beliefs of humanity, with the burdensome business of material life. As long as a man dressed properly, walked decently and paid correctly, he was accepted, in spite of the fact that he might firmly believe the world was square. No one worried about those matters. We judge people ultimately by how they eat and drink and get up and sit down. What they say is of little importance in the long run. If we examine a person professionally, we merely ask him what day it is, where he is, what is his name and where he was born. We watch him to see if he washes, undresses and dresses, and eats properly. We ask him to add two and two, and to divide six by three, and then we solemnly give our verdict that he is either sane or insane.

The enormity of this revelation engrossed me with an almost painful activity of thought.

I gazed across at Sarakoff and wondered what appalling gulf divided our views on supreme things. What view did he really take of women? Did he or did he not think that the planets and stars were inhabited? Did he believe in the evolution of the soul like Mr. Thornduck?

A kind of horror possessed me as I stared at him and reflected that these questions had never entered my consciousness until that moment. I had lived with him and dined with him and worked with him, and yet hitherto it would have concerned me far more if I had seen him tuck his napkin under his collar or spit on the carpet. . . . What laughable little folk we were! I, who had always seen man as the last and final expression of evolution, now saw him as the stumbling, crawling, incredibly stupid, result of a tentative experiment—a first step up a ladder of infinitive length.

Whilst I was immersed in the humiliation of these thoughts Miss Annot entered. She wore a dark violet coat and skirt and a black hat. I noticed that her complexion, usually somewhat muddy, was perfectly clear, though of a marble pallor. We greeted each other quietly and I introduced Sarakoff.

"So you are an Immortal, Alice," I said smiling. She gazed at me.

"Richard, I do not know what I am, but I know one thing; I am entirely changed. Some strange miracle has been wrought in me. I came to ask you what it is."

"You see that both Professor Sarakoff and I have got the germ in our systems like you, Alice. Yes, it is a miracle; we are Immortals."

I studied her face attentively, she had changed. It seemed to me that she was another woman, she moved in a new way, her speech was unhurried, her gaze was direct and thoughtful. I recalled her former appearance when her manner had been nervous and bashful, her eyes downcast, her movements hurried and anxious.

"I do not understand," she said. "Tell me all you know."

I did so, I suppose I must have talked for an hour on end. Throughout that time neither she nor Sarakoff stirred. When I had finished there was a long silence.

"It is funny to think of our last meeting, Richard," she said at length. "Do you remember how my father behaved? He is different now. He sits all day in his study—he eats very little. He seems to be in a dream."

"And you?" I asked.

"I am in a dream, too. I do not understand it. All the things I used to busy myself with seem unimportant."

"That is how we feel," said Sarakoff. He rose to his feet and spoke strongly. "Harden, as Miss Annot says, everything has changed. I never foresaw this; I do not understand it myself."

He went slowly to the mantelpiece and leaned against it.

"When I created this germ, I saw in my mind an ideal picture of life. I saw a world freed from a dire spectre, a world from which fear had been removed, the fear of death. I saw the great triumph of materialism and the final smashing up of all superstition. A man would live in a state of absolute certainty. He would lay his plans for pleasure and comfort and enjoyment with absolute precision, knowing—not hoping—but certainly knowing, that they would come about. I saw cities and gardens built in triumph to cater for the gratification of every sense. I saw new laws in operation, constructed by men who knew that they had mastered the secret of life and had nothing to fear. I saw all those things about which we are so timid and vague—marriage and divorce, the education of children, luxury, the working classes, religion and so on—absolutely settled in black and white. I saw what I thought to be the millennium."

"And now?" asked Alice.

"Now I see nothing. I am in the dark. I do not understand what has happened to me."

"What we are in for now, no man can say," I remarked.

"It's the extraordinary restfulness that puzzles me," said Sarakoff. "Here I have been sitting for hours and I feel no inclination to do anything."

"The thing that is most extraordinary to me is the difficulty I have in realizing how I spent my time formerly," said Alice. "Of course, father is no bother now and meals have been cut down, but that does not account for all of it. It seems as if I had been living in a kind of nightmare in the past, from which I have suddenly escaped."

"What do you feel most inclined to do?" I asked.

"Nothing at present. I sit and think. It was difficult for me to make myself come here to-day." She smiled suddenly. "Richard, it seems strange to recall that we were engaged."

She spoke without any embarrassment and I answered her with equal ease.

"I hope you don't think our engagement is broken off, Alice. I think my feelings towards you are unchanged."

"Ah!" exclaimed Sarakoff. "That is interesting. Are you sure of that, Harden?"

"Not altogether," I answered tranquilly. "There is a lot to think out before I can be sure, but I know that I feel towards Alice a great sympathy."

"Sympathy!" the Russian exclaimed. "What are we coming to? Good heavens! Is sympathy to be our strongest emotion? What do you think, Miss Annot."

"Sympathy is exactly what I feel," she replied. "Richard and I would be very good companions. Isn't that more important than passion?"

"Is sympathy to be the bond between the sexes, then, and is all passion and romance to die?" he exclaimed scornfully. He seemed to be struggling with himself, as if he were trying to throw off some spell that held him. "Surely I seem to recollect that yesterday life contained some richer emotions than sympathy," he muttered. "What has come over us? Why doesn't my blood quicken when I think of Leonora?" He burst into a laugh. "Harden, this is comic. There is no other word for it. It is simply comic."

"It may be comic, Sarakoff, but to speak candidly, I prefer my state to-day to my state yesterday. Last night seems to me like a bad dream." I got to my feet. "There is one thing I must see about as soon as possible, and that is getting rid of this house. What an absurd place to live in this is! It is a comic house, if you like—like a tomb."

The room seemed suddenly absurd. It was very dark, the wall-paper was of a heavy-moulded variety, sombre in hue and covered with meaningless figuring. The ceiling was oppressive. It, too, was moulded in some fantastic manner. Several large faded oil-paintings hung on the wall. I do not know why they hung there, they were hideous and meaningless as well. The whole place was meaningless. It was the *meaninglessness* that seemed to leap out upon me wherever I turned my eyes. The fireplace astounded me. It was a mass of pillars and super-structures and carvings, increasing in complexity from within outwards, until it attained the appearance of an ornate temple in the centre of which burned a little coal. It was grotesque. On the topmost ledges of this monstrous absurdity stood two vases. They bulged like distended stomachs, covered on their outsides with yellow, green and black splotches of colour. I recollected that I paid ten pounds apiece for them. Under what perverted impulse had I done that? My memories became incredible. I moved deliberately to the mantelpiece and seized the vases. I opened the window and hurled them out on to the pavement. They fell with a crash, and their fragments littered the ground.

Alice expressed no surprise.

"It is rather comic," said the Russian, "but where are you going to live?"

"Alice and I will go and live by the sea. We have plenty to think about. I feel as if I could never stop thinking, as if I had to dig away a mountain of thought with a spade. Alice, we will go round to the house agent now."

When Alice and I left the house the remains of the vases littered the pavement at our feet. We walked down Harley Street. The house agent lived in Regent Street. It was now a clear, crisp afternoon with a pleasant tint of sunlight in the air. A newspaper boy passed, calling something unintelligible in an excited voice. I stopped him and bought a paper.

"What an inhuman noise to make," said Alice. "It seems to jar on every nerve in my body. Do ask him to stop."

"You're making too much noise," I said to the lad. "You must call softly. It is an outrage to scream like that."

He stared up at me, an impudent amazed face surmounting a tattered and dishevelled body, and spoke.

"You two do look a couple of guys, wiv' yer blue faices. If some of them doctors round 'ere catches yer, they'll pop yer into 'ospital."

He ran off, shrieking his unintelligible jargon.

"We must get to the sea," I said firmly. "This clamour of London is unbearable."

I opened the paper. Enormous headlines stared me in the face.

"Blue Disease sweeping over London. Ten thousand cases reported to-day. Europe alarmed. Question of the isolation of Great Britain under discussion. Debate in the Commons to-night. The Duke of Thud and the Earl of Blunder victims. The Royal Family leave London."

We stood together on the pavement and gazed at these statements in silence. A sense of wonder filled my mind. What a confusion! What an emotional, feverish, heated confusion! Why could not they take the matter calmly? What, in the name of goodness, was the reason of this panic. They knew that the Blue Disease had caused no fatalities in Birmingham, and yet so totally absent was the power of thought and deduction, that they actually printed those glaring headlines.

"The fools," I said. "The amazing, fatuous fools. They simply want to sell the paper. They have no other idea."

A strong nausea came over me. I crumpled up the paper and stood staring up and down the street. The newspaper boy was in the far distance, still shrieking. I saw Sir Barnaby Burtle, the obstetrician, standing by his scarlet front door, eagerly devouring the news. His jaw was slack and his eyes protruded.

The solemn houses of Harley Street only increased my nausea. The folly of it—the selfish, savage folly of life!

"Come, Richard," said Alice. "The sooner we get to the house agent the better. We could never live here."

"I'll put him on to the job of finding a bungalow on the South Coast at once," I said. "And then we'll go and live there."

"We must get married," she observed.

"Married!" I stopped and stared at her with a puzzled expression. "Don't you think the marriage ceremony is rather barbarous?"

She did not reply; we walked on immersed in our own thoughts. At times I detected in the passers-by a gleam of sparrow-egg blue.

My house agent was a large, confused individual who habitually wore a shining top hat on the back of his head and twisted a cigar in the corner of his mouth. He was very fat, with one of those creased faces that seem to fall into folds like a heavy crimson curtain. His brooding, congested eye fell upon me as we entered, and an expression of alarm became visible in its depths. He pushed his chair back and retreated to a corner of the room.

"Dr. Harden!" he exclaimed fearfully, "you oughtn't to come here like that, you really oughtn't."

"Don't be an ass, Franklyn," I said firmly. "You are bound to catch the germ sooner or later. It will impress you immensely."

"It's all over London," he whimpered. "It's too much; it will hit us hard. It's too much."

"Listen to me," I said. "I have come here to see you about business. Now sit down in your chair; I won't touch you. I want you to get me a bungalow by the sea with a garden as soon as possible. I am going to sell my house."

"Sell your house!" He became calmer. "That is very extraordinary, Dr. Harden."

"I am going out of London."

He was astonished.

"But your house—in Harley Street—so central. . . ." he stammered. "I don't understand. Are you giving up your practice?"

"Of course."

"At your age, Dr. Harden?"

"What has age got to do with it? There is no such thing as age."

He stared. Then his eyes turned to Alice.

"No such thing as age?" he murmured helplessly. "But surely you are not going to sell; you have the best house in Harley Street. Its commanding position . . . in the centre of that famous locality. . . ."

"Do you think that any really sane man would live in the centre of Harley Street," I asked calmly. "Is he likely to find any peace in that furnace of crude worldly ambitions? But all that is already a thing of the past. In a few weeks, Franklyn, Harley Street will be deserted."

"Deserted?" His eyes rolled.

"Deserted," I said sternly. "In its upper rooms there may remain a few Immortals, but the streets will be silent. The great business of sickness, which occupies the attention of a third of the world and furnishes the main topic of conversation in every home, will be gone. Sell my house, Franklyn, and find me a bungalow on the South Coast facing the sea."

I turned away and went towards the door, Alice followed me. The house agent sat in helpless amazement. He filled me with a sense of nausea. He seemed so gross, so mindless.

"A bungalow," he whispered.

"Yes. Let us have long, low, simple rooms and a garden where we may grow enough to live on. The age of material complexity and noise is at an end. We need peace."

Strolling along at a slow pace, we went down Oxford Street towards the Marble Arch. It was dusk. The newsboys were howling at every corner and everyone had a paper. Little groups of people stood on the pavements discussing the news. In the roadway the stream of traffic was incessant. The huge motor-buses thundered and swayed along, with their loads of pale humanity feverishly clinging to them. The public-houses were crowded. The slight tension that the threat of the Blue Disease produced in people filled the bars with men and women, seeking the relaxation of alcohol. There was in the air that liveliness, that tendency to collect into small crowds, that is evident whenever the common safety of the great herd is threatened. In the Park a crowd surrounded the platform of an agitator. In a voice like that of a delirious man, he implored the crowd to go down on its knees and repent . . . the end of the world was at hand . . . the Blue Disease was the pouring out of one of the vials of wrath . . . repent! . . . repent! . . . His voice rang in our ears and drove us away. We crossed the damp grass. I stumbled over a sleeping man. There was something familiar in his appearance and I stooped down and turned him over. It was Mr. Herbert Wain. He seemed to be fast asleep. . . . We walked to King's Cross, and I put Alice without regret in the train for Cambridge.

19

THE MEETING AT THE QUEEN'S HALL

The same night a vast meeting of medical men had been summoned at the Queen's Hall, with the object of discussing the nature of the strange visitation, and the measures that should be adopted. Doctors came from every part of the country. The meeting began at eight o'clock, and Sir Jeremy Jones, the President of the Royal College of Physicians, opened the discussion with a paper in which the most obvious features of the disease were briefly tabulated.

The great Hall was packed. Sarakoff and I got seats in the front row of the gallery. Sir Jeremy Jones, a large bland man, with beautiful silver grey hair, wearing evening dress, and pince-nez, stood up on the platform amid a buzz of talk. The short outburst of clapping soon ceased and Sir Jeremy began.

The beginnings of the disease were outlined, the symptoms described, and then the physician laid down his notes, and seemed to look directly up at me.

"So far," he said, in suave and measured tones, "I have escaped the Blue Disease, but at any moment I may find myself a victim, and the fact does not disquiet me. For I am convinced that we are witnessing the sudden intrusion and the swift spread of an absolutely harmless organism—one that has been, perhaps, dormant for centuries in the soil, or has evolved to its present form in the deep waters of the Elan watershed by a process whose nature we can only dimly guess at. Some have suggested a meteoric origin, and it is true that some meteoric stones fell over Wales recently.

But that is far-fetched to my mind, for how could a white-hot stone harbour living matter? Whatever its origin, it is, I am sure, a harmless thing, and though strange, and at first sight alarming, we need none of us alter our views of life or our way of living. The subject is now open for discussion, and I call on Professor Sarakoff, of Petrograd, the eminent bacteriologist, to give us the benefit of his views, as I believe he has a statement to make."

A burst of applause filled the Hall.

"Good," muttered Sarakoff in my ear. "I will certainly give them my views."

"Be careful," I said idly. Sir Jeremy was gazing round the Hall. Sarakoff stood up and there arose cries for silence. He made a striking figure with his giant stature, his black hair and beard and his blue-stained eyes. Sir Jeremy sat down, smiling blandly.

"Mr. President and Gentlemen," began the Professor, in a voice that carried to every part of the Hall. "I, as an Immortal, desire to make a few simple and decisive statements to you to-night regarding the nature of the Blue Disease, the germ of which was prepared by myself and my friend, Dr. Richard Harden. The germ—in future to be known as the Sarakoff-Harden bacillus—is ultra-microscopical. It grows in practically every medium with great ease. In the human body it finds an admirable host, and owing to the fact that it destroys all other organisms, it confers immortality on the person who is infected by it. We are therefore on the threshold of a new era."

After this brief statement Sarakoff calmly sat down, and absolute silence reigned. Sir Jeremy, still smiling blandly, stared up at him. Every face was turned in our direction. A murmur began, which quickly increased. A doctor behind me leaned over and touched my shoulder.

"Is he sane?" he asked in a whisper.

"Perfectly," I replied.

"But you don't believe him?"

"Of course I do."

"But it's ridiculous! Who is this Dr. Harden?"

"I am Dr. Harden."

The uproar in the Hall was now considerable. Sir Jeremy rose, and waved his hands in gestures of restraint. Finally he had recourse to a bell that stood on the table.

"Gentlemen," he said, when silence was restored. "We have just heard a remarkable statement from Professor Sarakoff and I think I am justified in asking for proofs."

I instantly got up. I was quite calm.

"I can prove that Sarakoff's statement is perfectly correct," I said. "I am Richard Harden. I discovered the method whereby the bacillus became a possibility. Every man in this Hall who has the Sarakoff-Harden bacillus in his system is immortal. You, Mr. President, are not yet one of the Immortals. But I fancy in a day or two you will join us." I paused and smiled easily at the concourse below and around me. "It is really bad luck on the medical profession," I continued. "I'm afraid we'll all have to find some other occupation. Of course you've all noticed how the germ cuts short disease."

I sat down again. The smile on Sir Jeremy's face had weakened a little.

"Turn them out!" shouted an angry voice from the body of the Hall.

Sir Jeremy held up a protesting hand, and then took off his glasses and began to polish them. A buzz of talk arose. Men turned to one another and began to argue. The doctor behind me leaned forward again.

"Is this a joke?" he enquired rather loudly.

"No."

"But you two are speaking rubbish. What the devil do you mean by saying you're immortal?"

I turned and looked at him. My calmness enraged him. He was a shaggy, irritable, middle-aged practitioner.

"You've got the Blue Disease, but you're no more immortal than a blue monkey." He looked fiercely round at his neighbours. "What do you think?"

A babel of voices sounded in our ears.

Sir Jeremy Jones appeared perplexed. Someone stood up in the body of the Hall and Sir Jeremy caught his eye and seemed relieved. It was my friend Hammer, who had tended me after the accident that my black cat had brought about.

"Gentlemen," said Hammer, when silence had fallen. "Although the statements of Professor Sarakoff and Dr. Harden appear fantastical, I believe that they may be nearer the truth than we suppose." His manner, slow, impressive and calm, aroused general attention. Frowning slightly, he drew himself up and clasped the lapels of his coat. "This afternoon," he continued, "I was at the bedside of a sick child who was at the point of death. This child had been visited yesterday by a relative who, two hours after the visit, developed the Blue Disease. Now—" He paused and looked slowly about him. "Now the child was suffering from peritonitis, and there was no possible chance of recovery. Yet that child *did* recover and is now well."

The whole audience was staring at him. Hammer took a deep breath and grasped his coat more firmly.

"That child, I repeat, is now well. The recovery set in under my own eyes. I saw for myself the return of life to a body that was moribund. The return was swift. In one hour the transformation was complete, and it was *in that hour* that the child developed the outward signs of the Blue Disease."

He paused. A murmur ran round the hall and then once more came silence.

"I am of the opinion," said Hammer deliberately, "that the cause of the miracle—for it was a miracle—was the Blue Disease. Think, Gentlemen, of a child in the last stages of septic peritonitis, practically dead. Think again of the same child, one hour later, alive, free from pain, smiling, interested—and stained with the Blue Disease. What conclusion, as honest men, are we to draw from that?"

He sat down. At once a man near him got to his feet.

"The point of view hinted at by the last speaker is correct," he said. "I can corroborate it to a small extent. This morning I was confined to my bed with the beginnings of a bad influenzal cold. At midday I developed the Blue Disease, and now I am as well as I have ever been in the whole of my life. I attribute my cure to the Blue Disease."

Scarcely had he taken his seat again when a grave scholarly man arose in the gallery.

"Gentlemen," he said, "I come from Birmingham; and it is a city of miracles. The sick are being cured in thousands daily. The hospitals are emptying daily. I verily believe that the Blue Disease may prove to be all that Dr. Sarakoff and Dr. Harden claim it to be."

The effect of these speakers upon the meeting was remarkable. A thrill passed over the crowded Hall. Hammer rose again.

"Let us accept for a moment that this new infection confers immortality on humanity," he said, weighing each word carefully. "What are we, as medical men, going to do? Look into the future—a future free from disease, from death, possibly from pain. Are we to accept such a future passively, or are we, as doctors, to strive to eradicate this new germ as we strive to eradicate other germs?"

Sir Jeremy Jones, with an expression of dismay, raised his hand.

"Surely, surely," he exclaimed shrilly, "we are going too far. That the Blue Disease may modify the course of illness is conceivable, and seems to be supported by evidence. But to assume that it confers immortality—"

"Why should we doubt it?" returned Hammer warmly. "We have been told that it does by two responsible men of science, and so far their claim is justified. You, Mr. Chairman, have not seen the miracle that I have seen this afternoon. If the germ can bring a moribund child back to life in an hour, why should it not banish disease from the world?"

"But if it does banish disease from the world, that does not mean it confers immortality," objected Sir Jeremy. "Do you mean to say that we are to regard natural death as a disease?"

He gazed round the hall helplessly. Several men arose to speak, but were unable to obtain a hearing, for excitement now ran high and every man was discussing the situation with his neighbour. For a moment, a strange dread had gripped the meeting, paralysing thought, but it passed, and while some remained perplexed the majority began to resent vehemently the suggestions of Hammer. I could hear those immediately behind me insisting that the view was sheer rubbish. It was preposterous. It was pure lunacy. With these phrases, constantly repeated, they threw off the startling effect of Hammer's speech, and fortified themselves in the conviction that the Blue Disease was merely a new malady, similar to other maladies, and that life would proceed as before.

I turned to them.

"You are deliberately deceiving yourselves," I said. "You have heard the evidence. You are simply making as much noise as possible in order to shut out the truth."

My words enraged them. A sudden clamour arose around us. Several men shook their fists and there were angry cries. One of them made a movement towards us. In an instant calmness left us. The scene around us seemed to leap up to our senses as something terrible and dangerous. Sarakoff and I scrambled to our feet, pushed our way frantically through the throng, reached the corridor and dashed down it. Fear of indescribable intensity had flamed in our souls, and in a moment we found ourselves running violently down Regent Street.

20
THE WAY BACK

It had been a wet night. Pools of water lay on the glistening pavements, but the rain had ceased. We ran steadily until we came in sight of Piccadilly Circus, and there our fear left us suddenly. It was like the cutting off of a switch. We stopped in the street, gasping for breath.

"This is really absurd," I observed; "we must learn to control ourselves."

"We can't control an emotion of that strength, Harden. It's overwhelming. It's all the emotion we had before concentrated into a single expression. No, it's going to be a nuisance."

"The worst of it is that we cannot foresee it. We get no warning. It springs out of the unknown like a tiger."

We walked slowly across the Circus. It was thronged with a night crowd, and seemed like some strange octagonal room, walled by moving coloured lights. Here lay a scene that remained eternally the same whatever the conditions of life—a scene that neither war, nor pestilence, nor famine could change. We stood by the fountain, immersed in our thoughts. "I used to enjoy this kind of thing," said Sarakoff at length.

"And now?"

"Now it is curiously meaningless—absolutely indecipherable."

We walked on and entered Coventry Street. Here Sarakoff suddenly pushed open a door and I followed him. We found ourselves in a brilliantly illuminated restaurant. A band was playing. We sat down at an unoccupied table.

"Harden, I wish to try an experiment. I want to see if, by an effort, we can get back to the old point of view."

He beckoned to the waiter and ordered champagne, cognac, oysters and caviar. Then he leaned back in his seat and smiled.

"Somehow I feel it won't work," I began.

He held up his hand.

"Wait. It is an experiment. You must give it a fair chance. Come, let us be merry."

I nodded.

"Let us eat, drink and be merry," I murmured.

I watched the flushed faces and sparkling eyes around us. So far we had attracted no attention. Our table was in a corner, behind a pillar. The waiter hurried up with a laden tray, and in a moment the table was covered with bottles and plates.

"Now," said Sarakoff, "we will begin with a glass of brandy. Let us try to recall the days of our youth—a little imagination, Harden, and then perhaps the spell will be broken. A toast—Leonora!"

"Leonora," I echoed.

We raised our glasses. I took a sip and set down my glass. Our eyes met.

"Is the brandy good?"

"It is of an admirable quality," said Sarakoff. He put his glass on the table and for some time we sat in silence.

"Excuse me," I said. "Don't you think the caviar is a trifle—?"

He made a gesture of determination.

"Harden, we will try champagne."

He filled two glasses.

"Let us drink off the whole glass," he said. "Really, Harden, we must try."

I managed to take two gulps. The stuff was nasty. It seemed like weak methylated spirits.

"Continue," said Sarakoff firmly; "let us drink ourselves into the glorious past, whither the wizard of alcohol transports all men."

I took two more gulps. Sarakoff did the same. It was something in the nature of a battle against an invisible resistance. I gripped the table hard with my free hand, and took another gulp.

"Sarakoff," I gasped. "I can't take any more. If you want to get alcohol into my system you must inject it under my skin. I can't do it this way."

He put down his glass. It was half full. There were beads of perspiration on his brow.

"I'll finish that glass somehow," he observed. He passed his hand across his forehead. "This is extraordinary. It's just like taking poison, Harden, and yet it is an excellent brand of wine."

"Do get these oysters taken away," I said. "They serve no purpose lying here. They only take up room."

"Wait till I finish my glass."

With infinite trouble he drank the rest of the champagne. The effort tired him. He sat, breathing quickly and staring before him.

"That's a pretty woman," he observed. "I did not notice her before."

I followed the direction of his gaze. A young woman, dressed in emerald green, sat at a table against the opposite wall. She was talking very excitedly, making many gestures and seemed to me a little intoxicated.

Sarakoff poured out some more champagne.

"I am getting back," he muttered. He looked like a man engaged in some terrific struggle with himself. His breath was short and thick, his eyes were reddened. Perspiration covered his face and hands. He finished the second glass.

"Yes, she is pretty," he said, "I like that white skin against the brilliant green. She's got grace, too. Have you noticed white-skinned women always are graceful, and have little ears, Harden?"

He laughed suddenly, with his old boisterousness and clapped me on the shoulder.

"This is the way out!" he shouted, and pointed to the silver tub that contained the champagne bottle.

His voice sounded loudly above the music.

"The way out!" he repeated. He got to his feet. His eyes were congested. The sweat streamed down his cheeks. "Here," he called in his deep powerful voice, "here, all you who are afraid—here is the way out." He waved his arms. People stopped drinking and talking to turn and stare at him. "Back to the animals!" he shouted. "Back to the fur and hair and flesh! I was up on the mountain top, but I've found the way back. Here it is—here is the magic you need, if you're tired of the frozen heights!"

He swayed as he spoke. Strangely interested, I stared up at him.

"He's delirious," called out the emerald young woman. "He's got that horrid disease."

The manager and a couple of waiters came up. "It's coming," shouted Sarakoff; "I saw it sweeping over the world. See, the world is white, like snow. They have robbed it of colour." The manager grasped his arm firmly.

"Come with me," he said. "You are ill. I will put you in a taxi."

"You don't understand," said Sarakoff. "You are in it still. Don't you see I'm a traveller?"

"He is mad," whispered a waiter in my ear.

"A traveller," shouted the Russian. "But I've come back. Greeting, brothers. It was a rough journey, but now I hear and see you."

"If you do not leave the establishment at once I will get a policeman," said the manager with a hiss.

Sarakoff threw out his hands.

"Make ready!" he cried. "The great uprooting!" He began to laugh unsteadily. "The end of disease and the end of desire—there's no difference. You never knew that, brothers. I've come back to tell you—thousands and thousands of miles—into the great dimension of hell and heaven. It was a mistake and I'm going back. Look! She's fading—further and further—" He pointed a shaking hand across the room and suddenly collapsed, half supported by the manager.

"Dead drunk," remarked a neighbour.

I turned.

"No. Live drunk," I said. "The champagne has brought him back to the world of desire."

The speaker, a clean-shaven young man, stared insolently.

"You have no business to come into a public place with that disease," he said with a sneer.

"You are right. I have no business here. My business is to warn the world that the end of desire is at hand." I signalled to a waiter and together we managed to get Sarakoff into a taxi-cab.

As we drove home, all that lay behind Sarakoff's broken confused words revealed itself with increasing distinctness to me.

Sarakoff spoke again.

"Harden," he muttered thickly, "there was a flaw—in the dream—"

"Yes," I said. "I was sure there would be a flaw. I hadn't noticed it before—"

"We're cut off," he whispered. "Cut off."

21
JASON

Next morning the headlines of the newspapers blazed out the news of the meeting at the Queen's Hall, and the world read the words of Sarakoff.

Strange to say, most of the papers seemed inclined to view the situation seriously.

"If," said one in a leading article, "it really means that immortality is coming to humanity—and there is, at least, much evidence from Birmingham that supports the view that the germ cures all sickness—then we are indeed face to face with a strange problem. For how will immortality affect us as a community? As a community, we live together on the tacit assumption that the old will die and the young will take their place. All our laws and customs are based on this idea. We can scarcely think of any institution that is not established upon the certainty of death. What, then, if death ceases? Our food supply—"

I was interrupted, while reading, by my servant who announced that a gentleman wished to see me on urgent business. I laid aside the paper and waited for him to enter.

My early visitor was a tall, heavily-built man, with strong eyes. He was carefully dressed. He looked at me attentively, nodded, and sat down.

"My name is Jason—Edward Jason. You have no doubt heard of me."

"Certainly," I said. "You are the proprietor of this paper that I have just been reading."

He nodded.

"And of sixty other daily papers, Dr. Harden," he said in a soft voice. "I control much of the opinion in the country, and I intend to control it all before I die."

"A curious intention. But why should you die? You will get the germ in time. I calculate that in a month at the outside the whole of London and the best part of the country will be infected."

While I spoke he stared hard at me. He nodded again, glanced at his boots, pinched his lips, and then stared again.

"A year ago I made a tour of all the big men in your profession, both here, in America, and on the continent, Dr. Harden. I had a very definite reason for doing this. The reason was that—well, it does not matter now. I wanted a diagnosis and a forecast of the future. I consulted forty medical men—all with big names. Twenty-one gave me practically identical opinions. The remaining nineteen were in disagreement. Of that nineteen six gave me a long life."

"What did the twenty-one give you?"

"Five years at the outside."

I looked at him critically.

"Yes, I should have given the same—a year ago."

He coloured a little, and his gaze fell; he shifted himself in his chair. Then he looked up suddenly, with a strong glow in his eyes.

"And now?"

"Now I give you—immortality." I spoke quite calmly, with no intention of any dramatic effect.

The colour faded from his cheeks, and the glow in his eyes increased.

"If I get the Blue Disease, do you swear that it will cure me?"

"Of course it will cure you."

He got to his feet. He seemed to be in the grip of some powerful emotion, and I could see that he was determined to control himself. He walked down the room and stood for some time near the window.

"A gipsy once told me I would die when I was fifty-two. Will you believe me when I say that that prophecy has weighed upon me more than any medical opinion?" He turned and came up the room and stood before me. "Did you ever read German psychology and philosophy?"

"To a certain extent—in translations."

"Well, Dr. Harden, I stepped out of the pages of some of those books, I think. You've heard of the theory of the Will to Power? The men who based human life on that instinct were right!" He clenched his hands and closed his eyes. "This last year has been hell to me. I've been haunted every hour by the thought of death—just so much longer—so many thousand days—and then Nothing!" He opened his eyes and sat down before me. "Are you ambitious, Dr. Harden?"

"I was—very ambitious."

"Do you know what it is to have a dream of power, luring you on day and night? Do you know what is to see the dream becoming reality, bit by bit—and then to be given a time limit, when the dream is only half worked out?"

"I have had my dream," I said. "It is now realized."

"The germ?"

I nodded. He leaned forward.

"Then you are satisfied?"

"I have no desires now."

He did not appear to understand.

"I don't believe yet in your theory of immortality," he said slowly. "But I do believe that the germ cures sickness. I have had private reports from Birmingham, and to-morrow I'm going to publish them as evidence. You see, Harden, I've decided to back you. To-morrow I'm going to make Gods of you and your Russian associate. I'm going to call you the greatest benefactors the race has known. I'm going to lift you up to the skies."

He looked at me earnestly.

"Doesn't that stir you?" he asked.

"No, I told you that I have no desires."

He laughed.

"You're dazed. You must have worked incredibly hard. Wait till you see your name surrounded by the phrases I will devise you. I can make men out of nothing." His eyes shone into mine. "I once heard a man say that the trail of the serpent lay across my papers. That man is in an asylum now. I can break men, too, you see. Now I want to ask you something."

I watched him with ease, totally uninfluenced by his magnetism—calm and aloof as a man watching a mechanical doll.

"Can you limit the germ?" he asked softly.

I shook my head.

"Can you take any steps to stop it or keep it—within control?"

I shook my head again. He stared for a minute at me.

"I believe you," he said at last. "It's a pity. Think what we could have done—just a few of us!" He sat for some time drumming his fingers on his knees and frowning slightly. Then he stood up.

"Never mind," he exclaimed. "I'm convinced it will cure me. That is the main thing. I'll have plenty of time to realize my dream now, Harden, thanks to you. You don't know what that means—ah, you don't know!"

"By the way," I said, "I see you are suggesting that food may become a problem in the future. I think we'll be all right."

"Why?"

"Well, you see, if there's no desire, there's no appetite."

"I don't understand," he said. "It seems clear that if disease is mastered by the germ, then the death-rate will drop, and there will be more mouths to fill. If everyone lives for their threescore and ten, the food question will be serious."

"Oh, they'll live longer than that. They'll live for ever, Mr. Jason."

He laughed tolerantly.

"In any case there will be a food problem," he said in a quiet friendly voice. "There will be more births, and more children—for none will die—and more old people."

"There won't be more births," I said.

He swung round on his heel.

"Why not?" he asked sharply.

"Because there will be no desire, Mr. Jason. You can't have births without desires, don't you see?"

At that moment Sarakoff entered the room. I introduced him to the great newspaper proprietor. Jason made some complimentary remarks, which Sarakoff received with cool gravity.

I could see that Jason was very puzzled. He had seated himself again, and was watching the Russian closely.

"The effects of last night have vanished," said Sarakoff to me. "My head is clear again and I have no intention of ever repeating the experiment."

"You got back, to some extent."

"Yes, partly. It was tremendously painful. I felt like a man in a nightmare."

I turned to Jason and explained what had happened at the restaurant. He listened intently.

"You see," I concluded, "the germ kills desire. Sarakoff and I live on a level of consciousness that is undisturbed by any craving. We live in a wonderful state of peace, which is only broken by the appearance of physical danger—against which, of course, the germ is not proof."

Jason was silent.

"Do you mean to tell me," he said at length, in a very deliberate voice, "that the effect of the germ is to destroy ambition?"

"Worldly ambition, certainly," I replied. "But I believe that, in time, ambitions of a subtler nature will reveal themselves in us, as Immortals."

Jason smiled very broadly.

"Gentlemen," he said, "you are wonderful men. You have discovered something that benefits humanity enormously. But take my advice—leave your other theories alone. Stick to the facts—that your germ cures sickness. Drop the talk about immortality and desire. It's too fantastic, even for me. In the meantime I shall spread abroad the news that the end of sickness is at hand, and that humanity is on the threshold of a new era. For that I believe with all my heart."

"One moment," said Sarakoff. "If you believe that this germ does away with disease, what is going to cause men to die?"

"Old age."

"But that is a disease itself."

"Wear and tear isn't a disease. That's what kills most of us."

"Yes, but wear and tear comes from desire, Mr. Jason," I said. "And the germ knocks that out. So what is left, save immortality?"

When Jason left us, I could see that he was impressed by the possibility of life being, at least, greatly prolonged. And this was the line he took in his newspapers next day.

22
THE FIRST MURDERS

The effect of Jason's newspapers on public opinion was remarkable. Humanity ever contains within it the need for mystery, and the strange and incredible, if voiced by authority, stir it to its depths. The facts about the healing of sickness and the cure of disease in Birmingham were printed in heavy type and read by millions. Nothing was said about immortality save what Sarakoff and I had stated at the Queen's Hall meeting. But instinctively the multitude leaped to the conclusion that if the end of disease was at hand, then the end of death—at least, the postponement of death—was to be expected.

Jason, pale and masterful, visited us in the afternoon, and told us of the spread of the tidings in England. "They've swallowed it," he exclaimed; "it's stirred them as nothing else has done in the last hundred years. I visited the East End to-day. The streets are full of people. Crowds everywhere. It might lead to anything."

"Is the infection spreading swiftly?"

"It's spreading. But there are plenty of people, like myself, who haven't got it yet. I should say that a quarter of London is blue." He looked at me with a sudden anxiety. "You're sure I'll get it?"

"Quite sure. Everyone is bound to get it. There's no possible immunity."

He sat heavily in the chair, staring at the carpet.

"Harden, I didn't quite like the look of those crowds in the East End. Anything big like this stirs up the people. It excites them and then the incalculable may happen. I've been thinking about the effect upon the uneducated mind. I've spread over the country the vision of humanity free from disease, and that's roused something in them—something dangerous—that I didn't foresee. Disease, Harden, whatever you doctors think of it, puts the fear of God into humanity. It's these sudden releases—releases from ancient fears—that are so dangerous. Are you sure you can't stop the germ, or direct it along certain channels?"

"I have already told you that's impossible."

"You might as well try and stop the light of day," said Sarakoff from a sofa, where he was lying apparently asleep. "Let the people think what they like now. Wait till they get it themselves. There are rules in the game, Jason, that you have no conception of, and that I have only realized since I became immortal. Yes—rules in the game, whether you play it in the cellar or the attic, or in the valley, or on the mountain top."

"Your friend is very Russian," said Jason equably. "I have always heard they are dreamers and visionaries. Personally, I am a practical man, and as such I foresee trouble. If the masses of the people have no illness, and enjoy perfect health, we shall be faced by a difficult problem. They'll get out of hand. Depressed states of health are valuable assets in keeping the social organization together. All this demands careful thought. I am visiting the Prime Minister this evening and shall give him my views."

At that moment a newspaper boy passed the window with an afternoon edition and Jason went out to get a copy. He returned with a smile of satisfaction, carrying the paper open before him.

"Three murders in London," he announced. "One in Plaistow, one in East Ham and one in Pimlico. I told you there was unrest abroad." He laid the paper on the table and studied it "In every case it was an aged person—two old women, and one old man. Now what does that mean?"

"A gang at work."

He shook his head.

"No. In one case the murderer has been caught. It was a case of patricide—a hideous crime. Curiously enough the victim had the

Blue Disease. The end must have been ghastly, as it states here that the expression on the old man's face was terrible."

He sat beside the table, drumming his fingers on it and staring at the wall before him. I was not particularly interested in the news, but I was interested in Jason. Character had formerly appealed little to me, but now I found an absorbing problem in it.

"Harden, do you think that son killed his father *because* he had the Blue Disease?"

I was struck by the remark. For some reason the picture of Alice's father came into my mind. Jason sprang to his feet.

"Yes, that's it," he exclaimed. "That's what lay behind those restless crowds. I knew there was something—a riddle to read, and now I've got the answer. The crowd doesn't know what's rousing them. But I do. It's fear and resentment, Harden. It's fear and resentment against the old." He brought his fist down on the table. "The germ's going to lead to war! It's going to lead to the worst war humanity has ever experienced—the war of the young against the old. Not the ancient strife or struggle between young and old, but open bloodshed, my friends. That's what your germ is going to do."

I smiled and shook my head.

"Wait," said Sarakoff from the sofa; "wait a little. Why are you in such a hurry to jump to conclusions?"

"Because it's my business to jump to conclusions just six hours before anyone else does," said Jason. "I calculate that my mind, for the last twenty years, has been six hours ahead of time. I live in a state of chronic anticipation, Dr. Sarakoff. Just let me use your telephone for a moment."

He returned a quarter of an hour later. His expression was calm, but his eyes were hard. "I was right," he said. "Those two old women had the Blue Disease, and a girl, a daughter, is suspect in one case. Can't you imagine the situation? Girl lives with her aged mother—can't get free—mother has what money there is—not allowed to marry—girl unconsciously counts on mother's death—probably got a secret love-affair—is expecting the moment of release—and then, along comes the Blue Disease and one of my newspapers telling her what it means. The old lady recovers her health—the future shuts down like a rat trap and what does the poor girl do? Kills her mother—and probably goes mad. That, gentlemen, is my theory of the case."

He strode up and down the room.

"You may think I'm taking a low view," he cried. "But there are hundreds of thousands of similar cases in England. God help the old if the young forget their religion!"

For some reason I was unmoved by the outcry. It was no doubt owing to the peculiar emotionless state that the germ induced in people. Jason was roused. He paced to and fro in silence, with his brows contracted. At length he stopped before me.

"Do you see any way out?"

"There will be no war between the young and the old," I replied. "In another week everyone will get the germ and that will be the end of war in every form."

He drew a chair and sat down before me.

"You don't understand," he said earnestly. "Perhaps you had a happy childhood. I didn't. I know how some sons and daughters feel because I suffered in that way. People are strangely blind to suffering unless they have suffered themselves. When I was a young man, my father put me in his office and gave me a clerk's wages. He kept me there for six years at eighteen shillings a week. Whenever I made a suggestion concerning the business he was careful to ridicule it. Whenever I tried to break away and start on my own, he prevented it. There were a thousand other things—ways in which he fettered me. My only sister he kept at home to do the housework. He forbade her to marry. She and I never had enough money to do anything, to go anywhere, or to buy anything. Now, to be quite frank, I longed for him to die so that I could get free. To me he was an ogre, a great merciless tyrant, a giant with a club. Well, he died. When he was dead I felt what a man dying of thirst in the desert must feel when he suddenly comes to a spring of water. I recovered, and became what I am. My sister never recovered. She had been suppressed beyond all the limits of elasticity. As far as her body is concerned, it is alive. Her soul is dead."

He paused and looked at me meditatively.

"If your blue germ had come along then, Harden, I might— Who knows? I have often wondered why our pulpit religion ignores the crimes of parents to their children. I'm not conventionally religious, but I seem to remember that Christ indirectly said something pretty strong on the subject. But the pulpit folk show a wonderful facility for ignoring the awkward things Christ said. In about three years' time I'm going to turn my guns on the Church. They've sneered at me too much."

"There will be a new Church by that time," murmured Sarakoff. "And no guns."

Jason eyed the prostrate figure of the Russian.

"I refer to my newspapers. That's going to be my final triumph. Why do you smile?"

"Because you said a moment ago that it was your business to be six hours ahead of everyone else. You're countless centuries behind Harden and me. We have taken a leap into the future. If you want to know what humanity will be, look at us closely. You'll get some hints that should be valuable. I admit that our bodies are old-fashioned in their size and shape, but not our emotions."

The telephone bell rang in the hall and Jason jumped up.

"I think that's for me."

He went out. I remained sitting calmly in my chair. An absolute serenity surrounded me. All that Jason did or said was like looking at an interesting play. I was perfectly content to sit and think—think of Jason, of what his motives were, of the reason why a man is blind where his desires are at work, of the new life, of the new organizations that would be necessary. I was like a glutton before a table piled high with delicacies and with plenty of time to spare. Sarakoff seemed to be in the same condition for he lay with his eyes half shut, motionless and absorbed.

Jason entered the room suddenly. He carried his hat and stick.

"Two more murders reported from Greenwich, and ten from Birmingham. It's becoming serious, Harden! I'm off to Downing Street. Watch the morning editions!"

23
AT DOWNING STREET

That night, at eight o'clock, I was summoned to Downing Street. I left Sarakoff lying on the sofa, apparently asleep. I drove the first part of the way in a taxi, but at the corner of Orchard Street the cab very nearly collided with another vehicle, and in a moment I was a helpless creature of fear. So I walked the rest of the way, much to the astonishment of the driver, who thought I was a lunatic. It was a fine crisp evening and the streets were unusually full. Late editions of the paper were still being cried, and under the lamps were groups of people, talking excitedly.

From what I could gather from snatches of conversation that I overheard, it seemed that many thought the millennium was at hand. I mused on this, wondering if beneath the busy exterior of life there lurked in people's hearts a secret imperishable conviction. And, after all, was it not a millennium—the final triumph of science—the conquest of the irrational by the rational?

There was a good deal of drunkenness, and crowds of men and women, linked arm and arm, went by, singing senseless songs. In Piccadilly Circus the scene was unusually animated. Here, beyond doubt, the Jason press had produced a powerful impression. The restaurants and bars blazed with light. Crowds streamed in and out and a spirit of hilarious excitement pervaded everyone. Irresponsibility—that was the universal attitude; and I became deeply occupied in thinking how the germ should have brought about such a temper in the multitude. Only occasionally did I catch the blue stain in the eyes of the throng about me.

I reached Downing Street and was shown straight into a large, rather bare room. By the fireplace sat Jason, and beside him, on the hearthrug, stood the Premier. Jason introduced me and I was greeted with quiet courtesy.

"I intend to make a statement in the House to-night and would like to put a few questions to you," said the Premier in a slow clear voice. "The Home Secretary has been considering whether you and Dr. Sarakoff should be arrested. I see no use in that. What you have done cannot be undone."

"That is true."

"In matters like this," he continued, "it is always a question of taking sides. Either we must oppose you and the germ, or we must side with you, and extol the virtues of the new discovery. A neutral attitude would only rouse irritation. I have therefore looked into the evidence connected with the effects claimed for the germ, and have received reports on the rate of its spread. It would seem that it is of benefit to man, so far as can be judged at present, and that its course cannot be stayed."

I assented, and remained gazing abstractedly at the fire.

He continued in a sterner tone—

"It may, however, be necessary to place you and Dr. Sarakoff under police protection. There is no saying what may happen. Your action in letting loose the germ in the water supply of Birmingham was unfortunate. You have taken a great liberty with humanity, whatever may result from it."

"Medical men have no sense of proportion," murmured Jason. "Science makes them so helpless."

"I see no kind of helplessness in rescuing humanity from disease," I answered calmly. "Please tell me what you want to know."

They both looked at me attentively. The Premier took out a pair of pince-nez and began to clean the lenses, still watching me.

"France is unwilling to let the germ into her territory. Can measures be taken to stop its access to the Continent?"

"No. It will get there inevitably. It has probably got there long ago. It is air borne and water borne and probably sea borne as well.

The whole world will be infected sooner or later. There is no immunity possible."

The Premier put on his pince-nez and warmed his hands at the fire.

"Then what will the result of the germ be upon mankind?" he asked at length.

"It will begin a new era. What has made reform so difficult up to now?"

"People do not see eye to eye on all questions, Dr. Harden. That is the main reason."

"And why do they not see eye to eye?"

"Because their desires are not the same."

"Very good. Now imagine a humanity without desires, as you and Jason understand desire. What would be the result?"

"It is impossible to conceive. The wheels of the world would cease turning. We should be like sheep without a shepherd." He surveyed me quietly for some time. "Then you think the germ will kill desire?"

"I know it. I am a living example. I have no desires. I am like a man without a body, I am immortal."

Jason laughed.

"You are above temptation?" he asked.

"Absolutely. Neither money, power nor woman has any influence on me. They are meaningless."

"You have, perhaps, reached Nirvana?" the Premier enquired.

"Yes. That is why I am immortal. I have reached Nirvana."

"By a trick."

"If you like—by a trick."

"Then I cannot think you will stay there for long," said the Premier. "I shall look forward to my attack of the Blue Disease with interest. It will be amusing to note one's sensations."

It was clear to me that he was defending himself against my greater knowledge, but it was a matter of no importance to me. I was faintly oppressed by the dreary immensity of the room. I had become sensitive to atmosphere, and the feeling of that room was not harmonious.

The Premier stood in deep thought.

"If the germ prolongs life, it will lead to complications," he remarked. "The question of being too old has attracted public attention for some time now, which shows the way the wind is blowing. Oldness has become, in a small degree, a problem. The world is younger than it used to be—more impatient, more anxious to live a free life, to escape from any form of bondage. And so people have begun to ask what we are to do with our old men."

He paused and looked at Jason.

"My friend Jason thinks these murders are caused indirectly by the germ."

"It is possible."

"It seems fantastic. But there may be something in it." The Premier raised his eyes and studied the ceiling. "There is certainly some excitement abroad. We are dealing with an unprecedented situation. I therefore propose to say to-night that if, in the course of time, we find that life is prolonged and disease done away with, new laws will have to be considered."

"Not only new laws," I said. "We shall have to reconstruct the whole future of life. But there is no hurry. There is plenty of time. There is eternity before us."

"What do you eat?" demanded the Premier suddenly.

"A little bread or biscuit."

He clasped his hands behind his back and surveyed me for quite a minute.

"I don't believe you're a quack," he observed. "But when you walked into the room, I was doubtful."

"Why?"

"Because you wouldn't look at me squarely."

"Why should I look at you squarely? I looked at you and saw you. I have no desire to make any impression on you, or to dominate you in any way. It was sufficient just to see you. As Immortals, we do not waste our time looking at one another squarely. An Immortal cannot act."

The Premier smiled to himself and took out his watch.

"I am obliged to you for the instance," he said. "Good-night."

I rose and walked towards the door. On my way I stopped before a vast dingy oil-painting.

"Why do you all deceive yourselves that you admire things like that? Throw it away. When you become an Immortal you won't live here."

The Premier and Jason stood together on the hearth-rug. They watched me intently as I went out and closed the door behind me. A servant met me on the landing and escorted me downstairs. I observed that he was an Immortal.

"What are you doing here?" I asked.

"I am a spectator," he said in a calm voice. "And you?"

"I, too, am a spectator."

24
NIGHT OF AN IMMORTAL

I passed a most remarkable night. On reaching home I went to bed as usual. My mind was busy, but what busied it was not the events of the day.

I lay in the darkness in a state of absolute contentment. My eyes were closed. My body was motionless, and felt warm and comfortable. I was quite aware of the position of my limbs in space and I could hear the sound of passing vehicles outside. I was not asleep and yet at the same time I was not awake. I knew I was not properly awake because, when I tried to move, there seemed to be a resistance to the impulse, which prevented it from reaching the muscles. As I have already said, I could feel. The sensation of my body was there, though probably diminished, but the power of movement was checked, though only slightly. And all the time I lay in that state, my mind was perfectly lucid and continually active. I thought about many things and the power of thought was very great, in that I could keep my attention fixed hour after hour on the same train of thought, go backwards and forwards along it, change and modify its gradations, just as if I were dealing with some material and plastic formation. Since that time I have become acquainted with a doctrine that teaches that thoughts are in the nature of things—that a definite thought is a formation in some tenuous medium of matter, just as a cathedral is a structure in gross matter. This is certainly the kind of impression I gained then.

It was now in the light of contrast that I could reflect on the rusty and clumsy way in which I had previously done my thinking, and I remembered with a faint amusement that there had been a time when I considered that I had a very clear and logical mind. Logical! What did we, as mere mortals full of personal desire, know of logic? The reflection seemed infinitely humorous. My thoughts had about them a new quality of stability. They formed themselves into clear images, which had a remarkable permanence. Their power and influence was greatly increased. If, for example, I thought out a bungalow situated on the cliff, I built up, piece by piece in my mind, the complete picture; and once built up it remained there so that I could see it as a whole, and almost, so to speak, walk round it and view it from different angles. I could lay aside this thought-creation just as I might lay aside a model in clay, and later on bring it back into my mind, as fresh and clear as ever. The enjoyment of thinking under such conditions is impossible to describe. It was like the joy of a man, blind from childhood, suddenly receiving his sight.

As ordinary mortals, we are all familiar with the apparently real scenes that occur in dreams. In our dreams we see buildings and walk round them. We see flights of steps and climb them. We apparently touch and taste food. We meet friends and strangers and converse with them. At times we seem to gaze over landscapes covered with woods and meadows.

It seemed to me that the magic of dreams had in some way become attached to thought. For as Immortals we did not dream as mortals do. In place of dreaming, we created immense thought-forms, working as it were on a new plane of matter whose resources were inexhaustible.

That night I built my ideal bungalow and when I had finished it I constructed my ideal garden. And then I made a sea and a coastline, and when it was finished it was so real to me that I actually seemed to go into its rooms, sit on the verandah, breathe in its sea-airs and listen to the surf below its cliff. I remember that one of its rooms did not please me entirely, and that I seemed to pull it down—in thought—and reconstruct it according to my wish. This took time, for brick by brick I thought the new room into existence. One law that governed that state was easy to grasp, for whatever you did not think out clearly assumed a blurred unsatisfactory form. It became clear to me as early as that first night of immortality that the more familiar a man was with matter on the earth and its ways and possibilities, the more easily could he make his constructions on that plan of thought.

The whole of that night I lay in this state of creative joy and I know that my body remained motionless. It seemed that only a film divided me from the use of my limbs, but that film was definite. At eight o'clock on that morning, I became aware of a vague feeling of strain. It was a very slight sensation, but its effect was to make the thoughts that occupied my consciousness to become less definite. I had to make an effort to keep them distinct. The strain slowly became greater. It had begun with a sense of distance, but it seemed to get nearer, and I experienced a feeling that I can only compare to as that which a man has when he is losing his balance and about to fall.

The strain ended suddenly. I found myself moving my limbs. I opened my eyes and looked round. The graphic, visible quality of my thoughts had now vanished. I was awake.

I have given the above account of the night of an Immortal, because it has seemed to me right that some record should be left of the effect of the germ on the mind. I would explain the inherent power of thought as being due to the freedom from the ordinary desires of mortals, which waste and dissipate the energies of the mind . . . but of that I cannot be certain.

25
OUR FLIGHT

I got out of bed and began to examine my clothes. They were strewn about the floor and on chairs. The colour of them seemed peculiar to my senses. My frock coat, of heavy black material, with curious braiding and buttons, fascinated me. I counted the number of separate things that made up my complete attire. They were twenty-four in number. I discovered that in addition to these articles of actual wearing material I was in the habit of carrying on my person about sixty other articles. For some reason I found these calculations very interesting. I had a kind of counting mania that morning. I counted all the things I used in dressing myself. I counted the number of stripes on my trousers and on my wall-paper; I counted the number of rooms in my house, the articles of furniture that they contained, and the number of electric lamps. I went into the kitchen and counted everything I could see, to the astonishment of my servants. I observed that my cook showed a faint blue stain in her eyes, but that the other servants showed no signs as yet of the Blue Disease. I went into my study and counted the books; I opened one of them. It was the British Pharmacopoeia. I began mechanically to count the number of drugs it contained. I was still counting them when the breakfast gong sounded. I went across the hall and counted on my way the number of sticks and hats and coats that were there. I finished up by counting the number of things on the breakfast table. Then I picked up the newspaper. There were, by the way, one hundred and four distinct things on my breakfast table.

The paper was full of the records of crime and of our names.

The account of the Prime Minister's statement in the House was given in full. Our names were printed in large letters, and apparently our qualifications had been looked up, for they were mentioned, together with a little biographical sketch. In a perfectly calm and observant spirit I read the closely-printed column. My eye paused for some time at an account of my personal appearance—"a small, insignificant-looking man, with straight blue-black hair, like a Japanese doll, and an untidy moustache, speaking very deliberately and with a manner of extreme self-assurance."

Extreme self-assurance! I reflected that there might, after all, be some truth in what the reporter said. On the night that I had spoken at the Queen's Hall meeting I had been quite self-possessed. I pursued the narrative and smiled slightly at a description of the Russian— "a loosely-built, bearded giant, unkempt in appearance, and with huge square hands and pale Mongolian eyes which roll like those of a maniac." That was certainly unfair, unless the reporter had seen him at the restaurant when Sarakoff drank the champagne. I was about to continue, when a red brick suddenly landed neatly on my breakfast table, and raised the number of articles on that table to one hundred and five.

There was a tinkle of falling glass; I looked up and saw that the window was shattered. The muslin curtain in front of it had been torn down by the passage of the brick, and the street without was visible from where I sat. A considerable crowd had gathered on the pavement. They saw me and a loud cry went up. The front door bell was ringing and there was a sound of heavy blows that echoed through the house.

My housemaid came running into the room. She uttered a shriek as she saw the faces beyond the window and ran out again. I heard a door at the back of the house slam suddenly.

A couple of men, decently enough dressed, were getting over the area rails with the intent of climbing in at the window. I jumped up and went swiftly upstairs. So far I was calm. I entered Sarakoff's bedroom. It was in darkness. The Russian was lying motionless on the bed. I shook him by the shoulder. It seemed impossible to rouse him, and yet in outward appearance he seemed only lightly asleep. I redoubled my efforts and at length he opened his eyes, and his whole body, which had felt under my hands as limp and flaccid as a pillow, suddenly seemed to tighten up and become resilient.

"Get up," I said. "They're trying to break into the house. We may be in danger. We can escape by the back door through the mews."

The blows on the front door were clearly audible.

"I've been listening to it for some time," he said. "But I seemed to have lost the knack of waking up properly."

"We have no time to waste," I said firmly.

We went quickly downstairs. Sarakoff had flung a blue dressing-gown over his pyjamas and thrust his feet into a pair of slippers. On reaching the hall there was a loud crack and a roar of voices. In an instant the agonizing fear swept over us. We dashed to the back of the house, through the servants' quarters and out into the mews. Without pausing for an instant we ran down the cobbled alley and emerged upon Devonshire Street. We turned to the right, dashed across Portland Place and reached Great Portland Street. We ran steadily, wholly mastered by the great fear of physical injury, and oblivious to the people around us. We passed the Underground Station. Our flight down the Euston Road was extraordinary. Sarakoff was in front, his dressing-gown flying, and his pink pyjamas making a vivid area of colour in the drab street. I followed a few yards in the rear, hatless, with my breath coming in gasps.

It was Sarakoff who first saw the taxi-cab. He veered suddenly into the road and held out his arms. The cab slowed down and in a moment we were inside it.

"Go on," shouted Sarakoff, "Drive on. Don't stop."

The driver was a man of spirit and needed no further directions. The cab jerked forward and we sped towards St. Pancras Station.

"Follow the tram lines up to Hampstead," I called out, and he nodded. We lay gasping in the back of the cab, cannoning helplessly as it swayed round corners. By the time we had reached Hampstead our fear had left us.

The cab drew up on the Spaniard's Walk and we alighted. It was a bleak and misty morning. The road seemed deserted. A thin column of steam rose from the radiator of the taxi, and there was a smell of over-heated oil.

"Sharp work that," said the driver, getting out and beating his arms across his chest. His eyes moved over us with frank curiosity. Sarakoff shivered and drew his dressing-gown closely round him.

26
ON THE SPANIARD'S WALK

I paid the man half-a-sovereign. There was a seat near by and Sarakoff deposited himself upon it. I joined him. On those heights the morning air struck chill. London, misty-blue, lay before us. The taxi-man took out his pipe and began to fill it.

"Lucky me comin' along like that," he observed. "If it hadn't been because of my missus I wouldn't have been out so early." He blew a puff of smoke and continued: "This Blue Disease seems to confuse folk. My missus was took with it last night." He paused to examine us at his leisure. "When did you get it?"

"We became immortal the day before yesterday," said Sarakoff.

The taxi-man took his pipe out of his mouth and stared.

"You ain't them two doctors what's in the paper this morning, by any chance?" he asked. "Them as is supposed to 'ave invented this Blue Disease?"

We nodded. He emitted a low whistle and gazed thoughtfully at us. At length he spoke I noticed his tone had changed.

"As I was saying, my missus was took with it in the night. I had a job waking 'er up, and when she opened her eyes I near had a fit. We'd had a bit of a tiff overnight, but she got up as quiet as a lamb and never said a word agin me, which surprised me. When I 'ad dressed myself I went into the kitchen to get a bit o' breakfast, and she was setting in a chair starin' at nothing. The kettle wasn't boiling, and there wasn't nothing ready, so I asked 'er quite polite, what she was doing. 'I'm thinking,' she says, and continues sitting in the chair. After a bit of reasoning with her, I lost my temper and picked up a leg of a chair, what we had broke the evening previous when we was 'aving a argument. She jump up and bolted out of the house, just as she was, with her 'air in curl-papers, and that's the last I saw of her. I waited an hour and then took the old cab out of the garage, and I was going to look for my breakfast when I met you two gents." He took his pipe out of his mouth and wiped his lips. "Now I put it all down to this 'ere Blue Disease. It's sent my missus off 'er head."

"There's no reason why you should think your wife mad simply because she ran away when you tried to strike her," I said. "It's surely a proof of her sanity."

He shook his head.

"That ain't correct," he said, with conviction. "She always liked a scrap. She's a powerful young woman, and her language is extraordinary fine when she's roused, and she knows it. I can't understand it."

He looked up suddenly.

"So it was you two who made this disease was it?"

"Yes."

"Fancy that!" he said. "Fancy a couple of doctors inventing a disease. It does sound a shame, don't it?"

"Wait till you get it," said Sarakoff.

"It seems to me you've been and done something nasty," he went on. "Ain't there enough diseases without you two going and makin' a new one? It's a fair sickener to think of all the diseases there are—measles and softenin' of the brain, and 'eaving stummicks and what not. What made you do it? That's what I want to know." He was getting angry. He pointed the stem of his pipe at us accusingly. His small eyes shone. "It's fair sickening," he muttered. "I've never took to doctors, nor parsons—never in my life."

He spat expressively.

"And my wife, too, clean barmy," he continued. "Who 'ave I got to thank for that? You two gents. Doctors, you call yourselves. I arsk you, what is doctors? They never does me any good. I never seed anyone they'd done any good. And yet they keeps on and no one says nothing. It's fair sickening."

There was a sound of footsteps behind me. I turned and saw a policeman climbing slowly up the bank towards the road. Like all policemen he appeared not to notice us until he was abreast of our seat. Then he stopped and eyed each of us in turn. His boots were muddy.

"These gents," said the taxi-man, "'ave been and done something nasty."

The phrase seemed attractive to him and he repeated it. The policeman, a tall muscular man, surveyed us in silence. Sarakoff, his hair and beard dishevelled, was leaning back in a corner of the seat, with his legs crossed. His dressing-gown was tucked closely round him, and below it, his pink pyjamas fluttered in the thin breeze. His expression was calm.

The taxi-man continued—

"I picked these gents up in the Euston Road. They was in a hurry. I thought they'd done something ordinary, same as what you or me might do, but it seems I was wrong. They've been and done something nasty. They've gone and invented this 'ere Blue Disease."

The policeman raised his helmet a little and the taxi-man uttered an exclamation.

"Why, you've got it yourself," he said, and stared. The policeman's eyes were stained a vivid blue.

"An immortal policeman!" murmured Sarakoff dreamily.

The discovery seemed to discomfit the taxi-man. The tide of indignation in him was deflected, and he shifted his feet. The policeman, with a deliberation that was magnificent advanced to the seat and sat down beside me.

"Good-morning," I said.

"Good-morning," he replied in a deep calm voice. He removed his helmet from his head and allowed the wind to stir his hair. The taxi-man moved a step nearer us.

"You ought to arrest them," he said. "Here's my wife got it, and you, and who's to say when it will end? They're doctors, too. I allus had my own suspicions of doctors, and 'ere they are, just as I supposed, inventing diseases to keep themselves going. That's what you ought to do . . . arrest them. I'll drive you all down to the police-station." The policeman replaced his helmet, crossed his long blue legs, and leaned back in the corner of the seat. Side by side on the seat Sarakoff, the policeman, and I gazed tranquilly at the figure of the taxi-man, at the taxi-cab, and at the misty panorama of London that lay beyond the Vale of Health. The expression of anger returned to the taxi-man's face.

"And 'ere am I, standing and telling you to do your duty, and all the time I haven't had my breakfast," he said bitterly. "If you was to cop them two gents, your name would be in all the evenin' papers." He paused, and frowned, conscious that he was making little impression on the upholder of law and order. "Why 'aven't I 'ad my breakfast? All because of these two blokes. I tell you, you ought to cop them."

"When I was a boy," said the policeman, "I used to collect stamps."

"Did yer," exclaimed the taxi-man sarcastically. "You do interest me, reely you do."

"Yes, I used to collect stamps." The policeman settled himself more comfortably. "And afore that I was in the 'abit of collecting bits o' string."

"You surprise me," said the taxi-man. "And what did you collect afore you collected bits of string?"

"So far as I recollect, I didn't collect nothing. I was trying to remember while I was walking across the Heath." He turned to us. "Did you collect anything?"

"Yes," I said. "I used to collect beetles."

"Beetles?" The policeman nodded thoughtfully. "I never had an eye for beetles. But, as I said, I collected stamps. I remember I would walk for miles to get a new stamp, and of an evening I would sit and count the stamps in my album over and over again till my head was fair giddy." He paused and stroked his clean-shaven chin thoughtfully. "I recollect as if it was yesterday how giddy my head used to get."

The taxi-man seemed about to say something, but he changed his mind.

"Why did you collect beetles?" the policeman asked me.

"I was interested in them."

"But that ain't a suitable answer," he replied. "It ain't suitable. That's what I've been seeing for the first time this morning. The point is—why was you interested in beetles, and why was I interested in bits o' string and stamps?"

"Yes, he's quite right," said Sarakoff; "that certainly is the point."

"To say that we are interested in a thing is no suitable explanation," continued the policeman. "After I'd done collecting stamps—"

"Why don't you arrest these two blokes?" shouted the taxi-man suddenly. "Why can't you do yer duty, you blue fathead?"

"I'm coming to that," said the policeman imperturbably. "As I was saying, after I collected stamps, I collected knives—any sort of old rusty knife—and then I joined the force and began to collect men, I collected all sorts o' men—tall and short, fat and thin. Now why did I do that?"

"It seems to me," observed the taxi-man, suddenly calm, "that somebody will be collecting you soon, and there won't be no need to arsk the reason why."

"That's where you and me don't agree," said the policeman. "I came to the conclusion this morning that we don't ask the reason why enough—not by 'alf. Now if somebody did as you say, and started collectin' policemen, what would be the reason?"

"Reason?" shouted the taxi-man. "Don't arsk me for a reason."

He turned to his taxi-cab and jerked the starting handle violently. The clatter of the engine arose. He climbed into his seat, and pulled at his gears savagely. In a few moments he had turned his cab, after wrenching in fury at the steering-wheel, and was jolting down the road in the morning brightness in search of breakfast.

27
LEONORA'S VOICE

"My theory," said the policeman, "is that collectin'—and by that I mean all sorts of collection, including that of money—comes from a craving to 'ave something what other people 'aven't got. It comes from a kind o' pride which is foolish. Take a man like Morgan, for instance. Now he spent his life collecting dollars, and he never once stopped to ask 'imself why he was doin' it. I 'eard a friend of mine, a socialist he was, saying as 'ow no one had wasted his life more than Morgan. At the time it struck me as a silly kind of thing to say. But now I seem to see it in a different light." He meditated for some minutes. "It's the reason why—that's what we 'aven't thought of near enough."

I was about to reply when a motor-car stopped before us. It was a large green limousine. It drew up suddenly, with a scraping of tyres, and a woman got out of it. I recognized her at once. It was Leonora. She was wearing a motoring-coat of russet-brown material, and her hat was tied with a veil.

"Alexis!" she exclaimed.

Sarakoff roused himself. He stood up and bowed.

"What are you doing here?" she asked.

"Leonora," he said, "I am so glad to see you. We are just taking the air, and discussing a few matters of general interest." He patted her on the shoulder. "I congratulate you, Leonora. You are an Immortal. It suits you very well."

She was certainly one of the Immortals. The stain in her eyes was wonderfully vivid, but it did not produce a displeasing effect, as I had fancied it would. Indeed, her eyes had lost their hard restless look, and in place of it was an expression of bewilderment.

"What has happened to me?" she exclaimed. "Alexis, what is this that you have done to me?"

"What I told you about at the Pyramid Restaurant. You have got the germ in you and now you are immortal. Sit down, Leonora. I find it warmer when I am sitting. My friend and I had to leave Harley Street somewhat hurriedly, and I had not time to dress."

She sat down and loosened her veil.

"Last night a dreadful thing happened," she said. "And yet, although it was dreadful, I do not feel upset about it. I have been trying to feel upset—as I should—but I can't. Let me tell you about it. I lay down yesterday afternoon in my room after tea to rest. I always do that when I can. I think I fell asleep for a moment. Then I felt a curious light feeling, as if I had suddenly been for a long holiday, and I got up. Alexis, when I saw myself in the glass I was horrified. I had the Blue Disease."

"Of course," said Sarakoff. "You were bound to get it. You knew that."

"I didn't know what to do. I wasn't very upset, only I felt something dreadful had happened. Well, I went to the Opera as usual and everyone was very sympathetic, but I said I was all right. But when my call came I suddenly knew—quite calmly, but certainly—that I could not sing properly. I went on the stage and began, but it was just as if I were singing for the first time in my life. They had to ring the curtain down. I apologized. I was quite calm and smiling. But there the fact remained—I had lost my voice. I had failed in public."

"Extraordinary," muttered Sarakoff. "Are you sure it was not just nervousness?"

"No, I'm certain of that. I felt absolutely self-possessed; far more so that I usually do, and that is saying a lot. No, my voice has gone. The Blue Disease has destroyed it. And yet I somehow don't feel any resentment. I don't understand. Richard, tell me what has happened."

I shook my head.

"I don't know," I said. "I can't explain. The germ is doing things that I never foresaw."

"I ought to be furious with you," she said.

"Try to be—if you can," smiled Sarakoff. "That's one of the strange things. I can't be furious. I have only two emotions—perfect calmness, or violent, horrible fear."

"Fear?" she exclaimed.

"Yes, fear of the worst kind conceivable."

"I understand the perfect calmness," she said, "but the fear—no."

"You will understand in time."

The policeman listened to our conversation with grave attention. Leonora was sitting between Sarakoff and me, and did not seem to find the presence of the visitor surprising. The green limousine stood in the road before us, the chauffeur sitting at the wheel looking steadily in front of him. The Heath seemed remarkably empty. The mist over London was lifting under the influence of the sun.

I was revolving in my mind a theory as to why Leonora had lost her voice. I already knew that the germ produced odd changes in the realm of likes and dislikes. I remembered Sarakoff's words that the germ was killing desire. My thoughts were clear, easy and lucid, and the problem afforded by Leonora's singular experience gave me a sense of quiet enjoyment. If the germ really did do away with desire, why should it at the same time do away with Leonora's wonderful voice? I recalled with marvellous facility everything I knew about her. My memory supplied me with every detail at the dinner of the Pyramid Restaurant. The words of Sarakoff, which had at the time seemed coarse, came back to me. He had called her a vain ambitious cold-hearted woman, who thought that her voice and her beauty could not be beaten.

My reflections were interrupted by the policeman.

"The lady," he remarked, "has lost her voice sudden-like. Now I lost my 'abit of arresting people sudden-like too. I lost it this morning. Any other time I should have taken the gentleman in the dressing-gown in charge for being improperly dressed. But this morning it don't come natural to me. If he wants to wear a dressing-gown on the Spaniard's Walk, he presumably 'as his own reasons. It don't concern me."

"It seems to me that the germ takes ambition out of us," said Sarakoff.

"Ambition?" said the policeman. "No, that ain't right. I've got ambition still—only it's a different kind of ambition."

"I have no ambition now," said Leonora at length. "Alexis is right. This malady has taken the ambition out of me. I may be Immortal, but if I am, then I am an Immortal without ambition. I seem to be lost, to be suddenly diffused into space or time, to be a kind of vapour. Something has dissolved in me—something hard, bright, alert. I do not know why I am here. The car came round as usual to take me for my morning run. I got in—why I don't know."

Sarakoff was studying her attentively.

"It is very strange," he said. "You used to arouse a feeling of strength and determination in me, Leonora. You used to stimulate me intensely. This morning I only feel one thing about you."

"What is that?"

"I feel that I have cheated you."

"Cheated her?" exclaimed the policeman. "How do you come to that conclusion?"

"I've destroyed the one thing that was herself—I've destroyed desire in her. I've left her a mind devoid of all values tacked on to a body that no longer interests her. For what was Leonora, who filled the hearts of men with madness, but an incarnation of desire?"

28
THE KILLING OF DESIRE

We drove in Leonora's car through London. The streets were crowded. I do not think that much routine work was done that day. People formed little crowds on the pavements, and at Oxford Circus someone was speaking to a large concourse from the seat of a motor lorry.

Leonora seemed extraordinarily apathetic. She leaned back in the car and seemed uninterested in the passing scene. Sarakoff, wrapped up in a fur rug, stared dreamily in front of him. As far as I can recall them, my feelings during that swift tour of London were vague. The buildings, the people, the familiar signs in the streets, the shop windows, all seemed to have lost in some degree the quality of reality. I was detached from them; and whenever I made an effort to rouse myself, the ugliness and meaninglessness of everything I saw seemed strangely emphasized.

When we reached Harley Street we found my house little damaged, save for a broken panel in the green front door and a few panes of glass smashed in the lower windows. The house was empty. The servants had vanished.

Leonora said she wished to go home and she drove off in the car. Sarakoff did not even wave farewell to her, but went straight up to his room and lay down on the bed. I went into the study and sat in my chair by the fireplace.

I was roused by the opening of the door, and looking up I saw a face that I recognized, but for the moment I could not fit a name to it. My visitor came in calmly, and sat down opposite me.

"My name is Thornduck," he said. "I came to consult you about my health a few days ago."

"I remember," I said.

"Your front door was open so I walked in."

I nodded. His eyes, stained with blue, rested on me.

"I have been thinking," he said. "It struck me that there was something you forgot to tell me the other day."

I nodded again.

"You began, if you remember, by asking me if I believed in miracles. That set me thinking, and as I saw your name in the paper, connected with the Blue Disease, I knew you were a miracle-monger. How did you do it?"

"I don't know. It was all due to my black cat. Tripped over it, got concussion and regained my senses with the idea that led up to the germ."

He smiled.

"A black cat," he mused. "I wonder if it's all black magic?"

"That's what Hammer suggested. I don't know what kind of magic it is."

"Of course it *is* magic," said Thornduck.

"Magic?"

"Of course. Have you even thought what kind of magic it is?"

"No."

"A big magic, such as you have worked, is just bringing the distant future into the present with a rush."

"Sarakoff had some such idea," I murmured. "He spoke of anticipating our evolution by centuries at one stroke."

"Exactly. That's magic. The question remains—is it black magic?" He crossed his thin legs and leaned back in the chair. "I got the Blue Disease the day before yesterday and since then I've thought more than I have ever done in all my life. When I read in the paper this morning that you said the Blue Disease conferred immortality on people I was not surprised. I had come to the same conclusion in a roundabout way. But I want to ask you one question. Did you know beforehand that *it killed desire?*"

"No. Neither Sarakoff nor I foresaw that."

"Well, if you had let me into your confidence before I could have told you that right away in the general principle contained in the saying that you can't eat your cake and have it. It's just another aspect of the law of the conservation of energy, isn't it?"

"I always had a doubt—"

"Naturally. It's intuitional. The laws of the universe are just intuitions put into words. You've carried out an enormous spiritual experiment to prove what all religions have always asserted however obscurely. All religion teaches that you can't eat your cake and have it. That's the essence of religion, and you, formerly a cut-and-dried scientist, have gone and proved it to the whole world for eternity. Rather odd, isn't it?"

I watched his face with interest. It was thin and the complexion was transparent. His eyes, wonderfully wide and brilliantly stained by the germ, produced in me a new sensation. It was akin to enthusiasm, but in it was something of love, such as I had never experienced for any man. I became uplifted. My whole being began to vibrate to some strangely delicate and exquisite influence, and I knew that Thornduck was the medium through which these impulses reached me. It was not his words but the atmosphere round him that raised me temporarily to this degree of receptivity.

"It is odd," I said.

He continued to look at me.

"You have a message for me?" I observed at last.

"Why, yes, I have," he replied. "You have done wrong, Harden. You have worked black magic, and it will fail out of sheer necessity."

"Tell me what I have done."

"You have artificially produced a condition of life many ages before humanity is ready to receive it. The body of desire is being worked up by endless labour into something more delicate and sensitive—into a transmutation that we can only dimly understand. At present the whole plot of life is based on the principle of desire and in this way people are kept busy, constantly spurred on to thought and activity by essentially selfish motives. It is only in abstract thought that the selfless ideal has a real place as yet, but the very fact that it is there shows what lies at the top of the ladder that humanity is so painfully climbing. As long as desire is the plot of life, death is necessary, for its terrible shadow sharpens desire and makes the prizes more alluring and the struggle more desperate. And so man goes on, ceaselessly active and striving, for without activity and striving there is no perfecting of the instrument. You can't have upward progress in conditions of stagnation. All that strange incredible side of life, called the Devil, is the inner plot of life that makes the wheels go round and evolution possible. It is vitally necessary to keep the vast machinery running at the present level of evolution. Desire is the furnace in the engine-house. The wheels go round and the fabric is slowly and intricately spun and only pessimists and bigots fail to see evidence of any purpose in it all. Now what has your Blue Disease done? It has taken the whole plot out of life at its present stage of development at one fell swoop. It has killed Desire—put out the furnace before the pattern in the fabric is nearly complete."

"But I never could see that, Thornduck. How could I foresee that?"

"If you had had a grain of vision you would have known that you couldn't give humanity the gift of immortality without some compensatory loss. The law of compensation is as sure as the law of gravity—you ought to know that."

"I had dim feelings—I knew Sarakoff was wrong, with his dream of physical bliss—but how could I foresee that desire would go?"

"As a mere scientist, test-tube in hand, you couldn't. But you're better than that. You've got a glimmering of moral imagination in you."

He fell into a reverie.

"You are keeping something back. Tell me plainly what you mean," I asked.

"Don't you see that if the germ lasts any length of time," he said, "the machinery will run down and—stop?"

29
THE REVOLT OF THE YOUNG

Amid all the strife and clamour of the next few days one thing stands out now in my mind with sinister radiance. It is that peculiar form of lawlessness which broke out and had as its object the destruction of the old.

There is no doubt that the idea of immortality got hold of people and carried them away completely. The daily miracles that were occurring of the renewal of health and vigour, the cure of disease and the passing of those infirmities that are associated with advancing years, impressed the popular imagination deeply. As a result there grew up a widespread discontent and bitterness. The young—those who were as yet free from the germ—conceived in their hearts that an immense injustice had been done to them.

It must be remembered that life at that time had taken on a strange and abnormal aspect. Its horizons had been suddenly altered by the germ. Although breadth had been given to it from the point of years, a curious contraction had appeared at the same time. It was a contraction felt most acutely by those in inferior positions. It was a contraction that owed its existence to the sense of being shut in eternally by those in higher positions, whom death no longer would remove at convenient intervals. The student felt it as he looked at his professor. The clerk felt it as he looked at his manager. The subaltern felt it as he looked at his colonel. The daughter felt it when she looked at her mother, and the son when he looked at his father. The germ had given simultaneously a tremendous blow to freedom, and a tremendous impetus to freedom.

Thus, perhaps for the first time in history, there swiftly began an accumulation and concentration of those forces of discontent which, in normal times, only manifest themselves here and there in the relationships between old and young men, and are regarded with good-humoured patience. A kind of war broke out all over the country.

This war was terrible in its nature. All the secret weariness and unspoken bitterness of the younger generation found a sudden outlet. Goaded to madness by the prospect of a future of continual repression, in which the old would exercise an undiminished authority, the younger men and women plunged into a form of excess over which a veil must be drawn. . . . There is only one thing which can be recorded in their favour. Chloroform and drowning appear to have been the methods most often used, and they are perhaps merciful ways of death. The great London clubs became sepulchres. All people who had received the highest distinctions and honours, whose names were household words, were removed with ruthless determination. Scarcely a single well-known man or woman of the older generation, whose name was honoured in science, literature, art, business or politics, was spared. All aged and wealthy people perished. A clean sweep was made, and made with a decision and unanimity that was incredible.

It is painful now to recall the terrible nature of that civil war. It lasted only a short time, but it opened my eyes to the inner plan upon which mortal man is based. For I am compelled to admit that this widespread murder, that suddenly flashed into being, was founded upon impulses that lie deep in man's heart. They were those giant impulses that lie behind growth, and the effect of the germ was merely to throw them suddenly into the broad light of day, unchained, grim and implacable.

Fortunately, the germ spread steadily and quickly, killing as it did so all hate and desire.

Jason, still free from the germ, flung himself into the general uproar with extraordinary vigour. It was clear that he thought the great opportunity had come which would eventually bring him to the height of his power. To check the growing lawlessness and murder he advocated a new adjustment of property. Big meetings were held in the public spaces of London, and some wild ideas were formulated.

In the meantime the medical profession, as far as the men yet free from the germ were concerned, continued its work in a dull, mechanical way. Each day the number of patients fell lower, as the Blue Disease slowly spread. Hammer, himself an Immortal, came to see me once, but only to speak of the necessity for the immediate simplification of houses. It was odd to observe how, once a man became infected, his former interests and anxieties fell away from him like an old garment. In Harley Street an attitude of stubborn disbelief continued amongst those still mortal. There is something magnificent in that adamantine spirit which refuses to recognize the new, even though it moves with ever-increasing distinctness before the very eyes of the deniers. I was not surprised. I was familiar with medical men.

Meanwhile the Royal Family became infected by the germ, and passed out of the public eye. The Prime Minister became a victim and vanished. For once a man had the germ in his system, as far as externals were concerned, he almost ceased to exist.

The infection of Jason occurred in my presence. He had come in to explain to me a proposed line of campaign as regards the marriage laws.

"This germ of yours has given people the courage to think!" he exclaimed. "It is extraordinary how timid people were in thinking. It has launched them out, and now is the time to bring in new proposals."

"In all your calculations, you omit to recollect the effects of the germ," I said. "Surely you have seen by now that it changes human nature totally?"

He stared at me uncomprehendingly. He was one of those men, so common in public life, who have no power of understanding what they themselves have not experienced. He continued with undiminished enthusiasm.

"We must have marriage contracts for definite periods. With the increased state of health, and the full span of life confronting every man, we must face the problem squarely. Now what stands in our way?"

He got up and went to the window. It was a dull foggy day, and there was frost on the ground. He stared outside for some moments.

"What, I repeat, stands in our way?"

"Well?"

"The Church, and a mass of superstitions that we have inherited from the Old Testament. That's what stands in our way. We still attach more value to the Old Testament than to the New. The Scotch, for example, like the Jews. . . . Yes, of course. . . . What was I saying?"

He left the window and sat down once more before me, moving rather listlessly.

"Yes, Harden. Of course. That's what it is, isn't it? Do you remember—diddle—yes it was diddle, diddle—"

He paused and frowned.

"Hey diddle diddle, the cat and the fiddle," he muttered, "Yes—hey, diddle, diddle, diddle—that's what it is, isn't it?"

"Of course," I said. "It's all really that."

"Just diddle, diddle, diddle?"

"Yes—if you like."

"That is substituting diddle for riddle," he said earnestly. He frowned again and passed his hand across his eyes.

"Yes," I said calmly. "It's going a step up."

I suppose about half an hour passed before either of us spoke again after this extraordinary termination to our conversation. In absolute silence we sat facing one another and during that time I saw the blue stain growing clearer and clearer in Jason's eyes. At last he rose.

"It's very odd," he said. "Tell me, were you like this?"

"How do you feel?"

"As if I had been drunk and suddenly had been made sober. I will leave you. I want to think. I will go down to the country."

"And your papers?"

"We must have a new Press," he said, and left the room.

That same day the great railway accident occurred just outside London that led to the death of sixty people, many of them Immortals. Its effect on public imagination was profound. All dangerous enterprises became invested with a terrible radiance. Men asked themselves if, in face of a future of health, it was worth risking life in rashness of any description, and gradually traffic came to a standstill. Long before the germ had infected the whole populace all activities fraught with danger had ceased. The coal mines were abandoned. The railways were silent. The streets of London became empty of traffic.

Blue-stained people began to throng the streets of London in vast masses, moving to and fro without aim or purpose, perfectly orderly, vacant, lost—like Sarakoff's butterflies. . . .

Thornduck came to see me one day when the reign of the germ was practically absolute in London.

"They are wandering into the country in thousands," he remarked. "They have lost all sense of home and possession. They are vague, trying to form an ideal socialistic community. What a mess your germ is making of life! They're not ready for it. The question is whether they will rouse themselves to consider the food question."

"We need scarcely any food," I replied. "I've had nothing to eat to-day."

"Nor I. But since we're still linked up to physical bodies we must require some nourishment."

"I have eaten two biscuits and a little cheese in the last twenty-four hours. Surely you don't think that food is to be a serious problem under such circumstances?"

"It might be. You must remember that initiative is now destroyed in the vast majority of people. They may permit themselves to die of inanition. Can you say you have an appetite now?"

I reflected for some time, striving to recall the feeling of hunger that belonged to the days of desire.

"No. I have no appetite."

"Think carefully. In place of appetite have you no tendencies?"

"I feel a kind of lethargy," I said at last. "I felt it yesterday and to-day it is stronger."

"As if you wished to sleep?"

"Not exactly. But it is akin to that. I have some difficulty in keeping my attention on things. There is a kind of pull within me away from—away from reality."

He nodded.

"I went in to see your Russian friend. He's upstairs. He is not exactly asleep. He is more like a man partially under the influence of a drug."

"I will go and see him," I said.

Sarakoff was lying on the bed with his eyes shut. He was breathing quietly. His eyelids quivered, as if they might open at any moment, but my entrance did not rouse him. His limbs were relaxed. I spoke to him and tried to wake him, without result. Then I remembered how I had stumbled across the body of Herbert Wain in the Park some days ago. He had seemed to be in a strange kind of sleep. I sat down on the bed and stared at the motionless figure of the Russian. There was something strangely pathetic in his pose. His rough hair and black beard, his keen aquiline face seemed weirdly out of keeping with his helpless state. Here lay the man whose brain had once teemed with ambitious desires, relaxed and limp like a baby, while the nails of his hands, turquoise blue, bore silent witness to his great experiment on humanity. Had it failed? Where was all that marvellous vision of physical happiness that had haunted him? The streets of London were filled with people, no longer working, no longer crying or weeping, but moving aimlessly, like people in a dream. Were they happy? I moved to the window and drew down the blind.

"This may be the end," I thought. "The germ will be sweeping through France now. It may be the end of all things."

I rejoined Thornduck in the study.

"Sarakoff is in a kind of trance," I observed. "What do you make of it?"

"Isn't it natural?" he asked. "What kind of a man was he? What motives did he work on? Just think what the killing of desire means. All those things that depended on worldly ambition, self-gratification, physical pleasure, conceit, lust, hatred, passion, egotism, selfishness, vanity, avarice, sensuality and so on, are undermined and rendered paralysed by the germ. What remains? Why, in most people, practically nothing remains."

"Even so," I said, "I don't see why Sarakoff should go into a trance."

"He's gone into a trance simply because there's not enough left in him to constitute an individuality. The germ has taken the inside clean out of him. He's just an immortal shell now."

"Then do you think—?"

I stared at him wonderingly.

"I think that the germ will send most of the world to sleep."

He got up and walked to the window. The clear noonday light fell on his thin sensitive face and accentuated the pallor of his skin.

"All those who are bound on the wheel of desire will fall asleep," he murmured. A smile flickered on his lips and he turned and looked at me.

"Harden," he said, "it's really very funny. It's infinitely humorous, isn't it?"

"I see nothing humorous in anything," I replied. "I've lost all sense of humour."

He raised his eyebrows.

"Of humour?" he queried. "Surely not. Humour is surely immortal."

30
THE GREAT SLEEP

On that day the animals in London fell asleep with few exceptions. The exceptions were, I believe, all dogs. I do not pretend to explain, how it came about that dogs remained awake longer than other animals. The reason may be that dogs have some quality in them which is superior even to the qualities found in man, for there is a sweetness in the nature of dogs that is rare in men and women.

Many horses were overcome in the streets and lay down where they were. No attempt was made to remove them. They were left, stretched out on their sides, apparently unconscious.

And many thousands of men and women fell asleep. In some cases men were overcome by the sleep before their dogs, which has always seemed strange to me. It was Thornduck who told me this, for he remained awake during this period that the germ reigned supreme. He tells me that I fell asleep the next evening in my chair in the study and that he carried me upstairs to my room. I had just returned from visiting Leonora, whom I had found unconscious. He made a tour of London next morning. In the City there was a profound stillness.

In the West End matters were much the same. In Cavendish Square he entered many houses and found silence and sleep within. Everywhere doors and windows were wide open, giving access to any who might desire it. He visited the Houses of Parliament only to find a few comatose blue-stained men lying about on the benches. For the sleep had overtaken people by stealth. One day, passing by the Zoo, he had climbed the fence and made an inspection of the inmates. With the exception of an elephant that was nodding drowsily, the animals lay motionless in their cages, deep in the trance that the germ induced.

From time to time he met a man or woman awake like himself and stopped to talk. Those who still retained sufficient individuality to continue existence were the strangest mixture of folk, for they were of every class, many of them being little better than beggars. They were people in whom the desire of life played a minor part. They were those people who are commonly regarded as being failures, people who live and die unknown to the world. They were those people who devote themselves to an obscure existence, shun the rewards of successful careers, and are ridiculed by all prosperous individuals. It seems that Thornduck was instrumental in calling a meeting of these people at St. Paul's. There were about two thousand of them in all, but many in the outlying suburbs remained ignorant of the meeting, and Thornduck considers that in the London district alone there must have been some thousands who did not attend. At the meeting, which must have been the strangest in all history, the question of the future was discussed. Many believed that the effect of the germ on those in the great sleep would ultimately lead to a cessation of life owing to starvation. Thornduck held that the germ would pass, arguing on principles that were so unscientific that I refrain from giving them. Eventually it appears that a decision was reached to leave London on a certain date and migrate southwards in search of a region where a colony might be founded under laws and customs suitable for Immortals. Thornduck says that there was one thing that struck him very forcibly at the meeting at St. Paul's. All the people gathered there had about them a certain sweetness and strength, which, although it was very noticeable, escaped his powers of analysis.

He attempted on several occasions to get into telegraphic communication with the Continent, but failed. In his wanderings he entered many homes, always being careful to lay out at full length any of the unconscious inmates who were asleep on chairs, for he feared that they might come to harm, and that their limbs might become stiffened into unnatural postures.

All the time he had a firm conviction that the phase of sleep was temporary. He himself had moments in which a slight drowsiness overtook him, but he never lost the enhanced power of thought that I had experienced in the early stages of the Blue Disease. So absolute was his conviction that a general awakening would come about that he began to busy his mind with the question as to what he could do, in conjunction with the other Immortals who were still awake, to benefit humanity when it should emerge from the trance. This question was discussed continually. Many thought that they should burn all records, financial, political, governmental and private, so that some opportunity of starting afresh might be given to mankind, enslaved to the past and fettered by law and custom. But the danger of chaos resulting from such a step deterred him. He confessed that the more he thought on the subject the more clearly he saw that under the circumstances belonging to its stage of evolution, the organization of the world was suited to the race that inhabited it. All change, he saw, had to come from within, and that to alter external conditions suddenly and artificially might do incredible harm. We were constructed to develop against resistance, and to remove such resistances before they had been overcome naturally was to tamper with the inner laws of life. And so, after long discussion, they did nothing. . . .

It is curious to reflect that they, earnest men devoted to progress, having at their mercy the machinery of existence, walked through the midst of sleeping London and did nothing. But then none of them were fanatics, for Thornduck stated that the fanatics fell early to sleep, thus proving that the motives behind their fanaticism were egotistical, and a source of satisfaction to themselves. He made a point of visiting the homes of some of them. Philanthropists, too, succumbed early.

On the seventh day after the great sleep had overtaken London the effects of the germ began to wane. Those who had fallen asleep latest were the earliest to open their eyes. The blue stain rapidly vanished from eyes, skin and nails. . . . I regained my waking sense on the evening of the seventh day and found myself in a small country cottage whither Thornduck had borne me in a motor-car, fearing lest awakened London might seek some revenge on the discoverers of the germ. Sarakoff lay on a couch beside me, still fast asleep.

The first clear idea that came to me concerned Alice Annot. I determined to go to her at once. Then I remembered with vexation that I had wantonly smashed two vases worth ten pounds apiece.

I struggled to my feet. My hands were thin and wasted. I was ravenous with hunger. I felt giddy.

"What's the time?" I called confusedly. "It must be very late. Wake up!"

And I stooped down and began to shake Sarakoff violently.

Coachwhip Publications

CoachwhipBooks.com

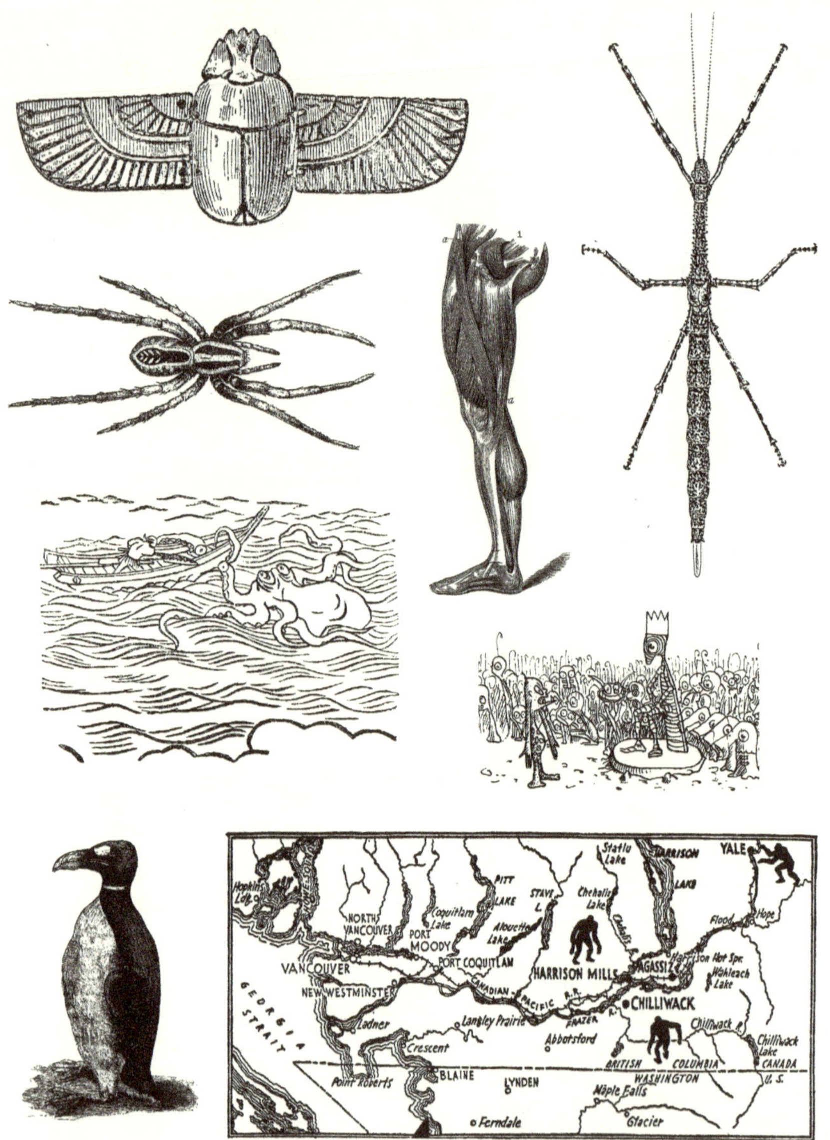

Coachwhip Publications

Also Available

Classic Stories of Botanical Marvels

Flora Curiosa

ISBN 1-930585-56-X

Coachwhip Publications

Also Available

Further Tales of Mysterious Vegetation

Botanica Delira

ISBN 1-61646-025-3

www.ingramcontent.com/pod-product-compliance
Lightning Source LLC
LaVergne TN
LVHW041056080826
845145LV00007B/1587

9781616461041